THE
SAND
GOD

THE
SAND
GOD

JAN E. HOUSLEY

THE SAND GOD

iUniverse books may be ordered through booksellers or by contacting:

iUniverse
1663 Liberty Drive
Bloomington, IN 47403
www.iuniverse.com
844-349-9409

ISBN: 978-1-6632-2125-4 (sc)
ISBN: 978-1-6632-2126-1 (e)

Library of Congress Control Number: 2021909687

Print information available on the last page.

iUniverse rev. date: 05/14/2021

PROLOGUE

I don't know if all of what I think I remember going through really happened to me. Was some of it just a figment of my over-active imagination or did it all really happen? I guess I'll never know for sure. I do know one thing for sure, though. I did experience some very traumatic events, and most of the memories aren't good. Like my uncontrolled arrival in the town, seeing the Dust Devil change form, and all of the mental messages to Tawamiciya, and several others that were just as frightening as these three events.

Today, as I sit writing this, it has been five years to the day since I left those experiences behind me up there in the mountains. Or did I? I don't know because it seems like they just happened yesterday. I do know one thing for certain. I am safe and away from the strange happenings that overtook and overwhelmed me back in June of 1980.

I am a lot older, and I hope a little wiser now, but as I listen to the tapes I made while I was there and look over my written notes, I shiver violently. As I sit here in a warm room, covered with a blanket, the memories renewed by those notes and tapes provoke shivers all over my body and the sweat pours from my face uncontrollably. The sweat comes, not from the warm weather outside but from the fright the notes and tapes rekindle in my psyche. I don't want to relive those days, but I'm drawn irresistibly to those memories again, and again.

Was I there for days, or just hours? I don't really know, now. At the time I felt like a normal person, who was just experiencing some traumatic events over a period of many days. I lost track of time and never really gained it back. The time there in the town I will refer to as Bullsnort as I tell you about my experiences. Part of the mystery is gone. Some of it is only dust covered memories that make me shudder. In a way I'm glad I'm here. Nobody believes my story when I tell it to them. They say it just couldn't have happened like that, things don't work like that. Well, they did work like that, for me, there.

My relief is absolute now. The town, the people, Mrs. Hernando, Martin, Rosalie, Carmelita, the Sheriff and the lady lawyer (No, that's not right, the lawyer was no lady!) are all just memories now. Some of the memories I know are good, and I accept them with pleasure. Others I know do me harm to remember them. I loved it up there, but also hated it up there, and I was reluctant to leave. I hope they are all happy now that the horror of what happened there is settled.

I am sane now. At least I have convinced the doctors here that I am not a danger to anybody. They didn't really believe what I told them at first when I checked myself into this facility but, then, they're a bunch of greedy bastards who couldn't pass on the fees I would pay for their meager help.

But I needed some help to find my way out of the fog that had enshrouded me. They found my story too incredulous to believe and labeled me with a plethora of medical terms that only they understood while I was in their care. I no longer try to tell my story and that seems to make them a lot more at ease with me. I've stopped taking their medications and am about ready to check myself out of here. I am ready to start living my life again.

Believe me when I tell you my story. It actually happened to me. I'll understand if you don't believe all of what I tell you. I know it happened. I just haven't been able, yet, to figure out many of the whys.

Why was I directed there? Why was I selected to receive the mysterious messages? Why was I the only one to experience these strange things?

I have hard evidence that it all happened, well, most of it, anyway. Will you believe me? Read on and then decide. Make up your own mind about it.

Maybe a little sympathy will be coming from you for my plight. I won't disclose where I am but rest assured, I am far away from that town. I won't reveal the real name of the town or its location for your protection. You see, I don't want you to come looking for me, or try to find the place where it all happened. If you do happen to know me or find me accidentally I'll deny all of it. I won't talk to you about the town either, so don't ask for specifics. I don't want what happened to me to happen to you. I don't want that on my conscious too.

Here's my story. Believe it if you choose. Please do just one thing, let your imagination soar with the Eagles and dance with the Kachinas.

Andrew I. Bling

ONE

"Andy, can you come into my office for a minute, I have something interesting here I want you to look at," I heard Dan, my Managing Editor, call to me over the intercom from his desk.

"Sure Dan, be there in a minute, I have some finishing touches to put on my latest column and I'll be there."

Damn, I thought to myself, here it is Sunday morning and I'm at work, essentially overtime without any expectations of overpay, to get this done and now he wants me for something. I shuffled the papers on my desk and made ready to leave it all in my usual disorderly way of filing, what other reporters call my neat piles of files and walked down the hall to see what awaited me. I guessed it was another assignment.

You see, I work for Dan. Dan Morenci is the Managing Editor for the *Albuquerque Journal* and I am the Indian Desk. What is an Indian Desk? You're probably asking. Yes, I would, too, if I weren't in New Mexico. That's what I am here at the paper. I handle and research all news articles regarding the many Indian events and happenings in the state. Granted, most of what I do involves the Indian tribes that surround Albuquerque, but occasionally I have to travel to Grants or Gallup or down to the southern part of the state to check on something for my column. I know of no other paper either statewide or nationally that has an Indian Desk so I do the best job I can because I love my work.

Right about here would be a good place for introductions and some explanations about my situation at the Journal.

My name is Andrew I. Bling. My friends and, even what enemies I have, call me Andy. I never use my middle name that begins with I.

There's a very good reason why I don't. The long version is tedious, so I'll give the short version.

My parents were archeologists who, at the time of my birth, were excavating the tomb of the legendary King of Crete named Idomeneus, who supposedly was a suitor of Helen of Troy. I guess they couldn't be bothered to take the time to give me a good logical first name. I don't know nor care now, but I sure cared in school when all the other kids called me Idiot.

If I wanted to be generous I would say that maybe it was because they couldn't pronounce the name, Idomeneus. But let's face it, it was more likely they just needed some feeble excuse to feel superior.

1

Fortunately, those taunts and jeers, because of my middle name don't keep me awake at nights because of some delayed stress something or other. I like my good night's sleep now, so I'll just introduce myself as Andy. Enough said about the I.

After graduating from high school I went into military service because I had no plans at all of going to college. I had no idea what kind of job I wanted to do. Besides, I was only eighteen and what do teenagers know about their future? Not what they think they know, that's for sure. I can vouch for that. For me, serving my country was a rite of passage into what the civilized world called manhood. All my male relatives from my fourth great grandfather had served in the Armed Forces. I was to find out later, after a great deal of genealogical research, that I was a direct descendant of a Patriot who fought in our Revolutionary War.

I am an active member of an organization called The Sons of the American Revolution now and, along with all the other members, I am very proud of my heritage. It was expected that I would also serve. I did, for three years as a Military Policeman. After that experience, mostly in Germany, I knew that my future livelihood would not be gained by being any kind of cop. Don't get me wrong. I enjoyed my time in the U.S. Army very much and have some very good and some very funny, memories of those times. Police work is an honorable profession and I respect both the police and the firefighting professions greatly for having the testicular fortitude to do the work they do every day.

It just wasn't for me anymore.

TWO

"Carmelita, can you come in here for a minute, I have something important to discuss," said Ms. Robin Charles, Bullsnort's only female lawyer. The only lawyer for that matter.

Carmelita knew better than to say that she'd be there in a minute after she decided that a minute was long enough to stall. She could blame the delay on paperwork, but then again, Ms. Charles knew exactly how much paperwork she had to handle, and didn't like to be kept waiting, even for a minute when she summoned someone into her presence.

What a bitch, Carmelita thought.

If I could find another job here I'd quit in a heartbeat and leave her stranded. Carmelita knew that nobody else in town would want to work for her boss.

Most of the younger townsfolk, who did clerical work, had worked for Ms. Charles at one time or another and they had all quit because she was such a damned tyrant and a hard-assed boss.

After about a minute, Carmelita pushed back her chair, made her way into Ms. Charles' office and said in a pleasant voice, "Yes, Ms. Charles, what do you need?" She had a very hard time keeping a civil tone as she spoke. She didn't like Ms. Charles at all and justifiably so, she thought.

Ms. Charles answered without even looking up at Carmelita, "I have some business on a new contract in Santa Fe this weekend and I want you to go with me so that in the future you can represent me and I won't have to make the trip again to complete all the details. My office will pick up the bill for your hotel and you can charge your meals to my account. I will also allow you two hundred dollars for incidental expenses. However, I want you to itemize and I'll reimburse you when you return. How does that sound?"

"Will the trip be for just one day or more? And when do you want to leave?" Carmelita inquired calmly.

"We will leave tomorrow morning to go down to Santa Fe and we will travel in my car" said Ms. Charles without the slightest regard for any personal plans Carmelita might have for the weekend.

"We should be back by Sunday night. But, when you go down by yourself the next time, you can take your own car. We will plan to meet with the clients on both Saturday and Sunday if that much time is needed to complete our preliminary contract negotiations. If most of the work gets done on Saturday and you want to go to Sunday church services in the Cathedral there that's perfectly fine with me, Carmelita."

When Carmelita did not say anything, Ms. Charles continued.

"We'll leave here at seven o'clock in the morning and that should get us to Santa Fe about eight thirty. The meeting with the new clients is set up for nine o'clock in the new Hyatt Towers Hotel, where I have reserved rooms for us. I have also reserved a small hotel conference room for our meetings. We'll break for lunch at about noon for an hour and then finish up the day's work about three or four o'clock. Sunday we follow the same schedule for this initial two day meeting, assuming we need the entire day to come to agreement. Just pack enough clothes and toiletries for two days. Can you be ready to go at seven on Saturday morning?" Ms. Charles asked as she looked up at Carmelita.

"Yes, I'll be ready to go" said Carmelita, trying to keep the animosity out of her voice. "Will we meet here at the office or at your house?"

"We'll meet here so I can make a last minute check to ensure I have all the information and forms we will need for the new clients" as she looked back down at the papers on her desk. "I want us to make a good impression. Contracts like this one are paying your salary and providing your comfortable office equipment" said Ms. Charles in a dismissive tone.

Damn it all to hell, Carmelita thought to herself. Now Mark and I have to put off our plans for a week-end picnic up at our favorite hide away. This surely won't end it for us. We'll just have to make other arrangements, but then maybe this might not be such a bad thing since it is all on Ms. Charles's expense account. She had to laugh to herself about that.

After forcing herself to get up early to meet Ms. Charles at the office, the drive was uneventful and pleasant for Carmelita since they had very little conversation. After checking into the hotel and making a quick trip to their rooms, they met in the dining room for a breakfast of orange juice and some good hot coffee. They didn't order anything to eat because Ms. Charles didn't want to risk being late for the meeting.

The meeting with the new clients, Cannon and Strife, went as Ms. Charles had planned and major details of the contract were settled in a surprisingly short time. Carmelita wasn't involved with the actual contract negotiation but took careful notes and was favorably impressed with the partners. They were good looking as well as rich. She was pretty sure they wouldn't be at the second meeting, but maybe their representative would be just as good looking. They finished for the day at about four o'clock and the partners agreed to send their representative to another meeting on Sunday at about ten o'clock. They wanted time to give everyone time to attend the early mass at the Cathedral.

Carmelita's time that evening was her own and no plans were made with Ms. Charles to associate together anywhere, so she walked around the plaza, window shopped and had a great time listening to all the great music that came through the open doors of the bars she passed. She was very tempted to go in and have some fun dancing and maybe have a few beers with the men, but decided she wouldn't take a chance on Mark hearing that she was cheating on him. Their plans weren't settled yet, but she had some long-term dreams in which he was definitely included. She didn't want to do anything to jeopardize her future with him. They could always come down to Santa Fe after she persuaded him to get married.

At the meeting on Sunday, the new representative, Frank Kirby, was introduced all around. He was older than Carmelita had expected, but he was good looking and she enjoyed looking at him despite the fact that he had a big solid-looking gold band on his third finger, left hand. She decided that was fine because, just no way was she going to have an affair with a married man. Although her current most significant other was un-married and said that he planned to stay that way for a long time, she was confident that she could persuade him to change his mind. Mark had joked that he wasn't above messing around but not with a ring on his finger. That gave Carmelita high hopes.

The drive back to Bullsnort late on Sunday afternoon was uneventful, and thankfully, a quiet ride.

Let's just see what happens next time, Carmelita thought, with a grin on her beautiful face, as she watched Ms. Charles negotiate the curves and switchbacks of the highway.

When they got back to town after the scary mountain drive, they went to the office, put the contract in the safe, cleaned up a little and then locked the doors. Carmelita went home. She was ready to see Mark if he called her. She didn't much care where Ms. Charles went or who she was seeing.

Carmelita decided that she was looking forward to the next trip to Santa Fe. Maybe Mark would decide to go with her. She would have to work on him to convince him that spending the weekend with her was his own idea and decision.

THREE

Thinking back on my years after high school was not always pleasant. I had had a series of uneventful go nowhere jobs at various places around the country until I drifted into New Mexico with a salt dome drilling company.

The company had a short contract to drill two exploratory holes on the outskirts of Albuquerque. I got a small, and I do mean *small*, apartment and bought a shabby, disrespectful looking car. My workday wardrobe consisted of several pairs of ratty jeans and grubby work shirts that needed some major patching at the elbows. I had two pairs of what I called my good pants, three respectful looking sport shirts, and a pair of loafers that had seen their better days long ago. I didn't have much to my name, and very little prospects for acquiring more unless I got some really lucky breaks.

On any day of the week, when I was unshaven for a couple of days, I could have very easily joined the homeless persons in their parade up and down any Main Street in any town and nobody would have known the difference. I knew I didn't want to wind up on the street but that was exactly where I was headed on a straight as an arrow path, if I didn't do something to change my economic outlook. What I'm trying to explain is that I was poor.

One day I found myself looking at a mean looking woman over a desk with a nameplate that said Registrar.

She was scowling at me over her half-frame glasses as she scanned my application to become one of her Lobos at the University of New Mexico. I had registered as a freshmen under my rights as a Veteran which would help pay for some of my classes. I signed up for 15 hours of classes that she said I would need to take the first semester. We made a plan for the entire year. I signed all the papers she handed me and then, with a look which I thought bordered on pleasure, she addressed me as "Mr. Blaing", and told me I could leave.

She acted like some ancient twelfth century queen dismissing her vassal. I sure didn't much care for her attitude toward me, but I had had some experience in dealing with piss-ant bosses so she didn't bother me much. I guessed that she really did intimidate the younger kids who were away from home for the first time though. I laughed at their plight, but I was glad that I wouldn't have to see her or her office again till next year when I registered as a sophomore.

I was a Lobo now! I still had no idea what I wanted to be when I graduated in four years' time. Hopefully I would stand here with my degree in hand looking happily at that wrinkled up old prune, probably still wanting her approval.

You see, *I frighten easily*. That's why I chose not to pursue any career that included the words policeman or cop in them.

Surprisingly, I made it through those four years there at the University of New Mexico and earned my degree in Anthropology and Journalism. I guess I remembered how excited my parents always were about exploring those ancient tombs. My grades were satisfactory, not exemplary mind you, but still high enough that I should be able to get a job in my chosen field.

I could write a clear, concise, declarative sentence with all the punctuation in the correct places and most of the spelling correct, so I was satisfied. I used to joke with my classmates in English 405 that I hadn't had to use a dictionary for at least ten years, but that about eight years ago I thought I had misspelled a word until I looked it up and confirmed that I was correct, just brag factor among students.

My main problem was that my satisfaction and bragging about being a better than average speller didn't put gas in my car or hamburgers on my table. I needed a job. My G.I. Bill monies were all used up, the rent was due and my stomach had resumed its natural hungry growling.

I wanted to go to Graduate School to major in either Anthropology or Archaeology because of the influence of my parents, but money was a problem. Yes, I could have asked them for the funds but I was on my own and didn't want to burden them with supporting me. Actually I guess I didn't want the strings that would be attached since I hadn't had any contact with them for all these years. Besides, I still wasn't too happy with the name they had given me. Then too, we hadn't talked or written a letter to each other for so long, I didn't really know where to look for them. Since I had no easy way of finding out, I just eliminated them as a source of income or sustenance.

I wanted to work at some of the Indian sites around the state and there were thousands of places I could be really happy working. I just needed to get attached to some professor who was getting together an expedition or a dig at an ancient campsite or a long forgotten burial site. My employment in that arena wouldn't be a problem, or so I thought, until I contacted several professors who usually organized digs during the summer months.

Funding was not as available as it had been in the past, and it appeared that they had their quota of workers already. They wouldn't be hiring for another three months for all those reasons that made my stomach growl a little louder. I needed a job now to stave off hunger. I didn't much care what kind of a job I got, or where it was.

Grad school would have to wait awhile until my usable funds were replenished. I began to think maybe my training in journalism could be useful. I definitely knew how to write and how to do research. I could try to freelance for magazines but that was iffy at best for an unpublished writer.

I certainly had no grandiose ideas of becoming a news anchor at one of the six major T.V. stations in town. I had had only one class in broadcast media and I certainly wasn't good at it. Every time it was my turn to give a presentation in front of the class my normally resonant *basso* voice developed this uncharacteristic squeak that made me sound like I had just inhaled a tank full of helium. Needless to say, I was a mess as a broadcaster and the brunt of a lot of jokes from my classmates. I should have gone into the standup comic field because I sure made everybody, including the professor, laugh at my efforts. But, I stuck it out, and had actually earned credit for that class, although barely. So here I was thinking about a job in Journalism, the writing end of the profession.

I scanned all the papers in town for a few days until an opening at one of the local newspapers, The *Albuquerque Journal*, showed up. It was for a reporter, experience not required, would involve extensive travel, and a willingness to learn the business.

This was exactly what I was looking for.

I dressed in my best, and only, threadbare suit. Tied a respectful knot in a tie I had bought from Goodwill, scraped most of the dirt off my loafers, went to the library at school to put together a decent resume, and showed up at the Journal's office at the announced time for the interview. As I entered the office I noticed there were three or four of my classmates already waiting. They were obviously also still unemployed and wanted this job. We chatted about what the job might entail, what the possible salary might be, and how interesting a reporter's job could be. We wished each other luck and then lapsed into silence until we were called, one at a time, into the inner sanctum to begin the interview process.

I did notice that nobody came into the outer office after me. I was the last in line. I waited as all the others disappeared through the door and one-by-one they had emerged not looking too happy about what had happened in there. It made me sweat a little about my chances. "Just have to take 'em," I thought.

When someone called my name, I revived from my deep thoughts and went through the door into my unknown future. I did notice that the title on the door said Managing Editor with the name, Dan Morenci painted under it.

As I entered, a stern looking man was sitting behind a very large oak desk holding a few papers I hoped were my resume and the job application. The expression on his face gave no indication of either approval or disapproval, or for that matter, any interest in them. His inaction made me wonder if I had made a mistake applying for the advertised position.

Maybe he was just reading an article about to be published. I didn't know.

I stood at some sort of loose attention in front of him until he motioned for me to take a seat. I wondered if the chair was designed like those used by some English kings of the distant past that made sure the subjects sitting in them would feel as uncomfortable as possible. They shortened the front legs so that the person had to hold on to keep from sliding off the chair. This trick kept the person very ill at ease in front of the king.

Fortunately though, this chair was normal but I still sat on the first six inches of the seat. I surely didn't want to appear casual to this man who held my future in his hands. We made our brief introductions as I covered my nervousness by crunching up a small notebook I carried specifically for that purpose.

I talked with Dan and answered his many questions. Our conversation must have lasted for at least a half an hour. I expressed my interest in Indian culture and happenings because I wanted him to know I thought they were a very important part of the history of the state. I also, very boldly, expressed my opinion that the three local papers were making a mistake by not doing more to cover the events, festivals, and feast days held at the many Pueblos each year. The Indian events at the State Fair always made the papers, but the other numerous Indian events were just given lip service. I didn't know what his reaction would be to my condemnation of the local papers, but he had asked for my opinion and I gave him my honest one. I'd just have to take my chances.

He surprised me.

"Those are my sentiments exactly Andy, and I plan to correct that oversight here at the Journal. I've had this idea for a long time now that I would like to establish what I would call the Indian Desk. My main problem hasn't been funding, but the fact that I haven't located the right person for the job until now."

My heart practically leaped into my throat. Had I blown any chance of a job with the Journal with my comments? I had better learn my lesson and in future interviews keep my personal feelings to myself.

I was only half listening when I heard Dan say, "You seem to be the first person who is both interested and qualified for this job, Andy. Can I interest you in taking the position?"

"Did I hear you correctly?" I asked finding it hard to accept my sudden good luck. "You are offering me the job of reporting on Indian affairs for the Journal?"

I hoped that I didn't sound too overly enthusiastic in my reply but, when Dan made me the offer of a salary higher than I had dared expect, one that couldn't, in all good conscious, turn down, I became "The Indian Desk."

He assured me that I had and that he wanted me to start as soon as possible. I asked him if Monday was too soon to start. He laughed and said that Monday would be soon enough. We shook hands on the deal and he told me to go directly to the Personnel office and sign some papers so I could get all the things I'd need to get on the payroll as a reporter. I would need to have a Journal ID card made, complete all the payroll forms, and get everything else that might be required to become the official Indian Desk.

That all took about an hour. I waited till I was several blocks from the Journal building before letting out the loudest war whoop that Albuquerque had ever heard. I had two days to wait until I went to work. I had some inkling about the job but I really knew nothing specific about what it would involve. The salary, which, as I said before, was more than I expected, was surely enough to keep me eating happily for a long time.

Who knows, I thought, I might just like being a reporter.

Now, I could afford gas for my car, maybe even an upgrade to a more reliable one and most assuredly, a better looking one, put some food in my fridge, and maybe up-grade my wardrobe. I wanted to appear respectable in my new job. When I got home I went through my apartment and reviewed my journalism textbooks, trying to recall those things that I seemed to have deliberately forgotten.

I stood in front of Dan that most important Monday morning at six forty-five. I was raring to go. He showed me where my office was. I noticed that the sign on the door read Indian Desk. Amazingly, I noticed my name below it. He hadn't wasted any time getting it painted there. I felt great!

My own office with my name on the door! As I looked over my desk, I noticed a little oblong box with my name on it. Business cards! He had had business cards printed for me with my title, "Indian Desk, *Albuquerque Journal,*" printed in big black letters. I made up my mind right then and there that I was going to enjoy this job, come hell or high water. My plans for graduate school quickly faded from memory.

All of that happened three months ago. Things have stayed at the same pitch all this time. Dan and I get along great. He has gone out of his way to give me some much needed advice and pointers and hasn't been too critical of the articles I have submitted to him for the paper, seven of which have been published. The copies are in frames hanging on my office walls. At this rate, I would have the walls covered in no time. Dan seems satisfied. I am improving too.

I write the Drumbeat, a regular weekly Indian column. I have traveled to almost all of the Pueblos close to Albuquerque. I haven't gone much upstate yet, but I'm sure I will eventually. There's a lot going on here in Old Town and at the Indian Cultural Centers. Somebody out there must like my columns because the mail and phone calls haven't slowed a bit since I got my first one. I get invitations to all kinds of ceremonials and events. I've met some of the tribal elders and leaders and have learned a lot about their tribal histories. I plan to write long articles on that topic one of these days. I like the free and easy management style Dan has used to bring me along and I feel like I am definitely developing my skills. I decided I might just make this a career and forgo grad school.

"What's up Dan?" I asked as I entered his office in response to his call.

"I've got something interesting here that a reporter from upstate sent to me," he replied. "It came from a small local paper in Bullsnort. Ever heard of it? Here, look at this clipping and tell me what you think," he said as he held up a small piece of newsprint.

I thought to myself, "where the hell is Bullsnort?"

"Sure, Dan, let me see it." I scanned the clipping and read that there was a young woman missing in Bullsnort. No one had seen or heard from her in three days. Her name is Carmelita Mendosa. The fact that no one knew what happened to her sounded strange because in small Spanish towns like Bullsnort, everybody knows everybody for generations and they all look out for one another. For someone to have disappeared without a trace just didn't fit the rule book.

What does Dan want me to do with a missing person? She isn't an Indian so what is he looking for? I asked myself. There was only one way to find out.

"What exactly are you looking for here, Dan? This is obviously a missing person case for the Police. How can I help? Where is this town called Bullsnort anyway?"

"In answer to your first question Andy, this clipping was sent to me by a former student who worked for me at another paper before I came to the Journal and he went off to make his fortune. He must consider it important that the Journal gets involved or else he wouldn't have sent it to me. I realize that it is a disappearance and not exactly the usual Indian Desk stuff, but I think you can investigate and write an article as well as I can. Besides, I can't take the time to go and check it out like you can," Dan said in a tone that indicated that this was my assignment.

"Bullsnort is up North in the Sangre de Cristo Mountains. Look it up on the map," he said as he pointed to a map of New Mexico on the wall of his office.

"Oh yes, you don't have to use your own car for this. Get a car and gas credit card from the newspaper motor pool, go to the Finance office and get an advance for your expenses, and be sure you keep a record for whatever reimbursement charges you may have. Keep in touch with me by phone and if this develops into anything newsworthy write it up and I'll see if we can publish it. Have a good trip and I'll expect a phone call with your initial report in a couple of days."

I didn't feel like I could find fault with his instructions so I said, "OK, just let me put the finishing touches on what I'm working on right now and I'll be ready to go this afternoon, or first thing tomorrow, at the latest."

I could hardly keep from letting out a loud whoop, as I eagerly accepted this assignment.

FOUR

The clean up on my article took about twenty five minutes and the trip to my apartment another thirty. I packed a ratty old tote bag with a couple pairs of underwear, T-shirts, some clean jeans and shirts, my ever present tape recorder, about nine cartridges of tapes, my camera with eight extra rolls of film, some necessities of clean living and made my way to the car I had picked up from the motor pool. I stopped at the nearest gas station, filled the tank, and bought a map of the state that showed me how to get to the mysterious town of Bullsnort.

It was a place represented by a dot on the map that looked like the period at the end of this sentence. It was located Northeast of Santa Fe, North on I-25, which was not the way I chose to go because of the ever present tourists intermingled with the normal heavy traffic due to local people going about their regular daily activities. Tourists are the easiest bunch to blame bad traffic on. Relaxed travel on that thoroughfare is virtually impossible and sometimes it becomes downright hazardous. Being the coward that I am, I chose the back, two lane roads that wound through many small towns and away from the bigger ones.

I didn't have to say goodbye or make any explanations about where I was going to anybody except my landlord, because my latest most significant other and I had parted ways a few weeks after graduation. I guess that happened mainly because of her constant picking at me to get married. I just wasn't ready yet and wasn't at all sure I wanted what she had to offer me in the way of marriage. I felt that her reason for wanting to get married was more to prove to her family that she could do it rather than to her desire for me to be her husband.

She was from some unpronounceable town in Massachusetts. Her accent was atrocious! She kept telling me that her family was very rich and they would make sure we were given good paying jobs, and maybe even our first house, by her father who owned several businesses. She seemed to think that this was perfectly alright, but for me it smacked of being a kept man which I wanted no part of. She adamantly refused to stay in the heathen infested Southwest where she said, no sane person can live comfortably.

I differed with her and we had some good arguments, me for, and her against Albuquerque or anywhere else in New Mexico. I love it here and wasn't about to knuckle under to her outrageous demands. Besides, I argued, the winters were cold as hell in New England. She settled the arguments when she left for home the next day. Funny thing about her leaving, she didn't even ask me to take her to the airport. I probably wouldn't have, at any rate. Remarkably, the constant headache that seemed to hover around when she was close by, was gone an hour after she left.

Now I was glad to get out of town for who knew how long. The drive north was comfortably slow going through town after town. I had decided that this trip to Bullsnort was going to be a great experience. Besides, I would probably get some contacts for later trips up there. I guessed that place, however small, had become, like so many places in New Mexico, a retirement community of snowbirds from the northern tier of the country getting away from the extremes of weather. One thing you can say about the weather in New Mexico is that it is constant. Most find it boring after a short period and return to wherever they came from. Some can't stand the solitude and quiet of the sand and cactus covered desert.

I guessed that Bullsnort was somewhere in this broad category-either in the throes of expansion or closing down due to a mass exodus. I would just have to hold back my building sarcasm about the place until I got there. Maybe Bullsnort had adjusted and the place had an exploding population of over a thousand. If you didn't love a town immediately, or had a hard time adjusting, you just left.

One of the biggest adjustments a new arrival to New Mexico had to make was to the distances between towns. From a relatively high hilltop you could probably see, on a clear day, in excess of fifty miles in any direction. Most days the sky was a clear azure blue with no clouds to mar the coloring. People from big eastern cities weren't used to anything that didn't go straight up for hundreds of stories. Most eastern city folks didn't drive a car because they never learned how or needed to. Those that did drive acted like they were in a bumper car at a carnival.

After getting all my gear stowed in the paper's car, I headed north driving casually through the many small Spanish towns along the way. I lost track of time and it seemed that I had been driving for hours when in reality I had only been on the road for an hour when I reached Santa Fe. I found the route out of town and followed it. All of my actions driving north out of Santa Fe seemed to be on some form of auto pilot. I drove, but was pretty much unaware of my actions for some unexplained reason.

Somehow the broken white lines on the highway had mesmerized me. Slowing down as I traveled through one small town after another became a blur to me. I'm not a true believer in the occult or ESP or any of those unexplained phenomenal things that some people say happen to them, but I sensed that something had indeed happened to me on the drive north.

It was as though I was under some sort of remote control. I just seemed to know where I was going and got myself there with no overt actions on my part. It was strange to say the least. Nothing like that had ever happened to me before. I shivered all over when I realized what was happening, but I could no more change it than anything I ever did in the past. I hoped I would soon come back to reality.

FIVE

I hadn't realized when the countryside changed from desert to mountains or when the mountains had changed again into a relatively flat plain in a dark green valley. When the double white lines had stopped zipping through my vision, I realized where I was, but I had no recollection of how I got there. Had I been under some kind of guidance? Was I supposed to be there at this place? Had I no choice? I wondered about those questions as the fog began to clear a little and I became a little less befuddled. It was like I had just materialized here, or had been transmuted here, whatever that means.

Either the broken white lines of the road I had been following had suddenly gotten much whiter or the street had gotten much darker. The grey road had suddenly become very black, like new asphalt. The white lines on the road, that led into the small town, just a short distance away, appeared to be freshly painted.

Was this Bullsnort? I had no idea. I didn't remember passing a road sign with that name on it. I was on the edge of the vegetation between two mountains that seemed like they started at the road's edge and went directly vertical.

I pulled over to the side of the road in a wide space and got out of the car to get my bearings. Ahead of me I could see a line of trees obviously fed by some underground water source. These cottonwood trees were about thirty feet tall and in full foliage. I got back into the car and drove on a little ways down the road to the edge of the small town. I stopped again just on the edge of town and looked.

I noticed that the place had only one major street. I estimated that the street ran for about one hundred yards then made a sharp right turn and disappeared. I saw twin silver rails embedded in the asphalt running the length of the street. Trolley rails? There was only one street light, one intersection, and some light pickup truck traffic, with what appeared to be the business district on both sides of the street. I noticed that there were very few people on the sidewalks.

I drove slowly down the street, behind a big silver slug of a thing that had appeared as I drove. I assumed that this was a farm vehicle of some sort. The rear license plate was covered with what could have been road kill innards, but probably was nothing more that hard caked mud. I could read only three of the five numbers there. The license plate was yellow like the New Mexico state plates and I made out the Zia sun sign, the yellow cross-hatched design that appears on all New Mexico plates. Below these numbers I could make out LAND OF ENCH. I knew by those letters that I was still in state, but still not sure if I was in Bullsnort.

There were only a few other vehicles on the street besides the silver slug, mostly old, battered pickup trucks. I recalled that in the few minutes of cognizance I had had on the road up here I had passed and had been passed by only a few vehicles. The few cars I saw were going too fast for me to get the license number, and the single farm truck amazed me because it had, in the bed, a gigantic black bull. I had never seen a bull that big or ugly. It reminded me of Paul Bunyon's blue ox, Babe. What amazed me most was that the dilapidated truck could carry that much weight without collapsing into a scrap heap.

As it passed me I noticed that the right front fender was held on only by the merest piece of metal and looked like it could launch itself into my driving space easily if the truck hit the slightest bump. Where the rear window should have been was an open space with jagged pieces of glass sticking up like razor wire around the perimeter of a prison. I did see two rifles in the rack strung across the open space in the back window. I couldn't see the driver because he was wearing the biggest brimmed cowboy that I had ever seen. It blocked my view of his whole face and even his ears.

I looked closely at the large black bull in the truck bed. I guessed the weight of the beast to be about two tons. The horns were about two feet long and stuck out straight from its head. It was definitely the ugliest thing I had ever seen because the front of the face looked like it had been beaten in with a four-by-four. I laughed and thought as it went by, I pity the cow that thing mates with.

I had no idea what I had gotten into here in this town but my expectations were high. I was here to do a job, however distasteful it might turn out to be. It felt like I had been directed here by some unknown powerful force. I had no choice but to be here. I had been just slowly drifting down the street toward the turn, not paying attention to what was happening around me, when all the sudden a pickup truck pulled right on my bumper and the driver let go with a blast of his horn that sounded a lot like it came from an eighteen wheeler. I had one choice then, either pull over in the nearest space or get pushed to somewhere I might not want to be. I didn't know if the driver of the truck was hostile or what, but I didn't want to take any chances. That blast scared the hell out of me.

As I sat at the curb waiting for my jangling nerves to come back to normal I wondered if the locals do this to all drivers in town and think nothing of it, or was I somehow singled out as a target. As the truck sped on down the street I decided that a target I wasn't and settled down a little to survey the street.

The sounds and smells of the place hit my senses like a cloud of fog settling in over the bay in San Francisco. Quickly and totally the fog seemed to engulf most of what I assumed was Bullsnort. There were pleasant smells of food in the air and my mouth started to water. I had to swallow several times to keep from slobbering all over my shirt. My stomach growled in sharp revolt to it's being slightly empty. I looked around for some sign of a restaurant and decided that a big juicy breakfast of steak and eggs would do nicely.

On my meager meal budget at home I normally ate hamburgers and pizza on a regular basis. I always tried to save what leftovers I had but after a few days they started to grow hair, turn black, and had to be thrown out. While I was on the newspaper's budget for meals I was going to take advantage of it and eat well while I was here in Bullsnort.

I secured my stuff, locked the car, and followed my nose to the source of the smells wafting from a small place that had a sign painted on the window in Spanish. I didn't bother to read it just then because I was too hungry. The place was decorated in a motif that included some extremely large sombreros, colorful pottery and some really good music was coming from speakers mounted on the walls.

I sat down in a booth that had a very large and dangerous looking cactus on the window sill and waited for the waitress. As I waited, I looked around the place and liked what I saw. I saw her looking in my direction as she raised one hand with her index finger extended to indicate that she would be at my side in a minute or so. In less than a minute she came to my booth with a large and a small folder in her hand, which I assumed was the menu and order book. She was wearing a pink blouse and jeans with white shoes on her feet. Not the typical waitress dress I guessed, but I was too hungry just then to complain. She greeted me and asked me what I'd like to drink and handed me the menu.

I should have known that the chance of steak and eggs being on the menu wasn't realistic. As I looked over the list which not to my surprise, was in Spanish, what I saw looked very exotic and new to me. Although I could speak a little Spanish and recognized some items, I didn't have a clue what most of them were. When I looked for obvious road kill, jokingly, and found none I was a little relieved. I would have to eat this stuff for as long I was in town.

What I found was some very interesting and potentially delicious food items:

Chuleas de Puerco	$4.74
Chamarones al MOJO de Ajo	$5.25
Carne Asada Y Cameron	$6.45
Paras en su Cascara	$5.75
Taquisa	$4.75

I had to let the waitress, when she came back to me, help me decide what it was I wanted. She was very patient as I asked all my questions and brought me a bowl of salsa and a big pile of tortilla chips to eat while I was waiting for my order to arrive. The chips were obviously homemade because they looked like saucers they were so big. I had taken her suggestions, not fully knowing what it was that I had ordered. As she walked back to the kitchen I tried the chips and dip.

I liked to think I could eat just about anything hot or cold, spicy or not, but that chip and dip proved me wrong.

Oh so wrong!

With the first swallow, my mouth was immediately on fire from the spicy chili in the dip. I took a big gulp of water to cool the volcano in my mouth but all I succeeded in doing was washing the terrific heat down into my stomach where it grumbled, burned, and felt like it was all going to erupt all over the place. After about ten minutes or so, the heat cooled enough for me to take a normal breath and another slug of cold water.

WOW! This stuff was so hot I guessed it would take the paint off my car. I wondered what the meal would taste like, or if I could eat it at all. I needn't have worried.

When it came it was beautiful with color and tasted great, and was mild enough that it didn't cause another eruption in my stomach. I guess the waitress had seen my reaction to the dip, and had taken pity on me by bringing something that was not too spicy. I had to admit it was one of the best Mexican meals I had eaten in a very long time. My reservations about eating here disappeared fast. The extra cold *Dos Equis* beer hit the spot too. I sat there admiring the décor when the waitress came back and removed the few remnants of my meal and cleared the table.

I asked her name just to be friendly.

"My name is Anna Marie Rodriguez. And what is yours?" she said in a heavily accented voice that had a very light touch of laughter in it.

"Andy Bling," I replied. "I'm new in town and I will be here on business for a few days. I was wondering what there was to do here other than sit and drink beer. I haven't seen much of the town yet so I don't know where to go looking. I thought you might be willing to help me get my bearings."

I realized that this wasn't much of an opening line but then again, I wasn't much for opening lines with women. Frankly, women tend to scare the hell out of me for some unknown reason. They all seem to have a built-in dislike for men in general. I certainly never did anything to make them hate me or give me a hard time. I hoped this one would be friendly. She had been so far, but then again, I was a customer and not someone she dated. I hoped that maybe that would change for the better, hopefully before I had to leave town.

She smiled at me. I get a little nervous and weak-kneed when strange girls smile at me, but this one was different and I smiled back at her.

"I don't know what you have in mind as far as fun goes, Andy, but here we make our own entertainment. We are a small out of the way place with not much going on. You did get here at a good time right now though. Today is Wasping Day".

I immediately thought, "Wasping Day? What kind of town and situation have I gotten myself involved with?"

I'd soon find out.

I had attended many festivals and Indian celebrations since I became the Indian Desk and had never heard of a Wasping Day celebration being held anywhere in the state. But then again, I was in Bullsnort and anything could, and obviously did, happen here.

The most famous celebration I could draw to mind was the one that happened in Santa Fe in September each year. It was the burning of "Old Man Gloom – Zozobra". The festival in Santa Fe dates to 1712 but the burning ritual, started in 1924, involves a giant figure in the form of a marionette called "Zozobra".

The brochures I have read described him as an empty headed, hideous but harmless bogeyman. He has no guts and doesn't have a leg to stand on. He never wins. He moans, groans, twists his head, his mouth gapes open and he chomps at nothing. His arms flail about in frustration.

Each year they string him up and burn him down, taking away the troubles of everyone for another year. He is stuffed with shredded paper, fire crackers, obsolete police reports and divorce decrees. He stands about fifty feet high and when lit, goes up in a great flame. Everybody is happy to get rid of their troubles while he burns.

I wondered if Bullsnort's Wasping Day was somehow going to involve a nest of wasps in which each bug would be zapped by a ball of flame.

I guessed that I was about to find out.

Wasping Day? I've never heard of a day to celebrate wasps. I don't particularly like them and stay away from them as much as possible. They rank right up there with black widow spiders and poisonous snakes, where I am concerned.

"Please tell me. What do you folks do with them, Anna Marie," I asked. I didn't want to sound too sarcastic or put her off, but I wasn't really interested in anything that had to do with having contact with very dangerous wasps. It sounded crazy to me but what could I say if I wanted to become friends with this woman?

"You heard me right, Andy. We catch wasps by snagging their nests in a plastic bag. We try to get at least one pretty large nest. Sometimes the wasps don't want to get into the bag and fight back and some of the catchers get some really bad stings, but we get a lot of volunteers to catch them anyway. Then we take the bag with the nests and carefully put a small dish of beer in it so it lays flat and doesn't spill. Then we wait. Filling the dish only takes about half of a can of beer so whoever puts the dish in the bag gets to drink the rest of that can. The rest of us get to drink the other six packs we've brought along while we wait for the wasps to do their thing. Just sitting there watching is not very exciting. It's kind of like watching a worm race, unless you happen to get stung, and it doesn't take long for that to happen to someone, either."

"This sounds a lot like weird to me, so, let me see if I understand it," I said.

"You find a wasp's nest, some not so smart volunteers to take it out of the tree and put it into a plastic bag. Then you put some beer in a saucer and feed the beer to the bugs, right? Then what happens?"

"Well once the wasps calm down a little they smell the beer and go to investigate it," she said with a laugh. "They get into the saucer, suck up some of it, apparently, and get drunk, I guess. Then, because they can't fly very well, they crash into each other on takeoff while some fall back into the beer and drown. Some never get out of the saucer they like the beer so much."

"We don't want the whole nest to be killed off so we open the bag after a few have been done in and the rest can fly away and make a new nest. You ever seen a drunken wasp stagger?" she inquired with a serious look on her face.

"It's hilarious! Believe it or not, Andy, this works for the critters around our houses too. Granted, this kind of entertainment doesn't last very long, and probably is a lot less exciting than you are used to wherever it is that you come from, but up here it's just something we do for entertainment. Of course the catchers get stung a few times and the bugs that get away aren't too friendly to us watchers, so we have to be careful so we don't get stung too."

She looked at me and a very bright twinkle came into her eyes like she had just put me on and was wondering if I believed the story.

I didn't say I did or didn't but asked her when the Wasping thing happened.

"You're in luck, Andy. Today some of the guys are going to collect a few nests. We will all meet out there on the street at three. Everybody is welcome so if you want to come you can. I will certainly be there."

I thought seriously about turning her invite down but what the hell, I didn't have anything else better to do right now, so I said sure, "I'd be there."

A funny thought came to mind just then. I had read somewhere that the sailors and airmen who happened to be stuck in the Pacific on Midway during World War II used to spend their off duty time betting on the gooney birds. Seems that was the great fun then, watching a big 20 -25 pound albatross trying to take off after a running start. After running about fifteen or so yards most of these birds got up only enough lift from their gigantic wings to crash and burn in a long drawn out tumbling act. The sailors thought those landings were hilarious, too. I understood. I wondered how funny the Wasping would turn out to be.

"And, if you're here two weeks from now we will be having our Snaking fun, continued Anna Marie.

I didn't want to hear about any fun with snakes, so I just ignored her as she walked away. The meal sat heavily on my stomach as I continued to wonder what kind of town I had wandered into.

I finished my now lukewarm beer, paid the bill and went outside under the clear blue sky. Things were looking pretty good so far, at least there was one pretty good looking girl in town who was at least a little friendly toward me, maybe single and if I played it right maybe she'd agree to go on a date with me.

Where do the locals go? I mused.

Wasping, or Snaking? How could I say no?

I didn't want to think about what other kind of sports they had come up with involving some other critter.

As I reached the street I looked around to get my bearings and was amazed at what I saw. I expected to see a town like the one I came from that was basically all one color of stone or brick fronts with grey concrete sidewalks.

Every building was painted with multiple colors. None were alike and none were just one color. The doors on some were one color and the rest of the place another, or two or three colors had been used to create an interesting pattern. The building directly across the street had a blue door, red shutters, yellow window sills, brown stucco, and green flower boxes that held a myriad of colorful flowers. It was a vivid splash of colors that I hadn't seen anywhere else in New Mexico, especially on the drive up into these mountains. The brilliant sunshine magnified the colors to their maximum effect into a bouquet not to be forgotten. The blues ran the gamut of sky blue to rainstorm grey, the yellows reminded me of ripe bananas and yellow delicious apples, the greens shone like pale grapes and avocado rinds, and the brilliant reds looked like bunches of ripe cherries. There was a smattering of purples of all shades and what amazed me most was that there were no basic whites anywhere to be seen except in the line running down the exact center of the paved street.

I turned around to look at the restaurant I had just left. It had a maroon door, green shutters, black window sills, and its walls were colored deep earth brown stucco. I looked up at the restaurant's sign, which I hadn't bothered to read as I went in. I read, "The Cueva Del Zorro". "The Cave of the Fox".

I wondered if the food I had just enjoyed was some variation of wild game, roadkill or a homemade mixture of things that I didn't want to think about. I laughed at the thought of having just eaten something like smashed squirrel or prairie dog casserole. My stomach was still settling down from the meal and it growled at the thought. I burped but I really didn't care, the food was delicious and I knew, roadkill or homemade, I'd definitely come back to the "Cave" to eat.

As I walked along admiring the colors, I thought of the cafeteria at the University of New Mexico and the food we endured as students there. Probably every college student who lived in the dorms and had to eat in the cafeteria was a victim of creative cooks on a tight budget wherever they attended school. Every Friday without fail students at UNM were served a concoction that was a basic ovoid shape with a brown crust that was obviously deep-fried something. It had no specific taste but was textured, and not at all tasty.

We who ate it at least once surveyed the guesses of what it might be and the best that we could come up with was that it was all the leftover meat from the previous week's meals that had been ground into pellets like rabbit food, compressed into the shapes and then fried. Nobody could come up with a better name than mystery meat because nobody could distinguish any particular taste, say of hamburger, or steak, in it. One good thing about it was these things were fried so hard they could, in an emergency, be used as Frisbees, or with a little mustard as glue, as heels on shoes, if nothing else was available.

We guessed the cooks figured that if they covered the stuff with enough pungent sauce then we'd eat it all. Well, they were wrong. There was a lot left that they did something with. I don't think they dared to feed it to domestic livestock for fear of poisonings. On Fridays, none of us ever took left over's to our dorm rooms for a snack. I'll guarantee that. I never saw any of the dogs that roamed the campus eat any of it if we offered it to them. I never saw any of the cooks eat the stuff either. You don't have to be stupid to be a cook in a college kitchen I guess.

As I walked down the street, my thoughts returned to the present and I became more and more enamored with the colors. Most of the small towns I had driven through were colorless, almost like the folks who lived there had drained it all away over the centuries the towns had existed. This place was surely different.

Bullsnort looked like it could have come from the pages of Architectural Digest it was so perfect. It was too perfect. As I would quickly find out.

There were only two people walking on the street, no children playing there, no trash had blown in on the ever present wind. The sidewalks were aged wooden slats, just like in the old timey western towns in the movies. It was beautiful, to say the least.

As I looked up the street, a large building directly across from me caught my eye. It looked like it had heavy steel bars on the windows. I wondered if it was the jail or the bank. It looked like a place I would want to investigate. I saw that it had a very old, weathered sign where I could make out some peeling raggedy hand painted letters that read

Mot Cou t Ro with Kitch ettes. I assumed that it had once said "Motor Court Rooms with Kitchenettes".

On the roof was what appeared to be a full sized Conestoga wagon. The wagon looked to be an original one as far as I could tell. Maybe some of the original settlers of this town had traveled in it on their way West. On the pink building next to it was a gigantic wagon wheel that looked like it was twice as big as the one over the motor court. I wondered where it had come from, maybe a freight wagon? The building next to it had a sign over the door that read "Cantina" from which I heard guitar music, singing, and much laughter. I decided to go there after I found out whether the motor court had any rooms to rent. Since there was no traffic I meandered across the street in that general direction.

When I reached the other side of the street, I looked both ways. I noticed a large screen that was obviously part of a drive-in movie theater at the opposite end of town. I could see some movement of the actors on the screen. I wondered why there would be an outdoor movie at this time of day. I decided that someone was probably just previewing it or maybe they always started the movies at sundown.

On the screen a larger than life cowboy was kissing his horse and saying something to a beautiful girl who was in tears and appeared to not want to hear what the cowboy was telling her. I couldn't hear the sound but could imagine what the cowboy was saying to her. I laughed at the thought of him kissing the horse instead of the girl. Not a chance in hell I'd be so stupid I'd kiss a horse, especially with a beautiful girl standing right there. But, then again, I wasn't a cowboy and didn't know what it would be like to love a horse.

As I looked up the street the other way I saw some very interesting architecture. The building on the corner had a very large yellow five pointed star on the roof. I didn't even try to guess what it stood for and continued to scan the street. The gas station on the opposite corner sported a sign that had a large, and very menacing looking ugly dinosaur as a mascot.

An overly large concrete teepee was attached to the entrance of a red building that was very long with a very low ceiling. It had no identifiable features, other than the teepee, to indicate what might be inside. On the plaza in front of a building that had five floors, was a double life sized concrete Indian in full regalia and feather headdress. The feathers were painted blue and white and ran the length of the Indian's body to the ground, a distance of about twenty feet.

As I looked over these buildings I caught sight of the glowing end of what was apparently a lit cigarette in the shadows between two of the buildings. As my eyes adjusted to the shadows I could make out the outline of a lone figure wearing a large high domed cowboy hat with the business end of something wrapped in a paper bag held to his lips. Best just leave that alone, I thought, as I scanned the rest of the street.

I noticed a bakery, an Indian arts store, a barbershop with a spinning candy cane outside, and a western wear clothing store. On my side of the street I noticed the Sheriff's office and a sign for a lawyer's office. I couldn't tell if they were open or not. I might have to go to both places for help in gathering what information I could about this missing girl. I'd decided that I'd present myself as an investigative reporter looking into a story for my paper as I questioned people about her.

After all, I was assigned to investigate and send stories back to Dan. I'd hold back on my intention to actually find out what happened to her until I talked to some people first to determine who might not be friendly to inquiries about the missing girl.

In this small town I was sure there'd be someone who didn't like her for whatever reason. I just had to find out who had the wherewithal to do away with her, if that was indeed her fate.

The other interesting feature I noticed immediately about this town was that there was very little traffic on the street. There were no cars, the big silver trailer that I had followed into town was now nowhere in sight, and right now there were no people walking around. The traffic on the main street was sparse and the vehicles were mostly pickup trucks. They were older, battered, dust covered, and most of them looked like they were in the final stages of decay before their ultimate collapse into rust colored salvage parts. A few looked as though all that held them together was the rust. The three or four I looked at had rifles of various calibers in the rear windows. Then I noticed that most had the glass broken out of the rear window, just like the truck I had seen earlier with the big bull in it.

Almost every one of the trucks looked like they had been involved in some raging gun battle, or maybe some variation of target practice, somewhere out on the desert. They had multiple bullet holes and shotgun pellet holes in the doors and beds of the trucks. None were completely unscathed. Another interesting thing caught my eye just then. None of the trucks were even near new in this small parade. I guessed that none of them were newer than the early sixties. Most were late forties and fifties Chevys and GMC's. All had some kind of mongrel multi colored dog in the bed that was doing a precarious balancing act while the trucks bounced along making their way to who knows where. None of these dogs fell out though. None were tied in the beds, either.

I had seen some dogs like these in trucks in Albuquerque. There, I figured that they were some kind of special New Mexican breed used only by pickup drivers. Here they were the prime noise makers in the area. They barked furiously at the other dogs to protect their trucks. They lunged and barked at each other while staying in the truck beds and keeping just out of range of the other dogs. Smart. Some had even barked and lunged at me as I watched the spectacle. If the noise levels were any indication of how ferocious they were they could have torn a man limb from limb with very little effort. I laughed as I guessed that if once given a chance to get out on the ground for a real face off they probably just all lie down meekly under their trucks and go to sleep.

What kind of a place had I driven into? Or been directed to?

Bullsnort had a strange aura about it. It looked like a throwback to the early fifties and those Route 66 Travelogues.

I re-scanned the street both ways. It was as if I were standing in the center of a painting. I was in the picture but not painted there. That feeling heightened my sense of foreboding and caution about the place. I decided that I didn't want the sinister amorphous shape with the glowing cigarette to take out his frustrations on me. If this first impression was truly Bullsnort, then I had a lot to look forward to.

I shook myself out of my thoughts and remembered that I needed a place to spend the next few days and as I looked I didn't see any place other than the motor court that might provide rooms for rent. I didn't relish the idea of sleeping in my car so I meandered over that way still not knowing what to expect from this town.

SIX

I didn't know what to expect as I climbed the three steps to sidewalk level and entered the front door of the motor court. There was nobody there and on the big log counter I spotted one of those silver bell affairs so I smacked it a good one to alert whoever might be in the back office that I was there to do business. As I waited for someone to answer the bell I looked around the place. I had spotted the heavy steel bars on the windows from the street. I now noticed that the side windows also had these bars on them too. I wondered if this place might have once been the town jail or the bank.

A sense of history enveloped me as I stood there. It was as if I had walked back a century as I came through the door. The floors were very rough and obviously made of hand-hewn boards that were at least two feet wide and irregularly shaped on the edges. They were sturdy though, with no squeaks or movement as I walked on them. There was also no paint or varnish to be seen anywhere, just well-aged wood. The counter top was made of heavy log planking and the front of it had what appeared to be bullet holes in it. There were wanted posters around the walls that appeared to be originals.

All of the posters were slightly browned with age. The mustachioed men looking back from them were definitely not the type of men anybody would want to tangle with, even if fully armed. Most of the pictures had the names, offenses for which they were wanted and the reward offered for their capture. A few of the more grisly looking ones simply read:

WANTED
DEAD OR ALIVE
DON'T MATTER NONE

I assumed this information was meant as further incentive for capturing the crooks. One poster of a murderer had a price tag on his head of fifteen hundred dollars, Gold.

The US Marshalls must have wanted him awfully bad for that kind of reward. I read the description of the crime and found out that he had killed two Deputy Marshalls in a bank robbery in 1876.

I was still studying that poster when a gruff, whisky soured voice from behind me proclaimed, "Most of them was caught and killed for the reward. Only one or two, as best I recall, ever spent time in this here jail."

"You've already seen all those bullet holes in the desk and walls? Well, we had some doozy shootouts here. I reckon that three or four of these wanted hombres was killed right out there in the street along with one or two Sheriffs unlucky enough to go after them. This here town was a real good place to be far away from in those days."

When I heard that voice I spun around to see a wizened old man who had the grayest, and scraggliest beard I'd ever seen. It could be best described as a fly's nest. What hair he had hung in strings from a cleared ring on the top of his head down to his shoulders. He looked like the pictures I'd seen of tonsured monks of the twelfth or thirteenth century monasteries. The top of his scalp was as smooth as a cue ball. He was about five foot two and stood no more than a couple of inches above the counter top. The black clothes he wore can best be described as decrepit. They were supposed to be black but their color was predominately just dirt. I gave him the benefit of the doubt. After all, he could have been working in a garden somewhere out back. Maybe he was also the local grave digger. That thought gave me a shudder. I just stood there looking at him trying desperately to suck enough air into my lungs so that when I was able to speak it wouldn't seem like I had just inhaled a lungful of helium and sound like Donald Duck.

The old man glared at me like I was a piece of dog dung that had happened to be dropped into his office off the bottom of someone's boot. It wasn't pleasant looking at him. "I'll bet he doesn't get much return business if he looks at all his customers that way," I thought.

The old man was obviously disturbed at my ringing his damned dinger summoning him to come from somewhere in the back of the building. He was bent over and leaned heavily on the big gnarled stick he carried to support himself. His face and hands were heavily liver spotted with obvious age. I guessed his age to be somewhere between eighty five and one hundred years. He didn't sound or look overly friendly toward me.

At that second I wasn't inclined to be too friendly toward him either.

If he doesn't like the sound of his bell going off, why the hell does he have it sitting on top of the worn counter, I thought as I waited for him to speak lest I say something to offend him more.

"You must be new in these parts ringing that bell like that. It must be forty years since it's been rung. Surprises the hell out of me that it's not rusted shut. Nobody ever rings that thing because they know how it aggravates me to hear it. Remember that if you ever come back here young feller," he said in a loud scratchy voice. "You want a room, just sign in, take a key, and pay up when you decide to leave. Word of advice, though, don't even think about not paying because the Sheriff will sure as hell get you," he continued.

"That way you don't have to bother me and cause me to have to come all the way in here. But we're both here now so just sign one of them cards and I'll get a key for you. How long you reckon on staying?" All of which he said without taking a visible breath of air.

"Okay," I replied sheepishly to his admonishment, "I'm just passing through Bullsnort. I might be here maybe two or three days till I get my work done then I'll be gone." I filled in the blanks on the guest card and quickly handed it to him.

I didn't know then that I'd have to extend this initial time by several more weeks, but that is the rest of the story.

I sure didn't relish the idea of being this close to the nasty old man but the alternative of sleeping in my car up here in the mountains where it gets very cold at night didn't float my boat either. People who are not from this part of the country who try it are sometimes found very much dead from the fumes they breathe while trying to keep warm in a running car. I signed the card, retrieved the key, got the directions to my home away from home, and left without another word from the old man. I guess he just wanted me gone so he could go back to his dirt.

I wondered what he had out back there that was so interesting that he didn't want to waste time doing business with me.

I knew better than to ask him.

SEVEN

I drove around back the way the old man had pointed and found the rustic log cabin that had the same number as my key on the door. The surface of the driveway gave absolutely no clue that another car had been over it any time in the recent past. I assumed that the clandestine meetings that did take place here were done within walking distance and very anonymously. I got my one bag out of the trunk, unlocked the very heavy log door, and entered the room.

To say that the room was sparsely furnished was a gross understatement. Bare would be appropriate.

The room had one window with the thinnest piece of material covering it that blocked no light at all from coming in. The bed frame was made of smaller logs that had aged to a dull gray color. The mattress that covered the frame looked like it had just been dumped there from the chicken feather factory. It was nothing more than a very large mound hidden below the coverlet. It left a lot to be desired in the way of comfort potential.

There was a little table only large enough to hold a medium sized lamp that had a shade with a woodsy scene painted on it; the kind you can get in any souvenir shop. The chair appeared to be made of tree limbs and definitely looked like it could wreck your back the first time you sat in it. And when I spotted what appeared to be the bathroom, it looked initially like a converted outhouse that had been enclosed by building walls around it.

There was a sink and a shower but I seriously doubted that there was even a remote chance of hot running water. Cold bathing didn't appeal very much to me at this point. I wasn't going to like staying here very much I decided then and there.

I put my meager belongings away in a dilapidated chest of drawers that had seen its better days a hundred years ago. Then I walked back outside to try and find the Cantina where the good guitar music I'd heard earlier had come from.

I followed the good sounding music and as I walked into the dark room from the bright sunlight outside, I was blinded until my eyes adjusted. In that space of less than a minute I guessed that I had been scrutinized and found acceptable because I felt all the eyes in the place focus on me and then move on to other things more important. Ever have that feeling? It was definitely present here in this place. The music didn't miss a beat. I guessed the word that a gringo was in town and staying at the motor court and already had eaten lunch at the Cave had spread around town.

It really is amazing how fast word travels in a small town. The pace of conversation in the darkness resumed as I made my way to an empty booth after weaving through a small bunch of angry looking cowboys who didn't say a word at me. A good looking waitress came up to me and asked what I wanted to drink. I ordered a beer and looked at the menu she handed me.

A few minutes later a bus boy came up and deposited a bowl of salsa and chips on the table for me. I was wary of the salsa from my last experience, so I took only a very small portion as way of testing the heat. I noticed then that the beer glass had a wedge of lime on it. I took the lime, bit into it and sucked some of the juice. It immediately puckered my mouth up so I took a big slug of beer to wash it down. The salsa wasn't nearly as hot as it had been at the Cave, so I snacked a little on it till the waitress came back and took my order for dinner. The food was fantastic with the second very cold beer. I was feeling a lot better after my experience with the old man and the Wasping tale from the waitress at the Cave.

The music was very good ethnic Mariachi. The four guitars were mellow, the trumpet was blaring and counterpoint to the singers. The five men had a natural harmony that was so close it reminded me of barbershop music.

The song was one I'd not heard before. It was great stuff to hear with dinner; soft and melodious. I hummed along with the rhythm because I didn't know the words and wasn't much of a singer, anyway. I wasn't tone deaf but my voice wasn't of operatic quality either, although I had sung in my high school chorus for four years and could carry a tune well. I noticed some couples dancing on the sawdust covered floor. Both men and the women had on the same basic costume. Cowboy boots that were scuffed up, blue jeans; the women's were definitely more form fitting than the men's were, a striped cowboy shirt and some kind of broad brimmed hat, mostly white straw it appeared. One guy's hat had a sad looking feather sticking out of the band. Some couples were just talking as they moved to the rhythm, while others were singing. All were having a good time with their partners. I had a few more beers while the music got better and better.

After a while I decided to go back to my room. I was tired from driving and content from the dinner I'd just consumed, which along with the extremely tasty beers would soon lull me into dreamland. Along the way back to the motor court I stopped and bought a local newspaper in one of the shops on the way.

I didn't know what to expect as I was an unexpected and unwanted visitors in this town so I made sure the two locks on the door were secure before getting ready for bed. The deadbolt made me feel a little more secure. I scanned the headlines as I undressed and climbed into the very soft looking pile of covers. As I looked over the paper my eyes were drawn to a story about a local girl, aged twenty one, who had mysteriously disappeared. It gave her name, Carmelita Mendosa, her address here in town, some of her friend's names, and a number to call at the Sheriff's office to inquire about the reward they offered for information leading to her being located. The name of the sheriff and the phone number were at the end of the article.

This news article expanded on the story that had prompted Dan to send me up here. I didn't know what would happen or develop out of my investigation of this disappearance, but I would spend a few days looking around and asking some questions. I had to gather enough information to write a follow-on story for Dan and the Journal. I had to write at least one article that was publishable to justify my expenses to the newspaper's finance department when I submitted my expense account for reimbursement.

Besides the story of Carmelita there was another article about the shooting of a local man, aged twenty, the same age as Carmelita. I didn't know if there was a connection between the two at this point but it wouldn't hurt to talk to this young man about his adventure. According to the article, he was still in the hospital with three gunshot wounds. One bullet had lodged in his shoulder, one in his arm, and one in his abdomen. The article said he was in serious condition but was expected to recover. His assailant was still unknown according to the source at the Sheriff's office.

There was an interesting sentence in the article that immediately caught my attention. It stated that the shooting victim's bullet riddled truck was found about three miles outside of town. There was no explanation of how the truck got there or how the victim had made his way back to town and to the hospital. There was nothing in the article about recovered casings.

I wondered about that and made a mental note to ask about them when I went to the Sheriff's office.

As I read the articles about the two seemingly unconnected young people, a very excruciating headache started behind my eyes. I never got headaches. What the hell was happening to me? Maybe the beers had started it. I swore to go easier on the salsa and beers tomorrow but my vow had no effect on the shooting pain behind my eyes. I pressed my thumbs to my temples to try and relieve some of the pain but it didn't help any. As I pressed my fingers to my temples, everything suddenly became a dark, mottled brown color. It must be some kind of effect from fatigue. I thought as the pain persisted.

The color hadn't faded at all when I thought I heard a voice talking to me from somewhere. Was my mind coming unglued or what? I had no idea what was happening. I just knew I heard the voice and felt the pain. The voice just seemed to come into me. I knew not how or from where it came. It began as a variation of what I guessed was Spanish or maybe some Indian dialect. I didn't understand many words of any Indian language so I couldn't even guess what the medium was. Strangely, as with all the rest of the strange experiences that had happened to me since I started on my journey to Bullsnort, I somehow understood what this voice was saying to me.

A male voice said,

"Tawamiciya,
I am the first Clan Father.
I am named "Crawls Along Slowly".
I am the spiritual leader of the Turtle Clan.
I will teach you to persevere.
When you are ready and need me, I shall return to you."

As I lay there thinking about the voice and the message, the tingling that came with it slowly diminished and my head returned to normal after a few minutes. I hadn't the foggiest idea what had just happened to me but it must have been important to someone to give me that message. My main problem now was what was I supposed to do with it? Were there more messages I was to get or was that it? The very large goose bumps on my arms looked like they were playing a game of marbles. Scared? That doesn't begin to describe what I was feeling right about then.

I quickly got out of bed and retrieved my notebook. After a minute I was able to remember the name the voice had called me and wrote it and the message down. I felt a tingle and knew that somehow this name and the message would be very important to my stay here in Bullsnort.

EIGHT

"You'd better be speaking the truth, you bastard, or I'll make sure that thing that you value more than anything else is severely shortened to the point where you won't be able to piss standing up without getting your pants soaked. If you're lying to me you won't be able to stick it in anything larger than a very small squirrel. You want that?" the lawyer asked the Sheriff who was looking very sheepish as he sat across the table from her at the Cantina where they had met for lunch. As she stared at the very pained look on his face a thought came into her mind and she almost broke out laughing, which wouldn't do at all,

"Damn! That was good!"

The lawyer continued, "I sent Carmelita to Santa Fe to confer with the new clients three weeks ago and guess what? You were very conspicuously gone from town that weekend. Same thing happened two weeks ago. Very convenient, you having Sheriffs' conventions every weekend in Santa Fe, isn't it?"

"I didn't say it was for a Sheriffs' convention, but I did have business there, and no, I didn't meet or sleep with Carmelita on either weekend. How is it that you don't trust me all the sudden? What's eating at you?" said the Sheriff in an irritated tone.

"I'll tell you what's eating me," she replied. "If you haven't noticed, I'm the only female lawyer in this little Spanish oriented town. The men don't trust me to do their business because they think that all women aren't as smart as they are and that we should stay at home, have as many babies as they want to make, and keep house. They are pigs for the most part that I wouldn't even come to the Cantina for a beer with any of them if they asked me, let alone go out on a date somewhere where we might be seen by others as ignorant as they are. I'm isolated here and you are the only man in town that gives a shit about my opinions or treats me halfway decently. Now I find out that you have been messing around with my clerk, for God's sake."

"How could you? If the concierge at the Hyatt was correct, he saw you come into the hotel on both weekends and then he saw you leave and return with Carmelita late every night. He saw you leave on Monday morning and saw Carmelita leave a little later. Do you deny it? Answer me now!" she demanded in a hurt voice.

"You are going to believe whatever you want to in spite of what I say," replied the Sheriff in a firm voice. "So no I won't either deny or confirm it. But if you want us to continue to be together you'll drop it, OK?"

"No, it's definitely not OK to just drop it as if nothing has happened between us," she said with anger in her voice and tears appearing in her eyes.

"I have to work with Carmelita sitting in my office every day! I can just imagine her laughing to herself that she has pulled a very fast on me and that I don't have an inkling about what's going on between you two juvenile delinquents. I have plans for her and I guarantee you one thing she will not like them one little bit. I'd like to believe I can count on you for help to carry out my plans, but, you can be sure, I am going to eliminate her as a bone of contention in our relationship with or without it!"

"You're not planning to do something really stupid are you?" he replied in the same tone he used when he interrogated suspects. "Like something that will get you and maybe me, if I decide to help you, in jail for a long time? Do you have any idea what life is like for any lawman who does time in a state or federal prison? I don't want to think about it, and neither should you. We'll work something out that isn't in the drastic category."

"When I make my final plan of action I'll let you know and then you'll have a choice of either me or her," she said as she regained her composure.

"WOW," the Sheriff thought later as he recalled this conversation about Carmelita, and then he really began to worry about the plan and whatever it might evolve into to eliminate Carmelita from our relationship.

He very quickly made a decision. "Whatever this plan turns out to be I want no part of it."

NINE

Later, as I thought about the message from the Clan Father, I realized that I had sensed the words more than actually hearing them. I had successfully written the message in my notebook so I wouldn't forget it. A million questions seemed to be buzzing around in my brain as I recalled what had happened.

What does the message mean and why did I receive it? Had I somehow chosen by this Clan Father to be a medium, or a go-between?

"A go-between for who, and for what?" The voice had come to me after I'd read the two newspaper articles.

Then a thought came to me. Maybe I was chosen to help solve Carmelita's disappearance or the attempted murder of the man out in the desert or both. I remembered that I had read a description somewhere about the Indian beliefs concerning Clan Fathers. There were several of them, all with different responsibilities, that guided the Indians of tribes and clans through their big decisions in life. Maybe the Clan Fathers are going to help me somehow solve these riddles.

As I re-read the newspaper stories, I remembered the message and thought, "How should I persevere?" Will there be more messages, and in what form will they come?

I had a whole shopping list of unanswered questions. Is the truth not in the article? Is the Sheriff not being truthful in stating that this staff is doing all that can be done to locate Carmelita? Was he, or someone he knows, involved in the shooting? Those two questions put the seriousness of the problem up about four notches on the scale.

But more questions came flooding into my thoughts.

How am I supposed to go about solving, or helping those better equipped than I, to solve the problems and questions if the Sheriff was somehow involved? Who can I rely on to help? Who might come after me for mayhem or to put damage on me if I asked the wrong question to the wrong person? Who can I rely on for the two days I plan on being here?

It looked as though my stay might just be a lot longer than I thought. I would definitely have to be very circumspect in my questioning.

Enemies I didn't need at this point. Especially if they were the kinds of enemies that made their victims disappear.

I wondered what guidance the Clan Fathers, if there was more than one, would provide or to what information they would lead?

How many Fathers are there? I had absolutely no idea. I definitely needed to do some research on that subject for my own safety. If there is more than one, will they all have messages for me? What am I to do with the messages once I have all that are forthcoming from the Fathers? Who can guide me? Can I rely on anyone in town to back me up when trouble starts? Most importantly, how am I supposed to use the messages? Will I be permitted by the Clan Fathers to tell someone else about them when I ask for their help? All of these questions and more poured through my mind.

Am I supposed to go to the Sheriff and relay the messages? Can I rely on him at all? What about the deputies? Maybe there is a big conspiracy involving the Sheriff's office staff and others who would probably like to remain hidden from revelations that can put them out of business. Who will reveal themselves as friends to me?

I made up my mind right then and there that in the morning I would try and find the reporter who broke the story and sent the article to Dan, but right now what I needed and hoped to have was a good night's sleep.

I lay there with the thoughts of the Clan Father's message running rampant through my mind, but the great meal in my stomach, and echoes of the soft rhythmic sounds of good music eventually lulled me to sleep. I guess I fell off in less than two minutes.

The absolute quietude of the surrounding desert soothed whatever mysteries I had gotten involved in.

TEN

I awoke the next morning at sunup with light blasting its way through the flimsy curtains that did nothing to filter out any brightness brought by the oncoming day. The sunshine was out there warming the world and sending out beckoning rays of warmth to me to get started on whatever journey awaited me. I walked out into the sunshine and felt as one with this town as I warmed under the sun. I had a ravenous appetite so I made my way to the Cave for breakfast.

As I walked along I thought of a cowboy joke I'd heard years before about a hapless group of hunters who were many miles from camp. They had gotten no game, had no food with them, and felt like they were starving. The camp cook had prepared their meal but they were nowhere close to camp and had a long trek through the woods to get back to it. As they trudged their way back to camp one hunter remarked that he was so hungry that he'd attempt to eat the south end of a jackass that was moving north.

I didn't relish the idea of jackass meat for dinner so I let the smells coming from the Cave lead me on. I didn't care if what they had today was entirely road kill. I was hungry. Maybe I'd order a venison steak and eggs as long as they could guarantee that there wouldn't be any strange bumper parts or chrome splinters in it. On second thought, I'll just stick with the eggs.

I was greeted by one of the waitresses I had seen the day before, as soon as I entered the front door. I took the seat she lead me to and looked at the menu. I immediately ordered *Huervos Ranch*eros and as she stood writing down my order for bacon, eggs and lots of hot coffee, I asked her if she knew Carmelita Mendosa, the missing girl.

"Yes I know her," was the hesitant reply, "everybody in town knows her. She has lived here all her life, went to school here, her family comes from Bullsnort and she works at the lawyer's office down the street. Why are you asking? You are a stranger in town. Do you know her or her family?"

I was reluctant to tell her my real reason for asking questions. I didn't know if she was Carmelita's friend or just her competition. She was only the third young woman I'd met since I arrived. Maybe there weren't many more who were vying for the attention of the young men in town. In a small town like this, there was probably a lot of friendly warfare among the women as they drifted from one boyfriend to the next. She might be friendly but I didn't want to spook her because that would probably be the end of any cooperation I could get from anybody in town. That would mean the end of my stay here. I weighed my options very carefully before saying anything else.

"No, I don't know her or her family. I saw an article about her in yesterday's paper and was interested in it. What about the man who was attacked out in the desert, do you know his name and why he was shot?" I asked cautiously.

I sensed that she had accepted my interest in local happenings as natural curiosity and had decided she would pass along what she knew. After all, it was interesting gossip.

"As far as I know Carmelita hasn't called, written to anyone, or had any contact with anyone since she disappeared a few days ago. I don't think she has been kidnapped and held for ransom or anything like that because the Sheriff is still putting notices in the paper asking for information about her. If anyone had reported receiving a ransom note he probably wouldn't do that. We're not a rich town so a kidnapper wouldn't get very much money anyway, just a whole lot of trouble for doing that." she declared.

That last statement lent a whole new aura to the disappearance of Carmelita. If everyone felt that she hadn't been kidnapped, then what other motive for her disappearance was there? Did she just leave town on her own accord not telling her friends where she was going or when she'd be back, if ever? I didn't think so. I realized then that I really wanted to find out what happened to her so I continued with my questions.

"You said she worked for a lawyer here in town. Do you know anything about the lawyer she worked for? Is it the lawyer who has the Law office across the street near the Sheriff's office? I might just have to go there to see what the other people who work there know about her disappearance" I said, hoping she wouldn't be offended by all my questions.

"The lawyer's name is Ms. Robin Charles, but there's no Mr. Charles that anybody has seen around here," the waitress said in a lower voice. "Don't know what happened to him. And yes, her office is two doors up from the Sheriff's office," she added with a smile. "You can't miss it. It's the green building with the bright yellow door. That's how we give directions to newcomers in town, by the colors of the place they're looking for," she continued with a laugh as she walked away to order my food from the kitchen.

When she returned with my food, I continued to engage her in conversation with the hope that the information she would give me would be helpful.

"Thanks, for the information on the lawyer. That will be very helpful. After I finish breakfast, I'll go look her up. Do you know if Carmelita was dating anybody steady? Is he still in town? Was she engaged to anybody?"

I knew enough of small town politics to know that everybody knew everybody else's business, especially who was dating and sleeping with whom. I hoped the waitress might be able to help me since I didn't know much about anybody in Bullsnort yet.

"The only man she had recently been dating regularly was Miguel Membreno, one of the Deputy Sheriffs. I don't think they were engaged. They've dated on and off for several years. This was one of their off periods I think. Carmelita told me several times that they fought recently about her working after they planned to get married. After that, she seemed interested in a guy named Mark something-or-other, who recently moved into town, but I don't know if they actually ever went out together," the waitress said in a puzzled voice.

Since there were no other customers, except at the bar, I introduced myself (leaving out the, I) and learned that her name was Rosalie. Our conversation took on a more personal perspective as we talked about her and the town for another half hour or before I left saying I had to talk to the lawyer. I knew I'd be back because I had made up my mind that I wanted to see more of this beautiful black haired gal. I wasn't horny yet, but I knew a beautiful girl when I saw one, especially when I was talking to her up close and personal.

As I left the Cave, I did some lightning-fast math in my mind. One could go into one very nicely.

The field of my inquiry had just expanded to the lawyer, the deputies, and the Sheriff. I would be very wary of revealing anything about why I was here to any of them if and when I had a chance to talk with them.

ELEVEN

As I walked down the street, I was again amazed at the wide variety of colors for the buildings, doors, shutters, and flowers that were everywhere. As I walked I looked into the various storefronts. I stopped for a minute and scanned the entire street. It looked like a movie set. It was just too neat and clean to be a lived in town. The sidewalks looked as if they were made of two or three inch thick boards and the storefronts were set back several feet from the edge of the sidewalks. There were tumbleweeds in the corners of some of the buildings, but no other trash that one would expect to have blown in overnight.

I noticed some very ornately carved southwestern style furniture painted in bright colors in the window of the furniture shop. There were all kinds of strange figures carved and painted on them.

Next to the furniture store was the bakery from which there were rich smells of freshly baked goodies of all kinds, the predominate one being bread. The great smells assaulted my nose as I walked past the place. I could no more resist going into that shop and buying a few pieces of several varieties of pastry and bread than I could avoid breathing. I had to laugh. I almost slobbered on myself as my mouth filled with juices in response to the fresh bread smells.

I came out with a bag of pastries and a loaf of bread that I'd surely enjoy later, along with some homemade whipped butter and a small jar of Elderberry jam that I couldn't resist buying. I successfully fought the impulse to start eating right there on the street. I would enjoy them later in the comfort of my room.

I walked along the sidewalk until I saw the sign that proclaimed Indian Arts Store.

The display window was tastefully decorated with Indian things. A carved doll immediately caught my eye. I had seen many dolls in the many Indian shops in Albuquerque, but not as close up as I was with this one. It fascinated me.

It had an immediate hypnotic effect on my mind. It was a male, painted mostly a dull, flat white, like chalk dust. It was striped with black paint all over its body. It had two horn-like projections that came out of the top of its head with rawhide strips coming out the end of the horns. The eyes were bulging black circles with large white areas around them. Resting in the crook of the doll's right arm was a vivid green watermelon with a large wedge cut from it. The bright red pulp looked inviting and ready to eat. In the other hand was a silver wooden knife that was eagerly waiting to cut another wedge. The mouth was a black maw displaying stark white teeth that looked ready to devour the melon, seeds and all, and be anxious for more. This piece of Indian art was both grotesque and beautiful at the same time. It was sitting on the edge of a shelf that isolated it from the rest of the dolls in the window.

I knew that it was a Kachina but I was not familiar with its name, or what the symbolism of it was. I went into the store and asked the lady behind the counter about it.

"That is a Kachina that is called a *Koshare*, or clown," she informed me.

TWELVE

When I heard the word, "Kachina" I began to recall what I had learned about Kachinas since my arrival in the Southwest.

Kachinas or *Katsinas* are characters related to the spiritual and religious beliefs of the Pueblo Indians, specifically, the *Katsina* religion of the Hopi and Zuni Indians, so they can be considered religious figures. Kachinas represent the spirits of everything in the real world. As with all religions, The Hopi religion was developed in order to help people fulfill their specific needs. Many of the Kachinas were not developed by the Hopis themselves, but by other tribes before being adopted by the Hopi. The Kachinas are not worshipped in a religious sense but are accepted as spirits who are respected for the help they can bring to the culture and to the people.

During the *Katsina* ceremonies, the men who wear the masks are called Kachinas because they are thought to actually become the spirit of the Kachina. Some of the ceremonies take place in underground *Kivas* where only the initiated can see them. There are ceremonies that take place on the open pueblo plaza where tribal members are given small gifts by the Kachina. The dolls, like the Koshare, are a learning tool made for the young clan members to help them understand their deities and culture.

There are three main ceremonies held regularly by the Hopi.

The *Soyal,* or opening of the Kachina season, starts when some Kachinas come out of the Kiva and perform many functions for the clans and villages before they return to the Kiva.

The second ceremony, the *Powamu,* is held when the world is ready for new growth.

The third involves many Kachinas who hold dances to initiate the youth into the clans and the dances continue until the maturing of the crops call the Kachinas back into the Kiva.

The men who are the active Kachinas carve their likenesses into dolls and give them as gifts to the youth during the dances. Kachina dolls are usually carved out of the softer cottonwood tree roots and represent many figures in the Indian cultures. The Endangered Species Act now limits the kinds of animals that can be killed for feathers and furs, so chicken, goose, and duck feathers are the only ones used in making the Kachina dolls and costumes.

The figures can be decorated with just about anything that is available, but the carver will not add material just to make it gaudy. That is not the way it's done. The proportions of the doll are very important, because they need to be attention grabbing, but not so large that they are unrealistic in appearance. One misconception about Kachinas is that they must be carved from one piece of a root. Most dolls are made in pieces, assembled and then dressed in buckskin, fur, feathers, and maybe yarn. They can have rattles, bow and arrows, feathers, a small drum, wheat stalks, turquoise, and wooden knives. Rifles are almost never depicted with a Kachina figure.

Because of recent popularity in collecting Native American art, the Kachina has experienced a rapid growth in both style and sale price. The most popular ones are the Eagle Dancers, Sun Face, and Mudheads, which represent the singers during the ceremonial dances.

"We have all kinds of Kachinas here," the lady continued, bringing me out of my thoughts. "About one hundred I think. They come from all the Indian tribes in New Mexico and Arizona, and even some from Alaska. Most of the ones that are made locally come from the roots of the cottonwood tree but some, like this one, are carved from hardwoods and then burnished with a wood burning tool to get the effects needed. Like the feathers on the wings of this one."

The one she had pointed to was shaded in light and dark browns. It was beautiful. She leaned over and picked up another one and said that it was called Eagle Dancer.

"This one here is the Owl Man, she said as she pointed from one to the other. "That little one, there with the multicolored dots all over it, is called the Zuni Fire God. The name of the figure and the carver are normally on the base of the doll. If you want something specific I'll be glad to help you."

I thanked her and said I'd just like to walk around and look at everything she had in the shop. I knew I was drawn to the Koshare and that I'd probably buy it if the price wasn't too high. She told me to look around all I wanted and advised me to call her if I had more questions.

As I walked around the shop, I saw many paintings. Some depicted bright blue horses with blindingly white manes that flowed as if in a high wind. Others showed warriors with fierce stripes of black and red on their faces, and others were of beautiful women in repose. I saw many pieces of multi-colored pottery, some incised, others painted with extremely intricate designs.

I noticed all the geometrical designs on beautiful handmade rugs that were piled four feet high in a corner. There were so many different styles and color patterns on them that I had to look at the tag, and sometimes the attached picture of the weaver, to see where it had been made. One really soft rug, woven in earth tones of light and dark brown caught my eye.

The label said Two Grey Hills. It had the softest touch of the pile. It was also the one with the tightest weave. I guessed that it would keep me dry if I crawled under it in the fiercest desert rain storm. I also noticed with a lot of pain that the price was a very long way out of my available cash range, so I very carefully put it back in its place on the pile. That one would just have to wait a while to wind up in my collection.

There were rugs from places that I hadn't heard of like Wide Ruins and Klagetoh. One rug with several with dancing figures called Yei Bechai caught my eye. The thing that struck me hardest was that the figures were dancing around a sparking fire. I imagined the rhythmic drumbeat and could envision their feet shuffling to that beat. I had to blink a few times to break the spell of the rug. Unfortunately, it, like the others rugs that I was attracted to, was out of my price range.

Was I not to find a rug that I could afford to buy? I hoped that wasn't true because they fascinated me. I laughed as I thought of standing in front of a very irate Dan trying to justify spending hundreds, if not a thousand, dollars for one or two of these masterpieces. I decided I'd better not try that at this point in my career as a newspaper reporter.

As I walked around the shop, I began to total up the cost of those things I would like to have and at the end of one tour up and down the aisles, I found the total to be staggering, if not totally deflating. I walked around humbled from that point. I was enthralled and wondered at the talent it took to make all of the things I saw here. Carvings, dolls, paintings, weavings, and the fantastic jewelry were all museum quality right here in this little store.

I went up a short flight of stairs and on the upper landing I found ten very large wooden drums. Most were scraped clean of bark but two had the bark still on them. The patterns in that bark were truly terrific. A few of the drums were tall, about 5 feet high, while some were squatter about 2 to 3 feet high. Almost all were about 25 inches in diameter.

Some were maybe even cut from the same cottonwood tree. The drumheads were hard, dried, but still relatively flexible, animal skin that was tied on to the base of the drums in an intricate pattern with strips of the same type of animal skin. I noticed then that there were drumheads on both ends of the drum. I wondered why. I walked around hitting them all.

Then I picked up one that was light enough to lift and hit the head on the opposite end. Where the one head resonated with a deep basso tone, the tone produced by the opposite head was lighter and more vibrant. Fantastic! I hit them all again and one rather large one reverberated with a sound that seemed to go right through me sending a chill up my spine as it shook me. I had never felt anything like that before. Just as the horns had blasted me earlier out on the street, this sound made my nerves jingle. It took me a good ten minutes to settle down after that shock.

Why does it affect me like that? I wondered. Just then a really strange thought came into my mind. What kind of spirits will this drum call up if I buy it and hit it at home? I had to wonder at the consequences of that totally random thought. Or was it totally random?

As I hit the special drum once more, I put my hands on it palms down. The resonance of the drumhead felt like I had put a giant vibrator on my head and I tingled all over. I kept my hands there as the sound faded. I closed my eyes and waited for the shock to my senses to dwindle. I was back to almost normal in a few minutes and continued up the steps to meander around the upper level.

I spotted some woven reed plaques of various sizes and patterns hanging above the drums, the largest of which was about three feet in diameter. All sorts of symbols and animals were woven very dexterously into the plaques. I noticed that near the top of every one of the plaques there was an unfinished section about a quarter of an inch wide.

I knew that Indian legend said that there must be an escape route so the spirit of things can get out of an object. Pots have these unfinished spaces in the design and all the rugs I had looked at had them. The ultimate requirement, based on that belief, was that when a family member died a hole had to be knocked into the wall of the Hogan so the spirit of that person could escape. Otherwise, the spirit would wander forever inside the Hogan causing all kinds of problems. Normally, when that happened, that Hogan had to be abandoned and a new one built just to be sure the spirit could eventually escape.

I continued my examination of other objects. I knew I had seen the objects that consisted of woven threads arranged on circles and trimmed in feathers in some stores in Albuquerque but hadn't seen one this close up before. I knew they were called dream catchers but what exactly a dream catcher was supposed to do, I had no idea. Next to the larger weavings were some smaller items that were very unique. Apparently the lady had followed me up the stairs, so I inquired about the dream catcher story.

She graciously filled me in on the function of these objects. "Dream catchers are made of various materials, mainly buckskin wrapped around a small metal ring, with feathers, prayer beads, and sometimes turquoise attached as decoration. Each one has a web of string inside the ring. This web has a very specific purpose. The dream catcher is usually hung by a bedroom window or on a bedpost. It is hung there, as the name implies, to catch dreams in the web of string. Any good dream makes it through the hole in the center of the web, is caught on the feathers and then sent to the Great Spirit in the morning sun. Bad dreams are trapped there forever."

THIRTEEN

I walked around on this upper floor and slowly made my way back downstairs to the main counter with the lady close behind me. I made two more complete circuits around the main floor of the store before I came to the main glass display area. There I saw some beautifully made turquoise jewelry, bracelets, inlaid pieces, and other styles of things. There were painted gourds and rattles that had bits of fur and feathers for adornment.

I introduced myself to the lady and said that I hoped I hadn't bothered her by hitting the drums so many times, but one of them had fascinated me and I was drawn to it.

I told her that I was a reporter from Albuquerque and that I would be in town for a few days and that I really liked her store.

I told her that I was drawn back to the clown-like Kachina and asked her the price. She told me twenty five dollars. It was a good price and one I could afford right then so I said, "OK, it's mine now."

She laughed a little as she very carefully wrapped it first in bubble wrap and then newspaper to protect it. I knew exactly where I'd put the clown on top of my stereo so I could look at it every day.

"My name is Mrs. Hernando, and thank you for your comments about liking my store," she said. "I have lived here in Bullsnort for about 25 years now. Right here in this same building. My parents were born here and so was I. I went away to St. Johns College in Santa Fe, but after graduating I came back here and took over this store when my parents retired. My family loves it here and wouldn't think of moving anywhere else, especially not to Canyon Road in Santa Fe with all the big name galleries. I'm happy right here. I know all the Indian artists from all the Pueblos and they give me a constant supply of their arts to sell for them."

"Twice a year I have a major party in my home. I have the first one on a major feast day and I call it a Pot party. I know what you might be thinking, but no, it isn't a marijuana party. It's nothing of the sort," she said with a laugh. "I invite all the potters I know to this party. As their admission entry fee, so to speak, they all must bring a pot they've made in the past year. I collect them all and later I have a pot auction and the proceeds go to Indian Charities. I keep nothing for myself. If any pot doesn't sell, and that doesn't happen often, then I bring it here and sell it in my store. The artists also have to sign my curtains too as a sort of guest list for that year. I have some very famous potters' signatures on my curtains, like Maria Poveka, who most collectors know as Maria Martinez. I also have Lucy Lewis, Blue Corn, and Tony Da, who was the grandson of Maria. I have many boxes of these curtains put away for safe keeping."

"To my second party of the year, I invite only painters and they do the same thing. Each brings a painting and signs my curtains. I have some signatures of some great ones too, like Kirby Sattler, Frank Howell, Fritz Scholder, and R.C. Gorman. So, Andy, I can guarantee that anything you see and buy from me is genuine handmade work by genuine Indians, not a fake. What are you interested in that I can explain and help you with?"

I was beginning to appreciate Mrs. Hernando quiet a lot.

I knew that for some unexplained reason I was compelled to buy this clown-like Kachina now, so I didn't hesitate. It had certainly worked its magic on me. I also knew that I had to have that one special drum, again I didn't know why, and didn't question that either. I just knew I would have a hard time coming up with the money for it just now.

I wondered if Mrs. Hernando would be helpful in my investigation into the disappearance of Carmelita Mendosa and the attempted murder of the man out in the desert. I figured that she knew, and had her own opinions, about everybody in town. That's the way small towns are. She could be a potential goldmine of helpful information if I went about asking for it in a way that would avoid offended her by my questioning. Besides, I liked her immediately, and knew instinctively that I could come to depend a great deal on her in more ways that I realized. I loved her store, the Kachinas, and especially the drum, but I couldn't buy everything today although I wanted too. I was very tempted to ask her if she would put the drum on lay-a-way for me but thought better of that idea. Besides, with my small salary I had to be careful about my expenses.

"Thank you for all of the interesting information, Mrs. Hernando. Do you happen to have any books on the Clan Fathers?" I asked as she made out the sales slip for the clown.

She looked up at me with a quizzical look on her face and said, "Yes I do right over here in the book section. That is a really strange request. I wonder why you are interested in the Clan Fathers. Most of the Indian tribes here in New Mexico are Pueblo and all have some kind beliefs that relate to myths involving the Clan Fathers and Mothers."

I told her that I had done some research earlier in the UNM library on Indian symbols and myths for an article I was planning to write for the Journal. "One thing or another stifled that article but I still have my research and recall a lot of facts from the work I've done," I said.

Just from looking at the Kachinas here in the store and the decorations on them, I recalled that arrows denoted force of travel, direction and movement. When an arrow appeared on an animal, a bear for instance, the arrow denoted the life force and was called the heart line.

Feathers represented the creative forces. They were also used for their connection to the bird from which they were taken. For example, goose feathers were used on arrows for their long flight, turkey feathers were used to decorate Kachina masks.

Many other animals were depicted in the symbols used in jewelry, potters, and weavings. For example, the Frog is used to represent fertility, the Bear symbolizes strength and leadership while the Turtle is used to denote long life. The Owl represents departed spirits, and sharp-eyed hunters. The Badger is honored as a healing animal and is used to represent great hunters.

Many spirits are also represented in many ways. The *Kokopelli* figure is used as a common fertility symbol and is honored in most Pueblo cultures. Many patterns are used in weavings and sand paintings and have a wide variety of meaning, depending upon the tribe.

Mrs. Hernando surprised and delighted me when she said, "I happen to be Kiowa and that's how I know so much about Indian beliefs and their art work. Each tribe has a different name for spirits and natural things, but their messages are basically universal and similar throughout."

I wasn't sure right then if I should reveal to her the message I had gotten from the Clan Father or not so I chose to stay on the subject of Indians, in general. "You say you are Kiowa? Where do the Kiowa come from?"

"Yes, I am full blooded Kiowa," Mrs. Hernando replied. "Originally we came from the far reaches of northern Montana. Over the decades our migration patterns and routes have led us to where the current day Kiowa reservation is located now in the western panhandle of Oklahoma."

We talked for almost another forty five minutes on various Indian cultures, specifically the makeup of the clans, and the overall makeup of Kiowan society. In the short time I was in the store, I realized that she had provided me with as good an education on Indian affairs as I would get anywhere. I thanked her again for helping me with the Kachinas, blankets, paintings, and the jewelry, and I left the store knowing full well that I would surely return many more times. I just didn't have an inkling of how those times and circumstances would have a profound effect on my life.

FOURTEEN

I continued my leisurely walk down the street looking in awe at the multi-colored building facades with their bright doors, shutters, and flower boxes. An interesting thought passed through my mind. It makes the town look like a bouquet of flowers.

For me that comparison was acceptable, because I liked all kinds of flowers. When and if I could afford a place of my own I was thinking seriously about having a rose garden. That would be far in the future of course. I looked in the windows of several stores and saw that people were busily conducting their commerce, paying no attention to me. After a few more minutes of wandering along the street, I found myself in front of the lawyer's office.

I pushed open the door and went into the front office to introduce myself. I wasn't sure if the woman sitting at the desk was Robin Charles or her new office assistant. A very brief introduction told me that this was indeed, Ms. Charles, the lawyer that Carmelita had worked for. Apparently, she had not yet hired a replacement for her missing assistant.

I explained to her that I was a reporter from Albuquerque, sent to gather information so I could write stories on both Carmelita's disappearance and the attempted murder that had happened near Bullsnort and would appreciate whatever help she could give me. She begged off with a not too happy look that told me more than her words how she felt about this. She used the excuse of lawyer-client privilege that made it impossible for her to say anything about either case. When asked, she conceded that the name of the Deputy, who had found the wounded man, was Miguel Membrano.

This must be the same Miguel that Carmelita had been dating, I thought. I felt that with Ms. Charles's non-responsiveness, and even some outright hostility toward me, I was beating a dead horse, so the best I could do was thank her and leave her office. The feeling of dislike and wariness on her part, I was sure, didn't just stem from the innocent question about her employee. She was definitely hiding something. What, I didn't know just yet, but I was determined to circumvent her attitude and find out. I logged her under the category of check again.

As I walked past the Sheriff's Office, I looked in to see several people bustling around. Some were on the phone and not in uniform, probably clerks and whatnot. Some, two exactly, were in uniform looking at files very seriously and another, obviously the Sheriff, was talking animatedly on a phone. He was talking to someone who was giving him a lot of information he probably didn't appreciate because he didn't look too happy.

I didn't know at the time of the connection between the lawyer and him. That would come after much more digging and asking questions. I walked on down the street without drawing their attention to me because I wanted to talk to a few more people before I brought the Sheriff into my arena for questions.

A few doors down past the Sheriff's office I saw a building marked by a huge sign that identified it as the office of the *Bullsnort Press*. That was the paper that I read yesterday to gather added information I needed for my investigation of Carmelita's disappearance and where I had found the article about the attempted murder of the young man out in the desert. I passed by slowly while checking out who was in the newspaper office. I was becoming more wary because I hadn't had a chance to separate friendly and helpful from hostile and dangerous as far as the people in town were concerned.

I tentatively put the lawyer, who I had already decided was no lady, into the dangerous group. I definitely wanted to talk to the reporter, who had written the stories for the *Bullsnort Press,* hoping maybe he had withheld something so it could be used as evidence once some suspects were identified. I made a mental note to call him later and ask him to see me.

I continued my slow ambling down the street. I was still amazed at the colorful town. At the corner I went into a gas station and bought a newspaper. The attendant looked like he was having a sexual experience with a long fold-out from a Playboy magazine and wasn't too happy that I interrupted him. Whatever floats your boat, I thought as I walked away with a copy of the local paper. I didn't read it then, but folded it and stuck it in my back pocket for later that night. I had other things on my mind right now.

I walked the full length of the street admiring the buildings and saying hello to those townsfolk I passed. They were friendly enough to me, a stranger, but that's the way people are in small towns everywhere. Everybody is accepted as a friend until he or she proves unworthy of that honor and, then the town can be hell on earth till the stranger either amends his ways or leaves. I would hate to think about what this town could or would do to a not so friendly stranger.

At the corner I re-crossed the street and walked back up the other side, looking into storefronts on the way. There was the usual variety of shops: shoe store, drugstore, and a western wear clothing store. I spotted a magazine rack which I might just need if my stay extended longer than I had planned.

The noonday sun was getting hotter by the second so as I got close to the the Cave I decided that lunch and a good cold Dos Equis was in store for me. I came in out of the bright sunshine and as my eyes adjusted to the darkness of the place I noticed that I was alone there. I sat at the bar as the young and good looking waitress who'd served me breakfast came up to me.

"Hi Rosalie, remember me, Andy I. Bling? I'd like to talk to you some more about Carmelita, if you can find some time to spare from all the other customers in here right now."

I hoped my joking manner would help break the ice with her. I looked over my shoulder like someone was sneaking up behind me and laughed.

A laughing reply came back to me from Rosalie. Her smile made her face look even more beautiful. "Sure, Mr. Andy I. Bling, I'll just tell all these other roughnecks in here that your beer is more important than theirs and then I'll just see how much longer you sit here as comfortably as you seem to be right now. How 'bout that?"

She definitely has a great sense of humor, I thought, as I looked over both shoulders to make sure that the place was really empty. Then, I said rather sheepishly to her, "On second thought, just take some time when you get free. I'll be here for about an hour and if you'll please bring me a menu and a beer, I'll nurse it very slowly. I'm in no hurry."

I had decided I would surely like to get to know this beautiful black haired girl better, if she'd let me, of course. I laughed back at her.

The twinkle in her eye said that she'd just gotten me big time as she said, "Yes, Andy, I'll find time if it will help you find out what happened to my friend, Carmelita. What do you want to know?"

Rosalie extended her small delicately boned right hand as a final seal of our introductions as she asked, "What does the "I" stand for, Andy?"

As I took her hand and thought about it, I felt a slight electrical impulse flow between us. I didn't see or detect any reaction from her so I let it pass. It was the same impulse that I'd felt when I spotted the Kachina doll at Mrs. Hernando's Indian Arts Shop. Had I somehow made another connection to this town and maybe to Carmelita? I intended to find out. I replied, "You don't really want to hear about that right now, it's a long story."

I wanted to ask her if she'd go out with me, but I didn't want to turn her off so I decided to wait. I'd ask her before I left the Cave. Right now all I wanted was to talk to her. And talk we did for about an hour and a half before some more customers came in for lunch. I had built up my courage so when I was about to leave I asked her if she would like to go out with me, the time and place would be left up to her.

"Yes," came the reply," I'd like that very much. I don't have to work tomorrow, is tonight too soon? I do have to warn you, Andy, that this is a very small town and there's not much to do on a date. All we have in the way of recreation is the library, the drive-in, the cantina, and, of course, the cave. Which will it be for us?"

I was relieved that she hadn't turned me down cold. Acting like I really had to think hard to choose the place we would go to, I frowned for a minute then said, "that's really such a hard choice for a guy who is trying to impress a beautiful girl. What about having dinner here at the cave, afterward we can go to the drive-in for a movie, then to the cantina for some dancing and a nightcap? Or I could flip a coin to see which two we eliminate?"

"My, you are an original aren't you? How many guys would go the expense of taking a girl to three places on a first date? I'm impressed!"

As she laughed at me again, I was beginning to look forward to her laughing at me a lot during the time I was in Bullsnort. It made me feel good inside.

"How about having at dinner at six o'clock at the Cave, and then the movie afterward? All I need is an address where I can pick you up," I said, hoping I didn't sound too eager.

"Six is fine. I'll write my address on this slip of paper for you. If you tend to be like most men who almost always lose important pieces of paper, just ask anybody town for directions to my house. I've got a couple of customers to take care of now so, see you tonight, Andy."

She walked away laughing like I had just been gotten again. I liked the motion I saw as she walked away. I had some very interesting thoughts about her; something to do with intricate math again, something about how one could go into one very nicely. I finished my beer, bought three more to go, gave Rosalie my biggest smile and made my way to my room at the motor court.

FIFTEEN

I opened one of the beers, put the other two in the fridge, drew the paper out of my pocket and lay on the bed to read it as enjoyed my drink. As I read I took several short swallows of the cold brew. Delicious! The condensation dripped off the bottle onto my tee shirt but the taste was great. It helped settled my jangling nerves and those lingering sexual thoughts about Rosalie.

I had scanned only two pages when I felt the starting pangs of another headache.

No, I thought, not another of those Clan Father messages. I hadn't digested the first message yet, or figured out what exactly it meant. Was I going to experience two of those painful things in two days? I didn't have long to think about it. The pain got more intense so as before, I closed my eyes and pressed three fingers to my temples. As before, the lining inside my closed eyes changed color, this time to a very dark red, the color of a mature red fox, and as before, I heard another distinct male voice speaking to me. This voice was different from the first Clan Father in both tone and inflection.

"Tawamiciya,
I am the second Clan Father,
I am named "Hunts at Night".
I am the spiritual leader of the Wolf Clan.
I will teach you to be both sly and stealthy.
When you are ready and need me, I shall return to help you."

As the voice, the pain, and the red color faded, another surge of pain and color came on immediately. The color inside my eyelids changed, this time, to a dark brown, the color of riverbank mud. A third distinct voice spoke to me.

"Tawamiciya,
I am the third Clan Father.
I am named "Loves the Snow".
I am the spiritual leader of the Buffalo Clan.
I will teach you how to dig for the truth.
When you are ready and need me, I shall return to help you."

I wanted to ask these voices how and why they contacted me, but I knew instinctively that they would not give me an answer until they were good and ready, and were convinced that I was receptive to them. I realized that I was already receptive to a lot of things that had happened to me. Or would apprehensive be a better word to describe what I felt?

As I lay there, I decided to write down these messages in my notebook, just as I had the first one. Logically I thought that if they were important enough for the Clan Fathers to make contact with me and pass them along, then I should at least write them down for future reference. Maybe, when this was over, no matter how long that took, I'd write a book about my experiences. I opened my notebook to the page where I had written the first message and as I recalled the words of the two new messages, I wrote them down.

I felt a large blank space still existed concerning Carmelita but I hoped that it would be filled by later events, more headaches and more messages. One blank space that defied all answers so far was what was that weird sounding word that each of the Clan Fathers had used before giving me the messages. *Tawamiciya?* An Indian word obviously, but what meaning did it have for me?

I retrieved the book about the Clan Fathers that I'd bought from Mrs. Hernando at the Indian Arts store, opened it and began to read about them and the mysticism involved with Indian religious beliefs.

I read a brief history of the Kiowa tribe, the structure of the Clan Societies; the Warrior (Men), and the Mystical (Women) Clans. I read that there were twelve Clan Fathers in just about all tribes, especially the Kiowan, Lakotan, and Minniconjou tribes.

As I read this I realized that all twelve Clan Fathers were probably going to contact me to deliver specific messages. I also realized that the remaining nine couldn't come to me in the time I intended to stay here so, I decided, the best thing to do was to change the registration card at the motor court office and extend my stay for at least two more weeks. I could write some interesting articles to convince Dan that he could do without me for that time as long as what I was doing was worthwhile. I knew it was.

As I walked into the motor court office, I knew that this time I wouldn't make the mistake of hitting the dinger again. I didn't want to get the old guy too pissed at me. I would like to talk to him again about this town, the history of the Sheriff's office and especially the current Sheriff. The old guy had looked so mean that, I knew once I got off on his bad side, I wouldn't be able to get close to him with any questions.

To get the old man's attention I yelled in a voice so loud that it made the counter vibrate, "Hello. Is anybody here??" As I stood there waiting for him to appear many thoughts began going through my mind. The Clan Fathers and their messages, along with my feelings about the drum I couldn't explain.

Why was I, just a normal person, being caught up in these events? To what end? I couldn't explain any of it yet but hopefully more guidance would be coming my way. From what sources this guidance would come, I had no idea, but just at that instant a cold chill hit me and I shuddered to think of what that might bring.

I had re-read all three messages but they had given me no clue to use in finding Carmelita. I wasn't a homicide cop or an investigative reporter but I vowed then and there that I would do everything I possibly could to solve this mystery. Now, besides Carmelita's disappearance and the attempted murder of the young man, I had three new message mysteries with the possibility of nine more to solve. Was I supposed to be the conduit for information that would help someone else, like the Sheriff, to find Carmelita or would I find her myself? Since the Sheriff and his deputies were the only law officers I was aware of, they had to be the choice. But what if I was wrong? What if I was supposed to find her myself and the Sheriff or someone in his employ was responsible for her disappearance? Then what?

I'd just have to work that out when the time came.

When the old man did not appear, I decided to take the advice he had given me earlier. I filled out another card telling him how long I would be staying and just left it lying on the counter. I walked out of the office and headed back to my room.

As I lay down on the bed again, I realized that I had had a premonition. If I didn't give this my whole effort I might not be allowed to leave this town. I wondered to myself, "Now what does that thought mean?" I felt that I was being tested, but for what purpose and why? What if I failed? I shivered but didn't want to think about the consequences of that. I couldn't pin down the reason for my uneasiness, but the tingling of my nerve endings had given me adequate warning.

Then again maybe, just maybe, at the end of the two added weeks I might not be inclined to leave. After all, I had just asked Rosalie for our first date. I held out hope that it would develop into something lasting. Who knew what tomorrow would bring?

I smiled at that thought, finished my beer, and rolled over to go to sleep with a smile of satisfaction on my face.

SIXTEEN

The Sheriff was sitting at his cluttered desk after a eating a full lunch, which had been washed down by two cold delicious beers. His eyes were getting heavy in the afternoon heat. Both of his deputies were out and about in town doing what they could to help stem the rising tide of truck thefts and petty crime. He had to laugh at that thought,

"Not here in Bullsnort where everything that goes on has gone on for a couple of hundred years tradition." He was day dreaming again about his date with his lady that evening.

Their ESP must have been working well as he picked up the ringing phone and said, "Sheriff's office, how may I help you?"

With no introduction, hello, or anything else, he heard, "For one thing you can get up off your dead ass and do something about that nosy young reporter from Albuquerque who was in my office today asking questions about a former member of this town who we both know is not around anymore, and whom, I must add, is a former paramour of yours." She paused a moment before asking, "Is he an undercover cop or just a nosy bastard, asking all those questions, or what?"

"Oh shit," he thought, "Here it comes again. When will she drop the subject of Carmelita sleeping with me? How the hell did she find out anyway, we were very careful?" He immediately calmed himself down enough to respond to her questions. "Yes, I know he's here and asking questions about her all over town, but I can't just run him out of town for doing that now can I? He's definitely become suspicious of our efforts to solve her disappearance. Since we are the only ones with any idea of what really happened, I think it best to just let him run his course for a few more days then he'll go back to Albuquerque, write whatever story he can, and we'll be done with it. What I don't know is why the disappearance of a girl in this remote and dusty little town has generated so much interest at the Journal, but if it'll ease your mind a little, I'll have some of my people talk to him and get a feel for what he's up to. Okay?"

"You'd better do more than just talk to him!" she said as her voice reached a higher pitch. "You'd better convince him that it isn't healthy for him to stay here and dig into something that'll finish us both for good and ever. Send him back home and tell him to stay there. Remember, you *are* the Sheriff here. I don't want him digging up things that we've gotten buried nice and deep in this town. I like my position here, and if you like yours, especially with me, do something about him!" she demanded.

The silence following the click at the other end of the line was deafening.

Why did I ever let her force me into doing what we did that day out there on the desert? I hope I live long enough to regret it.

That, to say the least, was a sobering thought.

SEVENTEEN

I reviewed my past week in Bullsnort as I sat in my room. I had arrived in town on Sunday. The first Clan Father, from the *Bear Clan*, had come to me that night and two more messages came from the *Wolf* and *Buffalo* Clans on Monday. Rosalie and I had our first date on Tuesday night. Since then, we had been seen together at various places around town, like at the weekly dance and of course in the Cantina. We had gone to church together that next Sunday. By that time everybody in town knew, had heard rumors, or thought they knew, that Rosalie was seeing the Anglo from Albuquerque. The fact that they knew only my name and nothing else about me didn't seem to bother them.

It didn't bother me either because I wanted them to know as little about me as possible. I doubted that anybody, except maybe the Sheriff, would actually call the paper to check on me. Why would the Sheriff be suspicious enough to do that though? I'll call Dan later to see if the Sheriff has actually checked on me, I thought.

Dan had told me that if there was anything to the story of the girl's disappearance, he wanted me to submit an article for the Feature Section of next Sunday's paper. I hadn't gotten much in the way of facts so far on the missing girl, so I put together what I considered a pretty good article describing the town with lead-ins for further stories. Will Dan be satisfied with this? I wondered.

Later, I began to doubt that Dan was even a little bit satisfied, when I scanned the Sunday paper and discovered that my story wasn't there. Whoops! Maybe Dan has decided that my time in Bullsnort has to come to a screeching halt and that the expenses for the last couple of days weren't worth it, I realized. With that thought, I decided that a call to explain what was going on was necessary. The subject of the Sheriff calling to check on me could just come up very casually.

I called Dan and gave him more details of my findings and what I had planned to look into in the next few days. Luckily, Dan OK'd more time.

"Just one more week," Dan said. He didn't sound too happy but if something better came of it then maybe I could justify the stay. Of course, I didn't mention the messages from the Clan Fathers, or my involvement with Rosalie. From our conversation though, I learned that the Sheriff had not called to inquire about me, however, a lawyer from Bullsnort, by the name of Ms. Robin Charles had called to ask to speak to me. After that bit of information, I sensed that she was up to no good. She knew I was still here in town, so why else would she make a call like that?

The date with Rosalie went very well. She selected dinner at the Cave for us. I chose the wine. We had a good time laughing at the cowboy kissing his horse at the drive in movie. Apparently the same movie in Bullsnort ran for a week at a time. We talked a lot about our possible future together. Nothing very personal, just get to know one another kind of stuff. We really didn't have what was a modern relationship just yet. The night-cap at the Cantina included some good music and dancing and good conversation. The slow rhythmic music was great for just standing close together and getting to know each other. Her hair smelled freshly washed with a hint of flowers. I snuggled my mouth into her ear and hummed along with the music.

We really had a good time dancing and I could tell she enjoyed it as much as I did. I brushed my lips against her neck and I felt a slight shiver go through her. I really wanted to kiss her then but I didn't want to break the spell of our dancing. Maybe later on the way home I'd try.

I tried alright and got a stinging slap for my feeble efforts. As I thought about it later in my room I knew that she'd been right. I shouldn't have had my hand where it was. It was a poor attempt to get her interested. I should have known better.

We had both laughed at my attempt to get her to let me kiss her. I apologized for being so clumsy and so did she for the slap as she gently touched the reddening outline of her hand on my cheek.

She jokingly said, "I don't think it will leave a permanent mark there, do you?" Then she leaned over and put a small repair type kiss on the red spot.

Then I leaned over and put a big thank you kiss on her lips and it was all OK from there. I apologized again for being rude and crude and she said she was sorry for the slap being so hard.

We sat in the car and talked for a while with the time generously spaced with more kisses sans slaps. I had walked her to her door to part as friends, I hoped. I definitely wanted to get to know this beautiful girl a lot better and just needed to convince her to appreciate my efforts to do that.

The next morning, at a great sunny dawn, as I lay in bed thinking about Rosalie, I couldn't help wondering about some of her strange answers to my questions about Carmelita. I couldn't pin down exactly what bothered me, but I sensed an antagonism and some very strong feelings from Rosalie toward Carmelita. They were classmates and were supposed to be friends. Rosalie had told me that they had grown up together, were roughly the same age, and their adult social life had been centered around the time spent at the Cantina.

That Carmelita dated Miguel seemed to be a sticking point when I had asked about it. Was it jealousy or anger and if both were the reason, then why? Did one of the girls steal Miguel from the other? How many times in a small town like this one had that happened where there were only few eligible men and several girls, all with exploding hormones and the belief that they had only one chance to find a husband or wife and had better not blow that chance. Could Rosalie have conspired with someone, maybe Miguel, to get Carmelita out of the line of competition? This was another sharp thorn in the dilemma. How could I probe into the relationship between Rosalie and Carmelita without making her so angry she might call an abrupt halt to our relationship? But I had to find out about their relationship one way or the other. There was no question about that.

These were troubling questions for which I had no answers. What really bothered me at this point was Rosalie's explanation of what happened when she and Carmelita had gone horseback riding out onto the desert on the very day that Carmelita had gone missing. I didn't need to poke holes in Rosalie's story, the obvious inconsistencies stood out all by themselves.

Rosalie said that she had answered all the Sheriff's questions to his satisfaction and had not been questioned further. Yes, she had gone riding with Carmelita. They had left town about one o'clock in the afternoon, in the heat of the day. I thought that going out to the desert on a horse in the middle of a hot day wasn't real smart, but Rosalie had said that the Sheriff had not questioned their reasoning. I wondered why the Sheriff would accept this story with no collaboration. Did the Sheriff know something he did not reveal to the papers?

Yes, they had ridden together for several miles, through many deep arroyos that day. Rosalie had no idea exactly where it was, but at one point, when she had looked back for Carmelita, she was nowhere in sight. She had stopped in a shady spot, eaten her lunch and waited for Carmelita to catch up. When Carmelita didn't appear she had returned to town.

Rosalie said she hadn't been concerned because she knew that Carmelita was an experienced rider who got impatient if her riding companion didn't do exactly what she expected. Rosalie had just assumed that Carmelita had turned around earlier after yelling at her and had gone back to town on her own. No, she had not immediately reported her missing. Rosalie had known that Carmelita knew her way around the arroyos and wasn't the type to do anything dangerous or stupid like getting herself stranded out there, especially not in the hottest part of the day.

Rosalie said she had found out later that Carmelita's horse, an Appaloosa, along with another horse, a Pinto, both without riders, had returned to the stables, about an hour or so after she had returned to town. It was then that she had begun to get worried about Carmelita. Rosalie said she had no idea who had ridden the Pinto and couldn't believe that anyone, even Carmelita, would just abandon a horse and leave it to find its way back to town. Nobody did that to any horse, much less a rented horse. She said she had become very worried then about Carmelita because being stranded in the middle of the desert could put the life of any person in the gravest of danger. She had gone immediately to the Sheriff with her concerns and had tried to point out the approximate trail they had taken so he could investigate and make sure Carmelita was OK. He had refused her offer to go with him on the search and she didn't know if he had checked with the stable owner to see who had ridden the Pinto.

Rosalie hadn't known it, but the Sheriff had told others that her story had been considered very suspicious, but without more proof he could do nothing. Surely not arrest her. He told the reporters that before charges could be brought against anybody, Carmelita had to be found.

Rosalie said that later the Sheriff had explained his failure to organize an extended ongoing search for Carmelita by saying that there were hundreds of arroyos out there and Carmelita could be in any one of them. There was too much risk of somebody else getting lost out there. Of course, no one knew that the Sheriff had a very good idea where Carmelita was because he had been out in the same area where she was supposed to have been riding that same day, but on a very different mission.

When he had been questioned by reporters about his failure get the State Police involved, the Sheriff had rationalized, that with what little information he had to go on he couldn't justify calling them into the investigation. Everyone knew that the State Police choppers would come in handy in any search and they would have been able to cover many miles easier than a posse could on horseback.

After listening to Rosalie's story, I decided that I had to take a chance and talk to the Sheriff himself. I was able to do that by walking into the Sheriff's office, identifying myself and requesting an interview. My conversation with the Sheriff gave me no more information than I had gathered already from Rosalie. It did increase my suspicions of the Sheriff's motives, however. Although the Sheriff gave me logical answers to all of my questions, I noticed that he appeared nervous and eager to have me leave the office.

When I remarked that I intended to conduct a search, however meager, to try to find some clue to Carmelita's whereabouts, the Sheriff strongly advised me against it. He told me that such an effort would be just plain stupid because any effective search would have had to be done before the onset of the recent heavy rains further up in the mountains. The water comes down these arroyos in torrents, so powerful that it washes away everything in its path, the Sheriff warned.

I wondered why the sheriff was so adamant about everything being washed away. Maybe he had knowledge of where Carmelita was, especially if he had killed her. Maybe he was just waiting for the first flood to get rid of her body. What reason would he have to kill her though? Was she a threat to him in some way? Or maybe he just helping cover up the crime committed by someone else? I had to ponder those questions.

I began to think that maybe the Sheriff was suspicious enough of me to lure me out there and do away with me too. That thought gave me a lot of very uneasy feelings as my conversation with the Sheriff drew to a close. I had been told that in previous storms up in the mountains, the water had washed out some bridges and the cars on them had never been found. I didn't relish being part of storm detritus that piled up and was washed into some distant arroyo many miles downstate.

Back in my room, I considered my meager options. I just didn't have much information to rely on. Should I reveal my suspicions to the Sheriff? I asked myself. I hadn't talked to anybody else but Rosalie and the lawyer, briefly, so far. My impressions of the lawyer weren't favorable at all but what did that prove?

I decided that I would talk to the reporter who originally broke the story and then go back to talk again to the lady at the Indian Arts Store, Mrs. Hernando. Maybe I would even go see the old geezer who runs the motel, again. A thought entered my mind, "Maybe I should ask Rosalie to go out to the desert with me and try to retrace the path she and Carmelita took the day she disappeared. But, surely she'll see through that. I certainly don't want to spoil what we have going so far by making her suspicious of me. After all, she had already indicated that she could not remember the exact place where she and Carmelita became separated."

EIGHTEEN

" I 've got to go to Santa Fe on office business this next weekend,"
Carmelita told her current most significant other on Wednesday
before the trip was scheduled. I have no idea how long it will take this
time. The last time, which was the initial meeting with this new client,
we finished up on Sunday at about one thirty, and had the afternoon
off. Of course Ms. Charles didn't have any reason to stay there, so we
came on back home."

"If you go with me, we will definitely have some very good reasons
for staying after the meeting this week end won't we?" she said with a
glint in her eye and a chuckle in her voice as she anticipated making the
trip without Ms. Charles the coming weekend.

Ms. Charles and Carmelita had had very little friendly conversation
during the trip they had made together to Santa Fe, other than
instructions on conducting business during the coming weekend when
Carmelita would go to Santa Fe by herself. During the week Ms.
Charles had given all the forms to Carmelita and indicated where
the client's signature was to go and identified the copy that was to be
given to the clients. Initial payment by the clients would of course, be
by check, which would go into the trust account for initial services,
then as services like pre-trial conferences, postponements, and all
associated business were performed, the money would be transferred
to the operating account for payment of expenses like Carmelita's salary
and finally into Ms. Charles's personal account.

Carmelita and her new lover made arrangements to meet each
other on Saturday night at the hotel where Ms. Charles had made
reservations the previous weekend.

Now that she was back in Santa Fe without Ms. Charles, Carmelita
felt a great deal better about being there. The meeting with the clients on
Saturday went as expected; smoothly. Ms. Charles had communicated with
them by telephone and everything had been preplanned. Carmelita was to
finish up whatever incidentals the clients needed clarified and be back in
the office with a report on Monday. Carmelita anticipated a lot of free time
to spend with someone who was a lot more interesting than Ms. Charles.

"Well, what do you want to do in this beautiful town?" Carmelita
asked as she smiled warmly at her most significant other. I would like
to take a long walk up Canyon Road and just look at all the Indian stuff

there. Then let's go to a movie and have dinner and then back to the hotel for the night."

"Sounds like a plan to me." I said.

When they returned from their night on the town, they surveyed the room Ms. Charles had graciously reserved for Carmelita. Carmelita was sure that it was the clients who were actually paying for her room. The fees they were being charged by Ms. Charles certainly seemed exorbitant enough. The room was spacious, to say the least. The bed must have been a custom made one because it filled half of the very large room.

"I will have to make you chase me in this thing all night," Carmelita said with a joyous lilt to her voice. She thought to herself, "No way am I going to let him catch me on the first try," and giggled.

Their lovemaking that night was a culmination of several efforts of preliminary touchy-feely on both their parts, because if the truth about them were known, they were both virgins, at least he had told her he was. This experience was a new one for them and they wanted it to be the best it could be. As they held each other closely later in the early morning, they both felt a wonderful glow and a feeling of togetherness that neither had felt before.

"It must be love." Carmelita thought, but didn't say it out loud. It was a time just for closeness and feeling of great tenderness, and she wanted to do nothing to spoil it.

Sunday they would have the entire day to themselves and could do whatever they wanted and then the trip back home would take several hours. They would make sure to stop often to insure that the drive would be the culmination of a terrific weekend for both of them.

Carmelita had no idea that Ms. Charles was involved romantically with the Sheriff, hadn't considered her as a threat, and chalked her up to just being a crabby, frustrated, and probably sex starved, old woman. Nor did she know that Ms. Charles had her spies at the hotel and would get a detailed report about her Sheriff and her clerk and their activities of this weekend.

Her life was in grave danger but she was totally unaware of the threat.

NINETEEN

The best alternative to questioning Rosalie would be for me to ride out into the desert alone and search for clues. It would be like looking for a single bubble in a bathtub full. I didn't expect to find anything of value. But if I didn't try, then there was no hope of really understanding what really happened to Carmelita.

I certainly do not consider myself any kind of expert horseman so when I went to the stables I asked the owner for the gentlest animal he had. I didn't want it to take a serious disliking to me and try to throw me off, or even worse, take a bite out of me somewhere painful. I most decidedly did not want to be horseless out in the middle of nowhere, lost. The horse he gave me wasn't the ugliest thing in the stable and he assured me it was gentle. I joked and said, "Ugly is only skin deep, but meanness goes clear to the bone."

He was right though, gentle is what this beast was. We made our friendship on the way out of town. We had mutually agreed on a compromise of sorts, if that's possible between a horse and rider. She didn't want to bite me and I tacitly agreed not to prod her in any way. I certainly didn't feel safe in kicking her into a jump start race with me hanging on for dear life or falling off and impaling my ass on a cactus. She walked easy and just fast enough for me. After about twenty minutes though I came to know why people who ride horses a lot tend to be bowlegged.

I didn't have a clue where to start so I just let the horse take me wherever it wanted to go. As I rode, moving and adjusting to the slow hypnotizing movements of the horse, I wasn't paying much attention to how far we were going. It could have easily been five or ten miles out of town when, about fifty or sixty yards from where we were, I spotted a swirling dust devil. The horse just came to a gliding stop. I had never seen one this close but wanted to get even closer if the horse agreed. It did.

I knew that the Indians consider a dust devil some kind of God reincarnate. They are also very fearful of them. They believe that these whirling clouds of dust are wandering souls of those long gone from this life whose spirits are in turmoil for some reason. The Indians stay far away from them.

"Maybe this is a spirit that was unable to get out of the Hogan as it should have," I thought. These spirits were thought to come back to give messages, maybe like those I had received from the Clan Fathers, to a selected person. Maybe this one had come to give me a message or lead me somewhere. I knew that normally, only the Shamans of the tribes were the recipients of these messages, but I couldn't afford to pass up the opportunity to get closer. I was certainly interested, so I nudged my horse and rode closer to the devil.

For all intents and purposes it was a miniature tornado of spinning dust. The dust swirled about twenty five feet high and had a rough diameter of twenty or so feet. It moved a tremendous amount of dust around as it spun there, but I could see its shape clearly. It moved along the ground very slowly, somewhat like a tornado, but also like some ephemeral being, that was unable to generate enough power to move any faster and not going anywhere in particular. It moved on its own course over boulders, then through a small gully. I knew that when dust devils run out of steam and can't spin anymore they just collapse into a pile of very pure sand. These piles of sand can be seen over the desert. Nobody, especially Indians, ever disturbs a pile of devil sand. Superstition does not allow it. It is considered to be as bad as desecrating a grave. Nobody wanted to take that chance.

This one slowed, spread out and stopped right before my eyes, not twenty yards from me, as I sat on my horse. What had been spinning swirling sand a minute ago had spawned a walking mirage of sand. An ephemeral shape emerged from the dust. It was not a solid substance that I could see, but it had a definite form.

The sand that formed the shape of a figure consisted of two colors; lighter colored finer stuff to darker soil colored sand that appeared a little more solid. It was as if some of the dust was still attached to the ground from which it sprang. The figure itself seemed to float just inches above the ground below it. I wiped my eyes to make sure I had seen what I thought I saw. "Yes, it is still there," I decided. At this point I became a little more nervous and a whole lot more cautious.

What had been whirling sand a minute ago had now materialized into a semi solid, opaque shape that looked very much like a robe of some sort that flowed with the wind but didn't blow away. "What wind?" I asked myself. There was no wind. The air was absolutely still, but the robe looked like it was blowing. I blinked again. "Yes," the robe was still flowing. "What the hell is happening to me? I'm seeing a pile of sand that looks like a robe." I thought.

What appeared to be hair flowed out from the top of the figure and it was the purest white I'd ever seen. As a can of spilled paint spreads out, so did this hair. It almost touched the ground from a height of seven or eight feet. It was beautiful hair. *Pure white* was the only word I could think of to describe it. There was a face, too. It was dark and wrinkled like a roadmap with great age. A sand face was what came to my mind. "Am I going completely nuts? Is my imagination running wild or what?" I didn't know at this point but I was mesmerized and wanted to find out, regardless of the consequences for me. I did see a face there. The eyes appeared to be fiercely black like obsidian, sparkly and sharp. The horse shied a little but I calmed it and it stood still. I realized that looking at this dust thing was generating feelings of fear inside me. I looked back at the devil, or whatever it was called and noticed three dark brown featherlike shapes, like long, brown, eagle feathers. One stood straight up at the base of the devil's head. Each one of the other two was tied with what appeared to be rawhide to the end of two long braids of black hair that hung down the front of the devil to its middle, which was about four feet, from the top of the form.

Neither I, nor the sand form, had made a move or sound since it had appeared out of the swirling sand. It did not appear to have seen me. I guessed that no more than five minutes had passed since the spinning dust had stopped. I was very scared, yet still curious. I knew absolutely nothing about mythology but made a note to find out when I got back to town. If this thing would let me get back to town, I thought.

The Indian arts lady, Mrs. Hernando had been very helpful, maybe I'd just ask her for some help understanding what I was now seeing. I nudged the horse forward again. I wanted to see this thing even closer up.

As I approached the devil, I heard a slight humming sound. Heard it or felt it? I realized it was like the feeling of magnetic power you get when standing under high power lines, pure energy that makes every hair on your body stand on end. Whether or not this spirit was friendly or malevolent, I would soon find out.

It still had not shifted to look at me but I felt as though I was being watched. I closed the distance between us and stopped the horse about ten feet from it.

The devil scared the wits out of me by turning and looking directly at me. It was like it had been waiting for me to get closer before it moved. I didn't like it at all, this dust thing watching me. Those sharp black eyes penetrated to my inner soul and somehow I sensed that it knew what was there.

The terror of those eyes looking at me was unexplainable. I had never felt pure terror before. I definitely didn't like the feeling but I couldn't move away until I had satisfied myself about the specter. I very carefully looked down to verify that I had not wet my pants, when the thing turned to look at me again. My pants were still dry, but if this dust thing started to move towards me or, God forbid, say anything, I would definitely come totally unglued.

What had started as terror but suddenly, unexplainably, seemed to be gradually consumed by a pure inner peace. I knew then that this was a *God*, n*ot a Devil.*" I knew nothing bad was going to happen to me. Still, I wasn't ready to be consumed by it, or die out here alone in this desert. Shivers began to travel up and down my spine at racetrack speeds. The small hairs on the back of my neck stood like soldiers at rigid attention. "Ah shit", I thought gravely, "What have I let myself in for?" My horse was calm but I surely wasn't. I finally stopped trembling and stared, wide-eyed, at the specter of dust.

Was I imagining it or was I seeing the face of a dust God close up? I didn't have much time to think about it as the peaceful feelings again spread through me. I had never been around anything this peaceful. None of the great cathedrals of Europe that I'd visited gave me this kind of feeling of inner peace and calm. This feeling spread over me like a veil of some kind. I became assured that only good would come of this encounter.

The lines of the God's face were etched deeply into the darker brown colored dust. The obsidian eyes penetrated to my innermost place. No religion that I had ever studied had done that. I guess that I had found too many faults with all of them, therefore I considered myself a pagan. If this Sand God was a manifestation of paganism then I was a believer.

Wouldn't you be in my shoes?

The starkly white hair was flowing like a Frank Howell Indian in a snowstorm but not moving anywhere. No snow was falling around it. All around the Sand God was clear blue daylight.

Being within five feet or so of the Sand God took my breath away. It was awe inspiring to say the least. This thing was no devil.

That name was given to it by Anglos, who don't know any better and attach a name to something they don't really understand. There was no physical opening that I could see that could be a mouth yet I heard, or felt, words being directed to me, into my subconscious. I understood the meaning, if not the actual words, of the message. It probably came in some ancient language, maybe of the Anasazi, the Ancient Ones, a language that could only be perceived now because nobody who was now alive has heard it spoken.

The message I got from the Sand God was not like those I had gotten from the Clan Fathers, but thoughts were implanted into my mind for a future date when I must make decisions. "Make decisions about what? I thought. I had no idea at this point. All I knew was that I was receptive to these thoughts, whatever they meant. After what seemed like just a few minutes, all I felt was a great soothing inner strength and all fear and terror vanished. The message from the Sand God had cleansed me of fear. The message came through loud and clear.

> *"You are not in danger yet, but tread carefully where you may leave an imprint, either physically on the earth where you are, or in the minds of those with whom you must associate."*

Although I was close enough to the Sand God to hear this message, I knew that I was in no danger. I sensed when it had begun coming to me and now I knew it was at an end. I had received only three Clan Father messages so far. What their meanings were, I knew not. Now I was just as baffled at the meaning of the message I had just received from the Sand God. I had hoped the Clan Fathers would give me more guidance, but so far that had not happened. Was the same thing going to be true of the message I had just received?

Then I realized that while receiving the message from the Sand God, I had somehow involuntarily closed my eyes.

When I opened them the bright desert sun blinded me for a few minutes. I saw that the Sand God had collapsed into a very neat pile of light and dark sand. The sand for the hair, the pure white sand, was on top. Topping the pile were the three brown eagle feathers of the now sleeping Sand God. It seemed to me that the deliverance of the message was its sole purpose and once that was accomplished it collapsed.

I knew then that I had not been dreaming or hallucinating. It had been there. I knew that I should move away from that pile of sand and not touch it or lead anybody else to it. It had existed for me and now it was gone. I instinctively knew that once I moved away from this place I would never be able to find it again, no matter how much I would want to. I decided then and there that I would not try. The message was the important thing that I was directed here to get. The Sand God was at rest now. I would surely leave it that way.

TWENTY

The very deep feeling of total serenity did not dissipate as I moved away from the pile of sand that had been the Sand God just a minute before. It brightened into inner knowledge that I was protected and would be safe no matter what happened to the contrary. I also had a feeling of foreboding about this place I couldn't explain. The Clan Father messages were an enigma as to their meaning and impact on me and the search. Now I had the Sand God's message and I had no idea what to do about it, maybe someone will come into my small sphere of interest to help. I surely hoped so.

I rode with my eyes closed, letting the horse go where she may, contemplating what had just happened to me. I didn't know what an epiphany or rapture felt like, never having had one, but this, I knew instinctively, was a very sacred happening. I wouldn't soon forget the image of that God back there. The eyes would continue to pierce my soul for who knew how long. After about fifteen minutes of riding I opened my eyes to the bright blue of the desert day.

As I rode and let the horse have its way, I pulled the small notebook out of my pocket and began to write down the message I'd gotten from the Sand God.

After about twenty minutes of writing and swaying rhythmically, I realized that all movement had stopped. I hadn't been alerted by any noise and the horse was very calm. Maybe another God of the Desert was after me. I started to shiver again in anticipation.

I looked up from my notebook and saw that my horse was nose to nose with another horse!

Sitting very still and erect like a statue was a very big, craggy faced Indian in a policeman's uniform. I noticed that his hair hung like the Sand God's with two long braids hanging down the front of his shirt. The only exception was that he didn't have eagle feathers tied into the braids and I didn't see any flowing white hair from the top of his head.

Whoops! I thought, I'm in deep trouble now, as I looked at a big shiny badge, a black belt that had what looked to be a very large, and menacing handgun in a shiny black holster attached at his hip. He didn't look all that friendly but at least I hadn't noticed a scalping knife so maybe he was OK.

"I'm Deputy Martin Begay of the Tribal Police. Who are you and what are you doing out here all alone, on tribal lands?" he said in a deep voice.

My voice sounded like Mickey Mouse when I answered him.

"I am Andy Bling, Officer Begay. I came out here earlier today to look around to see if I could find some clues to a missing girl from town. I'm a reporter from the *Albuquerque Journal* on assignment up here. I didn't know my horse had strayed onto reservation lands. I wasn't paying as much attention as I should have but just let her loose to do her own thing. I'm sorry. I guess we've been riding for about twenty five minutes or so. I haven't been paying too much attention to where I was headed. I just let her go while I was writing some very important things in my notebook. I've been in town about a week now and have had some experiences I can't explain and I was just trying not to forget them. If you just point me in the right direction, Officer Begay, I'll head back to town."

I felt foolish, but what else could I say to him?

He just sat very still looking at me wondering if I was telling him a far-fetched story or what. He apparently made up his mind that I wasn't some terrorist out to do destruction to the land out here as he spoke in a deep resonant bass voice.

"A lot of strange things happen to people out here on the desert, Andy. Indian legend has it that there are many spirits roaming around at loose ends out here just waiting to find a contact. When that contact happens to be an Indian, sometimes they become a *Contrary*. Do you know what it means to be a *Contrary,* Andy?"

"No, I can't say that I do, Officer Begay. Please tell me."

"A *Contrary,* Andy, is a person whose mind isn't functioning as it should. To them everything has to be done in reverse. For example, when they are hungry they throw away food. When they need to sleep, they stay wide eyed. When they have to go somewhere they always walk facing the other direction. You get the idea? And you can call me Martin if you want."

"Tell me, Andy, what unexplained things have happened to you?"

"I've got a thermos of hot coffee in my saddle bag, Martin, let's find a little shade and I'll try to explain what has happened to me. Maybe you can help me understand it all. Right now I am at loose ends." I replied in a voice that sounded tired, even to me. I was relieved that he was friendly toward me.

As the steam rose from our cups, I told my story about the contacts and messages from the three Clan Fathers after reading about the disappearance of Carmelita in the paper. I told him about meeting her best friend Rosalie and the many inconsistencies in her story. I explained that Rosalie's story was the reason I was out here in the first place.

I didn't know how superstitious Martin might be so, despite my true feelings, when I told him what had just happened I called the sand figure a dust devil instead of how I felt (that it was a Sand God). I also held back on the actual messages that I had been receiving. I didn't want to break the trust the Clan Fathers and the Sand God had placed in me by revealing them to anybody. Until I was given some kind of permission to reveal them I wouldn't. Who knew what might happen to me if I betrayed that trust? I shuddered to think of the power that might be invoked against me.

Martin seemed sympathetic and very interested when I finished my story. I did tell him the only word that I hadn't been able to understand from the messages and asked him if he knew what it meant.

"You're telling me, Andy, that you have received three separate messages from someone who claim to be Clan Fathers of three different Indian Clans and that they have decided to help you do whatever it is you are doing here in Bullsnort? And you claim that all three of them used the word "*Tawamiciya*" before each message, and that you received a message from a Sand God out here, not thirty minutes ago?"

"Yes, Martin, that's exactly what I'm telling you. I also talked to Mrs. Hernando at the Indian Arts Store and she led me to believe that there are twelve Clan Fathers, so can I expect to receive more messages from them?"

"I am of the Minniconjou Sioux Tribe, Andy, and that word is one that our medicine men use in their incantations during one of our ceremonies. It means that the person for whom the incantation is sung is to belong to one's self, free of other men. Not to be an outcast, yet not hampered, or hindered by other tribe members. Kind of like a free spirit to come and go as he chooses. The way to pronounce it in the old dialect is just like it is spelled; tah-wah-mee-ch-ee-yah, if you are interested how to say it. It also means the *Selected One*. You have obviously been selected for some very important purpose."

I could see a look of disbelief on Martin's face that gave me the message that he thought, "Yes, and I'm superman too." I was relieved that Martin had called it Sand God, now I could call it by the proper name too.

"Yes, Martin, I have all the messages I've gotten so far written here in this notebook. I don't know their meaning, what guidance they will give me, or what decisions I'll have to make when the time comes, but I've obviously been chosen for this important purpose and I intend to do the best I can," I declared. I went on to explain how the final shape of the Sand God came to be, the eagle feathers in the braids, and the pile of pure sand layered into colors when it collapsed. I also described the eyes as well as I could.

"Can you find that pile of sand again, Andy?" Martin inquired.

I did not hesitate to reply, "No, Martin, I can't and wouldn't if I could. It would be like betraying the trust the Sand God placed in me. Don't ask me to do that. Please leave it alone, Martin. When I decided to write down the messages I let my horse walk free and so, I have no idea which way to go to get back there, even if I wanted to. It might be over that rise over there or it may be miles from here. I guess I was writing and thinking for about twenty five or so minutes. Until my horse nudged up against yours I wasn't paying any attention to where I was. Do you have any idea why I was chosen for the messages from the Clan Fathers and the Sand God, Martin? What other kinds of messages are there, Martin?"

"Well Andy, I have to admit that I've never received a Clan Father message, let alone all twelve of them. The only person I know who has gotten one from a Sand God is the Shaman of our tribe. I'm sure he'd be interested in talking to you about all of them. Most Indians only get one such message during their entire life and it is the form of a vision they receive during their Naming Ceremony as a thirteen year old.

Before the Naming Ceremony, the young boy goes into the mountains to a sacred place and stays there for three days of fasting with only water to drink. The hunger causes him to hallucinate slightly and hopefully during that time a vision that comes to him. This vision is interpreted by the Shaman at the boy's Naming Ceremony. All Indians have two names; the name given to them by their parents and their Indian name that they receive as part of their transition to manhood."

"My Anglo name is Martin Begay but my Indian name is *Etahdleuh,* which means Riding Horse. Maybe the thing for you to do, Andy, is to request that you be honored with a Naming Ceremony. That can be arranged if the Shaman approves. I'll speak with the Shaman, while you talk to Mrs. Hernando and ask for her help. How's that sound, Andy?"

"I would be proud to have an Indian name, and if the messages are significant, I'd be more than willing to share the wealth so to speak with the Shaman. You'll let me know what he says about meeting with me?"

I was very relieved when Martin said, "Of course I will. To your other questions, I don't know. Only the Shaman can interpret and give you guidance in understanding the meaning of the messages. I do know that to receive a message from the Sand God is extremely rare and extremely important. Normally only Shamans get them and then rarely."

"There are Kachinas that are made to look like a Sand God, but nobody knows for sure what they look like because so few people ever see one. Most people find piles of sand but they are not all Sand God piles, obviously."

"I will talk to the Shaman and tell him what you've told me, and I'll have to be the go-between because I doubt that you will be able to see him face to face. I will get in touch with you later in the week after I talk to him. The way back to town is down this path for about five miles, Andy. I'll see you in about a week if everything goes as I think it will."

"Thanks Martin, I hope you can help me figure out this riddle. I'll be waiting at the motor court to hear from you."

As I rode away from Martin I thought about what he had said about the significance of the messages. It made me more cautious and wary about what was in store for me over the coming weeks that I probably would be spending here. I also felt that Martin and I had made a connection with each other that would be long lasting and very fulfilling.

I didn't know it then, but I would come to depend more on Martin than either of us had planned on.

TWENTY-ONE

As I rode toward Bullsnort, I contemplated my next moves. I wouldn't confide in anybody else just yet, but decided that I had to talk to the reporter, Jose Montoya, about the information I'd gotten, and surmised, from both the Sheriff and the lawyer. Hopefully he had held back some facts about his findings that would also help me.

I'd definitely talk to the Sheriff, Bill Johnson, again and the two deputies. If there was a conspiracy among these three cops then I had a more serious problem; trying to stop them from disappearing me. If not, then perhaps I could persuade them to make more effort to help solve the mystery surrounding Carmelita. I figured that the Sheriff was probably too old for Carmelita but the deputies might just be closer to her age and maybe, both had dated her at some time.

I'd definitely talk to Mrs. Hernando about the Clan Father and "Sand God" messages and try to learn more about the legends and Indian beliefs surrounding them. There had to be some kind of symbolism involved and since she said that she was an Indian herself then maybe she could help me a lot. If, on the other hand, the stories she knew about them were just folk lore, then I would have more problems. Martin's reaction to what I had told him told me more than anything verbal he had told me. I knew that he truly believed that I had, somehow, been directed, or led, into a situation over which I had very little control or influence.

What would transpire in the coming days would be beyond my control. I was the interpreter so to speak. If Martin was concerned enough to approach the Shaman with what I had told him, then the importance of the messages and what I was destined to do here would tax all our abilities to control it. Something very powerful was working through me. It made me more wary and concerned about my safety at the hands of those who would be against whatever I was destined to uncover, and anxious for those who would become involved later. I certainly hadn't anticipated anything like this the day I'd interviewed with Dan and accepted the job as the Indian Desk.

I realized that by the time I got back to the stable that I was ravenously hungry. I paid the bill and thanked the owner for being right on with the assessment of the horse, and walked to the Cave for lunch.

"Rosalie isn't on duty yet," the waitress told me with a knowing grin, "She'll be in later for the evening shift. She told me to tell you to be sure you come back then, Andy."

I was becoming known all over town as Rosalie's friend. I hadn't even seen this girl before and she knew me by sight. I thanked her, ordered lunch and scanned the newspaper I'd bought as I waited for my food. I found a follow-up article about Carmelita that said the Sheriff was offering a small reward for information that might lead to finding out what had happened to her. The article was sparse on any new information gathered so far. As I started to read the fifth line of the article I felt the starting of another headache.

"No," I thought, "Not another Clan Father message here in the Cave."

But that's exactly what it was. As before, the pain increased and I pressed my fingertips into my temples to relieve the pain. That didn't help this time either. A bright, sunshine yellow color ushered in the voice of the fourth Clan Father. I heard the male voice say to me,

"Tawamiciya,
I am the fourth Clan Father.
I am named Runs Fast.
I am the spiritual leader of the Deer Clan.
I will teach you how to be fast in seeing the truth.
When you are ready and need me, I shall return to help you."

I started to write this message into my notebook as soon as the pain faded a little. But just a few seconds later it intensified again, the color changed from bright yellow to the most intense blackness I had ever seen, or felt. "This must be the way Death is, total blackness," I thought as a shiver of apprehension raced up my spine. As before, I pressed my temples as the message came to me. I heard the voice,

"Tawamiciya,
I am the fifth Clan Father.
I am named Listening to Sounds.
I am the spiritual leader of the Horse Clan.
I will teach you how to carry the load of the truth.
When you are ready and need me, I shall return to help you."

As this voice faded, I felt a hand on my shoulder and a very soft concerned voice in my ear. It was the waitress with my chips and beer.

Andy, are you alright? You looked like you had fallen asleep on the table here. You were swaying from side to side like you were listening to some Mariachi music. I became concerned because you did this for about four or five minutes. I didn't want to bother you so I waited till you stopped and put your head down on the table."

I felt embarrassed at the question but couldn't tell her the real reason for my odd behavior. She would think I was some kind of nut talking in riddles like that, so I did the next best thing. I lied about having a headache after being out on the desert in the bright sun earlier in the day. "I guess it made me a little woozy," I said, hoping that would satisfy her curiosity. "I'm OK now and thanks."

She looked at me with a little askance as if to say, out in the sun, huh? Right! She didn't ask any more questions and I didn't volunteer anything so she just turned and walked away towards the kitchen. After a few minutes of gathering my wits while I waited, she brought me my lunch and walked away without saying anything.

I didn't have a funny retort for her at any rate. The meal was terrific. The stuffed sopapillas were smothered in a green chili sauce, which in turn was covered with chopped tomatoes and lettuce. The rest of the platter was filled with refried beans and Spanish rice. Remembering the spiciness of the salsa that came with the chips, I cautiously put a little of it on the rice to spice it up a little. As I ate, I sopped up the green chili sauce with a flour tortilla.

I recalled a story someone had told me, or maybe I'd read it somewhere, about one of the early Spanish explorers who went into what was then the unexplored wilds of northern Mexico. His travels took several years and in his reports back to the Grandees in Mexico City he reported that everywhere he went the people were unusual in that they didn't use the same utensil from one meal to the next meal but had many at their disposal. He apparently was trying to glorify the peasant folk a lot more than was justified in order to make his discoveries look a lot better and to have his explorations considered a success.

He was trying to justify his travels because he had not found Cibola, the seven cities of gold, that he had been sent to find. The church officials thought from his reports that he had discovered a lot more than he actually had. What he had written about was not riches but the native way of eating; with flour tortillas, then unknown in Spain. The tortillas were consumed and never used a second time. The joke was on the Grandees. But eventually they found out the truth of the reports and they certainly weren't happy with him.

I stretched a little. I was tired from the experiences of the day out there with the Sand God. I finished my beer, left a generous tip, and left the Cave. I decided to walk down the street to the Indian Arts store and if possible, have another long talk with Mrs. Hernando.

TWENTY-TWO

I entered the store and looked around for Mrs. Hernando, but she must have been back in her office. I gave a loud, "hello", just to let her know I was out in front. In a few seconds she came down the hallway.

She greeted me warmly and told me that she had received a new bunch of dolls and other things that I might be interested in and invited me to make myself at home while she finished some paperwork that she needed to catch up on. She'd be back as soon as that was done. She turned away from me and went back down the hall to her office.

I walked around the now familiar store. I saw some new paintings that were out of my price range. I used the leather bound knocker and hit the big drum again. It reverberated through the store and started my nerves jangling as the sound echoed loudly around the walls.

I heard Mrs. Hernando laugh lightly at the sound as she said, "Andy, you're going to have to buy that drum so I can get some work done while you're somewhere else banging on it." She had come back to the hallway entrance.

I laughingly said, "You can't possibly want me to go deaf by banging on this drum in my super small room over at the motor court do you? That crotchety old manager would probably call the Sheriff on me if I hit it in my room there. And, by the way, please don't sell this drum until I can scrounge enough money to buy it."

I felt some overriding compulsion to have this drum. I didn't tell her that though.

But she agreed not to sell it and continued walking back to her office. She said "I won't go so far as to put a Sold sign on it but I know that it is yours now."

After about twenty minutes of walking circuits around the shop I called to her to please come out so I could ask some questions about a couple of the dolls I'd looked at.

"What is this one here, the one that looks like it's made of mud, Mrs. Hernando?"

She seemed happy to answer my questions.

"That's exactly what it's made of, Andy, and it is called a Mudhead. They are sometimes made of red clay and other times light brown clay, like this one. Mostly they are not painted but left the natural color. They aren't like the other dolls here, Andy. These Mudheads have to be fired just like pottery. Interesting aren't they?"

"What about this little one here that doesn't look like the other Mudheads?" I inquired, picking up another one of the Kachinas.

"That one is a representation of what we call a Sand God, Andy. It is from the Zuni and it represents what you Anglos call a Dust Devil. Nobody I know of has ever seen a real Sand God, so these are based just on guesses what one actually looks like," she continued.

With that information my senses picked up about a thousand points as I examined the doll more closely. The one that fascinated me was about six inches tall. It had feathers and a little piece of downy rabbit fur at each ear. It had on a black leather breech cloth with pieces of red cloth to tie it on. It had no discernible face but there were black paint spots for the eyes and mouth. It had a piece of black yarn tied at each knee and in both upraised hands held what looked like wheat stalks. It was the plainest Kachina in the store but it surely held my fascination for about ten minutes. It was the most beautiful thing I had ever seen. I knew that whenever the price I had to have this doll. "My own private Sand God. WOW!" I thought. I knew that it didn't look like the Sand God I'd seen.

Suddenly a thought came to me. Mrs. Hernando had been very sympathetic and helpful in giving me information about the Clan Fathers, maybe she would help me with the messages I had received from them and the Sand Gods message as well. Somehow, I felt that confiding in her would not anger the spirits.

I asked her the price for the Sand God doll and the price she quoted seemed very reasonable. I would go into debt to have this doll. It would sit next to the clown I'd bought from Mrs. Hernando earlier. If I weren't careful, I thought with a chuckle, I'd wind up having a whole houseful of these creations. On second thought, that's OK, I can live happily, surrounded by these beautiful things in my house. My biggest problem right at this time in my young life: I didn't have a house.

After we'd talked a few minutes about the new dolls and all the other new stuff I finally got up enough courage enough to ask her. "Is there anything you can tell me about Sand Gods, Mrs. Hernando?"

She looked at me like she had done after I'd asked her about the Clan Fathers.

"Yes, Andy I've read the legends of how the Sand Gods came into being, what they are supposed to be, and how rare they are. As I said before, nobody I know of has seen one. Although, out on the desert there are piles of sand that are supposed to be their remains, I can't verify that that the stories are true. I personally have never seen one.

I've seen what they call that consists of whirls of sand picked up are by different wind currents, though. I do know that to see a Sand God is extremely rare and that it is considered to be an important and sacred thing."

"The books I've read about them sometimes mention a message that is given to the person who is chosen to see one, which is again extremely rare. The books also said that if a message is received from a Sand God, it should never be revealed to anyone, except maybe the Shaman. Why are you so interested in the Sand Gods now, Andy? Is there some connection between your interest in the Clan Fathers and the Sand God myths?"

"That's what I need to talk to you about. I don't know what is going on with me and this town but there have been some very strange and exciting things that have happened to me since I got here. I can't begin to explain them. I need to confide something in strictest confidence to you, Mrs. Hernando."

She replied, "You can trust me with anything you wish to tell, or ask me, Andy."

"You do know someone who has seen a Sand God, Mrs. Hernando." I said cautiously.

She had a very puzzled and surprised look on her face when she asked me, "What did you just say, Andy? That I know someone who has seen a Sand God?"

"Yes, that's exactly what I said. I have seen a Sand God. This morning I was engaged briefly by a Sand God out on the desert."

"I went riding this morning to see if I could find the place where Carmelita was last seen and about a hundred yards or so ahead of me was a spinning Dust Devil as we Anglos call them. I was curious and nudged my horse to get closer. I stopped about five feet from the spinning dust entity. All the sudden it stopped spinning. A sort of face appeared on the swirling sand. There was a brown eagle feather sticking in the pure white sand that was its' hair. This pure white sand went down to what should be its' waist, about four feet long. He also had two strands of black hair on the sides of his face. The hair that hung down was braided and had another feather at the end of each of the braids."

I was so excited at being able to tell someone who I thought would understand what I felt, that I wasn't sure my words were even making sense.

"I just sat there mesmerized," I continued, "and as soon as I felt that the Sand God had given me a message somehow and its mission was completed, it collapsed into a pile of sand, with the white sand on top and the three eagle feathers on top of that.

After that I nudged my horse away from there and was writing the messages in my notebook when the horse stopped walking. I looked up and saw a Tribal Policeman on another horse. We talked for a long time and I explained to him about the strange things that had happened to me and he wants me to talk to the Shaman as soon as he can arrange it. We'll meet later after he's gotten it all set up. I didn't tell him what the messages were." I was out of breath when I finally finished my tale.

As we talked, I began to trust Mrs. Hernandez enough that I began to tell her about the five messages from the Clan Fathers I'd received. I somehow felt that I would not be violating any code of secrecy if I told her what the Clan Fathers had said. I needed her opinion on what I thought their messages might mean. I felt that our confidence level was high enough that I could trust her not to reveal what I told her to anybody else. I followed Martin's advice, though, and saved the Sand God message for the Shaman only.

"I was somehow directed to come on a reporting job that was shaky at best."

I began by relating how Dan had concocted the job and sent me to Bullsnort. "My feelings on arrival in town were very strange and what has happened since then has been pretty much unbelievable."

As I told her about all the messages from the Clan Fathers, I watched her reactions to them. Obviously she was thinking very deeply about what I was telling her but didn't say anything, just waited for me to keep talking. She seemed to understand when I told her about Martin's advice not to reveal the actual message I had been given by the Sand God.

As I finished my telling I noticed that she was very intensely looking at me as if asking some very unknown and unasked questions of her own. I felt like I was sitting on some very sharp eggshells that were going to pierce this mysterious bubble I was in, and very soon.

Very solemnly she rose and spoke to me. "Please come with me, Andy. I have something in my office I want to show you. I don't usually let people into my office, but I feel that this is a very special case. Please come along." She touched my arm to lead me away to whatever she had in store for me back there. Of course, I followed her.

As I followed her along the very well-lighted hallway, I noticed some framed paintings. These must be special to be back here I thought as I looked at them. What I saw were miniatures, maybe three by three inches, of Indian dancers.

Their costumes were extremely elaborate and colorful and they were dancing to some unheard drum beat, maybe to the exotic sound of my basso drum that I had hit many times here in the store. That was a strange thought. My basso drum.

I followed her along till she opened the door to her office. "This is what I brought you here to see, Andy."

I was in awe and felt privileged just to be here with her and wondered what she had in this office that might just affect my life from here on. Some of those ubiquitous goose bumps rose on my arms like golf balls and I shivered like I had just passed through a dimension that separated reality from the unknown with a very cold, depth-defying area, somewhere between the warm now and the cold hereafter.

I didn't know what it was, but once having passed through it, I was not at all afraid of what I might find or what might happen to me. I had absolute trust in Mrs. Hernando even though we had only known each other a few days. I didn't really think of other dimensions being accessible but no other explanation of what I'd felt came to mind.

She pointed to a corner of the large room.

What I saw there I couldn't immediately interpret so she explained what it was. What I saw was about fifteen poles that went almost to the ceiling, which was about twelve feet above us. At the base of the poles was a pile of what looked to be animal hides with the fur still on them. In a neat pile in front of the hides were the most beautiful grey colored rocks I had ever seen. They were all basically the size of a grapefruit and of uniform color. Before I could ask the question she anticipated it with the answer.

"These things, Andy, are parts of a sweat lodge. You know what a sweat lodge is. Don't you?"

"Yes, I have a pretty good idea what it is and what it is used for, but please explain how all this works," I replied, wondering just how a sweat lodge was important to me.

She readily explained, "These poles are the frame of the lodge. These are buffalo hides and they are about two hundred years old and have been used for many a lodge. The river rocks there are used to heat the inside of the lodge. My great-grandmother collected them and they have passed through the matriarchal line of the family. I now have the honor of having them. I'll pass them on when I die. The stones are worn smooth by the action of the rapids of the river."

"They are beautiful and all the same shape and color. But, what connections does all this have to me?" I asked.

"Sweat lodges are what the local Indians use for purification and other special ceremonies. One of those ceremonies is the Naming ceremony. That is where every boy who is at least thirteen years old is to be given his adult name. The procedure has been the same for thousands of years. How it proceeds is this. The boy selected for the ceremony is taken to a sacred location out on a mesa in the desert by the elders, his father, and the Shaman of the tribe. The lodge is built, the rocks are collected and brought to one location, a fire is built, and a small group meeting is held. During his stay alone in the lodge, the boy is allowed only water to drink; no food to eat, and only a knife for protection."

"He is left there for three days with no contact with anybody from the tribe. During this time he should experience a vision of sorts that will be the basis for his adult name. At the end of that time, he will explain what he sees, if anything, to the Shaman. Occasionally, and rarely, the boy has no vision. If this happens, he must undergo the ceremony again later. The Shaman will interpret the signs the boy has experienced and a new name will be given. The elders will also return at the end of three days along with the boy's father and they will all escort the boy back to the tribe. Once he has his warrior name, he will never again be called his child's name."

"You said that Martin suggested that you should have this naming ceremony because of the experiences you have had. If the Shaman approves, you will use this lodge."

She said all this so matter-of-factly that I couldn't think of anything to say in response for a few minutes. I looked around the office and noticed a few other things that might be used in the ceremony and asked her about them.

"Yes, they are all used in the ceremony," she replied. "The fan of eagle feathers is used to pull the steam from the fire over your body. It is part of the cleansing process."

There was what appeared to be a turtle shell on the end of a short pole that had beadwork as sort of a handle. The longer part of the stem was wrapped in some kind of animal hide. Beside this item was what appeared to be a turtle shell ladle with the same pattern of beadwork and the same kind of hide wrapped around its' handle. I pointed to them and asked if these were also used.

"Yes, the stones are placed around the fire outside the lodge to get hot. Then you carry them inside the pitch black lodge and use the ladle to pour water over them. While you pull the steam over your body with the eagle feathers, you use the rattle to call up the spirits to you. Otherwise they wouldn't be able to locate you. The rattle calls up the good spirits and warns the bad ones to not come around. This is the cleansing ceremony that is done over the three days until the boy has a vision."

"I think the cleansing and naming ceremonies will help you to interpret the messages and help lead you in the right direction; so you can discover whatever you were sent here to find," she continued. "You said that Martin Begay will talk to the Shaman this week? If he agrees then I will arrange for a pack horse to take this lodge to wherever the Shaman says he will meet you. You should take about three gallons of water and no food for those days. When can you be ready to participate in these ceremonies, Andy?"

By the time she finished, I just sat in stunned silence. All this was happening so fast, the Sand God message, the Clan Father messages, and the possibility of both the cleansing and naming ceremonies. I wanted and could be getting an Indian name. I couldn't very well back out now, I thought, so I told her I'd be ready whenever Martin contacted the Shaman and arranged the ceremonies. I hoped that there would be much deliberation between Martin and the Shaman in order to give me time to build up my courage for this ordeal.

Now that I had some idea what was going to happen to me my senses seemed to explode with questions and sweat. I paid for the doll I'd selected and as I caught my breath I told Mrs. Hernando of my fears about what was going to happen to me.

"Do not worry, Andy, all will be fine," she reassured me.

Very meekly and quietly, I said, "I sure hope so."

TWENTY-THREE

L ater, after talking to Jose Montoya and getting some additional,
previously unpublished information, and after talking briefly to
the Sheriff who had just aggravated my negative feelings about him, I
went to the Cave. I needed a cold drink and hoped Rosalie would be
there because I needed to talk to her. She was.

As I sat in a booth, I considered the new information I had gotten
from Jose. He wasn't the least bit suspicious of Rosalie because her story
fit with what he had learned about both her and Carmelita. He didn't
think that Rosalie had any connection to Carmelita's disappearance.

The Sheriff, on the other hand, had raised both Jose's and my
hackles with the way he was conducting the so called investigation.
Jose had been wary of him for a long time. There were many things the
Sheriff had done in investigating other cases to arouse many questions
about his methods.

Jose couldn't explain why Carmelita had disappeared but had expressed
the hope that I could help him find out what had happened to her.

There were many questions to be answered and so far it seemed that
law enforcement officials were not making any progress. If Carmelita
had been kidnapped or murdered, where was she, or her body? Was
more than one person acting in a conspiracy against her? Did she just
choose to leave town and if so, why did she leave without telling anyone,
and where did she go? There were a multitude of unanswered questions
that neither Jose nor I could possibly answer yet.

That left me stuck again on the sharp horns of the dilemma. If
the person with the answers was not Rosalie, the Sheriff, or Jose, who
could it be? Maybe it was one of the deputies. What were their names
again? One, I recalled, was Miguel, who, according to Rosalie, had
been involved in a romantic relationship with Carmelita.

As I drank my cold beer, I asked Rosalie if she wanted to try
another date with me. Our previous date with dinner, followed by the
drive-in movie and the dancing at the Cantina had, in my humble
opinion, been a great success.

I was encouraged about our future relationship when she said
that yes, she'd love to go out with me again. I hoped her interest in
me matched mine in her and that we'd have a starry night instead of a
storm-wracked one. I told her that I had to go back to my room to work

on my story and that I'd come and get her around six, if that was OK with her. She said that would be fine.

Back in my room I pulled off my shoes to let them air out a little, sat on the bed and pulled the newspaper out of my pocket and began to read it. There was another short article about the young man who had been shot at out on the desert. Apparently he had been shot at a second time. The assailant, again, was unknown. I thought to myself, "Somebody wants this young man out of the way very badly to try to kill him twice." I wondered why.

The article, written by Jose, went on to say that the man had suffered no gunshot wounds this time, but that several windows in his house now were either totally minus their glass panes or had bullet holes in them. Jose had also asked for anybody with information about this shooting to come to the newspaper office and talk to him.

I had barely finished reading Jose's article when I felt the starting pains of another headache. This time a flash of brilliant fiery orange color invaded my senses. I heard a voice say to me,

"*Tawamiciya,*
I am the sixth Clan Father.
I am named Storyteller.
I am the spiritual leader of the Turkey Clan.
I will teach you how to bluff your way out of trouble.
When you are ready and need me, I shall return to help you."

Before I could retrieve my notebook and write down the message, the orange color was replaced by a flowery pastel pink color. Another male voice spoke to me.

"*Tawamiciya,*
I am the seventh Clan Father.
I am named Keeper of Knowledge.
I am the spiritual leader of the Owl Clan.
I will teach you how to tell the truth from lies.
When you are ready and need me, I shall return to help you."

I quickly dug my notebook out of my duffle bag and wrote down these last two messages. I had now received messages from seven of the Clan Fathers, with five more to go, in addition to the message from the Sand God. I looked at my list.

- • Perseverance
- • Slyness and Stealth
- • Dig for Truth
- • See the Truth Quickly
- • Carry the load of the Truth
- • Bluff my way out of Trouble
- • Tell the Truth from Lies

I had already started to fulfill the first message of perseverance by talking to Rosalie several times, the Sheriff once, Jose twice, the two deputies once each, and the lawyer once. I was determined not to give up because I still wasn't satisfied with either the Sheriff's or the lawyer's stories. I would have to go back to them and prod them again. I was a little leery about prodding the lawyer too hard because she looked like a lady who knew how to get revenge if she got pissed off enough. I felt that she would not hesitate to call on someone else to carry out her revenge for her if she felt unable to do it herself. If I could prove that the lawyer conspired with someone to kill Carmelita, or actually killed Carmelita herself, then she would certainly have ample reason to disappear me. I also didn't think that the Sheriff would have any qualms about eliminating me if I posed a threat to him. I would just have to be careful what questions I asked both of them since they already were suspicious of me.

Maybe Mrs. Hernando was also part of the conspiracy if such a thing had caused Carmelita's disappearance. I didn't know. The Cleansing and Naming Ceremonies would go a long way in helping me learn more in that regard. Martin Begay would be a valuable resource in solving the mysteries of both Carmelita's disappearance and the attempt on the life of the man who had been shot at. If the Sheriff was involved, Martin would be the only officer of the law I could turn to for help. I was confident that he would help me solve these mysteries, if he could.

I felt that I had already begun the process described by the Dig for the Truth message. I had talked to Jose to get the additional information that he had uncovered in addition to my efforts to learn more from Rosalie and Mrs. Hernando.

How the "Fast in Seeing the Truth and the Carry the Heavy Load of the Truth" messages would be fulfilled I hadn't a clue at this point in my investigation.

Would the clues and new information I was to find be so convoluted that I wouldn't be able to sift through them all for a cogent answer? I surely hoped not.

This whole business of suddenly being a criminal investigator was new to me. As a Military Policeman in Germany, I had investigated some automobile accidents, but this situation wasn't so cut and dried. Besides, the people involved in those auto accidents weren't a danger to me then. These people, whoever they might be, could be a definite threat to my continued health and well-being.

What trouble or dangerous situation was I to get into that I would need to use the advice promised in the "Bluffing" message? I pondered that for about a minute. I had never been prone to getting myself into trouble or into compromising situations where I needed to talk my way out real fast and would need the "Bluffing" advice, so it was hard to imagine needing it now.

The Liars message could apply to just about everybody that I had come in contact with so far here in Bullsnort. How I would sift through all of those questions was a mystery. But, then again, my whole experience in this town had so far been a mystery to me. Too many unexplained things had happened, and not all of them could be chalked up to chance. That sobered me up right quickly.

Somehow, deep down in my innermost places, I knew that the Clan Fathers would help me stay out of danger if they could. They would also lead me to the right conclusions by prompting me to ask the right questions, I had no doubt. That they would guide me was a given that I could not dispute at this point.

What I was doing was like trying to put together a large jig-saw puzzle with a blindfold on. The edges of the outside pieces could be distinguished but putting them together was the real challenge. The internal pieces would just be a jumble of clues with no meaning until I could see the entire picture. With the Clan Fathers help, I felt that I would eventually be able to do just that. The picture that I most wanted to see and complete right now was my date with Rosalie.

TWENTY-FOUR

I didn't know what expectations Rosalie had but when I picked her up at her house at six she seemed happy to see me. She was also in a good mood and was laughing at something. I had showered and put on clean non-horse-smelling clothes and was ready for a good time.

We decided that another horse/cowboy movie was OK. I guessed that was the only type of movie they ever got up here for some perverse reason. We went to the Cantina afterwards for dinner and dancing. We danced a lot and very closely. We hummed along with the mariachi music and whispered endearing things into each other's ears.

At midnight, by mutual consent, we decided the night had been full enough of enjoyment and decided to go home. The good cold beers we'd had were having a positive effect on both of us. As I drove towards her house she held my loose hand and said how much fun she'd had. I ventured to put my hand on her leg and assured her that I'd had a good time too.

"That's OK Andy, just drive with one hand and keep this one in sight, if you don't mind," she said as she laughed at my feeble attempts to let her know how I felt.

At least there was no slap this time. "Progress of a sort," I rationalized.

Along the way it began to rain with some thunder and lightning brightening up the night sky. She laughed a lot, not at me but with me. As I pulled up in front of her house with the rain pouring down and the moon blinking through occasionally in the very dark sky, we decided that it was best to wait in the car till the rain slackened in intensity or we would be soaked when we made our break for the front door.

As we sat there and talked, the windshield and then the side windows got all steamed up. We couldn't see a thing outside the car. I put my arm around her shoulders and gently pulled her to me and kissed her, hoping that she'd respond. She did and with what I would call enthusiasm. It surprised me the way she reacted to my kisses and caresses. I moved to her ear lobes, gently nibbling and sucking on them. She began to squirm a little as I moved down a little to the soft place on her neck below her ear.

As she didn't object, and seemed to be enjoying what I was doing to her ear, I moved a little further down her neck until I was at the V between her breasts. The kisses I put there left a taste on my lips like the perfume I had noticed while we were dancing. It was a soft and gentle fragrance that suited her well.

I lingered at that juncture for a few minutes and then unbuttoned two buttons of her blouse to reveal more of her soft flesh to caress. She didn't stop me after two buttons so I undid three more to her waist to reveal a black, lacy bra that covered her breasts seductively. The way she pushed against me as I gently kissed the deepest part of the cleft between her breasts made me more excited. I needed to see more of this beautiful girl. And right now!

I murmured for her to lift up a little so I could unsnap the silkiness. She arched her back as I slid my hand behind her and found the fasteners.

I thought to myself, "I hope I don't fumble with these damned hooks, turn her off and ruin it all right here."

I needn't have worried because they came undone quickly and the flimsy silk material immediately fell away from her soft breasts as I pulled her bra up. Her breasts fell free in my eager hands. I tentatively kissed one nipple and it immediately stood at rigid attention, just as a certain part of my anatomy was doing at this point. Then I kissed the other one. She pulled my head up to her lips after a few minutes and kissed me long and deep, thrusting her tongue into my mouth very seductively. This time it wasn't a "get to know me" type kiss but one of desire that gave me the impetus to get to know this beautiful girl a lot better. I surely was willing if she was and it sure did look to me like she was.

I responded by holding both breasts in my hands and began kissing and sucking both of her nipples at the same time. She moved her hips against me as I was doing this and I knew she was just as excited as I was. I just hoped that this wouldn't end too quickly.

Just as I thought about doing something more than I probably should have on a second date, a very large bolt of lightning, accompanied by an extremely loud blast of thunder ended our romantic activities. Judging from the vibrations created by the thunder, it felt like the lightening had hit within a block of us.

To say that it scared the hell out of us would be a gross understatement. We jumped apart, as much as the confines of the front seat would let us, she going to the passenger door and I to the driver's door.

I must have gotten one arm tangled in the steering wheel somehow as I fell back and jammed my elbow against the horn causing a second blast of noise. After I got untangled from the wheel, we noticed that some lights in the houses up and down the street had come on and people were looking out of windows to see what was happening outside. Rosalie had fallen back bare breasted against the door and was just lying there relaxed, seemingly not embarrassed at all. She looked at me with what I can only describe as a mixture of laughter and fear in her eyes.

Then I hit my head on the roof light because the noise had startled me badly and didn't feel so good either. We both broke into a paroxysm of laughter at my clumsiness. She fumbled with her bra trying to wiggle back into it and leaned forward so I could fasten it for her. She got into her blouse and buttoned it up as I watched her admiringly.

We rested against each other just enjoying the closeness of our mingled sweat wondering what passionate experiences had been erased by the bolt of thunder and the horn blast.

Then I remembered something my beloved grandfather had told me at age thirteen or fourteen, when I was busting through puberty with all kinds of boyish hormones exploding in me. I broke out in a very loud guffaw at the thought.

"I know what we have here is a funny situation, but why the hell are you laughing so hard?" she murmured as she finally got the top button on her blouse in place to cover herself.

"It was something my grandfather told me a long time ago about the way to a woman's heart," I explained. "I understood him, I think, to mean it was through her chest, which didn't make a bit of sense to me then. Being thirteen, without a very good understanding of anatomy, I misinterpreted chest to mean her breasts and asked him if he meant it was through her tits. My Grand Pa was very patient with me and told me that was not what he meant at all and I shouldn't call them tits because the proper word for them is breasts."

"I know now," I continued wisely, "That what he meant was that it was a good idea to keep the woman you love happy and laughing. I guess I made a good start on the laughing part tonight didn't I?"

"Right off hand I'd say we also started off rather well in the tits department. Didn't we?" Rosalie said, breaking up in laughter at our situation. "Maybe next time, if there is a next time, the weather will be a little better. And, I suggest that we do not include my neighbors if we can help it."

All I could manage was a very weak, "Yeah." It was night neither of us would forget anytime soon.

TWENTY-FIVE

I had waited no less than three anxious days for Martin to contact the Shaman and get back to me with his decision. Waiting anxiously for the call from Martin, I was lying in bed, playing out all the negative possibilities when the phone rang. I jumped out of bed and with a trembling, not completely awake hand, I answered the phone.

"Andy, Martin Begay here. I have some good news for you from the Shaman." I heard a distant voice say. His voice jangled me fully awake. I usually wake up nice and slow and easy which takes about ten minutes.

I knew that Mrs. Hernando was serious about the Cleansing Ceremony and apparently she had talked to Martin about it. I hoped that was what this early morning call was about.

I was very apprehensive about the ceremony because I didn't like unexpected things happening to me. Like I said before, I am a devout coward and have a severe aversion to pain. I would be at the mercy of the Gods of the desert or whatever else was out there that might not want me there. But, with the help of my newly found friends, I felt that this would probably turn out alright.

What Mrs. Hernando had told me was of no consolation either. I would basically starve myself for three days and hopefully have a vision of some kind. That vision would be interpreted by the Shaman and he would decide on a new warrior name, for me. What purpose would the new name serve? I hadn't a clue. I had had no guidance from anybody, on why I needed one, except for Martin getting excited about the connection between the Naming Ceremony and the messages I'd received. I had hoped for some sign or message of encouragement from the Clan Fathers but none was forthcoming so I assumed that I was on my own in this.

The anticipation of these events brought me wide awake and I bolstered my courage up a couple of notches before I answered Martin.

"Yes, Martin, you said you have good news for me? I have been sitting on very sharp pins and needles waiting for you to contact me."

"Yes, I do, Andy, the Shaman has listened to what I have told him and has approved your Cleansing Ceremony. If you have a vision out there, and you undoubtedly will, he has also approved a Naming Ceremony for you. He was very interested in your encounters and messages and wants to talk to you in person about them. He does speak English very well, so there will be no need to worry about him understanding what you have to tell him. He also gave his permission to use Mrs. Hernando's lodge from her shop. That lodge is a sacred artifact that we have used for many of these ceremonies."

I was relieved because I had not told Martin that I had discussed the messages with Mrs. Hernando.

"This is a very special occasion for you, Andy. It is a great privilege to have this done for you. You must be very special in the eyes of the Shaman. I congratulate you. I called Mrs. Hernando and found out that she has made arrangements for two pack horses to carry the lodge to the place the Shaman has chosen for your Cleansing Ceremony. The Shaman and I will take you to the place. Can you be ready at dawn tomorrow, Andy?" Martin asked.

"DAWN!" I gasped. "Martin, dawn is something I sleep through each morning. It is still dark then." My feeble attempt at humor did nothing to impress Martin. "I assume that we are going to ride horses out there, correct? Dawn is not the time I'd choose to go horseback riding. In answer to your question though, Yes, I can be ready at dawn tomorrow. What exactly do I bring with me?"

Mrs. Hernando had already told me just three gallons of water but I felt Martin might have some pity on me. He didn't.

"You can bring only three gallons of water, a knife for protection and a couple books of matches." Martin replied.

The only words that registered were "knife for protection." "Protect myself from what Martin?" I asked incredulously. "What is out there that I have to protect myself from?"

"Why, Andy, don't you know what's out in a desert, shame on you! There are foxes, snakes, mice, and all kinds of other critters that just might not take to you being in their territory," Martin said laughingly in a very low voice.

The laughing tone did nothing to dispel my already considerable, and now expanding, fear of the unexpected.

"Thanks Martin, you really know how to put a guy at ease about all this don't you?"

I heard a light chuckle from his end of the line. "Not to worry, Andy, all will be fine. See you tomorrow at dawn."

The click that ended the call was ominously loud.

After my nerves returned to normal and I had dressed, I walked to the Cave for some much needed breakfast. I asked the waitress if they had any empty milk bottles I could have. They had three one gallon empties, which I asked them to save for me. I got some funny looks but I didn't reveal why I wanted them.

I didn't feel that I would be cheating on the starvation ritual if I had a full complement of meals today. I sure didn't like the idea of not eating anything for three days. "Oh well," I thought, "I'm committed to this and can't very well back out now. Better just make the best I can of it."

The thought that this could change from just a vigil to a life or death situation didn't make me any happier about it.

I didn't do anything constructive all day but just rambled around looking at things I hadn't examined closely before. As I was walking down the street I again noticed the fired end of a cigarette butt in the shadows. That amorphous shape told me nothing of who it might be or for what purpose they were there. I didn't see anything ominously wrapped in a brown paper bag so that eased my thoughts a little. Was there only one of those folks in the shadows?

Why were they watching or following me? I didn't like that idea but what could I say to him or her if I were to confront them? "Hey you, are you following me or what?" Nope, that wouldn't work at all. I let it pass. I did look over my shoulder after I had walked down the street a ways to see if I was being followed. I wasn't.

I went into the Cave and talked to Rosalie for about an hour building up my courage to ask her for another date. I wouldn't blame her if she turned me down cold. The last two dates hadn't gone very well to say the least.

She said "OK let's just go to the afternoon movie, it's not a western this time, and maybe it won't rain or thunder on us." She was laughing as she said this so I felt as though she had forgiven me for the other night's fiasco.

The movie wasn't much to see or remember. I took her home afterwards and we said our goodnights without planning to do any more than that since I knew that dawn would come early tomorrow. She looked very skeptically at me when I didn't want to come into her house and I couldn't very well tell her why I couldn't. I drove away not feeling too good about myself.

I stopped at the gas station, bought two beers and a newspaper, came back to my room and started to read the paper while opening one of the beers. I was kind of hoping for another Clan Father message for guidance on the vigil I was to go through, but nothing came to me and I soon fell into a deep, restful sleep. I wondered if it was the high desert air or the depth of the darkness that made me feel so sleepy, but I had no answers. Anyway, I fell asleep in less than two minutes.

TWENTY-SIX

The room was totally black when, from somewhere deep in the dream I was having, I thought I heard a horse whinny. "Wait a minute here," I thought. "I wasn't dreaming about horses. I never dream about horses. I intrinsically don't trust, or even like them much."

As it turned out, I wasn't dreaming. I heard a sharp knock on my door and a disembodied voice somewhere calling my name. More horse sounds came after the calling and knocking.

I rolled out of bed and crawled to the window to see who was calling in the middle of the night. I saw that the sun hadn't risen yet and that it was very dark out there. Admittedly, I couldn't see much. What I did see though brought me wide awake in an instant and my plans for the day came flooding back into my mind.

I saw two pack horses loaded down with what looked like long poles on one horse, and a big dark bundle on the other one. On another horse was an Indian, I didn't recognize, and on a fourth horse was Martin. This time he wasn't in uniform but in Indian dress. I noticed another horse that had no rider on it. "Oh Shit. That one's meant for me!" I thought. "That's Martin and the Shaman and it must be dawn already. Here we go!"

I wasn't a good judge of horseflesh at any hour but in the dark the empty one, obviously mine, looked gigantic. I had read somewhere that a horse is measured in hands. The width of a hand is about four inches. If that bit of information was true, then the beast out there that was obviously for me was at least twenty one of them. I would need to pole vault to get on it. "No, Martin wouldn't do that to me!" I thought as the anxiety began to rise within me.

The horse's body was a light brown color, while its rump was white with brown spots. What looked like a blanket that was not big enough to cover the entire horse, was draped over its back. I hoped to hell it was at least tame.

I thought about the English history course I had taken in college. I especially liked to study the Crusades when the knights rode off to do battle with the Saracens. This horse reminded me of their steeds which were indeed robust, having to carry all that armor and weight. The most popular horse of the times was the French Percheron. Unlike this horse though, the Percherons were a deep purple color and were much larger than today's Clydesdales.

After a few more minutes I came more awake, my eyes began to focus and I determined that this one wasn't a warhorse of the Crusades, but an Appaloosa. I also re-judged the size downward to a normal sized horse. I might just be able to ride this one.

"Andy, are you awake yet? It's Martin here. It's time to get going. Open the door please."

"No Martin, I'm not awake yet and come on in and make a pot of coffee to take with us. I'll just be a minute. I'm ready to go. I've got my water, my knife, and I'm going to take a little notebook and my small tape recorder. Is that OK?"

"Yes, that's all OK, just no food, Andy."

"OK Martin, I wasn't going to sneak any into my bag. I want to do this the right way."

After the coffee was done and Martin had poured it into my thermos, we went outside where Martin introduced me to the other rider, who, turned out to be the Shaman. I had hoped he would say something at least encouraging but he didn't say anything. He just nodded his head.

I looped the strap of my tote bag over the pommel of the saddle and, after I got aboard without injuring myself, we rode away into the darkness.

We rode as quietly as five horses could through town. When we reached the edge of town I looked back and wondered if I were ever to see Bullsnort again. I hoped I would but that would depend, from here on out, on the two Indians who were riding with me. Not a sobering thought, coupled with being on horseback at dawn.

As we rode along at a trot, the sun broke over the horizon in a splash of fiery red color. Was it an ominous sign of coming danger? I hoped not. Before the sun had come up I was looking for shooting stars and had spotted three. Martin and I were close so I asked him what the Indians thought of them.

"They are the trails of lost souls trying to find their way home and their fiery re-entry into the world culminates their travels," he said quietly. The respect he had for them was obvious in the tone of his voice.

I was satisfied with that. I knew that they were meteorites on a re-entry path through the atmosphere as they were burning up but that wasn't as good a story as lost souls.

We rode silently after that with the Shaman leading the way, Martin leading the pack horses and me bringing up the rear. I didn't let them get out of my sight because I had no idea where we were or where we were going. We must have ridden about ten or fifteen miles out into the desert because the sun, by the time we stopped, was a giant fiery red ball in the sky. I reckoned that we were much further from town than where I had encountered the Sand God.

After about twenty or more minutes and a couple more miles I heard the Shaman say, "Here!"

We were in a small clearing that was spotted here and there with low lying creosote bushes. Not much here to inspire a vision, I thought to myself. Not much in the way of shade from the sun either.

We unloaded the pack horses putting the hides and the rocks into separate piles, with the poles sort of spread out across both piles. The rattle and the gourd were placed on top of this. The shovel and the water were put aside.

I noticed then that both Martin and the Shaman had brought what looked like intricately painted battle shields and sticks that had rounded heads on them. They were probably beaters of some kind. There were feathers on the other end of both sticks. The figures I saw on the Shaman's shield were stylized animals and a sun sign. I couldn't make out what was represented on Martin's shield.

As I stood there wondering what was to come next, suddenly both men started beating their shields, chanting in a high pitched tone and doing a shuffle dance around the pile of things. They went around the pile twice when the Shaman reached into his beaded pouch and got a handful of a powder. He threw it over himself, Martin, me, and lastly over the pile with the parts of the lodge, all the while chanting and dancing. This ceremony took about ten minutes. It didn't make me feel any differently, but if it worked for them, then who was I to say anything?

It was interesting to watch it, though. When the chanting and dancing were finished Martin retrieved the small collapsible shovel from beside the water jugs and began digging a fairly large hole beside the pile of logs. I asked him what that was for.

He explained, "Once we have the lodge built you have to have a fire. This is a fire pit. Right now you need to go out a little ways from here and collect up some firewood, and don't forget to find some kindling for starters. Pick up a sage bush too. And be watchful for snakes."

Like I needed to be warned to be watchful of snakes!

By the time I got back with the first armload of wood, the Shaman and Martin had arranged the poles in a very large circle and had tied them together at the top. The buffalo hides were heavy so I helped them pull the hides over the frame and secure them to the bottom and top of each the poles. I guessed that in a heavy wind they would be secure enough not to blow away. A flap of the hide was left unattached for the opening of the lodge. It was thrown back and pegged to the frame. Martin went into the lodge and began digging another small hole. This one wasn't as big as the fire pit so I figured it was for the rocks, once they were heated in the fire outside. I was right. We then piled the rocks outside the lodge next to the fire pit.

"When the sun goes down Andy, here's what you are to do," Martin explained.

The shaman still hadn't said a word to me. I wondered why he had looked at me when he thought I wasn't paying attention to either Martin or him. Checking me out somehow to make sure his approval was the right thing to have done? I didn't know nor care at this point. My big adventure was about to begin.

I heard Martin continue. "First of all build a fire here," as he pointed to the fire pit that had ten rocks around its edges. "Once it's going, break up several large pieces of the sage and put it in. Sit close to the fire and use the feather wand to pull the fragrant smoke to you. This is the part of the Cleansing ceremony that will help to ward off the evil spirits that live out here. It will also call up the good spirits to help protect you. In about twenty or so minutes, when the rocks are hot, use the shovel and take them inside the lodge to the hole there. Come back outside and put ten more rocks around the fire for later. Use as many logs as necessary to keep the fire going. The embers will be warm enough in the morning to start a new fire. When the second batch of rocks gets hot, put them on top of the first bunch inside the lodge."

"Close the flap and put some small pieces of sage on the hot rocks. Then use the ladle and drip water slowly over the hot rocks. The steam will heat the lodge. When there is a lot of steam, use the fan again to pull it to you while taking deep breaths. This will cleanse you internally. After you have inhaled the steam, use the rattle to call up only the good spirits. You don't know any Indian chants but if you want to hum some tones, that's OK."

Martin didn't answer when I asked him who the evil spirits were. He didn't volunteer to say who the good ones were either. I assumed that because of the messages I had received, the Clan Fathers and maybe the spirit of the Sand God would be looking out for me. They were on the good side of the spirit spectrum. At least I surely hoped so. I knew

I didn't know how to call them so I hoped they would be nearby to help when I had to leap over that hurdle when it came up.

Martin gave me the final instructions. "There's one hide inside to sit on and another to sleep under, Andy, so strip off your clothes and get into the lodge. Don't forget to drink as much water as you need. Do this for three nights and we'll see what happens. Hopefully you will have some kind of vision. Just don't try to force it. It will come naturally if it is meant to happen at all. We'll come back on the fourth day to get you."

With that small amount of encouragement and instruction I was left alone out there on that enchanted mesa at the whim of whatever may want me. I stared a long time at the small amount of dust they made riding away from me.

I was alone-totally alone.

TWENTY-SEVEN

I looked around the clearing and got my bearings. I looked up and guessed that I had several hours of daylight left. I thought I had enough firewood for the first fire. I felt like I would make it through this ordeal in good shape.

The site was on a high mesa which stood out above a very green river valley below. There were some large cottonwood trees down there that looked very small from where I stood. I guessed the altitude to be maybe eight hundred feet from the river below.

As I was looking at the sparkling water of the river, I noticed some movement. I watched intently. I soon realized that I was looking at an animal of some kind, possibly an elk that had come out past the tree line to browse on the succulent river grass along the banks. It was totally unaware of me way up above it. It seemed to feel totally free down there with obviously no fear of its environment. I must have watched it for ten minutes before it finished browsing, re-entered the trees, and disappeared.

That was peaceful, to say the least. After I thought about it for a couple of minutes I realized that that elk might be the only living thing I would see for three days. It was a sobering thought.

I wanted that elk to come back and provide some kind of company for me in my isolation but of course I had no control over it. Just watching it had made me more aware of my total isolation and very tenuous position, here alone.

I wasn't afraid-yet. I decided that maybe singing or humming to myself wouldn't hurt and maybe it would help to drive away some of those bad spirits Martin talked about. I didn't think that the Battle Hymn of the Republic counted as a hymn, but I sang it at the top of my lungs as best I could remember the words and tune, I doubted that it scared anything away that might have been intent on eating a part of me for dinner, but the sound and effort I put into singing it was soothing and I felt a little more at ease at my total loneliness.

I didn't have anything to do so I got one of the twigs I'd brought for firewood, sharpened one end, and jammed it into the sand near the lodge. Then I put a small rock where the shadow of the sun crossed it. I would make a great sun dial. I'd look at it again close to noon tomorrow, or when I was close to noon by my estimation. I'd also find rocks to mark the passing of each day. That way I'd have some estimate of how much time I had left to spend out here.

I said to nobody in particular, "I may be an amateur out here but I'm going to try and look like I am under control." I picked up four small sticks to start the fire with.

"WOW! This is going to be some kind of an experience," I said to myself. "Here I am out here, alone, with no one to talk to but myself. I wonder if, after three days, I'll have anything interesting to say to me. I wonder what kind of answers I'll have for my own questions?"

Will I be a completely raving nut when they come back for me? God, I hope not."

I had so many things to do. I had to find Carmelita, or her body, and those who did her in, plus find out who had tried to kill Jose. I had to try to develop a better relationship with Rosalie too. The first two dates hadn't gone too well. Gone to Hell would be a better description. I certainly couldn't afford to be a raving nut when I got back to Bullsnort.

I also wanted to visit Mrs. Hernando's store many more times to talk to her and examine her artifacts. She was a fountain of knowledge for Kachinas and Indian things in general and I wanted to learn so much more from her. A lot of unfinished business waited for me. Besides, I had five more Clan Fathers messages to get. Problem was I still had no idea where any of this would lead me.

TWENTY-EIGHT

My hand went involuntarily to the knife Martin had given me. I hoped it had a good point and was very sharp just in case I had to kill anything to stay alive for the next three days. Having it close by reassured me a little.

What if I saw a snake, or several snakes? What would I do? I knew that for one thing, I would stand very, very still and not breathe very much till they either tried to attack me or they left me alone. There also had to be lizards of all kinds out here. Maybe some were carnivorous and would enjoy a human snack, namely me. I didn't like to think of that at all.

Was I priming myself for a problem? I hoped not but I wanted to be totally aware of my surroundings. There were many rodents out here that could ruin a good day without trying too hard. Prairie dogs and ground mice, not to mention noisy chipmunks, were all over the place. I imagined thousands of snakes just waiting for a dinner (me?) to walk by.

I recalled reading in a book somewhere that snake meat was good to eat. It was supposed to taste like capon. I didn't care how it was supposed to taste. It would still be snake to me. I was never one to be interested in eating birds, other than chickens, but the taste wouldn't much matter, since I was not permitted to eat anything for three days.

"But what if Martin and the Shaman don't come back for me?" I asked myself. I will be desperate enough to eat anything if I have to stay here was longer than three days."

As I walked around the almost circular clearing, I noticed some ominous grey clouds that shrouded the mountains off in the distance. I guessed the distance to be about thirty miles but the altitude and clear air made the distance deceiving.

They were the Sangre de Cristo Mountains and I had read many stories about how they were named. When the first catholic missionaries who came to this part of the state, a territory back then, they saw the setting of the fiery red sun against the mountains and cried, "Sangre de Cristo", which means The Blood of Christ, three times. The name stuck and it is still used today.

I loved the look of this high desert landscape. There was a starkness that contradicted the beauty of it. I knew that the prickly pear cactus that was everywhere would bloom into spectacular colors. I had eaten some cactus jam made from the bloom and it was terrific.

"I have to stop thinking about food or I'll really be in trouble," I thought to myself. "Snake meat, lizards, and cactus jam."

What else would pass through my mind in three days?

I made myself busy by rearranging the kindling in the fire hole. It was just about time to get it going before the sun went down.

I went out to the edge of the circle and collected some larger logs. I picked up a pretty good load and separated them into piles based on guessing how long they'd burn. One limb in particular caught my attention for some reason. I felt that I shouldn't burn it. Why? It was just firewood. I didn't think too much about that feeling but laid that limb aside for later.

Later as I looked it over I measured it visually. It was about six inches in diameter and was made of red cedar with some intermingled white color. It really was a nice limb. It had a rather large knob on one end. The whole limb was about six feet long. It looked a lot like the English battering rams that I'd read about in history class. They were used by vast hordes of soldiers on foot and horseback when laying siege to a castle somewhere. Huge logs were fashioned into rams to break down the gates of the fortresses.

The knob on this one was bigger than a softball. It was large enough that I couldn't reach halfway around it with one hand. I didn't know what I would do with it but I knew instinctively that I should not burn it. Maybe I would receive some kind of message that would tell me how to use this stick. I knew not at this point. I'd do what the spirits wanted me to do in any case. I was getting used to being led and it didn't bother me so much anymore.

I knew that I couldn't start looking at everything that happened to me as some deep dark, mysterious thing from a God of something. I didn't feel that I was becoming more paranoid, but things seemed to be happening to me in very strange ways since my arrival in Bullsnort. Like these events were planned by someone.

After I had a good fire going and had arranged the rocks as Martin had instructed, I picked up the log to look at it again.

I sat down with it between my knees with Martin's knife in my hand, wondering if I should try to carve something on this limb. I wasn't a carver by any stretch of the imagination so I didn't know where to start.

Like I'd read somewhere; to start something, just start at the beginning and see what happens. I didn't know where the beginning was so I began by peeling off the remaining bark and scraping it clean.

I straightened up the end opposite the ball, smoothed down three small knots and was ready for whatever happened. I took a handful of sand and smoothed the entire surface of the limb from the end to the ball out a little.

The limb would be fine as a walking stick but instinctively I knew there was more in it than just that. How did I decide that? I had no idea. Things were getting stranger by the minute out here. I was getting messages from a limb of cedar? Unbelievable! Nobody would believe that story. Not even me.

I knew that whatever happened to me with this wood, I wanted the different colors to be the high points. I started at the smooth end and made several deep cuts in the wood. It carved easily. As I worked on it I began to feel a little sleepy since I had gotten up at dawn. As I sat there in what was left of the day, my eyes got heavy and my breathing a lot deeper and I felt myself getting more and more sleepy, and more peaceful.

When I awoke it was pitch black. I had obviously not slept for a few minutes but a couple of hours. The fire was low and the sun was gone. I looked at my feet and noticed a good sized pile of red and white wood chips. Something had happened to the stick that I had been working on but I didn't know what. I would look at it later when I had better light.

My first thing to do was put more logs on the fire. I didn't want a predator getting me. What I definitely didn't want was a snarling coyote at my door looking at me as its dinner. I needed that fire. I laid the stick aside and piled two logs on the fire. It flared quickly and warmed my bare skin very nicely. I had removed my shirt earlier in the heat of the day and now I felt chilly without it. I had heard that normally the temperature here drops an average of fifty degrees when the sun goes down.

I broke a bundle of sage and threw it into the blaze. It smoked heavily and I pulled some of the smoke over me. It smelled terrific. Just as Martin said it would. I was mesmerized by it and just sat there for a few minutes enjoying it. I looked into the dancing flames and let my imagination run wild.

As I looked into the flames and sparks, I thought I saw all kinds of shapes and forms. Just like seeing a face or some object in a cloud and then having it change to something else. The fire did that as I watched it. It changed colors from vivid red to blue, to black, and back to red again. I had never been hypnotized but if I were to be, then this fire would be the medium to do it. The fire suddenly materialized into the shapes of people.

No! They weren't just people. I saw in the flames what appeared to be a group of dancers wearing long feathered head dresses that went clear to the ground. They were carrying what looked like long curved sticks that had some kind of ball at the end just like the cedar stick I had been carving. Some of the Indians were beating an unseen drum while the others were dancing and chanting to the rhythm. They were doing a dance similar to what Martin and the Shaman had done here earlier. They danced around a huge bonfire that threw sparks skyward. Somewhere in the back of my mind I heard the rhythmic thump, thump of my drum, or the drum I had started to think of as mine.

I remembered the deep basso sound of the drum in Mrs. Hernando's shop that had chilled me then. These sounds did the same thing here. The goose bumps came up very quickly all over me.

Was this part of the hallucination and vision I was to have? I didn't know. I knew only one thing. The drumming and dancing were real. I can't deny what I heard and saw in this fire. Was this a message from some faraway place? What did it mean? Was this one just the beginning? I would make notes of it later. I didn't want to move. Didn't want to? I could no more move away from this fire than I could fly off the edge of this mesa. My logical mind told me that this was only the first night and that it was too early to have a major vision. I wasn't prepared yet. With what had happened so far, would I ever be ready? I sure hoped I would.

Maybe I was just sleepy and imagined the sounds, the Indians, and their dancing and singing as the flames danced and changed colors. Whatever it was it was working on me.

As the flames lowered the forms and the sounds faded away, I picked up each of the hot stones with the shovel and took them inside the lodge. When I had all the stones from the pit inside the lodge, I closed the flap, took off all my clothes and used the ladle to drip water on them. The steam rose in billowy clouds and it became stifling hot inside the lodge. I sweated rivers in the first few minutes. I had brought the pole inside with me but it was still too black to see it. I would have to wait till sunrise to see what I had carved there.

I put some sage onto the rocks and when I smelled the aroma I pulled some of it over my wet body. I could feel it clinging to me and "cleansing" me of worry and anxiety about my situation.

I had no idea what time it was, but it didn't matter. I was inside the lodge and protected from whatever was out there.

I had replaced the stones around the fire as soon as I had removed the hot ones so all I had to do now was to wait for something to happen. All that happened was that I fell asleep as soon as I crawled between the animal skins and got warm.

I awoke the next morning fully refreshed and as I pushed back the flap of the lodge the sun hit me full in the face with a blinding glare.

I had forgotten that all Indian Hogan entrances are placed facing the rising sun. The first thing I had to do was step out and to greet the sun the way the Indians do. I closed my eyes and looked at it directly. I felt the rising heat as it penetrated my body. I raised my arms and stretched them out to the side so I looked very much like a cross standing there. I said a little prayer of greeting and wished for a fortuitous day and wished the Gods well. I then went back inside, dressed and drank a few mouthfuls of water. It tasted great.

I went to the fire pit and noticed the embers were still warm. I didn't need a fire because I had nothing to cook so I just made sure I added a log to keep the glowing embers alive for the next few hours. I would need another blazing fire that evening to heat my stones. I went back inside the Hogan and brought all the stones out to the fire pit to be heated and used later tonight.

I looked for my pole and saw it lying near the pit inside the lodge. I picked it up and carried it into the sunlight. I was immediately amazed at what I saw there. Somehow, mysteriously as far as I could tell, there were twelve concentric rings carved into the end of the pole where I had made the initial cuts. They went up the pole about a foot and a half. I guessed that they represented all twelve of the Clan Fathers. I'm no carver and I know for sure that I definitely needed help to carve those beautiful rings. They were too perfect for my amateurish efforts.

"There has to have been a guiding hand from somewhere helping me do this," I thought. "Who or what, and better yet, why, was it done? Will there be more carvings to come up the length of the pole?" I wondered what it would be.

The coloring of the wood was something else to behold. The deeper red of the inner layers of wood shone brightly against the outer white wood. All it needed was a handful of sand and a little rubbing to take off the bits and small pieces that had not been removed in the carving. It was perfect! Maybe would need a little bit of linseed oil to brighten and preserve the wood and keep it from splitting. But it was already dry, so maybe it wouldn't split any more.

I put the pole down and looked around the mesa. It was totally and absolutely quiet. Not an animal sound broke the stillness. I had never experienced anything this quiet anyplace I had ever been before and I was stunned. There is always noise in our city lives, cars, busses, television, not to mention friends who always have something important to say. Here the silence was absolute. You can't imagine how quiet the world can be until you witness it alone firsthand.

I could see over the edge of the mesa for a distance of about one hundred miles in any direction. My vision at that distance was as clear as if it was at my feet. Was it just the altitude or something else associated with this enchanted mesa? These imponderables were adding up in the question column of my brain and would overflow like water soon. Martin had said that this place was sacred to the Indians and had been a place where people had experienced visions for decades. If the truth be known it was probably a lot longer than that, since the Indians had lived here long before the white man came to this continent.

I could see things that I could only imagine in other places. I was becoming overwhelmed with it all. I had often wondered what air would look like. Here, somehow, I saw the particles of it before me. I had wondered what colors smelled like. Now, the smells that proliferated from the trees and plants around the circle had a definite color to them. Not just the red of a delicious apple but the purple of the sage and the brown of the sand. I don't know how it came to be but here I could see silence, I could hear colors, and I felt the sky above me. As I looked around the mesa there were dancing prisms of light before my eyes. "What the hell is happening to me?" I wondered, but got no definite answer.

My senses were expanding to the point of overloading. This must be how a blind person feels, I thought. All of their senses are more acute because they cannot see things like the width of a smile or the glint of happiness or sadness in a person's eyes. I had never had any problems with my eyesight and it still affected me this way. What powerful feelings! How could I ever explain to anybody what was happening to me if they themselves had not witnessed it? I knew instinctively that I couldn't and wouldn't try to explain it to anyone.

I got out my notebook and tried to clarify my feelings but as I began to write about one thing, another would come flooding in and override the first and I had to skip to that one before it too fled for another and another. I gave up trying to put it all on paper and got my recorder and spoke into it for a long time. I left the lodge and walked out onto the mesa hoping that while I was out there my senses would return to normal and I would make some sense out of the words I spoke into the recorder.

As I looked out over the mesa I spotted a black speck high in the sky just floating there like a black cloud. At this distance I assumed it must be an eagle up there. As I looked at it, it went into a steep dive and disappeared from my view. Then I noticed that the thin grey line of mountains in the distance was covered with black clouds. It apparently was raining up there and I reckoned that sometime in the next three days I would have to deal with those clouds and whatever they decided to drop on me.

I walked the perimeter of the mesa which took more than an hour. It was funny. Here I was, fifteen or more miles from anywhere, and I was walking guard duty on the edge of my mesa! I laughed at that thought. The situation I was in wasn't laughable though. It was deathly serious.

I had started to call it my mesa. I thought that my weird behavior must be similar to a transformation prisoners sometimes make as they try to relate to their captors. I was giving this place a name so the unknown wouldn't be so scary when whatever was to befall me happened.

As I walked around the mesa I made all kinds of measurements to make my mind think about something else beside the horrible things that could happen to me. I counted exactly how many paces it took to make to complete one circuit around the edge, amazingly, three hundred and two. I put the trees into two categories.

Those over five feet high and then all the low lying bushes and shrubs. I mentally logged where the lodge was in relation to the other features. I triangulated it all into geometric forms. I also mapped out possible escape routes from the lodge. Escape routes? I had to laugh at that because there was only one way out and I had no idea which way we came in. I was here for the duration until Martin and the Shaman came and got me.

As I slowly resigned myself to that phantom time frame, I went back into the lodge and pulled the flap closed. I relished the absolute blackness of the dome. The place was heating up from the heat of the sun. I don't know how long I stayed there but very soon I fell asleep.

I knew exactly when I awoke though. I had apparently fallen asleep with both arms pinned under me. I couldn't move a muscle. It felt like there were thousands of pounds of something holding me down. My entire body was being stabbed with pins and needles as the blood tried to flow back into my outside parts again. I somehow got myself turned over onto my back.

My arms were useless. I tried to move my left one and only succeeded in slapping myself with a flopping, useless hand. I felt like there were a million bugs crawling over me. "Damn," I thought, "Mrs. Hernando has given me a bug infested hide to sleep on." Then I realized that my arms were still numb from lack of circulation, it wasn't bugs. It was my blood starting to circulate again. What a blessed relief! I surely did not want a bunch of unknown type bugs making me their current nest.

The sharp tingling told me that it would be another minute or so before my arms returned to normal. I lay there in the dark looking up through a hole in the top of the dome that I hadn't known was there. I saw blue sky up there. As my nerve endings came back to normal I took a big slug of water and lay back and thought about my first full day in my adventure.

I opened the flap and the sun's heat hit me. Sunburn wasn't a fun way to spend my time out here. I could not safely remove any clothes to be a little cooler. I needed my shoes for the rocks and sand. I sawed off the bottom third of the legs of my jeans and cut off the sleeves of my shirt to make them more comfortable in the heat. I had an old floppy hat to protect my face. I was ready to face my first day alone.

My sundial told me that a full twenty four hours had passed since my arrival on the mesa. The fire outside the lodge had burned to almost nothing so I carefully shoveled out the ashes around the edges and put them into a pile. Then I added a couple of small logs to the glowing embers to keep them alive before I broke up some kindling to put in the pit when I needed a hot fire. I put some smaller logs in a pile getting them ready for when I'd need them. I knew that I would need more firewood so I decided to walk out on the mesa in search of more.

I was very wary of snakes and critters that might not want me mingling with them. I found a berry bush but decided that only at the point of starvation would I break the rules and eat something. They did look appetizing though.

I gathered up an armful of wood and brought it back to the pit. I was ready, but ready for what? Whatever would happen would happen with or without me doing anything. But doing nothing was the easy way out. I could lie around all afternoon in the very warm lodge but that wasn't my style. I couldn't just sit and draw figures in the sand either.

I decided to prop open the door flap with a long stick so at least I'd have a little shade during the rest of the day. I picked up my log and knife and sat down under the flap.

I noticed that above the concentric rings a one inch barrier had been carved. What was that for? I had no control over what was to be on this pole and had no idea what this barrier was for. I guessed that its purpose would manifest itself in whatever the mystical carver would create above that barrier. As I sat in the shade surrounded by the sun-warmed air, I suddenly felt very drowsy.

I had begun to realize that every time I got the pole and the knife together I would fall into some kind of trance or stupor. I did it again this time. I just fell backwards onto the hides inside the dome. I had no control over my actions. Something spiritual was guiding my hand and the knife's will to do its bidding on the pole.

When I awoke the sun was way past the noon position so I went to the makeshift sundial and placed a rock on the shadow. As I went back to the shade and sat down, I noticed that there was another good sized pile of red and white chips of wood. I looked at the pole and was again amazed at what I saw.

Above the barrier there were now three Indian signs that I did not know the meaning of. I recalled seeing them in the books I'd read. They obviously had some significance to this pole.

Above these three signs was the outline of an eagle. The eagle's body went about two feet up the pole, the wings folded around the pole and were flared out as if in flight. Then I noticed that the eagle held a snake in its claws. As I looked closer at the snake I saw diamond shapes on its body. It was a rattler.

On the tip end of the carved snake, there were nine beautiful rattles that looked like they could make the ominous sound of a live rattler. The eagle was carved deeply enough so that the claws were a deep red color while the main part of the body went from red to white. Its wings looked like the genuine article with each feather perfectly shaped. The eagle's body was covered with smaller feathers and it was spectacular. The snake was red. The tips of the eagle's wings flared upward and went from red to white. The sharply hooked beak was white but the eyes somehow had been colored a fiery yellow! The carving reached more than a foot above the barrier. I was stunned and amazed, to say the least. I had no idea how this image, or any of the others, came to be there. I am not a carver. I had appreciated the carvings of the Kachinas in Mrs. Hernando's shop and I knew that whoever, or whatever, had done the work on this pole, was a master carver.

What, or who, was guiding my knife? Was the carving part of my vision? If it was then there were about four more feet of pole where something else would appear without any conscious input from me. What was the interpretation of the signs? I hoped for another Clan Father message but realized that the pole might be completed before that would happen. I rubbed a little sand on the rough edges of the eagle carving and called it good. There was absolutely nothing I could do to improve this carving.

My second day was starting with a bang, to say the least. I walked around the perimeter of the mesa again to see what was out there. I could see the mountains off in the distance to the north. To the south was open desert. To the west were more mountains. To the east was the lush green river valley spreading out below me. It was a glorious green panorama down there.

While I looked, in amazement I saw some movement along the tree line which I estimated was about eight hundred feet below my mesa. I focused as best I could without binoculars on the spot and saw the elk, probably the same one I'd seen the day before, coming out to graze on the grasses. It was followed by three smaller animals, probably doe. They grazed awhile and then went back into the trees again. The thought that they might be the only living things I might see out here besides mice and lizards sobered me.

I prayed a small prayer that Martin and the Shaman would keep themselves in good health and remember to come and get me. I've already told you that I am a devout coward. Wouldn't you be?

As I walked the mesa I heard the squeals and squeaks of a wide variety of small animals-chipmunks, squirrels, lizards and the like. Snakes are quiet so I didn't expect to hear anything from them. I don't know what I'd do if I heard a rattler going off. Talk about panic. I also hadn't seen any large cat type animals. I knew that an attack by a cougar wasn't designed to be fun.

The afternoon went by fast and when the sun was heading west for the day I put the twigs on the embers to build up my fire. I drank deeply of the now tepid water. My stomach growled as it went all the way down. I placed the stones around the fire pit and put some larger logs on the fire making the sparks shoot into the air. It reminded me of the scene of the ancient dancers from the previous evening. There weren't any drumbeats or chanting, nor did any dancers materialize. It wouldn't have surprised me if they had come out of the fire and smoke again. Out here anything could happen.

I just lay there looking up into the sky. At this height on the mesa I estimated that a billion stars were visible. As it got darker suddenly I heard something out of place. I didn't recognize it immediately so I looked around for the source of the sound.

As I looked towards the western sky I saw off in the blackness an amorphous shape coming at me at a height of maybe a hundred feet. The thing was about thirty yards from me. It was making sounds like an eagle or hawk might make after it had impaled a prey for dinner. It might be coming to ground to eat it. The wingspan I estimated to be about seven or eight feet. It didn't look like an eagle but I also knew that there were no California condors in our mountains.

Maybe it was a vulture. I couldn't tell what it was but didn't want it to get too close to me. My logic told me that if the thing really wanted to get to me there was no place for me to hide, except the lodge.

Was my over active imagination working again? I didn't think so. What I saw and heard was real. As I looked at the thing coming towards me I saw long black feathers around the head, or what appeared to be a head. There were longer blacker ones on the outspread wings. I then watched in fascination as it came in with a long slow glide to touch down like a small plane. I looked on in amazement because as soon as it touched down the talons and the feathered legs turned into what looked like human legs! The widespread wings turned into arms and the sharp beak turned into a nose! The sharp black shining eyes didn't take their focus off of me.

I didn't like the looks of this at all.

Right there before my eyes what I thought was a vulture had changed from a flying bird to a walking human-like image. I knew, once it had landed, that it was not just a giant owl. It was now an owl man!

"This is impossible," I thought. "Are my eyes playing tricks on me?" Had I actually seen this transformation? God, I hoped not! Or, was it the suggestion of the owl man I had seen in Mrs. Hernando's shop that had stimulated my vision of an owl man here?

It completed its landing and took about three more steps toward me. I stood there immobilized in awe of it. Before it came to a complete stop it let out a very loud piercing, "HOO! HOOO"! Then it rose into the air again as a complete owl.

As it rose and flew over my head, it cried again, "HOOOO"! Then whatever it had held in its claws was dropped at my feet as if it was a peace offering. Or was it something unknown? The Owl Man became a vague outline against a pitch black sky that had only a smattering of moonlight. I saw it flap its giant wings two or three times before it disappeared.

I rubbed my eyes to clear away the cobwebs and realized that I had just had my first vision. I quickly got the tape recorder going and described the bird, my feelings, and what I thought had happened to me. Without my words on tape surely nobody would believe my story about an owl changing into a man and then back into an owl that flew away into the night. I wouldn't have believed it before tonight. I am a believer now. I knew the Shaman would believe it but I still wanted the fresh ideas on tape.

It's ironic, I thought, that fear can't be shown on tape except for the fear in my voice. It was too bad that both fear and abject terror are two phenomena that are extremely hard to explain, let alone demonstrate to a listener.

When my rattled nerves had settled, I looked at what had happened objectively. I had just been visited by a Kachina Owl Man, given an offering, and had been left unscathed, but visibly shaken. I picked up a fire log to serve as a candle and walked to where the Owl Man had taken a few steps.

The sand was perfectly smooth! Not a claw or foot mark anywhere to be found! There were no feathers, no fur, no blood, no animal dropped as a sign, nothing had changed the mesa. Had I been dreaming? Had I actually seen the birdman and felt the animal as it had been dropped at my feet? Had I really heard the "HOO, HOO" sound it made as it flew away? Those now familiar goose bumps went up and down my body at racetrack speeds for several minutes.

I realized that my basic problem now was how I could handle it, or multiple its, without having some kind of terrible effect on my very fragile and shaky psyche. I knew that I had no choice but to endure what was to be sent my way by whoever was doing the sending, for two more days. I could only hope to survive intact, both physically and mentally.

In the minutes it took my racing pulse to return to normal, I fed another log to the fire god and watched as the red glow lit up a wide circle of the mesa.

Was my fire a circle of safety? I hoped so.

I moved the first series of rocks into the lodge for the night, then picked up my knife and the pole and sat down in the opening of the lodge and waited for the second set of rocks to get hot. As I sat there I wondered what would mysteriously appear on the pole this time. I knew I had no control over it. Maybe nothing would come this time. In another minute I was asleep.

When I awakened the fire was almost out, so I put more logs into the pit to keep it going. The rocks inside the dome had cooled a little so I replaced them with the second set of hot ones before I finally noticed that there was a new carving on the pole.

Above the eagle, running another two feet along the pole, was the carving of a male grizzly bear. I knew it had to be a male because of the white on its back. They are called silverback grizzly's. This one was true to form. The head was very large and the claws on all four paws were long, perfectly shaped, curved, and very sharply pointed. The teeth were also long and beautiful. There was absolutely no way I could have carved an eagle, a snake, and now a grizzly bear. Now I knew this totem pole had a major part to play in my visions. I would have to ask both Martin and the Shaman for their interpretations of the meaning.

I decided not to reheat the stones inside the dome and carried them back to the fire pit. I would be warm enough sleeping under the hide tonight. I picked up my pole, re-entered the dome and closed the flap. I lay back and in less than a minute I was asleep.

I knew instinctively when the sound, whatever it was, awakened me. I also knew that I had not been asleep all night. Possibly not even more than an hour had passed. I was jolted awake by a thunderous crashing noise outside the dome but inside the circle of the mesa. The heavy pelts and the frame of the dome shook with the tremblor. It felt like a violent earthquake had hit the mesa. I hadn't heard of any earthquakes this far North in New Mexico but it could happen here as well as anywhere.

After about a minute of this loud rumbling, I heard a sound that just didn't fit with an earthquake. It sounded a lot like the whinnying of a lot of horses.

Was it a stampede with my lodge at the center of it? God, I hoped not. I just didn't feel like being crushed under a thundering herd of wild horses. The ground shook, the cacophony of noise was deafening, and the frames violent movement made it look as if the lodge would come crashing down on top of me along with whatever was out there. A sobering thought.

The noise of the horses reached a tremendously loud crescendo.

The sound was all around me and seemed to be magnified by the dome. It lasted about three minutes and then as quickly as it had started, it faded away. As the noise faded the poles settled back into their holes, the pelts stopped shaking, the ground stopped vibrating, and there was complete silence again.

I had survived the stampede! Amazingly, I was unhurt, the dome was intact, and the horses had gone. Gone where? Over the rim of the mesa into space, to all be killed as they hit the rocks almost eight hundred feet below? It seemed to me that there must have been several hundred horses, the way everything shook, but I wouldn't know for sure till morning and I could investigate the damage and determine which way they came and went.

The silence was deadening. I quickly got my recorder going and it must have taken half an hour for me to translate my experience into words. When I finished, I lapsed into a very fitful sleep. What else could or would happen to me out here? I tried to think positively as I said aloud, Better not to think about that. Don't want the Gods who are doing this to me to get any new ideas of how to terrorize me. I didn't want a self-fulfilling prophecy to take over here.

I aroused myself at sunrise on my second day, greeted the sun with a small prayer, and went out to survey the damage done by the stampede. Unbelievably, nothing was damaged!

There were no hoof prints of the hundreds of horses that I had heard run through here last night. The fire pit and logs were exactly as I had left them. The bushes and small trees were still upright with no damage. Even my makeshift sundial was intact.

Was I going crazy with loneliness and isolation or what? Had I imagined the dome shaking, the noise of horses running, the whinnying, and the entire mesa shaking? Had my own imagination been playing tricks on me again? Or, was it part of the vision? Was someone, or something, playing with me? If so, then I was completely at their mercy. I had absolutely no control over my destiny while I was out here. I just hoped they were just testing me instead of being malevolent towards me. I hoped that my third full day wouldn't be as eventful as the first two had been.

My nerves were becoming extremely frazzled.

TWENTY-NINE

I walked to the eastern edge of the mesa and looked down at the riverbed far below me. I wondered if the elks would return to browse. To my surprise, all four of them were there browsing on the rich, green river grasses. As I watched them I caught a glint of something shining in the sunlight at the south end of the section of the river bank that was within my view.

I focused on the spot and soon I was able to distinguish two human figures crawling slowly along the edge of the tree line toward my elk! They were wearing camouflage clothing and would be invisible to the animals as they crawled towards them. I watched in horror as they got within about sixty yards of the elk and one brought his rifle to his shoulder, aiming at the male elk. He apparently fired at it because even though I couldn't hear the report of the rifle, I saw a small white puff of smoke rise into the air. I looked to where the animals had been to see the big elk laying quietly on the ground. As I was looking at the elk I heard the report of the blast that had killed it.

I stood there mesmerized. I couldn't have called out to alert the elk, it wouldn't have made one whit of difference to them. I watched as the hunters, warily, approached the downed animal ready to shoot it again if it weren't dead. In a couple of seconds I did hear another finishing shot. I was relieved to see that the doe were gone. At the first shot they had made it to safety into the trees. One of the only living companions I had had was now dead. I was devastated. I sat down, put my head in my hands and said a small prayer for the elk.

I walked around the mesa after seeing the elk go down and didn't do much of anything. I rationalized its death, knowing that hunting is a way of life for the people who live up here in these mountains. If your family needs food, the best way to get it is to go hunting and bring it home to them. I had no problem with hunters. I knew that this part of New Mexico is on the migration flyway and millions of birds of all kinds flew over this land on the way south to the Bosque del Apache, a park south of Albuquerque.

It is a national wetlands reserve for migrating waterfowl. I also knew that there were hunters all over these mountains taking game of all kinds. Just because I wasn't a hunter didn't mean that others shouldn't do it to sustain themselves and their families. But I also knew that it would be very hard for me to get over the elk being killed for food.

I was still sane at this point and had used only one gallon of water, so I felt that I could survive whatever the mesa Gods threw at me. Ah Bravado! I feel that I needed the protective security that feeling gave me. The isolation was now starting to take its toll. I was more wary as I walked around the familiar mesa. I jumped when small critters called out their warnings to one another. I carried my knife all the time now in my belt. I began to jump at all the sounds.

Then, for no reason, I burst out laughing and started talking to myself. What the hell am I so scared of? Nothing is going to attack me out here.

Nothing but my own overactive imagination, if I'd let it.

Things that are destined or programmed to happen are going to happen and I can't do a damned thing to stop them. That thought calmed my nerves and I settled down to some semblance of normalcy.

THIRTY

That afternoon I went out of the protective circle again, this time to find more firewood.

I was ranging farther and farther from my dome but to cleanse myself I needed more and more firewood.

While I walked I made note of the sounds of the animals I couldn't see. The loud squeaking noise of a chipmunk, lizards making a smooth soft calling sound, squirrels fighting off the chipmunks that were eating the pinon nuts they had shaken from the bushes. I noticed sets of tracks going away from the dome which I guessed were made by either a fox or raccoon.

On the way back, maybe a quarter of a mile out, I spotted something strange stuck on a thorn of a creosote bush. As I got closer I realized that it was a dried snake skin. I then noticed the diamond shapes on it. A diamond back rattler! On my mesa! No, I had to admit to myself, I was on the snake's mesa. I was the intruder here, not the snake. The skin was about four and a half feet long and was inside out. The snake had shed it with the help of the thorn. I picked it off the thorn and carefully wrapped it a couple turns around a limb and carried it all back to the circle. I didn't know what I was going to do with it other than just keep it as a souvenir of the mesa. Maybe make a hatband out of it? I'm sure a taxidermist could cure it so it could be made into a usable hatband for me or maybe as a gift for Martin or Mrs. Hernando in appreciation for all their help.

I made my way back to the dome and the fire pit and unloaded the wood. I then took a long slug of water. Mistake number one! The warm water hit an empty stomach, rumbled there for about a minute, and came rushing back up in a torrent. I sprayed a goodly part of my surroundings. After the dizziness passed and the vomiting stopped, I went over to the upraised flap on the dome and sat down in the shade.

"SIP the water fool!" I told myself. "You've been out here two and a half days with no food. Think about what you're doing." Self, being kind of slow under these circumstances, just answered, "YUP."

I picked up my knife and the pole as I sat there in the shade of the lodge door flap wondering what would miraculously appear on my pole today. As usual, as soon as I had both of those items together I fell into a kind of stupor and was asleep for I don't know how long. When I awoke I immediately saw what had been carved on the pole.

Above the grizzly bear there were three more symbols as a sort of separator. Above these symbols there was carved, again to my utter amazement, a mountain lion standing on what looked to be a boulder. It too was shaded from white to dark red. The muzzle was especially beautiful for where it would naturally be a deep brown color, it was deep red. It took my breath away at first sight. The lion's body was about seven inches long and extended to the end of the pole with a tail that wrapped around it for several turns. The tip of the tail was dark red, as were the paws. It was beautiful. I knew, again, that I didn't have the talent to carve this beautiful animal. Who was the master carver that was giving me these gifts? I knew not from where they came.

As with the other carvings, it took a little sand to finish off the rough edges. I couldn't improve on it. I wondered aloud, "Why me?" What is the symbolism of this pole with the animals? I had no idea. Hopefully Martin or the Shaman would understand the reason. The only possible connection so far to the pole was the rattler skin I'd found. Was I going to see a bear and a cougar out here? I didn't like the idea of that, me being armed with only a small knife.

The only parts of the pole left untouched now were the big ball at the end and about a foot of wood near the nose of the lion. I wondered what would appear there.

After the experience last night and the carving on the pole today I welcomed the thought of a good thorough steaming.

I put the pole inside the dome and went to get the fire going. After about twenty five minutes it was blazing and the first set of rocks were hot so I carried them inside the dome, put a sprig of sage on them and closed the flap. When the second set was hot I put them on top of the sage and dripped a full ladle of water slowly over the entire pile. The steam rose and engulfed me. It felt great! I had even remembered to cover the hole in the top of the dome so nothing would escape.

I sweated and dreamed of Rosalie. Oh Rosalie! Would she still want me after being gone all this time without assuring her that I'd be back? I sure did hope so. There wasn't much, short of an ESP experience, that I could use to communicate with her while I was out on the mesa by myself.

"Have an ESP or telepathic communication with Rosalie?" I laughed at that thought. I didn't think it would work but what other choice did I have? What with everything else that had happened, why not try it? Maybe the sound gods, if there were such things, would make it work.

I settled into the heat and the hides and closed my eyes. As if closing my eyes in total blackness made a whit of difference but I did it anyway. I pictured her face in my mind and thought the words I would like her to hear. "Rosalie, I love you. Please wait for me. I will come back to you."

After repeating this message three times, I stopped. I had concentrated so hard on transmitting the message I had given myself a slight headache. Was this another Clan Father message? I didn't know, but after a few sips of water, both the image and the ache for her were gone. The heat and steam were making me very sleepy so I lay back and covered myself with a hide and was instantly asleep, a sure sign of a pure conscious.

There was no way of knowing how long I'd slept, or whether it was still daylight or dark outside, since the dome was so dark. Suddenly, I was awakened by a deafening roar, a crash of thunder, and the sound of what must have been very large hail hitting the dome. The hides were stretched so tightly that the hail, or whatever it was, made it sound very much like I was inside a very large drum. Every piece of hail that hit the hide reverberated through my body like an electric shock. The sounds continued for what I estimated to be about forty minutes. It sounded like a storm of epic proportions.

"WOW!" I thought, "The whole mesa must be flooded. The firewood won't be dried out for days, and I've got to have a fire."

I had wondered when the storm and I would come together. It sure hit with a vengeance. I was prepared for it though. I had dug a shallow trench all the way around the dome to funnel water away so everything inside would not get soaked. Apparently it had worked. Everything inside was still dry. I didn't want to see what damage had been done outside but I had to investigate.

As the noise of the storm faded into the distance and finally stopped, I ventured to open the door flap. I expected to see the fire pit flooded and the wood soaked and useless with standing water everywhere. It had been another illusion! The area around the lodge was all perfectly dry, just as I had left it. No puddles, no soaked firewood, nothing was disturbed. The sky was a perfect blue with a smattering of light fluffy clouds.

This was surely an enchanted mesa as far as I was concerned, no doubt about it! First a non-existent stampede, then a hail-less hail storm, carvings showing up mysteriously on my pole, not to mention the scary Owl Man manifestation that had scared the hell out of me.

As I looked around the mesa, I let out a yell, "YOU ARE STARTING TO SCARE THE CRAP OUT OF ME, WHOEVER, OR WHATEVER, YOU ARE!"

The echo that came back to me scared me even more. An echo up here above everything! Amazing!

I realized that the yelling didn't help at all and I did feel a little stupid for doing that. I laughed out loud at myself. I wouldn't survive another day at this rate. What had I said earlier about winding up talking to myself and wondering if I had anything interesting to say? Talk about a prophecy! I went back into the dome and stayed there the rest of the day doing nothing but sipping a little water. I slept very well that night despite my totally jangled nerves.

I awoke on my last day with nothing to occupy my time and efforts. I had plenty of firewood and water. That is, I had plenty of firewood and water if Martin and the Shaman came back to get me on time today. I opened the flap, greeted the day as solemnly as I could and picked up my knife and the pole, hoping some more carvings would appear on it today. I didn't think whoever was carving this pole would leave the end unfinished. I cleaned up some of the edges with a little bit of sand and sat back in the shadow of my door flap and waited.

I felt myself getting drowsy but I never knew if it meant the carver was taking over my body or just the heat combined with exhaustion that was affecting me. With the large knob on my mind I finally fell back asleep. There was absolutely no worry about what would appear on the knob.

What I saw when I awoke took my breath away. It was the most beautiful and striking thing I had ever seen, and I had seen hundreds of carved Kachinas. This wasn't a Kachina. It was the full head of an Indian warrior. The face was craggily with the typical high prominent cheekbones of Indians. The eyes were like those of the Sand God, dark and flinty looking. The carved hair was flowing down the sides of the face in braids. It went down the pole to touch the face of the cougar. The back of the head was carved into a headdress with about forty small feathers which again reached down to the cougar. Every inch of the pole was now covered with carvings. It was truly spectacular!

Could this head be a solid rendition of the Sand God? It sure looked like it. Like on the Sand God I had seen, there were two feathers at the ends of the braids. They were so detailed they looked like separate pieces of wood that had been attached to the pole there. Like the other carvings, it, too, took exceptional advantage of the wood's color shadings from white to red. There were steaks of red on the white face that looked like war paint. Like the eagle, the eyes were a flinty black color.

It took me several minutes to focus on the exquisite coloring. It was perfect and I didn't need to sand away any rough edges. All I would do would be to put a little linseed oil on it to heighten the color and preserve it. I reckoned that the Gods who carved this pole would not have done it if the wood were going to split.

As I drew my attention back to my surroundings, I noticed a large pile of red and white wood chips where I sat. I gathered up a large double handful, carried them to the fire and threw them in. The totally unexpected explosion rocked me and slammed me into the frame of the dome, rocking it on the foundation. As I recovered, I realized that I wasn't hurt at all just totally bewildered.

What the hell was going on here? Why had these chips exploded, and not the others? I couldn't venture a guess that made any sense.

Maybe this was some kind of warning message from the gods telling me that The protective coverage they had given me was coming to an end?

Was the protection of the Shaman, and the spell created by Martins chanting and dancing also ending? Was I in more, and possibly increasing, danger from this point on?

Was the completion of the head and the totem pole the beginning of the end of my safety? I didn't like the sound of that, even a little bit.

I immediately got my recorder and started talking into it so that whoever found my dead body would have some kind of explanation as to what happened to me. I still had a boatload of unanswered questions for Martin.

I had to be alive long enough to question him.

I still had one more night here, alone.

I sat in the opening of the dome and let the sun play over the carvings on the pole. The shadows accentuated the carvings in a way I hadn't seen yet. I vowed then that I would keep this piece of art forever *IF* I was allowed to leave this mesa.

I pictured myself out here alone for many more days, slowly starving and dying from lack of water, and nobody coming to get me. Not a pleasant way to go I thought. I vowed, with my pole thrust skyward, "I will survive, I will survive."

As I sat there contemplating my future a distant echo of voices came into my consciousness, from where, I was afraid to guess. I couldn't distinguish the individual voices at first because they were scrambled up in volume and tone. The harder I listened the more they separated into distinguishable voices that I began to recognize one male, one female talking to each other. "How the hell is this happening to me?" I thought. "I am listening in on a private conversation somehow. Talk about ESP!"

I somehow then heard the male voice say, "We've got to do something about him. He's been asking too many revealing questions around town about Carmelita. He's talked to you, the reporter, and will probably talk to both of my deputies if something isn't done to stop him. We have to eliminate him like…"

He was interrupted by a female voice that I immediately recognized.

"You're right. What do I tell him to throw him off the trail if he comes back to ask me some more questions? He did say he would, you know. Do I try to lead him to the same place where we took care of the other problem or what? He's getting too close for my continued tolerance and comfort. He claims to be a reporter from Albuquerque but he could very well be a cop or private investigator hired by Carmelita's family to find out about her. Maybe he's just bungling around to throw us off his trail. I think he might just be persistent enough to find out everything."

I listened a few more minutes, identifying the male voice and then they both began to fade. It was the lawyer and the Sheriff who were talking.

Some disturbing questions came to me immediately. Who had been eliminated? Carmelita? Was I next on their list? Where had the problem been taken care of? What was the other problem? Who could I go to for help? Was I about to be disappeared by these two? If they were out to get me they didn't know where I was. I was sure that Martin hadn't told them. Mrs. Hernando surely hadn't either. I was safe as long I was out here. I quickly put this new revelation into my recorder. At that point it stopped and I realized that I needed a new cassette.

I very quickly came back to my immediate problem: survival out here. My main question concerning survival was how? I had nothing but a small knife, my recorder, and the pole, which I would not use in defense for fear of breaking it. That was the list of my armaments.

If Martin and the Shaman did not return for me I would need to kill some kind of game. I sure couldn't do it with just a knife. I needed something more flexible and formidable. I needed a spear or something. Problem was, I had no idea how to make a spear or any kind of a weapon. I had read many books about Native Americans using spears and something called an "atlatl" to increase their throwing distance and effectiveness. I definitely couldn't fashion an atlatl.

Problem two: Even if I had a spear and an atlatl, I probably wouldn't be able to get close enough to an animal that wasn't already dead to use it. Now that is a sobering thought when one considered their survival.

I'd bet that young Indian boys knew how to make weapons of all kinds, like a bow and arrows. "That's it. I'll make a bow and some arrows," I said out loud to the empty space around me.

Problem three arose immediately. I had no idea how to make a bow, let alone arrows that would actually kill game. But then, I didn't know how to carve either and somehow, with guidance, I'd done it on the pole. I would just start at the beginning and use a process of elimination. If I could eliminate everything that didn't look like, and function as a bow and arrow, then what was left should be a bow and arrow. Kind of like telling a barber to cut everything off that wasn't a good haircut. It might work, but it sure as hell was a haphazard way to protect oneself, or even get a good haircut.

"What do I need for this possibly lifesaving project?" There I went again, talking to myself without getting any answers. Was this the first or second stage of insanity coming on? I hoped not. "Talking my way through this dilemma should help me identify what I needed to do about it," I reasoned aloud.

"First, I need a long and flexible limb that I can bend into a makeshift bow. It has to bend and not break. Second, I need at least three long straight sticks that can be used as arrows. Third, I need something to use for the fletching on the arrows. And lastly, I need something like glue to hold it all together so that when I shoot the arrows at an animal, it won't fly apart and maybe kill me."

I went out onto the surrounding mesa top looking for my bow and arrow parts. I quickly found three straight sticks about four feet long that only needed a little shaving. No problem there. I finally found a stick that was as long as I was tall, about six feet, that didn't break when I bent it almost double. That would do for the bow. I felt very lucky because the first two sticks I'd found and tried snapped in half easily.

"Now," I thought, "what can I possibly use for the fletching?" Would I be so lucky to find a downed bird or a grouse at my feet? I didn't think so.

As I walked around, I spotted many dried and brittle-looking prickly pear cactus leaves lying on the ground all over the place. I picked up several until I found three that wouldn't snap in half. They were as hard as wood. I cut away the thorns and put them into my pocket. The one last major problem reared its ugly head at this point.

"What can I use for some kind of glue to hold it all together?" I found a cactus and broke off a dozen fresh leaves. As I made my way back into the circle, I improvised on what I could do to make usable glue. Who knew, it might just work. My life might just depend on it working.

I put some logs in the pit and started a fire. I knew a little about how the Indians straightened their arrows from some of the books I'd read. They had a very ingenious method that worked very well. They scraped away all the bark and cut off the knotholes as best they could. Then they soaked the sticks in water for a few days. Then they used a rock into which they had gouged out a small groove as a brace to straighten the stick. They heated this rock near the fire and when the not-so-straight stick was flexible from soaking, they drew it through the groove in the rock. The steam softened the tissue so it could be shaped and straightened as it dried.

I didn't have a grooved rock or enough time or water to soak the sticks for three days so I scraped them as best I could. I did use a chunk of sandstone to grind down the few imperfections so that they were smooth. They were passable as arrows.

I needed something I could use as arrow heads now. I didn't have any flint at my disposal and anyway, I didn't know how to shape it to make an arrowhead. I had seen mountain men doing it several times, but since I didn't have any flint I didn't worry too long on that aspect of it. I did the next best thing.

I took one of the hardened cactus leaves and cut six triangles, each about three inches long. I then cut three of the triangles in half. I put them near the fire for a couple of seconds to harden. I did this four times, waiting for them to cool before doing it again. Hopefully this would temper them. After they cooled from the last heating, I shaved the edges to sharpen them. I knew they were sharp because I ran one over my thumb and it drew blood. I had to somehow glue the smaller triangles onto the larger ones to make a four edged arrowhead. I also had to figure out how to attach them to the arrow. I would work on that later.

Another major hurdle was the fletching. Maybe the remainder of the hard cactus leaves would work as well as the feathers I had no way of getting. I had nothing else to experiment with. I had shaped them into pointed heads for the arrows. Maybe I could make them into a feather shape, too. With a little ingenuity and a lot of luck carving them I did fashion them into shapes resembling feathers.

Using my knife, I cut three grooves along one end of each of the three sticks for the feathers and made a + shaped groove into the other end of each of them for the arrowhead. Then I returned to the most major problem again; how to glue them on.

Some experimentation with the soft cactus leaves I'd brought back was in order. I scraped away the green outer skin to reveal the white pulp of the three big leaves. I put this pulp into the shovel and used a smooth rock to mash it up, adding a little of my precious water to make it into mush. With the water it sure didn't smell good. Maybe if it were heated it might just work.

I took the shovel to the fire and heated it until the goop started to smoke a little. I used a stick and stirred it adding some more water. It turned to a clear liquid once it got hot. I wondered if it would stick to anything. To test it I picked up two sticks and dipped one end into the goop. Then I pushed it against the end of the second one and held it tight for a few minutes. Unbelievably, it stuck. But, a serious question arose. Would it stick well enough to hold the points and the feathers on the sticks?

Had I just lucked out and invented natural super glue? I sure wouldn't want to bet my life on that. I did bet that my high school chemistry teacher would give me an A for effort. That would be a great improvement over the "C" I'd gotten when I was in her class.

I hadn't wanted to become a chemist anyway. I never did like the sound of Magnesium Chloride for some strange reason. Funny thing, I thought, I still don't know what the hell it is.

I spread a little of the goop on a feather and gently slid it into the groove on the stick. It stuck OK. I did this with all three arrows with the grooves and put them aside to dry. I assembled the arrowheads and put them close to the fire so the glue could dry. Meanwhile I sat and contemplated how to make the bow so it wouldn't break. After about an hour I went back to the arrows, attached the points in the grooves with the glue and laid the three completed arrows close to the fire to harden.

Now I moved on with my plans on how to fashion the bow so it wouldn't break and kill me. I scraped off the remaining bark on the limb I had found, smoothed out the rough places with a rock, and sanded off the knots. I tapered the ends and cut a notch for the bowstring, when and if I ever found one. I carved the stick a little to make a handhold so it fit my hand. It looked like a bow but would it work like one? That was the big important question.

The only thing I had for a bowstring was the strings in my boots. I took them both out and glued them together with my home made superglue. I knotted the string on one end and applied a drop of glue to secure it, then tied it into the groove on one end of the stick. All I had to do now was figure out how to flex the bow and add tension to the string while attaching it to the other end. Not an easily surmountable problem for one who was making his first bow.

I used the logic that came to mind as I thought about the problem. I put the stick between my knees, wrapped my arm around the top where I needed to attach the other end of the string. I bent the stick into a bow shape, put the string into the groove and tied a makeshift double knot in it. I slowly let the bow relax until the knot was tight in the groove and hoped it would hold. I knew that if it didn't hold, I would have a hell of a time untying the knot. It held. I put a good daub of my new superglue on it to secure it and set it aside to dry and harden.

The arrows were ready, the feathers were tight in their grooves and the heads were hard and sharp. All I had to do now was test my new weapon and hope I didn't kill myself with it when it came apart.

I very carefully, and with great respect for my new bow and arrows, picked up the bow and one arrow. I locked it on the string and tested it by pulling it back an inch at a time until the bow was about half the length of the arrow. It held. I then pulled it all the way to the head and let it fly towards the dome. The gods must have been watching out for me as the arrow went home into the hides with a resounding THUNK!

I retrieved the arrow and wondered what I should do next? Act the part of the great white hunter out on the desert? And kill what; a squirrel? That possibility made me laugh at my situation. I had never killed anything before. Not even as a kid with a BB gun or a slingshot. I certainly wasn't a hunter that got a deer or elk every year. I just wasn't into having animal heads hanging on my wall.

I made up my mind right then that if I had to kill anything it would be for my own survival, for food to keep me alive. In my present state of mind, I wasn't at all sure if Martin would come and get me off this mesa before starvation became a threat.

The sun was settling in the west with a fiery glow on the mountain tops. I got the fire going, heated up the sets of rocks, carried them into the lodge and went to bed, content that if I had to, I could assure my own survival. I was very proud of my pole, but was doubly proud of my bow and arrows.

They might just save my life I thought as I went to sleep, nice and warm in the dome, with that pleasant thought.

I awoke on the fourth day with the realization that now I was totally on my own. If I were to survive it would have to be by my own ingenuity. I had about one half of a gallon of water left of the three I'd brought. There wasn't any way to replenish it so I would drink it very sparingly today. I took a pretty good initial drink, capped the rest and put the bottle in the dome. I sure didn't want a stampede of horses to smash it.

I decided then and there, after greeting the sun, to take my continued survival into my own hands. If I killed a bird or snake, then that's what I would eat. Just the thought of eating a snake made my mouth water. I thought of the breads and fresh butter and the good "road kill" and especially the good, cold beer I had had at the Cave. What I wouldn't give for a good cold beer right now. At this point I was thinking more about food than I was about Rosalie. I had my priorities right. I decided that if she asked me about my experiences out here I definitely wouldn't relate to her that food was a greater concern than she was at this point.

I pulled on my now string less and floppy boots, picked up my bow and the three arrows and started out onto the desert. I was going hunting. I knew instinctively that I would make a success of it. I tried to walk as quietly as possible but since my boots had no strings they kind of flopped on my feet at every step like two very large clown shoes. I cut two strips off the bottom of my shirt and tied it around the tops of my boots. There! That held OK and certainly made it easier to walk quietly.

I must have walked crouched over being very careful for about fifty yards when all of a sudden out of a corner of my eye, I noticed some movement. I immediately fell to the ground and almost stopped breathing.

When I came back to normal I started low crawling like I had learned in basic training. I moved slowly in the direction of the movement, hoping that whatever it was, it was still there. There was no cover except for a spindly creosote bush so I had to dig into the sand to get out of sight. Mistake number one!

The sand went down my pants and into my boots and was playing hell with my skin as I crawled along. Wasn't anything I could do about it now, so I just continued crawling along, just not as deep in the sand as I had been before. I must have moved another twenty yards or so when, right there before me, was what had made the movement I'd seen.

There, not ten yards in front of me now was a fully grown male mountain lion eating a jackrabbit it had obviously just killed.

Could I kill the mountain lion for my own survival? If he spotted me, I might just look better as a meal than that jack rabbit.

"Wait a minute!" I thought to myself, "The Clan Fathers are the guiding factors here, not me. The Turtle, Wolf, Buffalo, Deer, Horse, and the other Clan Fathers promised to help me and have led me to this mountain lion." I said a short prayer of thanks to them for the lion.

Very slowly I brought the bow up and sighted along the arrow to the vulnerable spot just behind the shoulder on the lion. I said another short prayer for a true delivery. Very slowly, lest the lion hear it, I pulled back on the bowstring, hoping that it would work as it had before.

As I sighted along the arrow, I saw the big, tan head of the lion turn to face me. The sharp black eyes focused on me as it stood perfectly still, waiting for me to let loose the arrow that would kill it. I let it fly. The path of the arrow was true and straight and I saw it impact and imbed itself to half its length in the lion's body.

Surprisingly, the lion made no move to run away, nor did it make any kind of painful cry as the arrow killed it. To my utter astonishment it just turned and looked at me full in the face as if to say,

"There human, I have sacrificed myself so you may live."

I suddenly felt very humble.

I didn't know what to do, or feel. Had this lion been another Sand God that had come and sacrificed itself so I could live? Had the Clan Fathers really sent this animal to me? I didn't know.

As I watched to see what it would do, possibly run away, it slowly fell to its knees and then rolled all the way over on its side and lay there. I didn't move toward it because I didn't think I could put another arrow into it if it weren't dead. I must have sat there for a full ten minutes, just admiring the lion. I couldn't just sit there all until darkness fell, so I got up and walked toward it. It was dead. I knew that I couldn't skin it or eat it unless I was on the verge of starving. What I would do was to have it stuffed and save it.

What I could do was eat the rest of the large, and very ugly, jackrabbit instead. I picked up the rabbit and skinned and gutted it. I threw the entrails into a hole and covered them with sand. I tied it to an empty belt loop.

I pulled the arrow out of the lion and cleaned it off in the sand. I grabbed the lion by its hind legs and began dragging it back to the circle. It was a mature male, maybe five or six years old. I guessed its weight at maybe one hundred thirty pounds. It was heavy work dragging it all the way back. It took me the better part of two hours to get the dome in sight. Sweat was pouring profusely from every pore of my body as I finally sat down, my muscles aching from the exertion. I rested a little while before moving to start a fire.

I got the rabbit skewered on a sharp stick and held it over the fire where it started to cook. It was a greasy thing. It dripped into the fire and sizzled seductively, not to mention, smelling great. The meat was getting a really nice brown and it smelled delicious, and I was hungry! I didn't know, nor care, what jackrabbit meat tasted like and it was all I could do to keep from slobbering all over myself at the great smells coming from the cooking stick.

The rabbit meat was turning a nice golden brown like a Christmas turkey and looked very tempting. My stomach had started to growl loudly like it was about to gnaw on my backbone if I didn't put something into it. I wasn't a cook so I had no idea how long a rabbit needed to be cooked so I kept turning it on the stick until it was a uniform black all over. I propped the stick against a rock to let the thing cool off before I ripped into it. A seared mouth didn't sound like too much fun.

Before I started to rip it apart I said a small prayer of thanks to the gods that had brought me good fortune. I threw in praise to the arts God for the pole and the hunter Gods for my bow and arrows and the Clan Fathers for looking out for me.

I was just about to dismember the rabbit leg when, off in the distance, I heard my name being called by someone. Someone was coming to save me! The feeling of relief was staggering. I didn't need the rabbit to survive any more. I was going back to civilization all in one piece and sound of mind. I hoped anyway. Would I ever be the same as I was before I came to Bullsnort?

I doubted it.

Never one to waste anything on purpose except mystery meat, I decided to offer the rabbit to whoever was coming for me. Off in the distance I could see a cloud of dust as some riders came my way. I saw two riders and three empty horses. I made up my mind that one of those empties was mine if I had to kill for it. I didn't care if it were a wild horse or a Percheron. I was using it to get the hell off this strange enchanted mesa. I would later realize that I no longer called it My Mesa.

As the riders got closer, I recognized Martin, but the other Indian I didn't recognize. It wasn't the Shaman. I was safe. They rode into my circle and dismounted. Martin walked over to me, looking me over, probably for injuries or wounds, he found none.

He asked me, "Andy, are you OK? Did you think we had forgotten you out here? We couldn't get time till today to get back out here because of a brush fire around the village. I bet that you are ready to leave here aren't you? Did you have any kind of a vision, anything interesting happen to you?"

He obviously was excited to find out what had happened to me as I was to tell him. "I'll play it cool," I thought.

"Well Martin, yes some interesting things happened, but I'll wait till I can get my wits organized before I tell you about them. Besides, I just want to get back to town now, if you don't mind."

He looked a little crestfallen at my not wanting to tell him so I handed him my pole to look at.

The look of amazement on his face made my day as he looked carefully at my pole. "Did you carve these figures, Andy? They're beautiful. What are these smaller figures here?" as he pointed to the figures that I had to admit I had no idea what they meant. He obviously admired all of the carvings.

"I didn't carve those things all by myself Martin. It's a long story best told over dinner and a cold beer. Oh, by the way would you like some recently killed jackrabbit, cooked over an open spit?" I laughed at my faked accent.

He looked rather skeptically at me and said, "Did you kill this rabbit, Andy? How did you do it?" He hadn't seen the carcass of the mountain lion yet.

"No, Martin, I didn't kill it, this mountain lion did before I killed it. I did it with this bow and arrows I made," I said with obvious pride in my voice. He took the bow and arrows and looked them over very closely.

"You made these, Andy? Why? Did you think we'd forgotten you out here? You didn't eat anything did you to ruin the visions?" All the while he was examining the bow and arrows very closely. "Andy, where did you get the ideas for these? They are almost an exact replica of some we have in the tribal museum that were made by the Anasazi people over a thousand years ago."

All I could answer was that I had some kind of divine guidance in carving the pole and making the bow and arrows. Other than that short explanation, I had no idea how the plans for them came to me. I didn't want to seem arrogant by saying that I just started at the beginning and the end product was as you see it. That wouldn't go over too well, I thought.

I told him how the lion had looked at me the instant I let fly with the killing arrow and then described what it did after it was hit.

Martin looked at me very strangely and said, "You mean the lion just looked at you, didn't cry out when it was hit, and didn't attempt to run away?"

I repeated what I had said once more, "No, it just looked at me in that mysterious way, and fell over dead."

"That's certainly not normal, but I can't explain it. We came prepared to carry the lodge but now we'll have to bring the lion also. The horses will probably shy away from the lion smell but that can't be helped. First of all we need to take down the lodge. We won't have time now to eat the rabbit, Andy, sorry."

After we took the lodge apart and piled it up Martin and the other Indian got their shields out of their saddlebags and started to beat them and chant as they danced around the lodge just as Martin and the Shaman had done when we arrived. The other Indian took some powder and threw it out over the mesa in a kind of reverse cleansing effort. Then they packed some of the lodge sections on a horse and put the lion on top of it all. They put the heaviest sections on the other horse and tied it all down as we prepared to leave the mesa.

I noticed that Martin and his friend were both very careful not to walk on my sundial. We mounted and started making our way off the mesa. After we had gone about one hundred yards, Martin turned around and said something to the open space that I didn't understand. I didn't ask him what he had said. Maybe it was a prayer of thanks for my safety or something. I also turned and looked in awe at the flat mesa where I had spent three eventful nights and four days. I said my silent good-byes as I rode away.

I carried my pole as a badge of honor. Maybe it was protection against those forces that were still out there and that still might be planning some mischievous antics to get to me. I didn't want to evoke any spirits; either good or bad, as I rode quietly away. I shivered for a long time until I saw the town's lights in the near distance. Only then did I relax a little in the saddle. What waited for me there? I hoped it wouldn't be malevolent.

My feelings at having left the circle were mixed. I was glad to be rescued by Martin and away from there. I was relieved that maybe, just maybe, no more strange and weird things would happen to me. Had those things really happened or was my imagination overworked to the point of wanting something to happen? I didn't know if my weakened state caused me to be that susceptible or not. Or was it just the place that affects whoever is there? Were there spirits living there all the time who were called up by the Cleansing ceremony? I'll never know because there's no way in hell that I'll ever go back out there alone. Had my receptivity called up the Owl Man, the horses, the mountain lion, the thunderstorm, and the hail storm?

I wondered about all of it as I swayed to the rhythm of the horse as it walked along. I thought again about the Clan Father messages and the vision of the Sand God. They were all becoming clearer to me as time passed. I needed their help to get the final answer but it would surely come. Would I like the outcome? I had no way of knowing if I were receptive to it or not.

My other feelings were mixed in that I was leaving the protection of the circle and leaving myself vulnerable to whatever might happen in the world of humans. My making it through the ordeal was a major accomplishment and I was proud to have done it. I had to laugh at that thought.

I had done absolutely nothing. What had been done had been done was to me not by me. That didn't lessen my pride at all. Now I would get a good Indian name from the Shaman, if he could interpret what had happened. Was what I had gone through some kind of a test? Was I supposed to panic and make the bow and arrows? Had I passed the first test with the killing of the lion? I thought it had sacrificed itself and let me kill it easily. I didn't have an answer for these questions, but I was glad that it was over, for now anyway. Were there more tests to come?

I vowed with the rocking of the horse that I never again would take on a test like the one I had just completed; for whatever gain, never, period! Being terrorized wasn't my idea of a fun thing to do in my spare time. I was a survivor now and wouldn't try my luck a second time.

As we walked along the lights of the town got brighter, the sound of Mariachi music filled my ears and brought tears to my eyes. The feeling of safety covered me like a warm blanket. I might feel fear again in my young life, but I instinctively knew that nothing in the future would begin to equal what I had been put through for this vision. I wondered anew if it was all worth it.

Yes, I decided, it was worth it to have the privilege of getting a new Indian name to go through the ordeal. I knew I'd never have to go through it again.

Now I was safe.

THIRTY-ONE

I had been in town for a total of about ten days when I returned from the experience of the harrowing multiple visions out on the enchanted mesa. I was once again safely away from the terror but I still remembered and dreamed vividly each night, and basically relived in my dreams what had happened to me out there. I awoke in the middle of the night the second night home and thought that I was still in the lodge. Sweat was pouring from every pore of my body and I had been dreaming of untold strange things happening to me. I knew I couldn't let those events be an obsession or I'd never recover so I tried to regain some sense of normalcy quickly.

I needed some activity to keep my mind occupied till I could get back to normal again. I decided to talk some more to the old man at the motor court. I needed to talk to him about several things, including the history of the town as he could recall it, about the current Sheriff, and what he might know about Carmelita, although their age difference would probably mean that he had just seen her as a child and had not paid much attention to her. I had to give him the benefit of the doubt, after all, he was the Motel owner and probably saw and heard a lot that people thought he just ignored in his eccentricity.

I knew very little about the town or its inhabitants, with the exception of Rosalie, Mrs. Hernando, and Martin. I had talked briefly to the Sheriff, his two deputies, Jose Montoya, the reporter, and Ms. Charles, the lawyer twice briefly. I knew absolutely no history of the town.

From the looks of it and the style in which the buildings were built, I could readily guess that it was a very old town. Who the original settlers were, where they had come from and why, I had no idea. Although there was only one main street in town, I hadn't even bothered to see if there were any side streets. Maybe the one main street was it. Surely the street where Rosalie lived wasn't the only other street. It didn't seem very likely that this was the case. I also had not found the church. I knew for certain that every one of these little Spanish towns had a church. I hadn't located the public library. Maybe there wasn't one here. I would take the time to ask Mrs. Hernando, if we could keep from getting sidetracked from talking about her Indian arts for a few minutes. I knew that she would want to know all about the visions, and especially the carving on the pole. I was eager to tell her. I wanted to see the Shaman first though, while the memory of the events was still vividly clear.

But first, I wanted to talk to the motor court owner about his memories of the town. As I entered the motor court office, which I supposed was just a front for his living area, two very large mangy, and dangerous looking dogs came bounding out of the back room heading straight at me. They were snarling and slobber was flying out of their vicious looking jaws all over the place as they ran. Their teeth looked like very sharp swords as they gleamed in the sunlight.

Probably meat eaters, I thought as they came closer and closer to me. I knew I should back up and try to get away from them but I had no place to hide or run to. I stood my ground as I looked around for something to use as a weapon in self-defense to prevent them from ripping out my innards or grabbing my throat and killing me right there. They looked so wild they might just try and devour me on the spot instead of dragging me out back. They sure looked hungry and mean. I didn't think that the small one bladed pocket knife I always carried would save me. Where are the most vital organs located in dogs like these? Probably their brains, however small, ran through my mind.

Luckily the heavy beam front counter that was between them and me was a formidable barrier that I hoped could stop them. I quickly realized that they were big enough to easily jump over it. If and when they did that they would be right at the same level as my neck. Their eyes were glowing with an odd yellow color which was, at the very least, a little disconcerting. They left pools of slobber all over the floor and flung gobs of that bubbly stuff all over each other as they galloped toward me. They probably had only traveled a few feet towards me but I was not taking any chances with them.

I had opened my small pocketknife I always carried and had my hand wrapped tightly around the handle, knowing that it wasn't big enough to do much damage. I backed away from the monsters and moved very slowly towards the front door so as not to agitate them further. I knew I could find no other weapon to defend myself with if they decided to attack me. I had my hand on the knob when the old man called to them from somewhere out of sight.

I had almost ripped the knob out of the door in fright. "I don't like this one damned bit," I said in reassurance and anger. I usually don't mind dogs but these two large uncontrolled brutes terrorized me. The ugly brutes, I guessed, weighed about one hundred pounds each.

The old man called the big brown one by name, something that sounded a lot like Dipstick, and the uglier of the two, the black one, he called Oil Slick.

At the sound of their names they skidded to a halt and fell back on their haunches with their snarling jaws open just inches away from the counter. The relief I felt was enormous to say the least. A head came out of the shadows and I recognized the old man.

He had a smirking grin on his face as he said, "Sorry 'bout the hounds, but I wasn't expecting company. What do you want? Glad you didn't ring the bell. That really sets them dogs off."

He glared at me after this brief introduction. The malevolent look in his eyes had a slight yellow glint to it, just like his dogs. Dogs from Hell was the name I silently gave them. I didn't know where the old man came from, probably the same hell hole as his dogs. I definitely didn't like him.

I still didn't know his name so I just started talking like the old man had done.

"What kind of dogs are those two anyway?" I thought maybe a crossbreed with some wild animal. Serve them right for being so damned ugly. Maybe he just uses them for protection and to terrorize every unsuspecting traveler who wants a room. Nah, there hasn't been anybody new check in since I got here. The old man didn't bother to answer me about the dogs–like I was wasting his time again.

As my nerves had settled a little I asked him "If you have a few minutes, I'd like to talk to you some more about this town when you were Sheriff here." Again, he seemed to ignore what I had just said, but at least he answered my question about the dogs.

"Oil Slick here is three parts wolf and I don't know what the fourth part is. Dipstick is all mongrel, and is just naturally mean and ugly. Just wait till I get these dogs back outside and chained in their cages then we'll talk. Hasn't been anybody come in here for years just to talk to me. Wait here. I'll be right back."

I was relieved to know he had consented to talk to me and watched as he turned and grabbed each dog by the scruff of the neck and hauled them somewhere out of sight, totally ignoring the opportunity to apologize.

Damn, I thought, as I watched him walk away with a dog in each hand, He's sure strong to be able to pick them up like that. He had raised their front feet up so they were walking on their hind paws as he led and pulled them away.

I guessed that he must be on the down side of eighty or maybe ninety from the whiteness of his thinning hair. It still looked like a monks' tonsure of the early centuries; a large round bald spot on top with a circlet of very long white hair surrounding it that hung almost to his bony shoulders. He also still had this gray fly's nest of a beard covering most of his face so I couldn't see his craggy features clearly. I did notice that it looked like he had tried to trim his beard since I last saw him.

Must have used a garden tool like clippers or a hedge trimmer, it looks so raggedy. I laughed to myself at the thought. The face what showed above the fly's nest was a wrinkled mass of skin that looked like a human roadmap. I knew that in New Mexico that alone wasn't a sign of old age. Most people who work a lot outdoors and don't wear a broad brimmed hat to ward off the sun have, over the long years, developed weathered wrinkled skin like that. Those who do wear hats normally have a white band of skin under the brim that gives them a clown look. He must have spent a good portion of his many years out in the bright sun. I decided to ask him about that when he returned; along with a lot of other important questions.

While I waited I looked over the room and the wanted posters again. I then noticed that there were bullet holes in places that I hadn't seen the first time. There were more posters too. I read about six of them before the old man came back and interrupted my trip back to the days of the old "wild west."

"You seem interested in the law sonny." He was pointing to the posters as he spoke to me.

"In their time these guys were the real bums of this area. They're the card sharks who stole the unsuspecting gambler's money, murderers, and bank robbers, the riffraff of the world that came here to hide out from the law of Santa Fe and Albuquerque. They didn't get to hide out long, about a week at the most for most of them, and was almost always found out and hanged. Some of them were shot trying to get away, but most had a trial and were hanged right outside there on them big rafters. Did what was called the Air Dance."

"This building was the jail for the first hundred years, and believe me, it was built sturdy. See that post there?"

He pointed through the barred window to a massive post that held up the roof. It must have been twelve inches square by about eight feet long, and the axe marks in it indicated that it was hand hewn. It, and all the other upright posts, held more massive beams of the same size, but these were about twelve feet long. These were the supports for the porch above this level. The ax and saw marks were still visible on all the larger timbers.

"Yes, you guessed right, they're hand hewn timbers from the forest that used to be out there. Took it all to build this town, it did. Not a tree left this size within fifty miles of here. It doesn't matter because the town will last another thousand years before these timbers give way. But you surely didn't come here to talk about the town's timbers did you?"

He gave no indication of having heard what I had asked him when I came in, so I repeated myself, this time closer so he could hear a little better if he was deaf.

"No sir, I came here because I would like to talk to you about the memories you have of this town. I've been here about ten days now and know absolutely nothing about the place. You did say the last time we talked that you were the Sheriff here before you retired. You seem to know a lot, that's why I came back."

"Where've ya been for the last couple'a days? I haven't seen hide or hair of you. Did you go back to Albuquerque on business? Bet you have a girl down there that misses you huh?" He sneered as he grinned at his own private joke, again ignoring what I had just said.

"No, I didn't go to Albuquerque and no, I don't have a girlfriend that's wasting away because I'm up here. I went out on the mesa after talking to Martin Begay and Mrs. Hernando and stayed there for four days. I went through the Indian Cleansing Ceremony, and I guess I had a couple of visions. The Shaman of the tribe has agreed to give me the Naming Ceremony. I can tell you that the Cleansing ritual is an experience that I'm glad I'll only have to endure once. Once was more than enough for me. I've been recovering sort of, for the last two days, but I'm in pretty good shape now."

"Yeah, I know about the Cleansing Ceremony. I can still recall when I went through it and the Naming Ceremony too. I agree with you that once is enough. You probably had yours the same place I had mine. They've been using that same mesa location forever it seems like. They say, and rumors tend to prove it, that the place does strange things to the boys who're sent up there."

The fact that he had experienced the Cleansing and Naming Ceremonies really startled and surprised me. Needless to say I was totally speechless for a minute or two. After this revelation from him I looked at him with a new respect.

"Yes, it probably was the same place but for the life of me I couldn't even begin to locate it again. I won't look for it either. Can you tell me your Indian name?"

I didn't expect him to reveal anything about himself at this question. He hadn't revealed anything so far in the times we talked. I figured I had to break the ice if I were to get him to talking about the town. I still didn't even know his name or anything about him other that the fact that he was Sheriff here a long time ago.

The old man was full of surprises. "Yeah, as a matter of fact I can tell you my Indian name. Not just because I went through the ceremony, but cause all Indians have a name. I am a full blood Lakota Sioux and my name is To-Nah-Pah. It means 'Sees Thru Time.' I got it because my vision was that I could see into the future. I knew I was going to be Sheriff here someday and that I'd be shot and killed if I stayed Sherriff longer than I was supposed to. Well, I grew up and became the Sheriff."

"As you can see I am alive but I was shot and wounded in a shootout," he continued. "I knew then that I'd been given the message and a second chance, so I quit the law business while I was still intact. I was thirteen when I had my vision and became Sheriff when I turned twenty one. I was Sheriff for twenty five years and then quit. I had other better paying jobs after being the Sheriff too. Have you been given your new name yet?"

"No, not yet," I replied. "The Shaman has to decide when he'll do it. Martin said he'd let me know. I hope I don't have to wait too long though. I'm getting a little antsy to get it over and done."

To-Nah-Pah seemed to be losing his willingness to talk about himself and said, "Well, that's all well and good, but what can I do for you now?"

He had obviously decided to become a bit friendlier toward me since he learned that I was going to get an Indian name. Was it because of our common quest for a vision out there on the mesa? I wondered. I wouldn't press my luck too far this first time so I just asked him about the basic history of the town.

"When was the town settled and where did the settlers come from?"

"You see that Conestoga wagon up there on the roof?" He pointed skyward through the bars to the building across the street.

"Well, that was one of the original wagons that brought the first Anglo settlers to this part of the country. It was called 'Indian Territory' back then, in the early 1830's. The original settlers come here from

Northern Mexico and Southern New Mexico before it became part of the United States and after the Mexican War in 1848."

"Most of the settlers back then were farmers," he continued. "There were a few shopkeepers who made sure the necessities could be bought though. Some of those shops are still open now. Back then this was a very fertile place, with the river running through it. They grew all the basic essentials. They opened a *Mercado*, that's a market for Anglos, to sell what excesses they had."

"There was some gold nuggets found in the river but the people didn't let the news of it get out of here cause they didn't want a gold rush to bring a passel of people here and ruin the land. They kept the whole thing a secret. What gold they found they'd put in jars and cans and buried them all over the place. If some treasure hunters came up here with metal detectors looking, they'd find jars and cans of gold dust and nuggets all over the mesa and in open spaces here in town. They put a lot of the foodstuffs in what was called root cellars. They were really just big holes in the ground with hinged doors for lids on them, but they kept things cold and away from the animals. Besides, in those days we didn't have electricity and ice boxes."

Did I hear him correctly? Did he say we didn't have those things? He had slipped up the first time I'd met him when he accidentally said eighteen instead of nineteen for the dates when he was Sheriff here. Now this new slip made me wonder exactly how old this gray haired old guy was. If he were a child in the 1830's that would make him over 160 years old. Impossible! Unless. Unless this place is in some sort of time warp and all who live here are that old but just appear to be normal age. No, that would be impossible and I wouldn't believe it. He just slipped up on the we accidentally." I told myself. Somehow, in the back of my mind though, it just didn't register as a slip of the tongue. Maybe I could find some irrefutable proof in the death records for the state or county. If not, maybe, there was some record in the local cemetery that could prove his name and age, one way or another, or maybe I could locate them in Santa Fe. That is, IF, I got a chance to go back there. I don't mind admitting that just being in close proximity to this scary old guy wasn't a pleasant experience. "He might be just what he appears to be, just a motel manager," I thought, "but why take the chance that he isn't?"

We talked for about an hour during which I was frantically taking notes of what facts he gave me. Stupidly I had forgotten to bring my ever present tape recorder for this interview. In addition to being cautious, I sometimes am very forgetful. I also tend to learn things the hard way. As we were about to end the talk, the old man suggested we take a walk up to Boot Hill and take a look at some of the tombstones up there.

An eerie suggestion which I accepted readily. I didn't even know that there was a Boot Hill in town, much less where it was.

Before we had a chance to get up and go, I felt a slight tingling in my head like the beginnings of a headache. Maybe another Clan Father message was coming to warn me not to get near the cemetery however badly I wanted to find something interesting up there. I begged off for a minute using the excuse that I had a headache and asked the old man if I could have a glass of water to drink. As the old man went into the kitchen to get it the tingling increased in intensity and I sensed another message coming on. It was different this time from all the others though. It wasn't just a message, but a warning from the Buffalo Clan Father.

"*Tawamiciya,*
Do not be misled away from your goal or distracted by meaningless junctures. Remember, you are digging for the truth of why you have been led here and why we are giving you guidance in your search."

What meaningless junctures were they warning me about? Were they referring to going anywhere with the old man; or just talking to him for information? I'd hoped he would be a good source of information, as well as rumors he'd heard, but maybe the Clan Fathers knew better. Or was I in some danger, that they sensed, and this was a serious warning? I didn't want to go against their wishes, but I had already agreed to go with him. I wrote the message down quickly before the old man returned with the water.

"Yeah," I said, quickly drinking the water while slipping the notebook into a side pocket, "let's go, we might just find something interesting on the headstones. I am also making a collection of epitaphs and who knows what's up there," I said as I followed the old man out the back door of the motel, past the snarling dogs, through what appeared to be a gigantic rose garden and up a winding path to what he called Boot Hill.

THIRTY-TWO

I hadn't noticed it when I came into town but there was a hill directly behind the motor court and jail. I was getting exhausted as I climbed the rocky path. We were both bent over due to the steepness of the climb, but the old man seemed to have endless energy and talked as we climbed. He explained briefly about the cemetery up there. After about fifteen minutes of climbing we came out of the scrub bushes into a well-manicured and obviously well cared for cemetery.

There were, I estimated, about forty grave markers and stones in this yard. Some were just two pieces of board wired together to make a cross with a name and dates crudely carved on them. Some were markers of marble and granite. A few had epitaphs on them.

One interesting one that caught my eye because of its size was a double one for husband and wife. The husband had died in 1875 and his wife had died in 1880. These were obviously not newly placed markers. The husband was 100 years old and she was 102. They had obviously had their tombstone carved at the same time because the letters of both epitaphs had weathered equally.

The husband's epitaph read:

> *Behold and see all that pass by*
> *An instance of mortality*
> *As I am now so you must be*
> *Prepare for death and follow me*

The wife must have been some kind of lady with a wild sense of humor. Hers was exactly the same but had an interesting and humorous addition. It read:

> *To that I won't consent until I know for sure which way you went*

We looked over the yard and more markers and I came to another humorous one. It was of more modern marble design. The man who was buried there was 99 years old when he died in 1899. His epitaph read:

> *I was somebody*
> *Who, is no business of yours*

We laughed at both of them. I told him of one I had found in Puxico, Missouri that was also funny. It read:

See there
I told you
I was sick

We walked and talked. The old man told me about his days as Sheriff. He pointed out markers at various places and told that person's story. He did this for about ten of the markers. He was visibly tiring but he continued to look and tell stories. The interesting thing about all of the stories was the fact that he seemed to know all of them personally. Some of them had lived and died before he could have possibly been around here. Quite a few had died in the late 1800's. Those he could have known, maybe, if he were as old, or older, than I had guessed him to be. It was as if he was the last living monument to their lives and existence. He had somehow been chosen to outlast them all so that their stories would never be forgotten and could be retold through the generations that followed them. Otherwise they would just lie here, forgotten in this Boot Hill and nobody would know about them.

We got separated as I was looking at one stone and he kept walking around the yard. When I looked up he was sitting near a stone about twenty yards from me and appeared to be talking to whoever was buried below it. He got up and moved to another one and started talking there too. This was just too much for me. Spooky it was! Eventually we met at a common stone and he carried on the conversation with me as if we had been together all the time. He obviously didn't know, nor care, that I had seen him talking to the stones. I certainly didn't want to ask him about it.

We started walking back down the path back to the motor court. As we walked, he talked about the many shootouts he had been involved in and about being wounded twice before he had retired. I halfway expected him to pull up his shirt and show me his bullet wounds but luckily he didn't. He said that the others who followed him as Sheriff weren't as lucky or smart enough to quit before getting killed in a gunfight. He said that every year the town has a major reenactment of the shootouts and jailbreaks.

"You probably have seen them pickups that have all them bullet holes in them driving around town haven't you? There's a real good reason for them to look like that. We don't want to endanger our horses so we stage the getaways in trucks. Only one man's got hurt over the years we've been doing the reenactments. It was just last year and I guess that it was a random shot that blew his right ear plumb off. I've always wondered where the shot came from because, you see, we're all supposed to fire blanks for the noise so nobody gets hurt. All the bullet holes are put in the trucks out in the desert just to make them look like they were in a gunfight."

"Anyhow, the man recovered, of sorts. Now he acts deafer than a doornail when anybody, especially his wife, talks to him if he's not in the mood to do what they want. I guess he's just playing the part now, as the one-eared hero of the shootouts. It may've been an attempted killing, I don't know and the current Sheriff never bothered to find out. That's why most of the trucks you see don't have a rear window but do carry rifles. It's an honor to be selected for the shootouts even if everybody in town usually is."

I thought that the shootouts would be a perfect place to commit a preplanned murder. The earless man could have very well been an intended victim who was lucky. I wondered why the Sheriff never did anything to find out what had happened. I needed to somehow try to find out whether maybe both that shooter and the person who tried to kill the man out in the desert were the same person. Maybe both the injured man and Carmelita were also somehow connected to both the Sheriff and the lawyer in some way. The plot had definitely thickened. I was brought out of my thoughts by more talking by the former Sheriff.

"You've seen, Andy, this is a relatively poor farming town with little to take away the harshness of everyday life except what we can do ourselves. Nobody bothers us here, being isolated in the mountains like we are. Nobody from the outside seems to care what happens in most of the other small mountain towns either. Shootouts are not the only events that're re-enacted in this town."

"We have yearly ceremonials showing the Crucifixion of Christ. The Catholic Church tends to ignore these reenactments, for the good of the people here. They are customs that've been followed since the early Spanish settlers first come here. The Church has always been a guiding force but there've been times in its history up here when it was like there was no Church like we know it now. In them years, the people devised a religious ritual that still exists and that's followed faithfully. The ritual includes self-flagellation, devout worship, prayer, and the crucifixion of a member. The people that follow these rituals are called the Penitentes and they're very active here and in other small towns in Northern New Mexico."

This last piece of information from the old man, spoken with obvious pride, perked my interest in talking to him and finding out more about the Penitente group, as well as others that might be active up here today. I doubted that what I had just been told would make a good front line story but I was definitely interested. I hadn't heard of, nor read any stories in the papers about the Penitentes. I made an excuse to leave; that I had other pressing paper business, and asked if I could come back to talk to him some more at a later time.

"Sure you can, Andy. I'm not going anywhere far away or fast at my age now am I? Be glad to give you all I know, or can dig up bout the town, been here a long time. Guess I'm the oldest original town member still left nowadays."

There, he slipped up again about his age, again. Oldest original member left.

What inference could I make from that? I quickly wrote it in my notebook along with all the other notes I'd taken, said my good-byes and walked down the street to the Cave. I was getting very hungry.

Rosalie was there and seemed surprised, to see me.

"Well if it isn't the long lost Andy? I haven't seen you since you got back and I was very worried about you. You didn't call or anything. I thought you might have left town for good. You look like whatever you did had some kind of really bad effect on you, huh?"

"Well to tell the truth Rosalie, yes, it sure did. I don't want to tell you all that happened before the Shaman has had time to interpret it and to help me understand what it all means, but I can tell you that I was out on the mesa going through something that I had never even imagined before I came to Bullsnort. I can say though, the experience was vigorous and extremely interesting, to say the least. I had some things happen out there that you just would not believe if I told you. But please believe me, they happened."

I was looking for a little sympathy and maybe a chance with her by playing on my troubles out there, but the way she looked at me sure didn't seem to be very sympathetic.

"I'm OK now, though," I continued. "I have had to go slow in introducing food back into my starved system. I've been eating mostly fruits and drinking a lot of juices for a couple of days now. Now, I am hungry. I'm ready for a man sized meal again. Feed Me!"

I beat on my chest with both fists like an aggravated gorilla. All I got for my efforts as a hungry caveman was a good laugh from her, and no sympathy for my sore chest.

I let Rosalie pick the meal. I also wanted a really cold beer, or maybe two or three. My mouth watered at the thought. I remembered the smells the cooking grease from the rabbit made and my thoughts went back to the mesa with the first Dos Equis. As I sat there I must have dozed off for a minute and when I awoke I heard another Clan Father voice speaking to me. There had been no headache this time but the color had come with the sound as usual. It was a deep chocolate soothing color. The male voice said,

> *"Tawamiciya,*
> *I am the eighth Clan Father.*
> *I am named One Big Growler.*
> *I am the spiritual leader of the Bear Clan.*
> *I will teach you how to fight for the Truth.*
> *When you are ready and need me, I shall return to help you."*

As the chocolate color faded, it immediately changed into hues of the brightest and purest, white color, other than the hair of the Sand God, that I had ever seen. The male voice said,

> *"Tawamiciya,*
> *I am the ninth Clan Father.*
> *I am named Flies on the Wind.*
> *I am the spiritual leader of the Eagle Clan.*
> *I will teach you how to catch your prey quickly.*
> *When you are ready and need me, I shall return to help you."*

I pulled the small notebook from my pocket and wrote both messages down with the others listed there. Since I had prior warnings like the headaches when the other message came, I'd taken to carrying the notebook and the recorder with me all the time just in case.

I didn't fall asleep or anything like I had done with the first seven messages, so when Rosalie came back with my beer, I was sitting normally as if nothing had happened. I hadn't revealed the messages to her. I was dozing–mesmerized by the music coming from the jukebox which was a current Country and Western love song about trains. It seems like they're all about either trains, convicts or some lost dog. I laughed at the thought of what one with all three would sound like. It would be a real tearjerker of a song. I remembered some of the words to one that filled the bill a little; "When Momma was released from jail I went to get her on a train in the rain."

As I sat there, I had time to ponder the messages, what the last three might be, and where they would lead me. I had received nine so far. What would happen after I had received all twelve messages? Would I not be under the protection of the Clan Fathers anymore? That didn't sound too good to me since I didn't know yet what the outcome of my searching would be, and how much danger I would put myself in by questioning people.

THIRTY-THREE

Would Carmelita be found dead or alive? Would I play a part in either scenario? I had an idea where it all might be heading but I couldn't confide in anybody just you about my many unsupported suspicions. I wouldn't even consider putting my suspicions into words, not until I could determine one way or the other who Sheriff Johnson was talking to that night out on the mesa when I had heard the one way conversation in my mind. It might just prove dangerous to talk to anybody, with the exception of Martin. I might be falling in love with Rosalie, I reminded myself, but until I can be sure she wasn't involved I can't confide in her about this.

When Rosalie returned with the meal, I asked her if she would be free later and if she was, maybe could we take in a movie. I didn't want to test my luck with a three part date again. I was still on an expense account from the paper and with only two articles submitted so far, I wasn't at all sure how much leeway Dan would give me with extra expenses, especially for movies. I definitely wanted to press my luck with Rosalie though, if she'd have me. I was definitely falling in love with her and I hoped the feelings were mutual.

She answered with some hesitation, "Yes, I am free tonight from all my other boyfriends who are out of town and you can pick me up at six at my house."

She laughed at me in the way I was beginning to like. I realized that although that laugh was seductive in my mind, to her it probably wasn't meant to be. In fact, she seemed more than a bit cold and less friendly toward me today. The last view I had of her at the doorway was with a wet dish rag in her hand wiping down the bar.

I was determined to get back to the old man before he forgot how to be friendly toward me. I definitely wanted more information from him, and if he had the older town records there in the motel, so much the better. I might just be able to get him to let me take a look at them.

I left the Cave and walked away toward the motor court with the hope of getting more interesting information about the Penitentes from the old man. What I didn't want was to be attacked by the two hounds of Bullsnort when I entered the front door. I hoped they had long chains around their necks somewhere away from the office. I was in luck. I heard them out in the back somewhere baying and yelping at something, or someone, when I got closer to the motel. I needed the dogs barking at me to get the attention of the old man because I still had no idea what name he was using. Although he had talked some about himself he still had not revealed much personal information that made sense. I entered the front office and the deathly quiet hit me like a wet sponge.

I approached the counter hoping to get a glimpse of what was going on out back but I couldn't see past the curtain over the hallway entrance. Did I dare ring the silver dinger again?

"Never!" "Not on your life!" I advised myself. He might just come running out of the back with an ugly looking six shooter in each hand and be more than ready to start blazing away at the villain who has done the dastardly deed. I didn't want the dead villain to be me.

Why did I feel that every time I got close to the old man or the office my life expectancy suddenly got very much shorter? I did the next best thing. I waited a few minutes, then walked closer to the entranceway and hollered out, "SSSHHHEERRRIIIFFF!!"

"That ought to get his attention," I laughed. I hoped that when and if he came out here it would be without those two bloody looking hounds. They had an evil glow in their eyes that somehow I took to mean that they would take absolute delight in tearing me limb from limb and enjoy it immensely.

I was reading another one of the wanted posters for a murderer when a voice behind me scared the bejesus out of me as it spoke. I hadn't heard the old man come up behind me.

"Oh, it's just you again. What do you want now? You can't keep pestering me, sonny. I got too many important things to tend to and I'm not getting any younger. If I don't get them done, they won't ever get done!"

The scowl on his face, coupled with the evil glint in his good eye, would melt an icicle.

"I'm sorry, Sheriff, I thought this might be a good time to talk a little more about things. This time I brought my recorder and I can stay as long as you feel up to it. I'd sure like to hear a lot more about the town history, your part in it, and the Penitentes in this area. If not today, just say when I can come back and I'll be here. You know where I live."

I could see immediately that my feeble attempt to humor him hadn't fazed him in the least.

"Yes, I've got time now. Follow me out back and we can talk while I do a few chores. You needn't worry about the hounds, got them chained up out of the way. Damned things are three quarters wild. It's all I can do to keep them from killing every animal round here. Damned things attacked a Texas long horned bull about a year ago and crippled it=chewed the *cojones* right off the damned thing. It kicked the hell out of them but fortunately, didn't kill them. I had to pay for it too. Should've shot both of them full of holes right then, but I didn't. Don't you even think twice about coming out here alone without me around here close by. You'd probably lose a hand, or worse, in the fight that you'd surely lose. I don't know if they'd kill a man or not but they'd sure as hell chew them up awful ugly if they were mad enough. Both have good sharp teeth. I feed them frozen slabs of meat and they don't seem to have too much trouble eating it all. But you didn't come here to talk about them dogs, did you? What do you want to know?"

I had a lot that I wanted to know and instinctively knew he was the person who knew it all. I wanted to know all about the town, what this man's part in it as Sheriff had been, and what he knew about the current Sheriff and the lady lawyer. I'd get to the latter parts after we had established the ground rules for the interview.

I showed him the tape recorder, got his permission to use it and assured him that before I published anything in the paper I'd get his permission for that. He agreed.

"This building was the jail and maybe the town hall back in the early days of the town wasn't it?" I began. "I wonder if the town records are still kept here." I already knew that this building was the jail in the past, but I probed for the location of the town records, hoping that they might still be here.

"If they are here can I possibly get a look at them? I'm sure there's enough interesting stuff there to make a really good article. I would also like to know more about you and the Penitentes and your part in their ceremonies. I recall that earlier you said they were a secret society so you probably can't reveal much about them, but whatever you can tell me would be greatly appreciated. Will you help me?"

I could see that he was reluctant to tell me anything until I promised not to attribute what he might reveal about the Penitentes directly to him if I happened to write a story later. He drank a full shot glass of some foul smelling stuff, wrinkled up his face like it burned all the way to his stomach, and started talking.

I punched the record button.

THIRTY-FOUR

The old Sheriff began. "I'm also a converted Catholic. My history begins with me being taken away from my family, this town, and my reservation."

As a young boy of seven, I was sent away to a Catholic school that was run by the Bureau of Indian Affairs, the BIA, they called it. That's where us Indian savages learned, not just the white man's religion, but their cruelty, too."

"Many thousands of us Indians were rounded up like cattle and sent away to them schools. It took me some time to learn enough English to understand the words I wasn't supposed to hear. Many times I heard the words, 'We must bring the uncouth savages into normal civilization' as the reason for us kids being there. We heard them from the teachers, nuns, and the visiting administrators. We didn't understand at first why they hated us but we learned quick enough. They stripped us of all things Indian. Our clothes, our names, our religious beliefs, our languages, and worst of all they tried to erase our culture."

"They had no idea that the beliefs and rituals we practiced long before they came here was a religion in its own right, and should be valued. We couldn't even braid our hair. They cut it off Anglo style. They tried to remake us into their image of what a normal person should look like. They didn't want anything Indian to be left. Nothing of the savage was to be left in us. They tried to beat it out of us. Sometimes they succeeded but most of us fought back quietly."

He drank another shot, winced, and continued.

"We hated it but were powerless to stop it. After all, we were just children. Who'd listen to our problems and take them seriously? Nobody would, or did then. We learned quick-like not to complain because it would only bring more punishment."

"For example, the standard daily punishment for speaking our own language instead of English was five smacks with the headmaster's paddle. For not pronouncing an English word right it was two smacks and for not saying grace at dinnertime was five smacks. For stuff they thought was more serious, it was one or two hours of total isolation in a dark room that didn't have any windows. Many a time I lost the privilege of having a meal because I broke one or the other of those rules."

He took a deep breath and continued, "That' no way to teach kids that Christ was forgiving and that if we were to follow his teachings it would lead to greater things. We rebelled and suffered for it. Those harsh practices surely wouldn't have been acceptable in an Anglo school but since we were just Indians nobody cared. Our treatment was ignored by those who should have known better."

"It was a bad example of your white government at work, Andy."

I didn't know what to say, so I kept my mouth shut tightly. I had read some articles about the BIA schools and knew he was exactly right. I waited for him to continue.

"After all these years away from there I still got the hurts inside me and physical scars they gave me. We all learned very quickly that if we were going to survive we'd better do exactly like they said, so we did for the most part. We'd speak our own languages quietly when we were isolated and out of hearing range of the headmaster and the nuns. We were always tightly controlled and regimented, kind of like when you join the Army and go away to basic training. You have to be together and the Sergeant has control over you every minute in your conversion from a civilian to a soldier. It was the same way with us in those BIA schools."

"One of our biggest things we faced in those schools that we never did get over **ever**, was the historical animosity between tribes. Old tribal enemies were now our new school enemies, but we mostly knew that we depended on each other so we'd put aside the personal grievances for the most part.

When we graduated from there we all tried to go back to the reservation and our own people. Some made it, some didn't.

On any street corner in any New Mexican town you can see the results of those BIA schools. One of our main social problems is alcoholism. The suffering victim doesn't feel like he's Indian or Anglo and most of the time alcohol takes care of the differences. Suicides are another great scourge among the Indian Nations. There's a lot of wanderers who seem to float around, going nowhere, and don't know who they are. The state social agencies want to help but I think they mostly do more harm than good because they don't have the understanding or are just plain indifferent to the problems we have."

"What would you feel like if right this instant you were grabbed by some authority figure of government and sent to Mongolia and told you were going stay there in captivity for thirteen years?" he asked. "You had no rights and you were totally under the powers of them Mongolians? You couldn't speak any English and you had to act like your captors or get beat for it? Not a pleasant thought is it? Well, Andy, that's exactly the meanness that happened to all of the Indians in the BIA schools."

After saying this, he just kind of slumped in his chair and sat very still for a long time just staring off into space-totally ignoring me sitting there watching him. I couldn't tell whether he had gone to sleep or had died. I just sat quietly looking at him, waiting for him to return to the present, I pushed the pause button on the recorder while he was quiet. I didn't want to intrude on his quiet time, even if it were just the recorder running. I waited and as I did I made some notes in my notebook recording my impressions of him, his feelings, his anger, the room in which we sat, the furnishings, which were sparse, to say the least, and the overall appearance of the place. I especially noted the hardships he had endured in the BIA schools.

He roused himself after about five minutes and continued talking as if no time had had passed. I pushed the record button again so nothing of this saga would be missed. I had no idea what kind of article, if any, would come from this talk but I wanted it for reference anyway.

"I'm Catholic now, but I'm still an Indian," he said defiantly, "And I practice my native religion from time to time. I'm also a Penitente. I practice those beliefs and customs too. I was initiated into the brotherhood almost fifty years ago, right here in this town. You might think that I'm older than I really am, Andy. I'm eighty nine years old now."

THIRTY-FIVE

"Back then the brotherhood was all that kept us going when the church failed us." He continued. "The brotherhoods' are legally incorporated nonprofit religious associations that are created to help people."

"Now they're organized into fraternities under church authority helping people in their own churches and towns. Their purpose is to help people get a better understanding of the life and death of Jesus and to help their own members, family and community get along better with each other."

"You see, the brotherhood is a secret group of townsmen who believe in devout prayer and penance for sins. We follow the Bible and Holy Scriptures real close. The formal name of the brotherhood is Los Hermano Penitentes. There are many levels of organization and each level has specific duties. Control over everything's given to the *Hermano Mayor* who is elected each year during Lent and Holy Week. The *Los Hermano* has many assistants who perform the ceremonies."

He handed me a printed list that he had obviously prepared in anticipation of my many questions. On the paper were some specific terms and a short explanation of each.

Morada	The stone building of the brotherhood where the rituals and ceremonies are conducted. These are usually located away from the town center.
Celador	Warden who maintains order within and outside the Morada, administers punishment.
Secretario	An agent and treasurer.
Maestro de Novios	Teacher of the novices.
Sangrador of Picador	Blood letter or picker
Rezador	Reader of the ritual prayers from a copybook.
Pitero	Piper of the homemade flute as musical accompaniment.
Enfermeo	Nurses who care for sick members and do many other charitable acts during the year.
Sudario	Prayer for the dead
Campo Santo	Cemetery

Coadjutor	Assistant who washes the whips and attends to the wounds of those doing penances.
Ayudantes	Helpers

I scanned the paper quickly, and put it in my notebook for safe keeping.

I expressed my thanks for the list that would certainly help me understand more of what he was saying.

He continued, "The whole ceremony starts with a meeting in the Morada, where a member is selected to play the part of Christ. It is a great honor to be selected for this. There's much prayer and at this point some of the members begin to flog themselves with branches with thorns on them. After the meeting the long procession starts."

"The method of the procession's always the same based on tradition. The Brother who's selected to be the Christ has to carry a heavy cross the whole way without help of any kind. That's not ever easy because the distance they walk barefoot can be many miles over dirt roads. He's treated exactly like Christ was. He's flogged along the way by townsfolk. He can't have any water. He has to wear a crown of thorns, and he's jeered by bystanders watching the procession. At the end of the procession is the crucifixion."

"This is a time of intense emotion. Onlookers kneel and pray and weep for Christ. Death of the Hermano can result from the stress of taking part in the procession and the hanging, but not always."

"After they take him off his cross, they move him into the Morada. Then the *Las Tinieblas*, or earthquake, takes place late on Good Friday night. The Penitente ritual uses one white and twelve yellow candles, representing Christ and the twelve apostles. The twelve Psalms are read with one yellow candle flame being put out after each one's read. When the flame of the last yellow candle is put out, noise comes from everywhere. Clackers, drums, cymbals, bells, whistles, banging pots, stamping, and screaming are part of the noise. The brothers who're doing penances whip themselves again for the last time. The white candle is brought out lit and all the yellow ones are relit. *Alabado* (songs) are sung, the ceremony ends, and everybody goes home. If the Hermano Christ has really died, he's buried in the cemetery."

I made a vow that this Lenten Season, if possible, even if I were back in Albuquerque, I would come back up here for the procession. I was sure the old man would allow me to participate by watching. I very much wanted to witness the ceremonies although I guessed that they were forbidden to non Penitentes, and especially outsiders. I also vowed that I would do more research on the brotherhood and learn more about them.

The old man and I talked for a goodly amount of time when suddenly, out of the blue for no discernible reason that I could tell, he said he couldn't talk anymore today.

The information gathering session was over for now, so I thanked him for his time and the great help he had given me. I would need time to listen to the tapes and transcribe them into the notebook. I wasn't a shorthand taker so I would probably need to be refreshed by the tapes as to the specifics of the explanation. He had moved from subject to subject very rapidly and I didn't have time to note all the details in my notebook. I had made a sort of topical outline as best I could which would help a little. I had made sure that I had plenty of tape in the recorder before he started on each new subject. I had four used tapes in my pocket from this particular session. It would take me a long time to transcribe them all. We didn't make a date for me to come back. I'd leave that to him, when he was willing and had the time. I told him that I had a lot of work to do and that I'd be in touch with him in case I needed some point clarified. He nodded his assent. I felt that the session had gone smoothly enough and that the old man was very willing to talk, once he got started.

I wanted to find the town library, if there was one, and do some research on my own. I had a lot of ideas that needed some kind of verification. I wanted to look into the town's history and maybe some of the early newspaper obituaries in the archives to either confirm or refute the feelings that the old Sheriff wasn't exactly what he appeared to be. That specific thought sent a chill of apprehension traveling the now familiar route up and down my spine. I shivered all over again.

"Sure you can come back, Sonny," he had said in a quiet voice. "I haven't talked to **anybody** like you for a long time. It's surely unusual to find a young person as interested in learning about this old town as you are, especially in those people up there in Boot Hill. People tend to shy away from wherever I happen to be, especially up there. Just come back whenever you want to talk some more. I don't have any place to go, so I'll be here. Just remember the hounds, though. See you later Andy," he said as he walked toward the back of the hallway.

I wondered about that last statement and put it into my memory banks to be retrieved later. Why do people of the town tend to avoid him? I can understand not spending a lot of time in the cemetery, although I did find a lot of interesting things, including art, good epitaphs and carvings, on the stones up there.

THIRTY-SIX

B ack in my room I listened to my take recorder again and after making more complete notes on what the old Sheriff had told me, I listed about a dozen more questions in my notebook that I wanted to ask him. I called Mrs. Hernando and we talked for the better part of an hour about my very strange, but exciting experiences out on the mesa. It was my first contact with her since I'd returned. I told her of the two new Clan Fathers' messages, numbers eight and nine, that I'd received that day in the Cave. She seemed very interested in them.

I started telling her about some of the specific and more bizarre experiences I had out on the mesa. I left out the ESP conversation I'd overheard between Sheriff Johnson and the woman I believed to be the lady lawyer. Even without that particular bizarre experience, Mrs. Hernando didn't know what to make of the other weird experiences I had: the unnatural stampede, the non-existent thunderstorm, or the falling eagle man I'd seen. She was sorry about my seeing the elk being killed," but that's the way things go around here she said. If a family needs meat for the table, the best place to get it is from wild game. The men go hunting for deer and turkeys. It's a way of life here." She was glad the vision quest had been a success and was anxious for the Shaman to tell me what it meant and to approve and conduct the Naming Ceremony.

She was extremely interested in seeing the pole with the carvings. She also wanted to see the unique bow and arrows I'd fashioned. I explained that the Shaman had them all and she seemed to be satisfied with that for now. After I told her what Martin had said about the arrows and the way they had been constructed, according to the ancient tradition, I had to promise to bring them by the store for her to see as soon as I got them back from the Shaman.

At a break in our conversation, I asked her if she had any books about the Penitentes in her shop. The prolonged and ominous silence following that question made me wonder if she had put the phone down. I held on and waited. I surely didn't expect this kind of reaction from her.

After what seemed several minutes she came back on the line. "Why do you ask about them, Andy?"

For some unknown reason, her tone was a lot less friendly than it had been just a few minutes before.

I sensed a coldness that had never been there before whenever I had asked her about something in the shop. She had always been very helpful and tolerant of my efforts to learn about traditions around the area and I had certainly asked a lot of questions, which she very patiently answered. Was I prying into something that was personal for her? Was the idea of my looking into the Penitentes and their rituals revolting to her? Was she somehow a part of, or associated with, the brotherhood? I had no idea.

I decided to tread carefully as the Sand God message had suggested. Using the excuse that I had better take some time to work on my writing I ended our conversation, assuring her that I would come by the shop in the morning, and hung up the phone.

I again felt the tingling in my head that I now knew signaled another message from the Clan Fathers. I wondered which of them would come to me now that I had confronted Mrs. Hernando about the Penitentes. I sensed a Clan Father speaking to me.

From the Turtle Clan Father I heard:

"Tawamiciya,
Persevere in your efforts and results will surely come your way. This is your first test in telling truth from lies. We will help guide you but the ultimate decision will be yours."

As I recorded that message along with the others I had previously received, I realized with a feeling of relief that the advice from the Clan Fathers seemed to be getting a bit clearer to me.

After a long hot shower in anticipation of my date with Rosalie, I felt refreshed and was able to put all my questions aside for the evening.

THIRTY-SEVEN

I was definitely psyched up for the date tonight with Rosalie. I had showered and shaved and was even a little extravagant when I splashed on some really good smelling stuff. Believe it or not, I didn't have a clue what it was till I looked at the little green bottle with the gold emblem of a polo player on it. It obviously was called Polo. I am also at a loss as to how it came to be in my ratty tote bag, but that's a mystery for another time and place.

I needed to get ready for my date, and when I looked at my watch, I noticed that I had exactly 15 minutes to pick her up and then go to wherever it was we were going. I put on a clean shirt, a pair of my newly purchased jeans, my new fancy cowboy boots, combed my hair, and felt that I was at least presentable, and hoped that she wouldn't be too turned off by the way that I smelled.

This date would probably be more of the standard fare here in Bullsnort. First the usual cowboy kissing his horse movie at the Drive In, then for dinner at the Cave for the usual tacos or burritos and beers, and then who knows after that. Maybe to her house or my room at the motor court, maybe just to park under a big tree somewhere and watch the stars and moon shine through the clouds. Maybe something good mathematically will happen. I wouldn't want to wager a lot on that, though.

I arrived at Rosalie's house with five minutes to spare because the traffic in town was light. I rang the door chimes and waited for her to appear. I was totally surprised at what I saw when she opened the door.

I had pictured her in a nice flimsy and frilly blouse that would accent her ample figure, maybe a short skirt to emphasize other parts of her anatomy, some nice shoes and maybe a pair of stockings to set the whole combination in perfect order. Nothing could have prepared me for the shock I experienced when she appeared in the doorway!

She was dressed, to use the term loosely, like she had just this instant come from digging in a compost heap that she was using for a garden in the backyard. Her hands were filthy with dirt between her fingers, her nails were full of dirt like she had dug in whatever she was working in bare handed. She was wearing what was supposed to be a white T-shirt. I say supposed to be white because across the front of it were steaks of dirt like she had used it to wipe her hands after rooting around in whatever dark, and possibly foul smelling stuff, she was using before I arrived.

Her jeans were grubby with holes across the knees like they had either worn out or she had cut them like that on purpose. I have noticed jeans cut like that on kids in Albuquerque. They had done those cuts on purpose with scissors because they thought they looked neat. The holes in Rosalie's pants legs looked like she had used a rusty and very dull hedge trimmer to cut them. They were so ragged and uneven. I didn't care to ask her about the holes in her jeans just then. Her sneakers were completely covered with dirt. To say the least she sure didn't look like she was ready for a date with me then, or maybe ever again.

Her face had no makeup, but it was covered with dirt streaks that imitated Indian face painting that is so common in tribal festivities. Finger sized streaks of dirt covered her face from all angles. It was hideous, to say the least.

"Andy, what the devil are you doing here now?" she asked in what sounded like a very antagonistic tone.

"You obviously didn't get the message I left for you at the counter of the motor court, did you? I called about an hour and a half ago and because you weren't anywhere around I asked the old creepy guy if he'd pass on a message to you. He said he'd take a message and get it to you whenever you showed up again. I should have known better than to rely on him for anything!"

After saying all of that, she just glared at me for interrupting her work and waited for me to respond.

I said, defensively, "No I didn't get the message because I was at Mrs. Hernando's shop talking to her about a lot of things and we lost track of time. I didn't realize how late it was 'till I got back to my room to clean up in preparation for our date tonight. We do still have a date tonight don't we?"

I was almost struck dumb founded by her very caustic reply.

"Well Andy, let's look at our situation realistically now. You've been gone for several days, to who knows where. You didn't say goodbye, I'll see you when I get back, go to hell, or nothing. We saw each other at the Cave only once since you returned and you briefly hinted at something being very important that happened to you then you clammed up and didn't bother to explain. I've had it with your attitude that I just don't count in your picture of who is important in your life. Since I didn't know where you were or what you were doing, I didn't know what was going on with us, and still don't."

"I had a suspicion that maybe you went back to Albuquerque to see an old girlfriend who you decided was more your type than me. I don't know and don't really care if that's the case. Maybe you really did go out on the mesa to have what you described as an 'unbelievable experience,' but the least you could have done was let me know you would be spending time with the Indians and would be gone a few days."

"Another point I want to make it this. I don't like being ignored like I have been since you've been back from wherever it was that you went. You have been to see the Sheriff, Ms. Charles, and Mrs. Hernando, and who knows who else, but could you take time to call me and say that you were OK and that you wanted to see me again? NO, you didn't make the slightest effort to keep me informed. A couple of short phone call would have gone a long way to relieve my worrying about you. I realize now that I shouldn't have agreed to a date with you tonight."

Now that she had told me how she felt, I realized that there was no excuse for my not getting in touch with her before I left with Martin and the Shaman.

"You just don't do things like that to someone you care about." I thought, as I waited with baited breath for whatever axe she wanted to split my skull with, fell into place between my eyes. She didn't take long to swing that axe.

"Obviously, I am in no mood, or in any kind of condition to go anywhere with you, now, or in the future, unless I happen to have a complete and total change of heart toward you," she began.

"If that is hard for you to understand, or you have some problem digesting and believing it, I'll make it as clear as possible. I don't care if you come to the Cave for whatever meals you want to take there, but don't expect me to wait on you anymore. Don't ask me for any more dates because I may not be overly friendly when I tell you to stick those movie tickets up where the sun don't shine. In other clear words, Andy, don't darken my life or my doorstep anymore by coming here, or trying to get back into my good graces, because I am thoroughly and totally PISSED at you for treating me like you have. So, if you will kindly remove your foot from in front of my door, I will gladly close you out of my life, Good Bye Andy!"

She didn't look like she would listen to any reasoning I may have as an excuse, so I pulled my foot back from against the door jamb and the door slammed with a resounding CRACK! She was gone behind the solid yellow door.

I couldn't move for a minute or so till I finally came to my senses enough to realize that she had kicked me out of her life and I was to blame. I turned around, went to my car and drove all over town in frustration, thinking about my loveless situation now.

After driving up and down every street in Bullsnort two or three times, I drove back to the motor court, got undressed and went to bed. Maybe I'd get lucky and dream of some way to explain to Rosalie that I loved her and wanted to see her again. That didn't happen either, because the two tacos I ate and the beer I had for dinner gave me a terrific case of gas and I lay in bed making very weird music as I tooted all kinds of melodies all night long.

The next morning I left my room and went directly to Mrs. Hernando's shop. She seemed to have fully recovered from her hesitation to talk to me and smiled as I began to present my latest request for her help and advice.

"I was talking to the motor court owner about the Penitentes. He explained briefly that he is a member of that brotherhood and he gave me a short fact sheet explaining some of the terms used in their organizational structure. However, he seemed very cautious about giving me more information about them. His stories certainly raised my curiosity though, and I thought that you would be a great source of information on their beliefs and traditions. I thought since you own the arts store and have lived here all your life you might just be able to fill in the many gaps in my knowledge. I sure am interested in learning more. Can you please help me?"

"Yes, I can help you, Andy. I walked over to the bookshelf after you asked about the Penitentes and found a really good pamphlet and also a hardback book that should answer many of your questions. I put them at the front desk so you could find them when you came to the shop again. I'll be glad to help you any way I can."

Needless to say, I was greatly relieved that she would help me and sorry that I had misjudged her. I walked over to the desk, picked them up and said to her, "I'll look at them first chance I get."

I expressed my appreciation again for all the help, paid for the book and pamphlet and headed out the door toward the Cave.

As I walked the smells of food cooking at the Cave and the great music of the live mariachi band from the Cantina hurried me on my journey. I didn't like the idea of being hungry ever again. Little did I know at this point, that hunger wasn't going to be my major aggravation.

THIRTY-EIGHT

I walked along the boardwalk until I came to the first alleyway and paused there to look down the darkened path.

In what appeared to be a cubbyhole between buildings, about fifty feet from where I had stopped, there was an ominous glow. I recalled the first day I had seen something like this. I guessed then that it was a man standing in the alley smoking a cigarette and drinking from a brown paper bag that covered a bottle of some kind. I could see no definite shape there but only the slight glow.

Is someone following me, watching where I go, what I do and who I talk to?

I was talking to myself again and I didn't like the sound of what I was hearing at all. Too many strange things had happened to me since I got here to totally discount any potential threat. I didn't feel threatened now but was becoming more wary about things that didn't appear to be normal.

Seems like nothing in this whole damned town is normal!

As I tried to focus on the glowing shape it suddenly became a cloud of what looked like black smoke, or a dark mist. I tried but my sight couldn't penetrate the cloud. What had caused a cloud to suddenly appear? I didn't like this!

As I watched the cloud, it very slowly coalesced and started to move toward me! Up came those now familiar goose bumps on my arms and neck as I watched it move, ever so slowly, toward me. I looked down to my legs to see if I were involuntarily draining any internal bodily fluids there. Needless to say, I was becoming scared of what might happen but I couldn't get my legs moving to move away. I was stuck there! "Ah, Shit, what the hell is that thing?" I said aloud. I had no idea but didn't like it one damned bit.

I looked to the right and left, along the street to see if there was anyone I could call on for help. The streets were empty. Was that also planned so I would be alone and at the mercy of the thing coming towards me? I didn't have time to think about it because when I turned back to face it, it had moved to within an arms-length of me and had stopped. I hadn't hit the panic button yet but my finger was poised right over it.

As it sort of hovered there I heard, or thought I heard, something, or someone speak in a gravelly, smoke-choked male voice.

> *"You are on the right track. The main questions must be asked of the lawyer and the Sheriff. Only they can help provide the solution you seek."*

As I heard these words the mist, or cloud, or whatever the hell it was, started to dissolve before my eyes and in an instant it was gone. I looked up to see if it had risen into the blue sky, it hadn't. It just evaporated in less time than a snap of the fingers would take.

I took out my notebook and quickly wrote down the new clue. Then I just stood there for about five minutes until my breathing came back to normal.

I wondered how many more "helpers" like this frightening one would be coming out of nowhere to give me guidance? Weren't the Clan Fathers enough? Who, or what, was the guiding principal for the cloud? Would the next one be an animal of some description that would talk to me?

The question, "Am I being driven completely crazy by this town?" ran through my thoughts again. I gave some serious thought to just going back to the motor court, packing my meager belongings, and beating a path out of town and back to the relative safety of Albuquerque.

Talking to myself again, I said aloud, "No, I can't take the coward's way out. I'm committed for the duration. Besides, there's Rosalie and I can't just leave without seeing her. This cloud thing is just one more thing I have to talk to Mrs. Hernando about."

I looked carefully up and down the alley, making sure there were no more clouds that wanted my attention, and walked very quickly to the Cave for that much needed brunch.

THIRTY-NINE

Just as I had been warned by Rosalie the night before, she avoided me when I entered the Cave and another waitress seated me, took my order and watched attentively to see if I might need anything. When I had finished, she gave me the bill, took away the dirty dishes and even said "Have a great day, Andy."

With my desire for food temporarily satisfied, I left the Cave and headed back to Mrs. Hernando's shop again. I sure hoped she didn't mind all her time being taken up by me today.

We greeted each other warmly as I entered the shop. We talked for several minutes about things I didn't want to trust to the phone. There was no telling who might be listening. She was excited that I had "overheard a conversation" when I was up on the mesa and was doubly concerned when I revealed the context and who I thought the voices belonged to.

"You mean to tell me Andy, that you somehow overheard the Sheriff talking to someone who sounded like the lawyer in a conversation about getting rid of you, the way they did Carmelita for who knows what reason? That's definitely strange and potentially dangerous for you. Who else have you told about this?"

"Only Martin and the Shaman, but I also put my descriptions along with my feelings concerning all that has happened, including the "conversation," on tapes. Martin has them. He said he needed them to make an interpretation of the events."

"Be very careful who you tell things like that to here in town Andy," Mrs. Hernando advised with a nervous timbre in her voice. I immediately drew up from memory the message the Sand God had implanted in my mind.

> *You are not in danger yet but tread carefully where you may leave an imprint, either physically on the earth where you are, or in the minds of those with whom you must have associations.*

When I came back to reality I heard her continuing, "Especially those you might question about the Penitentes. Most people in town are Penitentes but most are very reluctant to talk about it outside the conclave and ceremonies, so be very cautious when you ask questions."

"Oh, by the way, here are two more books I have set aside for you. Since you've been gone I got some more new dolls and other things in. Feel free to wander. I'll be in the back office. Come on back when you want to talk."

Before she could walk away I told her about the dark cloud and the message that I had gotten from it in the alley on the way to her store. Her face showed concern that I might be in danger from some unknown source. I asked her some pointed questions about the Sheriff and the lawyer, which she answered truthfully, filling in a lot of the blank spaces in what I had already learned about them.

I told her that I wanted to take her up on her invitation to look around the shop a little. She assured me, again, that that would not be a problem since she had some work to do in her office. "Just call me if you need anything, or if another customer comes in and needs help."

I said that I surely would. This time I let her leave me alone with the artifacts.

I looked at the titles of the two books she had selected for me. Both of them looked like they could provide me with whatever information I wanted to know about the Brotherhood. I decided to buy both of them. I laid them by the register and wandered around the store refreshing my memory of what was there.

I hit the big drum and once again it resounded throughout my body like an electric shock. I didn't know if I actually shook at the sound and reverberations but I closed my eyes experiencing the feeling. With the sound still echoing, and with my eyes closed, I somehow saw some ancient figures dancing around a fire to drumbeats as they chanted. I also heard what I guessed were the wild horses stampeding around the lodge. It was if it all had just happened again with this drumbeat.

The whole experience out there on the mesa had been unreal from the start. I shivered involuntarily at the thought. I wondered how many more times I would relive a specific experience from my time out there. I wondered, "For the rest of my life?"

How long would that be if I remained here in this surreal town? I felt that I had no specific time period to stay here; just that I had an important reason now to be here and a mission to complete however long it took.

I leaned onto the big drum for support as I held my eyes closed and thought. I thought long and hard about the Clan Fathers, their messages, and what I was supposed to gain from them. As the drumhead stopped vibrating and settled back, I opened my eyes to see if I was still in the shop. I had felt, with my hands on the drumhead, that I had been, somehow physically transported back to the scene of the figures dancing around the fire. That feeling was real, but I was still in the shop. I walked away from my drum and saw some display cases and went to them. In one I spotted some items that I hadn't seen before.

There, on a black velvet display block, were about a dozen extremely small baskets and plaques. The baskets were no bigger than a dime, some with lids, some had no lids. All had very intricate designs woven into them. The other items were woven plaques about the size of a quarter. They also had intricate designs and symbols woven into them. I couldn't tell what material they were made of. I would have to ask Mrs. Hernando when she came out of her office.

In another case labeled Supplies I saw many beads of stunning colors and what appeared to be porcupine quills. I guessed they were porcupine because Mrs. Hernando had pointed out similar structures on a warrior's breastplate. She came out of her office about ten minutes later and we talked some more.

I bought the two books, thanked her for all her help and left the store on the way to the Cave. After dinner I made my way to my room. I wanted to get into the books I had bought as soon as possible. The brief list the old Sheriff had given me had strengthened my interest in the Penitentes even more. After reading only the brief introduction, I suddenly got very drowsy. I laid my head back on the pillow and fell fast asleep.

FORTY

It was dark and I was with a lot of waiting people who stood watching at the sides of the road. Faintly, ever so faintly, the sound of a flute's high and mysterious notes slowly edged their way into the people's consciousness. "Here they come," someone said quietly and anxiously. I saw nothing at first.

Then the procession came slowly into view, thirty men, for it was a male dominated group, these Penitentes. They were all dressed in white cotton shirts and white baggy cotton pants. All were barefoot. They came from the Morada to the church where they entered, walking on the backs of those doing penances who had prostrated themselves. They went into the darkened church and stayed in the church having a mass all through the night.

As dawn was breaking the group of men came out of the church. There were three brothers who had stripped off their shirts in the group now. One of these brothers, the Hermano, selected to be the Christ, went over to a large timber cross and hefted it to his shoulder. His head was covered with a white cotton sack so his identity wouldn't be known until the end of the procession. The other two shirtless men just joined the group as they started walking behind the *Hermano*.

Some of the brothers who were doing penances had fashioned scourges of cactus spines tied together with horsehair ropes and as soon as the procession started moving, every three steps they took they slapped the scourge first over one shoulder, took three more steps and slapped it over the other shoulder. They hadn't taken more than a dozen steps till the blood started flowing from the wounds they had inflicted upon themselves.

I saw the marchers wince and but heard none cry out from the pain caused by the sharp rocks that greatly damaged the soles of their feet. They all tried to ignore the pain and the bloody footprints that they left behind them on the road. The holy verses of religious songs were sung while the flutist, the Pitero, made the series of ascending and falling notes into a melody that led the cadence of the marchers and of the slaps of those doing penances when they purged themselves with the cactus spines and horsehair whips.

The sticks they used, sometimes with thorns, made cruel bloody marks after being slapped on the bare skin two or three times. These marks of blood accompanied the three gashes already there that represented the Trinity. The blood ran freely down their backs onto their white pants. Some who used no flagellants had wrapped their upper torsos with cactus which were tied tightly with woven horsehair ropes. These scourges were designed to cause severe pain at each step or movement. The Hermano had made a blanket of thorns, besides the crown he wore, and had it under the heavy beam cross.

The blood dripped from these wounds onto his back and his once white but now bloody pants.

The faces of the thirty marchers were covered with black hoods, not out of shame, for there was none, nor to hide from the Catholic priests, for the priests had no control over them, but as a way to humble themselves further in the eyes of God and to those who looked on them from the sides of the road.

While most of those doing penances walked to the cadences of both the flute and the alabados of the singers, some chose to make the journey on bloody knees, making the agonizing pain they suffered even harsher. This was done for the entire journey.

The dust raised by their shuffling feet rose only a few inches and settled back to be aroused by those who followed. The bloody white cotton trousers would be mud caked at the end of the journey.

At the halfway point of the procession the Hermano could, if he chose to, rest the cross off his bloody shoulder and have a drink of water. Taking food was not allowed during the march. This Hermano chose not to remove the heavy cross, but did rest as best he could.

At the end of this short break they continued going to the Calvarios, even those abandoned, to pay honor to these places and then back to the *Morada*. The distance they would cover would be several torturous miles over the rock strewn path.

I knew very little about the procession of the Penitentes because I had never witnessed one, so to be able to see one in living color and with such realism, was keeping my nerves on edge for I didn't want to miss anything. No one made a sound around me. It was very close to feeling, what I felt as I looked at the town for the first time, like being in a painting but not being painted there. I was in this scenario but not a part of it. The procession slowly wound its way back to the church where the crucifixion would happen.

As the procession of Penitentes reached the church on the return trip, three of the self-scourgers positioned themselves on the steps so that those entering would walk on their bloody and cut backs. No sound of pain ever was heard from these greatly injured men.

There were in this procession, this day, those who obviously, because of their age, were initiates to the order and were doing their first procession and penances. These novices were called a "Salir a Luz", literally coming out in the light of day. They carried the Bultos and the Retablos, the sacred carvings and paintings of the saints. All was peaceful and quiet as the time for the crucifixion drew closer.

When the entire procession reached the church it was time for the Hermano who was selected for crucifixion to be tied to the cross. The Mayor and the selectmen of the group indicated the penitent make his way, with his cross, to the sacred spot where the hole had already been dug. He laid the cross down with the base near the hole. He then, very reverently, and obviously with extreme pride, lay on the cross with his arms stretched out along the cross member. His hood still covered his face so I couldn't identify him. The members of the group them prepared him in the ritual manner by washing his hands and feet before tying him to the cross, and when ready, hoisted him and the cross upright as they sunk it into the hole. I noted with great relief that they didn't nail him to the cross. As the cross hit the bottom of the hole, the cowl that had covered his face fell away revealing who had been chosen. The main Hermano, the Christ, was in the middle of the two other men crucified this day.

At that point I sat bolt upright in bed, sweat pouring from my body, my heartbeat going at a tremendously fast rate. I had seen the face of the person hanging crucified as the Christ. It was me hanging there on the cross!

I was the Hermano!

After my nerve endings gained some semblance of normalcy, I asked a vital question.

What does this dream mean? Does it portend danger to me if I continue my hunting for Carmelita? I had about a thousand more things to ask about but because of the initial shock of me hanging on the cross, crucified, I passed out.

FORTY-ONE

Later, as I regained my limited composure, I thought of several of the Clan Fathers messages and what I was meant to do with and with them.

From the Turtle Clan Father, Crawls Along Slowly, I had gained insight about how to learn the truth about the disappearance of Carmelita. It meant that I should trust my instincts and not let anybody else's input affect them. I also had to be slow and very methodical in my research of this crime to find the guilty party, or parties, and bring them to justice. That I felt she had been plotted against by the Sheriff and someone unknown at this point was obvious. The Sheriff certainly was the number one suspect. Who number two would actually turn out to be would surely come later. I had a pretty good and idea, but no solid proof yet.

From the Deer Clan Father, Runs Fast, I now had an inkling of how to put my own values on what I had learned so far. I knew definitely that I had heard the plotting. I was not hallucinating then. I had been given this insight for a reason. As I used it in my evaluation against whatever other clues were to be discovered, I felt sure that the Sheriff would definitely be implicated. I vowed that I would prove it!

From the Buffalo Clan Father, Loves the Snow, I had learned how to accept the fact that I was a conduit somehow chosen to ferret out the person or persons who had done the crime or crimes, as they appeared to be. The clues or suppositions so far, were straightforward. There had been no diversions or sidetracking to throw me off the path. I knew I had the correct clues.

From the Horse Clan Father, Listening to Sounds, I definitely saw the truth in the several visions I'd had out there in the desert. I saw the dancers, the deer, the eagle, the fire, and the Owl Man. I could discern fact from fiction and both of those from hallucinations. I needed to apply this process to decide what was true and who the guilty party or parties were.

What I saw, I was supposed to see. This had been predestined, so to speak. The main question now, as I saw it, was, "Am I supposed to just find out what happened, if anything, to Carmelita, or are there larger and more ominous questions about the entire town that I am somehow responsible for answering?"

I didn't know just yet but with the help of the remaining Clan

Fathers and their messages, I felt that I, and I alone, was destined to find the answers.

From the Owl Clan Father, Keeper of Knowledge, I had gained an inner peace about the information I had been given so far. I also knew that there would be more messages and help forthcoming. From what sources, other than the Clan Fathers or maybe another Sand God, I hadn't a clue just yet but I would surely recognize the medium when it appeared to me. I knew instinctively that I would judge the clues and make the right decisions.

From the Eagle Clan Father, Flies on the Wind, I will learn to speak the truth when the truth will determine the outcome of this adventure. It may be at a trial, it may possibly be in an article, or in a book. It may not come at all. If that happens, I will be the longtime receptacle of this knowledge and I will become the teacher, helper, or maybe a leader in making it possible for someone else to find the truth.

From which Clan Father will I learn how to place value on all things, living or inanimate? Everything has value. Nothing is lessened in value by our judgments of it. One problem in passing judgment on anything is that we are routinely biased in our opinions, which makes our evaluation of anything that may be the slightest bit foreign or unknown to us very difficult to access. Out there in the darkness and alone I had learned that I had value other than just being a supposedly superior, thinking, speaking animal.

From my experiences so far I learned that my responsibility will not end when, and if, this situation is concluded by finding Carmelita alive or dead. No, it will only be complete when those who are responsible are brought to justice. I would play a big part in that ending, I realized.

I came to realize early in my stay here in Bullsnort that I must be the one to be truthful. I could not plot and deceive to find those responsible. I must work honestly and truthfully towards an honorable end. If the Clan Fathers lost trust in me they would not help me further. If I am not both honest and truthful, the message from the Sand God will have no value.

Both sources had somehow chosen me as the receptacle of their knowledge. I swore I would do nothing to dishonor that trust.

What I didn't know was what the last three Clan Fathers messages would give me but whatever guidance they gave me, it would be the crowning piece in the large puzzle they had called me here to complete for them. I felt absolutely in awe of their power over me. I also knew that if I didn't live up to their expectations and trust that something extremely unpleasant would befall me before I would be allowed to depart from this place. That wasn't a very happy thought.

My hunger attacked me and I realized that I'd slept till almost noon and had laid there just thinking for another hour. I got up, dressed and made my way to the Cave for some breakfast. Rosalie was the only waitress working so I took advantage of that and was able to prod her to talk a little as she took my order for Huervos Rancheros, (Spanish style eggs). When my meal came it was covered with the usual salsa looking dressing, chopped tomatoes and lettuce. This time though, I didn't wash it all down with beer but chose a more modest iced tea to start my day.

We talked a little more and before I left on my daily excursion and after extensive apologies from me, we made tentative plans for another date later that evening. I had tried as best I could to make my feelings toward her known and told her that I was truly sorry for having caused her any grief. I told her that I would explain it all to her if she would just give me another chance. She smiled a little, beautiful smile, and said she would. We brushed lips in a light kiss as I left the Cave a lot happier than I was last night and headed down the street.

I followed a direct path to Mrs. Hernando's store. I had some more very serious questions to ask her, specifically, about the Penitentes, I wanted to get her impression of my latest scary dream and the voice in the cloud that I had encountered in the alley.

FORTY-TWO

M rs. Hernando must have been in the back office when I entered because the storefront was empty. I walked around and found my target, my drum. I hit it a resounding smack and it reverberated through me for a full two minutes. I closed my eyes and experienced the feeling with both hands on the reverberating drumhead. As soon as I did that, an image came into view that astounded me with its clarity. Just like I was looking at a photograph, I could make out an Indian scene in the mist of my thoughts.

I saw a vast plain spotted with what must have been five hundred pointed, white teepees. There were warriors, riding around on their horses; some singularly, some in groups of four or five. Some, who were not mounted, were shooting arrows at a target. Others were throwing what looked like spears at another man-sized target. Younger children were mimicking their older brothers and fathers by doing the same things with their child-sized weapons. The women were carrying large bundles of something to a central location where a gigantic bonfire was being fed with logs. "Must be some kind of celebration," I thought. Then, before I could recognize anything more specific, the picture faded to a dull gray blur.

As I came back to the present, I opened my eyes and moved away from the drum. This large bass drum seemed to be the focal point of my visits here. I felt like the steel shavings that are drawn to a magnet. I admitted to myself that I could no more come into this shop without going to this drum and hitting it, than I could get up and stay undressed all day. The taut skin of the drum created its own sensations that tingled up my arms when I leaned on it. It was like a reservoir of knowledge that I alone was capable of tapping.

I wondered in awe how all these supernatural things worked. How was I chosen to be the conduit? Why? What else in this shop could be a source of energy for me? I was drawn to the Kachinas, but as yet hadn't gotten any kind of messages from them. Maybe the paintings would provide some insights. I knew instinctively that I was not the one to choose the medium. I was only the receptacle through which the spirits could give voice to their messages.

I looked over the new articles that Mrs. Hernando had put out for sale. A baby cradle board caught my eye because of the intricate work of multi-colored beads. Lying next it was several more beaded articles.

One was obviously a rifle scabbard and beside it was a knife scabbard. Both of these were covered with intricate designs in many colors of beads intermingled with what appeared to be porcupine quills. The handwork on these things was spectacular. I read the tags on them and saw that they were made by Plains Indians, one by a Pawnee artist and the other two created by Sioux. The prices were way out of my price range so I passed them up quickly.

One last item did catch my attention before I walked on. It was also beaded and appeared to be a bag of sorts that I had not seen before. It had a different shape than the other things around it. It was rectangular and measured about seven inches long by three wide. The eye catcher was the pattern composed of three triangles on one end of the piece. The beadwork included animal effigies and other symbols. The tag said it was a tobacco bag from the early 1800's. I was happy to see that the price was low enough that I could possibly afford to buy it.

Lying next to it in the case was a beautiful feather fan.

I examined it as closely as I could and counted eight deep chocolate brown feathers secured in a handle affair with more intricate beadwork. The tag identified it as an Eagle Feather Ceremonial Fan. It reminded me of the three feathers the Sand God had in his hair. Everything in this shop was beginning to symbolize some part of what I had been experiencing. I realized that I was definitely becoming more in touch with things here.

Next to this display case was another case labeled Supplies.

In it I saw many smaller containers of colored beads and what appeared to be porcupine quills. I guessed that was what they were because they looked a lot like the pieces on a warrior's breast plate that Mrs. Hernando had identified as having been made of porcupine quills. "Maybe the Indians from a nearby tribe come here," I thought, "to get these things when they make their dance outfits for their powwow's and festival dances."

I hit my drum a second time on the way back to the counter and Mrs. Hernando had appeared from her back office. She just smiled at me and shook her head. We talked for almost an hour. She was aghast as I explained, as best I could, about seeing myself at the end of the Penitente procession ending with the Hermano, who was actually me, being crucified. I told her about hearing the conversation between the Sheriff and a woman, who was probably the lawyer about Carmelita. Mrs. Hernando listened intently to my descriptions of my visions and then gave me a lot more insight into the goings-on of those two by elaborating on one or two rumors that had made the rounds in town before I got here. She was very helpful and sympathetic, but could offer no explanation for the many things that had happened to me. I didn't press her for her opinion. When she understood it more thoroughly, maybe then she'd offer some kind of explanation.

I bought and paid for another book and pamphlet she'd laid out for me and told her I'd probably spend the next few days reading and trying to digest what was in all the books I had bought about the Penitentes.

We said our good-byes and I headed toward the bakery to get some of the sweet smelling breads and a tub of fresh homemade butter that I could taste before I even got close to the store.

I completed my mission at the bakery and headed back to my room. I had about two hours left before I had to go pick up Rosalie for our movie date but first I wanted to get started on my reading.

I delayed starting to read just long enough to rip off two huge pieces of the still warm fresh bread and literally smeared them with rich creamy butter. "Boy," I thought, "I could sure get used to this diet!" The bread was delicious. I laughed at myself, "Man cannot live by bread alone. He needs sustenance of other kinds, too." I recalled a professor at UNM who jokingly listed the student's four main food groups as Beer, Cheese, Pizza, and Chocolate. I had to add Bread to the four because this bread sure was good.

The hardback books looked formidable with 350 pages each, so I started reading the smaller pamphlet. It only had 50 pages in it so I might get through it rather easily before I had to go and pick up Rosalie. I am a prodigious reader. In a week's time I might read ten full length books but I doubted that I could read 350 pages before I had to leave.

I scanned the pamphlet from page one to the end and went back to the specific topics that interested me. I read those more carefully.

In the 1540-1541 timeframe the Spanish conquest of the Southwest was undertaken by Coronado and the many missionaries who had taken part in all of the military expeditions. They came to the Northern reaches of New Mexico and established the Catholic Church's presence. It amazed me when I read that blood penances and sacrifices of the Aztecs were brought to this area by the conquering Spaniards. The motives for severe penances are usually explained by emphasizing that they are for the reparation of personal and other sins. They are considered necessary for demonstrating devotion to Christ, and self-discipline.

I got an inkling of why Mrs. Hernando had seemed uncomfortable with my questioning about the brotherhood as I read about the women, who are not always allowed to be full members of the Brotherhood, but more likely serve as auxiliaries, preparing meals, caring for the sick and wounded, and organizing the wakes or vigils. Women usually have a milder penance but it does sometimes include the scourging, or blood-letting, of the men. They can walk the length of the procession with either rice or stones in their shoes. Some women have been flagellants but none have been crucified.

One misconception, I read, that exists about the Brotherhood concerns the Descansos, or the piles of stones which sometimes have a small cross on them. These crosses and stones are scattered throughout the countryside. It is thought that they are the graves of crucified brothers. I read that they are not graves but places where those in the procession who are carrying a coffin, or pulling a rock laden death cart, could stop and rest and sing a song to the dead. Many times they added a stone to the pile so, over the years, many of these markers grew quite large.

I read of the Santos and Bultos, the religious carvings and paintings that are indigenous to New Mexico, but decorate most of the churches throughout the Southwest. The pictures were in color and spectacular. I knew then that I had seen some of them in Mrs. Hernando's shop but didn't know then what they were. I decided that I would go back and look at them more closely. I remembered seeing a calendar in the shop that had pictures of both the Santos and the Santero, the carver.

There was just too much valuable information in this little pamphlet to digest after only one short reading. I'd definitely have to go about this in a scholarly way or I'd wind up scrambling all the information and becoming really confused. I was fascinated by what I'd read so far.

FORTY-THREE

The strange feelings, and unexplained happenings, I had experienced continuously since driving into this town so long ago have not gotten any better. I didn't go out alone at night if I could help it. I stayed pretty much in my room, the Cave, or the Cantina after dark. I had an uneasy feeling that all was not as it appeared in this place. I had no solid proof but the circumstantial evidence led me to believe that some malevolent force is alive and well and working there.

Somebody was out to get me. I couldn't shake that feeling, but I also felt that there was some protective force working in my favor and was watching out for me. Would this protective cover end with the last Clan Fathers message and allow the malevolent force take over? I hoped that neither would happen. It's not that I am a coward, mind you, but some mighty strange and dangerous things had happened since I got back from the mesa.

I awoke one dark morning to the sound of gunfire that sounded like it was just outside my door. I know the difference between pistol and rifle fire. I was in the service as a Military Policeman and had to fire all kinds of weapons that were currently in the Army's arsenal, in addition to the .45 caliber pistol. I knew what an incoming round from a rifle or pistol sounds like, so I knew that these shots came from a rifle. I just didn't relish the idea of being on the receiving end of that fire.

No shots came through the windows at me but there was definitely shooting going on outside. I heard several slam into the heavy plank door and into the framing around the door. At the sound of the first shot, I rolled out of the bed and cowered near the back wall, trying to cram most of my body into a very tight corner away from the shooting. I heard at least a dozen or more shots before all was quiet again.

At daylight I went out to look at the damage. In addition to the holes in the door of my room, the windshield of my car had three neat holes in it at just the right height for the chest of the driver. I hated to think about what shape I would be in now, if I had been sitting there in the driver's seat. In the driver's side door window there were two more neat holes. I took this message to mean that I was in the crosshairs of at least one, maybe two, shooters. I doubted that the shots were random because of the holes in the seat.

The trajectories were planned for maximum effect. All three through the windshield would definitely pierce the heart of a person sitting in the driver's seat, while the others, through the side window, would probably enter under the armpit and come real close to the first ones. If I had been in the car all of them would have been killing shots, well planned for maximum effect.

There was absolutely no way to tell who had fired the shots. Somebody didn't want me doing what I was doing and wanted me out of town. Either dating Rosalie or asking leading questions about Carmelita, or both, had certainly offended someone. I had a strong suspicion just who that someone might be. I dug the five slugs out of the seatback and kept them. I scoured the ground around the small parking area and found an entire handful, maybe seventeen, shell casings.

They looked a lot like 30-30 caliber shells to me. There was no way to look at both the slugs and casings to see if they matched but the State Police lab had the technology to do it. I would give them to Martin or whoever was involved trying to solve the case of the attempted murder of the man out in the desert. I believed the two shootings I had read about in the paper, and the one the old Sheriff had told me about involving the shot off ear, and this shooting of my car, were related. I just had to prove it.

I would have to act like I did not understand why this had happened because I was sure that someone was watching my every move, watching who I talked to and where I went. I wouldn't put my few new friends in danger and I wouldn't let the shooter, or shooters, know how much the shots had heightened my awareness of them. I calmed myself down and then tried to go on about my business as usual.

I went to the cemetery office and asked about their records. I found that they had kept ledger books back to the day they opened, which was January 1st, 1900. I was in luck. I had several hours to scour their records. I found some interesting facts in their death records.

"Either some people here are extremely old or they have the same names as the people whose deaths are recorded." I thought, as I jotted down some of the more familiar names.

I climbed back up to Boot Hill and examined all thirty of the markers and stones located there. I was stunned to find markers on graves for three people with the same names as three people I had met in town. I went to the new cemetery, and discovered the same macabre thing there. I had a long list of names and as I walked around looking at the markers and headstones, I found a dozen more names of currently active people in town. All dead and buried long ago! Or are they? I didn't know and would not ask anybody about my fears until I was sure of the facts. I thought I might just go the newspaper office and look up some obituaries in the archives.

It looked as though I had found the real name of the motor court owner on one of the markers. It is Orlando Ordonez. I found his grave and marker in the new cemetery. It had his name, the date of birth as July 4, 1830 and a date of death as August 21, 1919. The epitaph read:

> *A good Sheriff*
> *May he do a good job*
> *Wherever he is*

Maybe my imagination ran wild here, but he did say that he was eighty-nine years old. The age on this gravestone showed Orlando Ordonez to be eighty nine years old when he died in 1919. If he didn't die then, or isn't buried here, then who the hell is the guy at the motor court that swears to be the old Sheriff? Who was this Sheriff right at my feet?

I couldn't answer that new quandary just yet but the way the old man had answered my questions and the slip ups he made earlier have come back to haunt me. I need to talk to somebody about this, but who? I could surely ask Mrs. Hernando or Martin. Most reassuringly I did not find either of their stones at either cemetery.

My nerve endings were tingling their old messages of caution again. It was obviously time to be very careful about what questions I asked certain people. I wanted to talk again to the lady lawyer. What was her name again? Robin something, oh yes, Robin Charles. I called and made an appointment this time. I had some specific, but very carefully worded, questions that I wanted her to answer. I casually walked the short distance over to her office (One of the benefits of living in a small town.)

FORTY-FOUR

As I approached the lawyer's office I was walking very slowly so she'd see me before I had a chance to look at her and see what she was doing. I had a feeling that Ms. Robin Charles didn't like surprises.

She had a cell phone to her ear when I entered her office. She motioned for me to have a seat and held up two fingers. I guessed that she needed about two minutes more on the phone before she could get to me. Five minutes passed before the one sided conversation ended and she was ready to talk. I was trying to listen to what she was saying but it made no sense to me, probably talking to a client. When she hung up the phone I turned and started to explain what it was I wanted from her. I assured her that I wouldn't take too much of her time.

I explained that I was still looking into the disappearance of Carmelita for another, possibly larger article, for my paper.

I lied and said that I had gotten some pressure from my editor who had told me to get something useful and interesting or that I would have to leave town without a story. I also explained that I hadn't had much luck in getting facts that I could use in a story and hoped that she could help me. After all, she was Carmelita's employer and maybe she knew her habits better than anybody else in town.

As I looked into her face, I recalled the open hostility of our first meeting.

When she started talking I realized she hadn't mellowed at all. She sort of pinched her eyebrows together and I could tell easily that she was agitated by the question.

She said, "I was her employer not her confidant and certainly not her watchdog. I didn't pay much attention to what she did after she left my office."

I definitely got a sense of hostility from her where Carmelita was concerned. Her tone and hostility were ever present and the change from the pleasant conversationalist to an angry person became even more evident as I asked more questions about her relationship with Carmelita. My main concern was why? What caused this animosity between them?

If this animosity was work related she could have just fired her. If it was personal then that was more serious. It was as if a light had flashed on in my mind. What if that was exactly the case? There had to be a personal connection between Carmelita and her boss to cause this hostility. Did it somehow involve the Sheriff? That would prove to be an interesting possibility. I gave her the benefit of the doubt though. I had no solid proof to back up my suspicions. I would have to take the Wolf Clan Father's message to heart. Be sly and stealthy in order to dig the truth out of her. If it meant making up a story to trap her, then that's what I'd do. If the three of them were somehow involved personally, then that would certainly provide a motive for Carmelita's disappearance.

Up to this point I hadn't seriously considered the lawyer as the actual murderer of Carmelita. But now, with her anger showing visibly as I asked my questions, I changed my mind on that. The obvious doesn't have to hit me too hard right between the eyes to make an impression.

I very carefully skirted the issue of the overheard conversation but alluded to it by asking her if she had talked to anybody anytime about Carmelita being gone.

She stuttered a little, caught her breath again, lowered her eyes to her hands and lied. She said she had been out of town that week and no, she had not talked to anybody about Carmelita's disappearance. I knew for a fact that this was a lie because I had learned from the Sheriff that he had talked to her two days after Carmelita disappeared about what she might know about it.

"That's Lie number one." Why?

It was beginning to look exactly like I had guessed it might. She and the Sheriff were somehow involved in what was looking more and more like Carmelita's murder. Could she be the voice at the other end of the conversation I had heard? If she was, then why did she want Carmelita out of the way and how did she do it? I couldn't come right out and ask her if she had a hand in it now could I? I had to trap her into lying again. If she lied a second time about something I already knew to be true, then I had her right where I wanted her.

"Where the hell is that?" I asked myself. I had no solid proof yet that she or the Sheriff did anything. All I had so far were guesses.

I asked the intimidating question anyway. "Do you have any idea why or even if she did leave town, Ms. Charles? Did she take time off or did you send her out of town on business for the firm or something? Did she give you any indication that she might be going anywhere out of town that week?"

"No she didn't confide in me about going anywhere, and no, I didn't and never have, sent her anywhere on company business. I go myself when required."

She told me this lie with such a straight, emotionless demeanor. Had I not known better, I would have taken her at her word. As it was I certainly wouldn't believe anything she told me from here on out.

"That's Lie number two." Again, why?

Rosalie had told me truthfully, and with no reason to lie, that Carmelita had told her once, about a month and a half ago, that she was going with Ms. Charles to Santa Fe on business. That trip was supposed to give Carmelita the experience she needed so that in the future Ms. Charles could send her to Santa Fe alone the next time travel there was needed. Carmelita had told Rosalie that she was sent alone to Santa Fe at least once by Ms. Charles. Carmelita didn't object because she had an expense account at the hotel where she stayed for whatever she needed and Ms. Charles picked up the bill. Ms. Charles had also given Carmelita a small amount of cash for incidental expenses. Rosalie thought it was about one hundred dollars.

Carmelita had told Rosalie that the trip only involved two days at the most. Rosalie had also thought it was strange that when Carmelita had gone to Santa Fe alone, the Sheriff had also gone out of town. Maybe he went to Santa Fe to be with Carmelita?

The triangle was now starting to take shape.

Also a possible motive was forming more solidly in my mind. Had Ms. Charles somehow discovered that Carmelita had spent time with the Sheriff in Santa Fe? The old saying, A woman scorned is a vicious woman. Or something like that came to my mind.

I decided to ask Ms. Charles one more question to add a nail to the already semi-solid plank of proof that she was involved. The third question, if answered with a lie, would make my feelings about her involvement irrefutable.

"Was Carmelita involved with anybody romantically, that you knew of, who might be able to help me?"

As I suspected, her facial features took on an ominous sneer and her voice became almost a growl when she answered with "Lie Number Three."

"I don't know. As I told you before I wasn't her friend, watchdog, or confidant, only her employer. Now, I have some cases I have to get busy on."

I decided to find the cement that would hold these mixed clues together. I needed to talk to the deputies about the extra duties they had been assigned during the two times the Sheriff was out of town. I thought I could come up with some obscure reason to ask them about his whereabouts for that week. I had the dates Rosalie had said Carmelita had been sent out of town, and which, according to Rosalie, the Sheriff was also out of town. The corroborating proof would be from the duty logs of the deputies and the hotel registers in Santa Fe. All this evidence together could show a solid motive for Ms. Charles and possibly the Sheriff to want Carmelita gone.

The flavor of the disappearance had very distinctly turned sour and was taking on the ugly stench of a murder and maybe even a conspiracy to commit murder by two of the town's major citizens, the Sheriff and the lawyer.

I didn't want her anger to cause Ms. Charles to stop talking to me so I very quickly and carefully changed the subject to the motor court owner and the old jail.

"I just have one more question," I said apologetically. "Do you know where the town's records are kept? Are they in the old jail? I would really like to look at them from a historical point of view and maybe write a story about the town. Can you help me find them?"

"I don't know for sure where the town's records are. They might be in the old jail, but I'd guess that they can be found in the City Hall building where the Sheriff has his office."

Her tone had changed from antagonistic to a more friendly and helpful one. "To tell the truth, I don't ever go near the motor court. I haven't even been on that side of the street near that place for about twenty five years. It's a long and sometimes boring story. Do you want to hear why I avoid that place?"

FORTY-FIVE

That surprised me. A couple of minutes ago she was ready to show me out the door. Now she was ready to tell me a long and boring story? She was ready and willing to get away from Carmelita as a subject and to change the subject to the motor court, no matter how painful the memory might be.

I wanted to encourage her to talk and be friendly toward me so I said "Yes, I do want to hear the whole story, but I don't want to keep you away from your work." I knew better than to just say, "I've got about twenty minutes left on my appointment time."

"The whole thing began about twenty five years or so ago, when I was a little girl. of about eight or nine," she began. "We kids always went out on the town for Halloween Trick or Treating."

"Well, this one year that old man, it seems like he was always old to me, did a really good job of fixing up the outside of the motor court for Halloween. He made it look like one of the crypts up at the cemetery. You know, with cobwebs and cornstalks and spooky noises coming from all over the place. I still don't know how he did it but the place even smelled musty like it hadn't been opened in a hundred years. To us it was real. To me it still is."

"Well, three of us went up to ring his doorbell. It must have been rigged somehow to start the strange noises and what sounded like organ music because it scared the hell out of all of us. We were too scared to run away and after a few minutes of waiting for something to happen and being terrified, the door slowly creaked open with squeaks and scrapings just like a heavy concrete crypt door would make when it moved."

"That old bastard came to the door in the remnants of a black suit and a raggedy tie covered with dusty looking stuff that just hung all over him. He had no shoes on and I didn't see many toes that looked like whole ones. He had made up his face and hands to look like they had been rotting away for a long, long time. Somehow he had made up his face to look like big patches of decaying skin were hanging on by small slivers. His hair was very gray and dirty. I doubt if it was a wig. One eye socket looked like it was empty, leaving a black nasty looking hole that had something in it that looked like maggots eating the flesh. He opened his mouth and it looked like his teeth were falling out and the hole that was left of his mouth was very black. One ear was gone and the hole it left was oozing blood, or as I think about it now, maybe red ink or ketchup. He was either wearing perfect makeup or a rubber mask. I suspect he actually made up his own face to look that gruesome."

"When I saw him dragging his feet and moving towards me, I got scared so badly I peed my pants right on the spot, screamed, and ran away. I don't know what the other two kids did, but I ran all the way home without stopping once to catch my breath. Wet my pants and screamed all the way. If he had used makeup it was extremely effective in scaring the three of us. To me he looked like what I imagined a corpse would look like after many years in a coffin but had just gotten up and walked out of it. I sure as hell wouldn't eat any treat he would drop in my bag."

"The next day we kids all got together and compared notes about where we'd been to get the best stuff. Nobody, out of all the kids, and there must have been about thirty there, had gotten anything from the old man at the motor court. Most of us vowed that we'd never go there again because he'd scared us so badly. I knew that after what I had experienced that Halloween night that I would never go back there again. Most kids I knew then only went to his place once and that was enough. Nobody ever dared anybody else to go there. Nobody wanted to be grabbed and dragged inside the motor court and never see the light of day again. We let our imaginations run wild after that. I still avoid that side of the street as much as possible. I never go close to the motor court."

"Another reason us kids were scared of him was the rumors going around town," she continued.

"What might those rumors be?" I asked her, sympathetically.

"Well, you know he grows all kinds of things in his back yard. We used to sneak up to his back fence and look to see what he was doing. There are three containers out there that I have come to find out are his compost bins. What I didn't expect to see were the pumpkins that he was growing."

"Pumpkins?" I asked with a sincerely puzzled look on my face. "I was in his yard and I didn't see anything that looked like pumpkin vines anywhere."

"Yes," she nodded. "He grew them then for Halloween, at least is what he used to tell the other adults in town. They were the giant variety, the ones that get to over two hundred and fifty pounds. Well, to continue with the rumor. The rumor was that there were three or four girls missing from Santa Fe one year. They were never found. One of the kids that went up to look into the back yard claimed that she had seen the big leaves of three pumpkin plants that had what looked a lot like human faces on them."

"Are you telling me that he was responsible for abducting three kids in Santa Fe, bringing them up here, killing them, then feeding their bodies to the plants, and that somehow the images of the victims showed up on the leaves that year?" I couldn't keep the doubt out my voice. I felt a twinge of something unusual as I asked her that question, I had noticed that she had started to visibly shake at the telling and her color had turned a pasty pale from the normal pink shades of her face.

"I don't know what the truth is, and I don't much give a damn. I know that he scared me so badly I don't go to that side of the street. If he killed those kids he needs to be brought to justice. I don't know if he still grows the pumpkins or not."

She continued to visibly shake and sweat broke out on her forehead with the retelling of the terror of twenty five years ago.

To say that I was shocked by her fright is putting it mildly.

This lady lawyer didn't strike me as the type of woman that would be frightened of an old man. I wondered if what she had just told me would bear out the suspicions that I already had about the motor court owner. Maybe he had died in 1919 and somehow wasn't dead.

That's impossible, I told myself. That would mean he is one hundred and fifty years old. There had to be another explanation for this anomaly. Maybe he was just good at making his house spooky at Halloween time. Maybe he took perverse pleasure in scaring the hell out of trick or treaters. I had to admit, the first time I saw him I was scared too, and it wasn't even Halloween.

It was an interesting story but not the one I had come to get from her. Maybe it was meant to distract me from pursuing Carmelita's murderer. I changed the subject again and saw her immediate relief. But when I asked about Carmelita again the hostility shone through again. Something very personal had obviously happened to her that had involved Carmelita but I didn't know what. The reaction was just not faked.

Was the conflict just between her and Carmelita or between her and the Sheriff? Was jealousy the motive for her anger? Had she somehow found out about the Sheriff's trips to meet Carmelita and confronted him with the issue of his affair with Carmelita?

Maybe Carmelita had not just been disappeared but was murdered and her body disposed of somewhere out there in an obscure arroyo.

Who had decided to get rid of her, the lawyer, the Sheriff, or both? A major problem became more obvious with that question. If both, then how could I set a trap that would reveal their involvement? If both know the pertinent facts of Carmelita's demise then how could I set one against the other and catch them both? I definitely would have to work on that strategy.

Maybe Carmelita, despite Ms. Charles' statement about her not being Carmelita's confidant, had confided to her that she was pregnant and had told her who the father was. She would have felt more confident talking to Ms. Charles because she knew enough about the law to know that it forbade Ms. Charles from revealing anything told to her in confidence. Carmelita wasn't her client in the strictest sense of the word but she would have felt that security. Carmelita couldn't have told Rosalie.

As I was rehashing this scenario, I didn't put my mouth in gear before I activated my mind as I blurted out "Did you know that Carmelita was pregnant?" I thought to myself, "Damn, that surely will get her blood pressure on the rise. She'll never answer that question."

Her reaction told me more than her answer did. She knew all right. I knew I had her then. I just had to find the proof of her involvement.

"No, she didn't tell me anything about her personal life away from the office, especially about being pregnant. As I said before, I am her employer, not her mother or confessor. I really must get back to work now."

She rose from behind her desk, walked to her office door and opened it and showed me the street without even a "Have a nice day," or a handshake. Her hostility had come back, big time hostility, toward me.

This, along with the lies she had already told me made me doubt what she had just told me. I knew deep down inside that she was involved. My appointment time had obviously come to an end. I had touched some very sensitive nerves and she didn't want me to see any more of her reactions.

"No, I have nothing else right now," I said politely. "But if anything comes up I might want to talk to you again. Would that be OK with you?"

The answer was less then friendly but she did accede to my request for now. I didn't really expect much response or much time to talk to her next time, if there was to be a next time.

That would depend entirely on the direction my search for clues led me. I felt certain that I would be back to talk to her before this whole thing was settled. I thanked her for her help and went quickly out the front door. I didn't like the feeling of her eyes staring at my back.

FORTY-SIX

As I got outside I slowed a little and saw her scowling at me, obviously unaware that I had seen her. As I took a few steps away I saw her hurry back to her desk, dial a number on her cell phone and talk very animatedly to someone. I could guess that it was the Sheriff and she was telling him all about our conversation about Carmelita. She may not have done Carmelita in by herself, more than likely she had hired someone to do it. Whatever the answer, she was involved. I knew it. Proving it legally would be another matter entirely.

Another problem raised its head with that call. Now the Sheriff would know that I was interested in him and Ms. Charles in connection with Carmelita. Every way I added it up it came to three. "A Lover's Triangle".

An older woman scorned in favor of a younger one.

The younger one pregnant by the Sheriff, and the older one jealous to the point of murder? If ever there was a motive for doing what I guessed they'd done, that was it.

I decided I needed insurance just in case something was to happen to me. I would alert both Mrs. Hernando and Martin about my talk with Ms. Charles. Just in case the two suspected perpetrators decided to disappear me. I had concealed a tape recorder in an inside pocket of my jacket so I had all the sounds and inflections, coupled with the obvious anger of her responses. If her involvement was that clear to me, it should be clear to anybody else who listened to it.

What would I have to do now to even support the extremely flimsy evidence for a case of murder against these two? Somehow, I had to lay a trap so that each would want to spill the beans and implicate the other in whatever had happened. Had they hired someone else to help them? I knew deep down they were guilty, but proving it meant having to solve many other problems.

If the Sheriff had done the deed and buried Carmelita in an isolated spot out on the desert, maybe Ms. Charles didn't know about the location. But, if they had plotted and connived together, then both would know where she was buried and one could be used to implicate the other and try to pass the blame. On the other hand, if they had hired someone to help them, maybe neither of them knew exactly where the body was buried.

My mind was full of possible strategies. Maybe an anonymous note sent to the newspaper giving some piece of information about Carmelita that only the two suspects knew would get some reaction from them. Maybe that would start an argument between them, and then the rift could cause one or the other to send their own letter claiming innocence and blaming the other. Someone would have to watch them both for their actions and reactions to the letter. That might just work. Play both ends against the middle.

The ends being Ms. Charles and the Sheriff, while the middle was obviously, Carmelita and her disappearance.

Maybe I could pose as a third party who had just happened on to the situation but hadn't told the authorities.

"Blackmail, that's an excellent idea!" I thought. I could threaten one or both of them with exposure if a large sum of money wasn't delivered to a certain place, in exchange for a mysterious video of the crime scene. Get the two suspects all primed to get the evidence and thus clear their names of the crime. Then nothing happens! Nobody is at the location for the exchange. No video. No proof. No witness. The suspects then have more time to sweat and confront the other partner in the crime.

If only somehow their phones could be tapped and their conversations monitored by the State Police. I wondered if Martin could convince them to do that. I'd have to ask him. On second thought, it probably would take a court order for them to do phone taps.

FORTY-SEVEN

As I walked down the street, I noticed the Barbershop that I'd seen but had not yet entered. There were two barbers busily cutting customers' hair. I waved and to my great surprise, they waved back. I must be recognized by everybody as a familiar face in town, I thought as I walked on past the Barbershop. I passed a shoe store and a drug store, but before I realized how far down the street I'd walked, I had come to the corner. As I reached the middle of the street I was brought back to reality with a cacophony of truck horns blasting away at me and at each other. Like staccato Morse Code in truck horn. It was like a ritual tattoo of bugles calling a Roman legion to formation over a distance of miles.

In addition to the horns blasting loudly away, the drivers were shaking their fists out their busted out windows and shouting invectives at each other. The Spanish words for parentage, (El Arbol Genealogico), combined with the word for sheep, (La Oveja), were used again and again. I didn't laugh because I didn't want to be the target of their combined anger. I wondered when the rifles were going to be taken off the racks and the firing would start. At the first sign of that happening, I was headed for the nearest building. It sounded like World War Three was about to start here.

One very skinny fellow of undetermined age, in a battered yellow Ford that looked like it was about to collapse any second, was yelling at another guy in an old Dodge truck. They had stopped dead center of the street, oblivious to the other trucks and yellers.

"Hector, you'd sure be ashamed to write to your mother in Mexico and tell her that you got your skinny ass kicked by someone as small as me wouldn't you?" said the barely visible driver of the Ford.

The reply that came from the old Dodge was just as jeering. "I would barely start to worry even if you could reach it, buster."

"How'd you like it if I put a dozen more "boolet" holes into your miserable looking truck amigo?" came the retort from Hector in the Ford.

"Go ahead, but I don't think that three dozen of your "boolets" will make it look any better."

Both drivers laughed then, gave each other the one finger salute and sped away, smoke pouring out of the muffler less tailpipes. This was 'cruising' at its best.

It was sort of a controlled demolition derby all in good fun. As I watched them from the curb through the gray haze of exhaust smoke, all of the sudden the street was empty. The trucks were gone, who knows where? They just went up side streets, into parking places, around corners and were gone.

"Make no imprint", immediately came to mind.

I quickly crossed the rest of the street and walked up the other side toward Mrs. Hernando's shop. I quickly passed the bakery with all the wonderful fresh bread smells.

I'll get some on the way back to my room, I assured myself. As I looked in the window of the Indian Arts shop, I saw that Mrs. Hernando had gotten some more dolls and other carved things since I'd been there. I decided not to go into the shop right then but maybe come back a little later. I didn't want to wear out my welcome there and I needed to put my thoughts in order before talking to Mrs. Hernando again.

I walked back to the bakery and got some rolls, butter, jam, a bottle of milk, and a paper. I made a beeline for my room to read about the latest developments the Sheriff had allowed to be published about Carmelita. I didn't expect much. I wasn't disappointed.

There wasn't much that hadn't already been said as far as the public having any additional information about her.

I took a warm roll, covered it with butter, poured a large glass of milk and started to read the article. I got one bite and one small drink down when I got the indications of another headache coming on. Maybe it was another Clan Father message. I had three more to get before I could start to make serious headway in solving this crime.

As before, as the headache intensified, I pressed three fingers on each side into my temples to relieve some of the ache. As I did, the color in my mind changed to a very pale gray color. From within the color I heard the voice say.

"*Tawamiciya,*
I am the tenth Clan Father.
I am named Hides in Plain Sight.
I am the spiritual leader of the Snake Clan.
I will teach you how to not be obvious when searching for the truth.
When you are ready and need me, I shall return to help you."

As happened before for multiple messages, this voice faded and the color changed from gray to a brilliant golden color. I heard the second voice say,

> *"Tawamiciya,*
> *I am the eleventh Clan Father.*
> *I am named Great Fighter.*
> *I am the spiritual leader of the Badger Clan.*
> *I will teach you how to fight for what is right about the truth.*
> *When you are ready and need me, I shall return to help you."*

This second Clan Father's voice had barely faded when the third headache started. "Wow," I thought. "These last three must be important messages." I had never gotten three at once before. The gold color faded and changed into the brightest purple I had ever seen. It looked similar to one of the sunsets I'd witnessed out on the mesa. I heard the third voice say,

> *"Tawamiciya,*
> *I am the twelfth Clan Father.*
> *I am named Gives Praise.*
> *I am the spiritual leader of the Coyote Clan.*
> *I will teach you how to be Grateful for the Truth.*
> *When you are ready and need me, I shall return to help you."*

As the last voice faded away, I reached for the notebook to record the three messages. I had now received all twelve messages. What must I do now? Would all of them somehow lead me on the right path to get evidence on the Sheriff and Ms. Charles? Or would they lead to something obvious that had been overlooked? I had no idea but I suddenly realized that with these last three Clan Fathers messages, I was near the end of what they could tell me and how they could help me. Who could I now rely on for my protection against the bad Gods or even the evil people out there?

What new path did Hides in Plain Sight mean for me to follow? Should I follow his advice and be creative in my investigation and the preparation of the traps I needed to set to seal the fate of the criminals, whoever they may turn out to be?

The messages from Great Fighter had me in a quandary. Just how would I need to fight for whatever I found if I knew it was the right thing to do? The last one, from Gives Praise, had me totally stumped. I knew I'd be grateful for whatever help I got, from whatever source, if it would bring this problem to a successful conclusion. That conclusion would only be limited by the length of jail time imposed by a judge.

FORTY-EIGHT

I thought about my precarious situation here; possibly being in the sights of a rifle belonging to whoever didn't want me to ask questions about Carmelita. The fact that I had become aware of the hostility of someone, or two someones, through their phone conversation about me in addition to all the strange things that had started to happen since I arrived here, made me very uneasy about my safety.

I needed to confide in someone or maybe several someone's to help me sift through the information, both solid clues, and the many suppositions, I had concerning my suspects. Who could I trust? Who might be a spy for the suspects? Could one or more of my choices have been in on the disappearance of Carmelita and I just haven't found them out yet? I would have to be extremely careful who I talked to and confided in about my suspicions.

As I approached Mrs. Hernando's shop it hit me squarely between my eyes. OF COURSE! The one person that I could trust was Mrs. Hernando! I need some answers and I need them now, I thought out loud. I had some clues but nothing that I could take to Martin. I certainly could not go to the Sheriff.

I entered the store and Mrs. Hernando greeted me, asking if I needed anything specific because she was busy filling out some orders for new merchandise.

"No." I replied. "I just need the solitude of the store, I won't bother you. I know where everything is now."

She nodded her head to that and bent over her forms again.

I walked slowly around, not looking closely at anything and not touching anything either, which was what I always did when I came in here. I was totally fascinated with all the Kachinas and paintings and everything in this museum.

I walked through the store looking at all the articles that fascinated me. When I had waited as long as I could, I walked over to her desk and stood waiting for her to look up.

"Yes, Andy, what can I help you find?"

"Nothing right now Mrs. Hernando, but I do have something on my mind I'd like to talk with you about, if I may interrupt you for a few minutes." She looked up at me with a question in her eyes, "Sure, Andy, pull up that chair and tell me what's on your mind."

"Well Mrs. Hernando, it's like this. I have been in town now for several days now. I never told you the whole story of what prompted me to come here in the first place did I?"

As she nodded her head I continued.

"I was sent up here by my Editor. I have already told you that I am a reporter for the *Albuquerque Journal*. I was sent up here to look into the disappearance of a young girl named Carmelita, who, as you know, lived here. I have been looking around, asking questions, doing some snooping, as part of my research, and have come up with some information relating to her disappearance, and the people I think might be involved. Two of those people have very important positions here in town, so I can't accuse them without a lot of undeniable proof. I have a lot of suspicions and suppositions and guesses. That's why I need your advice on how to go forward with this."

"Andy, I also want to know about Carmelita's disappearance, and if I can be of any help to you and to whatever officials you choose to talk to, I will be happy to do so," Mrs. Hernando replied quickly.

"Thanks a lot, Mrs. Hernando, I hoped I could depend on you. Here is what I have so far I've talked with the Sheriff, Ms. Charles, the lawyer, the two deputies, Rosalie, at the restaurant, and the motor court owner. I've collected the hotel's registers from Santa Fe for the days Carmelita was there on business for Ms. Charles. I also have the work logs for when the Sheriff was also in Santa Fe supposedly on business, which turned out to be the very same days Carmelita was there. I have a tape recording of my conversation with Ms. Charles about her work relationship with Carmelita."

I took a deep breath as the words continued to pour out of my mouth. "My suspicions are that the Sheriff and Carmelita were having an affair and took advantage of the time when they could both be in Santa Fe.

This greatly pissed off Ms. Charles, because she and the Sheriff had had a long standing romantic relationship, but only here in town. The work logs for the Sheriff and the hotel registers for Carmelita show that they were both in Santa Fe on the same two weekends, the weekends that Carmelita was there on business for Ms. Charles. I asked Ms. Charles if she had ever sent Carmelita out of town on business and she flatly denied it. Why did she lie about that?"

"Another interesting thing happened that is unexplained. I was with Rosalie and we were talking about each other having had ESP experiences. As we were about to start an experiment to see if we could read each other's thoughts, something totally unexpected happened to me. Right at the instant we were going to try our ESP powers on each other I heard something in my mind. I raised my hand for Rosalie to wait a minute, and she remained quiet as she realized that something I hadn't planned on was happening to me. I closed both eyes and concentrated. I knew that it wasn't a Clan Father's message coming in because there was not color and no headache, but didn't know what to make of it."

"I asked myself if this ESP business could really work or was it just my overactive imagination working on over-load? After all, I had already heard the Sheriff talking to someone while I was miles away from him out on the mesa. It's really strange this ESP. There's no telling who you might be in touch with and can hear in your mind. Have I become more attuned to things like this since I had those experiences out on the mesa? I don't know, but as I sat there with Rosalie, I heard the voices of two people talking to each other and what they were saying was not directed to me, but they were talking about me."

"There were definitely two people talking, a man and a woman. I actually heard them say to each other, 'You have to get rid of him. Look at him over there. There's no telling what he's telling that girl about us. He's been snooping around and I think he's suspicious of the two of us about what happened,' the female voice said. The male voice came back at her saying, 'Yes, I think you may be right. I talked with my deputies and now I know they are suspicious of me too. My rifle wasn't in the rack where I always keep it and they wanted to know why.'"

"The reporter at the Bullsnort paper is doing some snooping, too. Seems like this guy from Albuquerque has stirred up a hornet's nest and we are in the middle of it. I may just have to take him out on the desert and get rid of him like we did the girl.'"

"The male voice sounded very much like the Sheriff and the female one sounded very much like Ms. Charles, the lawyer," I concluded. "It's certainly not solid proof, but I can't ignore it."

"Then, later, my car was riddled with bullets while it was parked outside my room at the motor court. I think that was a threat to encourage me to stop what I am doing and to get the hell out of town, before something very serious happens to me."

I could tell that Mrs. Hernando heard the fear in my voice that I felt when I thought about that event.

"I caught Ms. Charles in another lie when I was in her office," I continued.

"I had asked her if she had ever talked to anybody about Carmelita's disappearance and she flatly denied talking to anybody about her. That could possibly be a provable lie because when I talked to the Sheriff about Carmelita, he told me that both he and Ms. Charles were concerned and had talked about her being missing. Of course, if the Sheriff is involved in Carmelita's disappearance or is protecting someone, he will certainly deny saying that," I lamented.

"Ms. Charles didn't know it but before I went into her office I turned on my small pocket recorder so I wouldn't miss anything, or misinterpret what she had said. When you listen to it you'll be able to hear and judge her reaction to both questions. I think you'll agree that she sounds very nervous and agitated."

I pulled the small recorder out of my pocket and hit the Play switch. The voice we heard was that of Ms. Charles answering my questions.

Mrs. Hernando listened intently to the voice and nodded at the inflections and tonal differences and made notes on a pad about those changes, especially the hostility, which she underlined for emphasis.

"What do you think I should do, Mrs. Hernando?"

Mrs. Hernando took a deep breath and made her suggestions. "Well Andy, if it was me and I had what you have, I would certainly let the authorities know of it. Now you obviously can't go to the Sheriff or his deputies. I also think that going to the F.B.I. would be overstepping the bounds by a lot. How about giving all that you have to Martin, the Tribal Policeman? Surely he can help, or point you in the right direction to get the help you need to settle this."

"Thanks Mrs. Hernando, that was my plan too but I wanted your advice before putting it into action. I am relieved that you see things the same way I do. I'll go see Martin in the morning."

Feeling better after finding someone to share my dilemma with, I stood up a bit straighter and assured her, "I have to go now, but you know I'll be back to keep you updated on the current standings of things. Goodnight, Mrs. Hernando."

FORTY-NINE

Due to circumstances beyond my control, I wouldn't get to see Martin for two more days and I needed to talk to Mrs. Hernando again.

I wanted to go to her shop and lose myself in the Indian things I had come to love and appreciate. I needed the basso of the drum to clear away what cobwebs of doubt that lingered in my brain. I walked down the street toward her place, ignoring the smells of the bakery, the furniture and all the people on the street.

As I entered the store, I found her filling orders. She greeted me and asked if I needed anything specific.

"No," I replied, "Right now, I just need the solitude of the store and all that's in it for a little while, I won't bother you. I know where everything is now. I'll bring you up to date later."

I walked around the cases until I came to my drum. I hadn't paid for it yet because I didn't have room for it in the small room, but Mrs. Hernando knew not to sell it because I had already claimed it.

As I approached it, I noticed that it gave off a slight glow that I hadn't seen before. I turned to see if Mrs. Hernando had seen it but she was face down looking at her forms. I got up next to it and there was a definite golden glow emanating from the hide drumhead. I put both palms on it to feel any warmth that might be coming from it. It was slightly warm to the touch.

That's sure odd, I thought. It had never glowed or felt warm all the other times I touched it or hit it and made the sound I'd come so to need.

As I held my hands on the hide, nothing happened for more than a minute. Then very slowly the hide of the drumhead seemed to fade into nothingness. My hands did not move any further into the drum but there was open space below them now. In this space I perceived an image in my mind. More visions-more messages from some unknown source or am I just hallucinating? What the hell is happening to me and my drum? I asked myself as my concern grew. I was concerned, but not afraid. Yet!

What I saw was almost the same image I had imagined before, the one with warriors dancing to a thumping, rhythmic drumbeat around a fire that was throwing sparks into the air. This image didn't have a fire, but there were warriors covered with brightly colored animal headdresses, wearing white deer hide leggings and beaded moccasins. The sound of a drumbeat was faint in the background; my attention was drawn to the warriors themselves, not the dancing.

There were *twelve* of them. Somehow I knew there would be exactly that number. I had seen a Yei Bechai rug on one of my earlier visits that had twelve dancers on it. As I looked closer at the dancing figures, I noticed that these men were dressed with very large masks of the totem of their respective clans. They were stunning. The intensity of this vision outshone anything that I could have ever imagined. These figures must be the Clan Fathers.

I found many questions running through my mind. What do they want? Why are they coming to me here in the Shop? Why all together like this? Am I going to get a collective message from them in addition to the singular ones I have already received? I didn't know what to expect. I stood in awe of them.

One interesting thing struck me as I looked at them. I couldn't make out their faces at all! Their headdresses totally covered their heads and where their faces were not covered by the masks there was only dark space. Their arms were covered with buckskin that extended into sharp angles as they danced. In each hand they held either an eagle feather fan or what looked like a hatchet. They were apparitions!

I didn't like the looks of this but I wasn't afraid. I was anxious to see them and hear what they meant to tell me. I wondered if Mrs. Hernando had seen the glow or heard the drumbeats. I was facing away from her and didn't want to break my connection with the drumhead, fearful that if I did the Clan Fathers would fade away.

As I stood looking into the hollowed out drum I saw a figure separate itself from the others and take a few steps away from the line. I heard a voice speaking. He was wearing a Turtle Clan headdress. The jaws of an extremely large turtle covered most of his face while his back was covered by a large shell. His new message was:

"If you are to learn the truth you will have to be very keen on unraveling the mysteries of the clues you now have, and those you will receive."

As soon as he finished speaking he stepped back and another Clan Father stepped forward. This one wore the Wolf Clan headdress. The entire head of a large grey wolf covered most of his head and face. His new message was:

"Honor the truth and discard the false ideas that are given to you. Develop your own new ideas."

I knew then that all twelve of the Clan Fathers were going to give me a new message. I was right. Each in turn came forward from their position in the dancing line, and spoke to me.

The Buffalo Clan Father, wearing the complete head of a large black buffalo, told me:

"You must accept the truth no matter what you find."

The Deer Clan Father, wearing a gigantic set of antlers, said:

"You must see the truth. You have the vision, use it wisely."

The Horse Clan Father, wearing the head and the entire hide of a black spotted Appaloosa, said:

"You must be able to use all the truth that you carry wisely."

The Turkey Clan Father, with his very large tail fan of feathers spread out, said:

"You must not be timid in telling the story. It will be your reward."

The Owl Clan Father, whose entire head was covered with the hide of a great horned owl, said:

"Finding the truth will be complicated but you must do it."

The Bear Clan Father, amazingly walked out wearing the entire hide of a grizzly bear, said:

"It is your duty to see the doers of evil brought to justice. It will not end until this happens."

The Eagle Clan Father, with the head of the eagle on his head, the wings on his arms, and the talons on a pendant around his neck, said:

"You must live the truth always."

The Snake Clan Father, who had the entire skin of a rattlesnake around his shoulders, took his turn and said:

"You must always use the truths set forth in our messages."

The Badger Clan Father, whose badger hide went down his back to the big bushy tail at his waist, said:

"You will lead the way to new paths and plans."

The Coyote Clan Father, who wore the skin of a large tan coyote, said:

"You must set time aside every day to give praise to the messengers."

He also paid me the biggest compliment that I had ever received when he said that I had become the Clan Fathers' vision for doing the right thing now.

After each had given his message to me he had returned to the dancing line facing the bonfire. When Gives Praise moved back into the line they all turned back to face me and I heard a collective message that said:

"You no longer need us to help you. Goodbye."

As I heard this final message from all twelve Clan Fathers, I felt an all-encompassing cold chill start between my ears and travel down my back the full length of my body and leave me through my feet. It was amazing; I had never had such a feeling in my life. I felt a great inner calm come over me as both the warmth and light faded back into the drumhead that was, once again, stretched tightly over the drum.

My hands rested once again on the skin of the drumhead and I was once again in Mrs. Hernando's shop. I looked around to see if she was still there and if she had heard the messages.

She was still at the front counter looking at the papers she was working on. Should I tell her what had just happened to me right here in her shop? Somehow I knew that she would understand.

Before I did that though, I wrote all twelve new messages in my notebook. Then I hit the drum a solid whack because I felt that it would send the sound back to the dimension where the Clan Fathers had gone. It was my only way of giving them the recognition signal that I had received, understood, and would do my best to act on all of their messages. I would be eternally grateful for their help.

Somehow I knew deep inside that wherever they were they heard my drumbeat of thanks.

At the sound of the thumping and rhythmic drumbeat, Mrs. Hernando looked up at me and smiled and said, "I know exactly how you feel when you hit that drum, Andy. And this time, I know why you feel so good." She didn't elaborate but I knew then that she understood that the Clan Fathers had chosen me for their purpose and that I was destined to carry out their advice regardless of any help from her, Martin, or the Shaman.

I did tell her, though, that I had not contacted Martin to relay my suspicions to him. She understood that too and nodded her agreement.

I wondered if I would be strong enough to face the struggle.

FIFTY

I was in my room reviewing the facts and suspicions that I had collected so far, when the phone rang. I was very surprised to hear the voice on the other end of the line. It was Rosalie. My hopes for us soared until she told me why she had called.

"Andy, I would like for you to come over to my house this morning. There is someone I would like for you to meet. This is someone who can be of great help to you in solving the mystery of Carmelita's disappearance."

I was disappointed that this wasn't a personal call and I tried not to let my feelings show in my voice and replied, "Sure, Rosalie, I need all the help I can get with that! I will be right over."

When I arrived at her front door a few minutes later, she calmly showed me into her living room and offered me a cup of coffee. I sat down and thought about how I could explain my inconsiderate behavior that had made her so angry, when she began explaining how she had been in contact with Jose Montoya and felt that I should meet him.

"He is a photographer and has some pictures you should see." She was interrupted by the ringing of the front doorbell. Rosalie got up from the couch to go answer it.

As she walked away, I thought, Jose? Maybe he is her newest love interest.

I heard muffled voices as she was talking to someone out in the hallway. Both of them came into the front room. I hadn't equated the name she'd mentioned to the newspaper reporter. Jose Montoya was the reporter I had talked to by phone on two separate occasions. I hadn't gotten too much help from him but did let him know why I was in town. We shook hands in greeting.

Jose spoke first. "Andy, Rosalie and I have been working closely on the problem of Carmelita's disappearance. I guess she's told you all about me and that I have something that may help you. I've been watching the Sheriff's comings and goings for several years now because I have my own suspicions about several unexplained things that have happened here in town, the most recent being Carmelita's disappearance."

"Yes, Rosalie has told me that you are a photographer and that what you have will probably be very helpful in putting the people involved in Carmelita's disappearance behind bars. What is it?"

I hoped I hadn't offended him by being so anxious, but I wanted whatever it took to put those two away for a long time, and I hoped he had it.

"Did you know it was me who sent Dan the original article on Carmelita?" He continued, "Yes, I sent it to Dan because I suspected foul play. I also knew that if the Sheriff was somehow involved and that if no outside effort was made, then nothing would ever be done to find her. With what I had then, I couldn't very well make an accusation like that to the State Police. I would have been a laughing stock and whatever I would have produced that proved their guilt would not have been taken seriously. I'm glad to help you in any way I can."

Now things were beginning to make sense as I replied, "You sent the article? I'm glad you did, Jose. My Editor, Dan, sent me up here based on his knowledge of your performance a long time ago. You must have made a very favorable impression on him. I'm glad you did too."

I could see he was proud of the connection with Dan and appreciative of the approval I'd just passed along to him.

"What I have is right here," Jose said as he handed me a very thick manila envelope. "I have another set hidden away in a safe place in case something happens to these, or to me."

What I saw when I lifted the top of the envelope was about twenty black and white pictures. When I finished spreading them out in front of me on the coffee table, I knew immediately that these were going to help a great deal in connecting the Sheriff and the lawyer in a conspiracy designed to cover up the attempted murder of the young man out on the desert.

The images I saw before me were Sheriff Johnson and Robin Charles on horseback heading out of town towards the desert. Another shot showed them riding down a slope into an arroyo with the sun in the sky and a shadow of a tree as an indicator of the time. Original, to say the least, the tree served as a sundial!

The next photo showed the Sheriff pointing his finger at something after they had dismounted. Ms. Charles was beside him looking in the direction he was pointing. A close-up of the sand in the arroyo showed two sets of tracks that appeared to be footprints that went toward the far bank of the arroyo. Another photo showed them again on horseback riding away from the arroyo. The date and time was printed conveniently at the bottom of each picture. I was glad that Jose's camera incorporated the latest technology. This allowed me to put the photographs in the same order they had been taken.

The most damaging photo showed the Sheriff kneeling and aiming his scoped rifle at something. The background desert features were clear and could possibly be found again with Jose's help. Another 8x10 had the both of them standing beside someone's bullet riddled truck looking into the driver's window. The rifle was still in the Sheriff's hand. Another damaging picture was one that was focused on Ms. Charles holding a large handgun in her hands which was being aimed at something, or someone, inside the truck. Another in the exact time sequence was a clear view of them riding away from the truck.

An excellent close-up of the bullet riddled truck showed three large holes in the windshield surrounded by many smaller ones. A bloody close-up showed a man's body sprawled out over the front seat. One was a close-up of the three wounds he'd taken.

These are great, I thought. Who is the victim laying there? I had another thought but Jose interrupted me before I had a chance to say anything else.

"After Sheriff Johnson and Ms. Charles rode away, I drove over to the truck. I saw someone lying there on the front seat wounded and bleeding," Jose said. "I couldn't see immediately who it was so I opened the door and turned him over, face up. It was Pablito. I felt for a pulse and found a very weak one so I knew he was still alive. I couldn't very well leave him there to die so I dragged him out of his truck and carried him over to mine. I brought him back to the emergency room at the hospital. They saved him there."

Rosalie and I said in unison, "You are the one who brought him back?"

"Yes. I was standing on a bluff overlooking an arroyo trying to get some shots I could sell to a magazine. Through the high powered lens of my camera, I had seen the Sheriff point at something in the arroyo before he aimed his rifle and fired at least three shots. I saw the three large holes in the truck big enough to put my index finger all the way through. I also heard Ms. Charles fire several shots into the truck. I put the three things together and after the Sheriff and Ms. Charles rode away, I drove my truck down to see what had happened and found Pablito, shot."

Jose continued, "Nobody goes out on the desert to shoot a large caliber rifle for fun. The bullets are too expensive to waste like that. It is always used for a specific purpose. To get a deer, or kill a coyote that is killing your sheep, or something important, not just to shoot cans or prairie dogs. Twenty twos are plenty powerful enough for that purpose. I think I can find the place where I took the pictures in the arroyo. Maybe that's where we will find Carmelita. We need some law enforcement officers to go with us though. But who can we trust?"

"I can call Martin Begay at the Tribal Police station and ask him," I said decisively. "We will have to show him these pictures, though. You will also have to testify as to what you saw when you took these pictures, Jose. Will you do that to put these two killers away?"

"I sure will testify against them, Andy. I loved Carmelita and I want to see them brought to justice for killing her. I gave up hoping that she was still alive weeks ago. If I can find the exact spot where I took these pictures of them in the arroyo I'll bet that's where we will find her body."

FIFTY-ONE

When I had arrived in town, almost a month ago, I had talked briefly to the Sheriff's deputies about Carmelita's disappearance. They were non-committal about what they had learned from their investigation so far, which, to me, meant that they had done absolutely nothing. Why? Was it under the direction of the Sheriff? Again, why? That was not normal. I understood the reluctance of the deputies to give me any specifics. Reporters don't readily give up their confidential sources either. Even with the threat of contempt of court charges police don't want to compromise their investigation and lose a conviction. I understood that, being a news reporter.

I made arrangements to talk to both deputies again that afternoon, when the Sheriff was out of the office. What I didn't understand, and couldn't rationalize, was the fact that they were still stonewalling me and were reluctant to use my help. They didn't seem interested in investigating my ideas on where to look for Carmelita or any of the other suspicions that I had.

They did show some interest in the phone conversation between the lawyer and an unknown person, but I refrained from telling them it was something I'd overheard while having trances and visions. I didn't really lie to them but just wanted to prod them into looking in other directions; namely at their Sheriff and the lawyer. They were definitely hesitant to even lean in that direction. Maybe this was out of fear of reprisals, or maybe even losing their jobs, if the Sheriff found out what they were doing. I didn't know for sure what their reasoning was, but I had given them the benefit of the doubt and didn't press them too hard.

I showed Deputy Jim Janson the original clipping that had prompted Dan to send me to Bullsnort to look into the problem and possibly write some newspaper articles and help in any way I could to help solve the case. Both he and Deputy Miguel Membrano said that they were doing all they were permitted to do to find the girl.

I didn't tell them about the pictures Jose had shown me, nor did I tell them that I very strongly suspected that the Sheriff and Ms. Charles had killed Carmelita. I'd let them find that out for themselves. If her disappearance was a four way action then getting these two deputies on my trail wouldn't be very smart. I had to test them somehow to try and get them to admit or refute the evidence I had to give them. I was in no way assured that they had not taken an active part in the killing.

They were law abiding police officers from all outward appearances, but I knew that cops are experts at doing things that CYA.

I also didn't tell them that Martin Begay of the Tribal police was coming to see me later to discuss the case. I suspected that Martin would also call either the State Police or the F.B.I., or both, in to help if he saw the value of it all.

Miguel was doubly concerned because Carmelita's disappearance cast a shadow of suspicion on him due to their on-off again relationship. He assured me that she seemed OK when he had seen her two nights before she disappeared. They had gone to the Cantina and had had a short argument in the car when he took her home. They both had agreed that it was best not to see each other for a while.

"She called it a cooling off period. She wanted it to be at least a month. I had no choice but to agree. That was the last time we dated. I saw her briefly the next day as she was going into work at the lawyer's office. I didn't see her after that. I definitely did not go anywhere near her house, follow her, or in any way cause her disappearance," Miguel stated matter-of-factly in response to my questioning.

I believed him. He had no reason to lie to me in front of Jim.

"As far as she and I were concerned," Jim said in his own defense, "We dated a few years ago and nothing came of it. I saw her around town all the time, going into work, and occasionally at the Cantina, but we never hit it off very well back then. I am, and have been dating another woman for a couple of years and hope to marry her, when she says yes. I hope this will be next month, after she graduates from college in Santa Fe. I don't know if we'll live here, Santa Fe, or just where. It will depend entirely on where we can both get jobs. I want to find Carmelita as much as Miguel, or you do. What else can we do to help find her, and, if she's dead, her killer?"

Their talking to me so openly made me change my mind about their reluctance to help me.

"I have been working with Martin at the Tribal Police and maybe he has some leads that he hasn't told me about. Maybe you should contact him and possibly coordinate efforts. I don't know what the Sheriff has done, or is doing now, but, as I have explained, I suspect that he had a hand in whatever happened to Carmelita and also in Pablito's shooting."

They definitely didn't like the sound of that. I detected a look of both a sour taste in their mouths and some angry feelings toward the Sheriff for putting them in this compromising position. They felt they had to cover for him when they didn't know the full truth of the story. They appeared to want to be more helpful if they could.

While we were in the Sheriff's office I noticed that there was a rifle case with maybe twelve rifles in it. I noticed that there was one empty slot in the case. I had to ask about the missing one. "Which rifle in the case over there is the Sheriff's favorite one? The one he practices on the range with? Maybe the one he uses to hunt with?"

They both turned and looked into the case and after a minute or two turned back to me. I saw a look of concern on both their faces.

"His special rifle, a Marlin 30-30 lever action, is missing from the rack," Jim said. "It's his own private weapon but he keeps it here so he can use it on the range and clean it whenever we have a slow time. He loves that weapon. He's gotten his deer with it every year for the last seven years. It has an excellent scope and he zeroes it in at least once a year at the range. He is an excellent shot. He can hit the silver end of a pop can at one hundred yards dead center. I think he used to be a Marine sniper in Vietnam."

"What the Sheriff aims at, he hits. He has some trophies in his house that he won while still in the Marines. Maybe a dozen or so that I've seen. He brags a little about his shooting skills," Miguel volunteered this interesting piece of information. He had just fitted another piece of the jigsaw puzzle into place. The overall picture was taking shape very nicely in my mind.

I didn't tell them that I already knew about this rifle or that I had taken five slugs from my car that may have come from it. I asked them about their work schedule whenever the Sheriff is out of town on either business or vacation-specifically, about maybe a couple of weeks before Carmelita's disappearance.

They went to a grey six drawer filing cabinet and pulled out a ledger book. They scanned it and came back with the information that the Sheriff had logged out four times in the month before Carmelita disappeared. The assigned destination for each trip was, in fact, Santa Fe. I had hit the nail right on the head-dead center!

Another piece of the puzzle just slid into place.

I had them write the dates down for me. I wanted to compare them to the dates Rosalie had said that Carmelita had told her that she was in Santa Fe for the lawyer's business. I didn't reveal this incriminating piece of information to either Deputy just yet. I didn't want it passed on to the Sheriff.

I needed to do some more research first. I did have a gut feeling though, that I could rely on them and that they had told me the truth about their relationships with Carmelita. I just hoped I could convince them that the Sheriff and the lawyer were the guilty ones here. After I had showed all the pictures to Martin, along with all the rest of the evidence I'd collected, then, maybe I'd confide in the two deputies. It sure wouldn't hurt the case, or the trial, to have two more honest cops on our side.

I thanked the deputies for their help and said that if anything else came up, either for or against my ideas, I'd definitely be in touch with them. My only hope now was that they would keep our conversation confidential and not reveal anything to the Sheriff.

I know from what I'd heard through my ESP experience the other night at the Cave that the Sheriff must already know that I was looking closely at his activities when he was out of town. When he found out that I was hoping to get his own deputies to take a good close look at his activities, he might just increase his efforts do what he and the lawyer were plotting to do. Get rid of me. I left the office and walked back down the street toward the Cave.

It was time for lunch.

FIFTY-TWO

I had spoken to Rosalie only once, other than briefly at the Cave, since she had literally kicked me physically out of her life and then, we had been so intent on talking to Jose and looking his pictures that there had been no personal interaction. I talked to her briefly again when I went for breakfast at the Cave, but still hadn't been able to explain the entire situation of my trip to the mesa to her. I needed to clear the air and tell her all of it. I needed to talk to her to explain more about what happened to me, so I had asked her for another date and she had very reluctantly said yes.

I picked her up at her house and we went to the Cave for dinner, the Drive In for a Hop-along Cassidy "shoot'em up" movie, and then to the Cantina for some drinks and dancing.

The mariachi music was great as we swayed together to the soft rhythm of La Paloma. The men's voices were soft and blended nicely on the "Ro-co-co-co-coo" and the high notes.

I hummed the music in her ear while she sang the words in mine. The deep bass Spanish guitars were enough to put me to sleep. I could feel her against me swaying to the rhythm. I said softly in her ear that I was having a great time. My hopes for our relationship began to soar again. She nodded in time with the music that she was having a good time, too. When the song was over we went back to the booth.

We ordered some beer and as we sat there drinking she hit me with a totally unexpected bombshell out of the blue. "Have you ever had an ESP experience, Andy/"

"What?" I asked her, incredulous at the question.

"I asked if you had ever had an Extra Sensory Perception experience. You know, it's like you can hear things like voices or music that someone says, or plays away from you, or make things move without touching them. Or, weirder you being somewhere, watching something, and nobody can see you. That's called an out of body experience. Being transported somewhere while people can see you, is a very different experience. I think that's called *telekinesis*. Have you had anything like that happen to you before?"

"Now that you mention it, yes, I have had several of what you might call ESP experiences. Once when I was in the Army before I came back to the University of New Mexico to go to school, I had a definite feeling that I was somewhere else other than in Germany where I was stationed. I felt like I was floating high over a few people and that I was watching them but they couldn't see me, nor could I hear them. The whole thing lasted maybe ten minutes and I woke up."

"Then, another time, I was just sitting on my bunk in the barracks and I started tasting gingerbread and when I wrote home about it, my mom said that on that night she had made a gingerbread cake. Nothing ever came of it. Why do you ask?"

I had a premonition of what she was going to say and the goose bumps started again. I hadn't told her about the Sand God message, the twelve Clan Fathers messages, or the very vivid Penitente dream, so I knew if she mentioned them, I would be astonished.

"I think I had an experience one night after you had gone away for those four days," she began. "I didn't know where you were so I was very worried that you may have gone back to Albuquerque without telling me. I was at home after dark watching T.V. and it was very quiet. While I sat there I thought I heard you say something. I knew you weren't in the house with me so I concentrated on what you were saying-or what I thought you were saying. I heard you say that you would return to town and for me to wait for you. You assured me that you would be back and wanted to see me again. I even think I heard you say that you loved me. Do you love me, Andy?"

Without waiting for my answer she continued,

"The whole thing lasted just a few minutes-less time than it takes for me to tell you about it. Did you do something like that out there on the mesa one night?"

I didn't know whether I should be relieved or more cautious. "Yes, I did. I was very much alone out there and I was watching the stars and wondered if I thought real hard about what I wanted to tell you if somehow you would get my message. Apparently my little experiment worked. I hope it didn't scare you too much." I thought I had skirted the question of love very nicely.

"You didn't answer the question, Andy. Do you love me?" She looked at me with those big brown doe sized eyes and my resistance turned to mush. She had me cold. I couldn't very well lie to her.

"Yes, Rosalie, I think I do love you. Is the feeling mutual?"

I waited with great anticipation for her answer which would either make, or break, what we had going for us.

"Yes, I think I do love you, Andy. And no, I wasn't scared too much. I had never before had something like that happen to me. I wonder if we could do it again if we both knew we were going to try?"

"I don't know. Are you willing to try?" I was skeptical about it working but what the heck, if she enjoyed trying it, why not, I had nothing to lose. "Yes, I'd like to see if I can send a message to you right now."

I laughed to myself and thought of something, and all my energy of the thought was directed toward Rosalie. Very quickly I noticed that the expression on her smiling face had changed.

"That's not funny, Andy," she said as her puckered up face looked like she was about to break out in tears. Had she heard me or was she just putting me on? I didn't know what I'd done to hurt her feelings and said so. The last thing I wanted to do was hurt her feeling by saying something wrong. I was definitely falling hard for this beautiful girl.

"Gotcha!" she laughed at me. Her scowl disappeared and a big toothy grin filled her beautiful face.

I was embarrassed that she might have actually heard my thought a minute ago. It was about me getting her into a bed somewhere but I didn't say anything more about it. I thought it again and she saw me looking at her. I must have scowled at wondering what had set her off because before I could ask or say anything I heard.

"Gotcha again, Andy," she said, laughing harder this second time.

Damn, I thought, she can be so much fun, why is she picking on me like this? Can she actually read my mind or hear my thoughts? If she can then I'm in real trouble. I probably shouldn't have thought about getting in her pants, but I did and she apparently heard it. I'm in deep trouble with her now, I thought. I'll just have to wait and try again, if there is an again, sometime.

It took both of us several minutes to stop laughing at each other. I had to take a long drink of beer to settle my choking.

She laughed, but not as hard as before. She asked me if I wanted to dance. I had to decline saying, "I just want to talk right now." I couldn't very well tell her that I would be too embarrassed to stand up with the big bulge in my pants showing.

The next thing I knew I was being shaken lightly around my shoulders by Rosalie. I heard her call my name several times before I dared open my eyes. I had no idea what had happened while I was thinking about her. I was lying flat on the floor and a towel of some kind was under my head.

"Andy, what happened to you?" I heard Rosalie ask me with a very worried look on her face,

"You were talking and then all of a sudden you seemed to pass out and wound up on the floor. You were muttering something about someone shooting someone. It sounded like you said, 'get rid of him and his snooping,' and 'He is suspicious of us,' and 'The deputies asked me about my rifle.' You also said something about like, 'What we did to the girl.' What does all that mean, Andy? Are you OK?"

I came to a little more as she asked me the questions. I sat up and rubbed the pain out of my eyes and tried to explain. I didn't want to get her involved more than necessary because my suspects might just do her in, like they were obviously planning to do to me.

"You know the ESP experiences we were talking about?" I said. "Well I just heard two people talking and I guess I just muttered what I was hearing them say. The two people were the Sheriff and Ms. Charles."

"I have been asking questions around town, to the deputies, and to everybody else I think might be able to help me. I didn't just show up in Bullsnort on my own, I was sent up here by my boss to investigate the disappearance of Carmelita."

I took a sip of the cold water that Rosalie gave me and continued. "I have some guesses and several solid clues that those two are the guilty ones in her disappearance and this ESP experience just reinforces those suspicions." I didn't tell her about the specific lies that Ms. Charles had told me when I talked to her.

I changed the subject back to us, apologized for my odd behavior and indicated that I wanted to have a fun night out with her, she nodded her agreement. We talked through the next song, while I regained my composure, and when the next song started we got up to dance. I was OK by then. This isn't working out like I planned, I thought to myself.

We danced and drank more beers till about midnight and then started for her house. As I parked in front I reached over, pulled her closer to me and kissed her. She responded. The night was a little cool and there were at least a billion stars that we could see out there in the desert sky. There was no sign of clouds or a rainstorm anywhere. Great! I could concentrate on what I had in mind instead of worrying about a lightening blast.

"Would you like to come inside, Andy?" she said with a smile.

"Sure, Rosalie, but what about your parents, will they be awake?" I asked.

"No Andy, my parents were killed in a multi-car and truck smash up out on the interstate three years ago. I live alone here now. I grew up in this house. There's nobody to bother us once we get inside. Come on, let's go inside."

It was a typical adobe house like all the rest in town. I followed her closely as she opened the gate in the wall and walked up to her very bright pink door, a very feminine color. She unlocked it and we both went in.

FIFTY-THREE

I hadn't noticed much about Rosalie's living room when I had been there to talk to Jose. Now I looked around and greatly enjoyed what I saw. Her living room was absolutely beautiful with the Spanish style painted furniture and Indian artifacts around the walls. There were paintings of Indians of all descriptions and pottery all over the place.

There were remnants of a small fire in the fireplace. "Go put a couple of logs on the fire while I go get us something to eat from the kitchen," said Rosalie, as she turned to leave the room. "I'll be right back."

I put three logs on the fire and they started to warm the room as soon as they caught. The warmth radiating from the burning logs felt great. I sat on the couch and waited for Rosalie to get whatever it was she went for. She came back carrying a big tray loaded with sandwiches and tequila drinks. She had even included several slices of lime.

She went to an alcove and as she turned back to me some very good music filled the room. "Want to dance some more, Rosalie?" I asked.

"That would be nice," she said with a smile. "But first, let's eat a bite. I'm a little hungry."

After about fifteen minutes, a few sandwiches, and one or two tequila drinks we started to dance. I didn't know, nor care, what the music was but it was danceable music and it was good feeling having her pressed against me. We went through three songs before we decided to sit down and relax.

"Let's get comfortable on the couch, Andy," she whispered as she led me toward the couch, removing her shoes and her blouse. Her black silk bra was very enticing. I did the same with my shoes and shirt. If she had actually read my mind there in the Cantina she was acting it out now, here at home. She bent over to grab her pants to pull them off as they fell down around her ankles. I liked the round shape of her buttocks under the sheerness of her black panties. When I saw her pants come off I didn't hesitate to unbuckle my belt and let mine fall to the floor, too. I would have loved to undress her slowly while caressing her bare body, but she obviously had other, more urgent plans for us. How could I object? I wasn't stupid. Rosalie seemed to know exactly what I wanted.

We made good use of the blanket that hung over the back of the leather couch as we snuggled up spoon style, me behind her. The leather was cold on our bare skin and feeling her against me warmed us both. She snuggled her hips into me and I put my hand on her hip. I began to caress her leg and her nice round bottom that felt so warm under the edge of her silky black panties. I moved my hand up her side till I came to her breast, around which my big hand cupped nicely. I wanted the silky material to be gone but I liked what I was holding. We looked into the dancing fire as I kissed the back of her neck and shoulder many times. All the while my hands were touching and caressing some very sensitive places as she shuddered a little at my touch. I sure liked what I was touching.

We didn't talk about anything in particular, just generalizations about where each of us wanted to be ten or fifteen years from now. I asked her if she ever wanted to get married and she was very non-committal in her answer. I thought that I was ready to get married but I didn't know if I should take the chance of asking her to marry me after that kind of response. I didn't want her to say no a second time. I thought I loved her but maybe she didn't love me enough yet to make such a serious commitment.

As we held each other close, I unsnapped her bra hooks and when she lifted her arm it fell to the floor. I turned her toward me and kissed her full on the lips with her tongue moving slowly over mine. The sensations that started with the touch of our tongues were making me more aroused.

I could feel her quiver a little in response. I kissed her neck a few times and nibbled on her ear lobe and then very slowly moved down to the V between her breasts, kissing her all the way. I cupped one beautiful breast in my hand, pulled it to me and kissed the deep brown nipple that was already standing rigid. I started sucking lightly on it, which caused it to get even bigger and harder. I rubbed my tongue in a circle around it and sucked some more. I was holding her other breast, as I slowly rubbed the nipple between my fingers. I heard her moan as and felt her nipples get even more rigid. A certain part of my anatomy was getting a lot more rigid too. I stopped caressing her breasts and as I let my hand slide slowly down her stomach to the top of her panties, she moaned again.

I slid my fingers under the elastic around her leg and moved to the soft fuzzy spot there. I pushed my fingers further and felt her get warm and moist. I wanted to take her panties off right then and make love to her but I was enjoying what I was doing. Rosalie must have been enjoying it too because she raised her hips and pressed herself into my hand. I was touching her where only a lover should touch a woman. My fingers entered her and I pushed them in and out slowly as I leaned over her and again started sucking one of her nipples.

I could feel her excitement as she moved on my hand and pushed her breast into my mouth. We could certainly make beautiful love, I thought, as she moaned again. She reached down and felt for me. I felt her slim fingers searching for me and I tingled all over when she found what she was searching for and tightened her fingers around me.

"Let's go somewhere a little more comfortable than this couch," she said and started to get up.

I followed her eagerly. Her bedroom was very feminine. Just as I imagined it would be. The bed was large enough to hold four people comfortably. I didn't hesitate to get totally naked after watching her remove her panties. The large fluffy down comforters felt soft and warm as we crawled under them.

Our lovemaking that first time was as frantic as we expected it would be as we satisfied our lust for each other. We continued to caress each other's vital spots and that excited us all the more. We were frantic for each other. Her thighs were warm and her body was willing as our bodies joined and we, all too soon, enjoyed the culminating pleasures of our love making.

Afterwards, with both of us still trembling, I held her close to me as we stretched out on the bed. We lay spoon style with me behind her. The feel of her warm backside against me was very pleasurable to say the least. Neither of us fell asleep. We just rested a little while.

I soon let my hand fall in place in front of her and caressed each nipple as we lay there. I could feel myself become aroused again as I felt her move against me. This time was much more pleasurable for both of us. Gone was the frantic rush we had felt the first time and we explored each other's body very slowly. At each touch we quivered with the enjoyment it gave each of us. The enjoyment of that lovemaking was the ultimate in pleasure.

I couldn't help but think back to what I had said when I had first met her the day I arrived in town. It had certainly come true. Mathematics was a true omen that day. One did go into one very nicely.

"I would love you like this always if you would marry me Rosalie," I whispered in her ear while holding her close to me.

She didn't respond, just acted as though she hadn't heard me.

After we had totally satisfied each other a third wonderful time, I whispered, "This is how it should be."

She still didn't answer me and so we just lay there and held each other closely. We were becoming more comfortable with each other, but the fact that she was not willing to make a long term commitment to our relationship disturbed me.

I must have dozed a little after the excitement and was brought back to reality when I heard water running, and the click of a cabinet or something snapping shut. I reached across the bed to where Rosalie had been and felt only a slight indentation, the space was empty. It must be her in the bathroom, I thought.

When I felt her crawl back under the covers, still naked, I reached over, pulled her to me and asked where she had been. "I was in the bathroom taking my morning after pill," she said very matter-of-factly. "I don't plan on getting pregnant any time soon."

I chuckled to myself and as I thought, "I probably shouldn't be saying this." I whispered playfully, "Sort of like an after diddle mint huh?"

"Yeah, you could say that." Her response had no laughter in it so I thought it best not to continue talking along that line.

We were lying face to face on the bed holding and kissing each other, when my thoughts returned to our experiences in the Cantina. I had to know. I had to ask her what had happened.

"What happened back there in the Cantina when I thought you had read my thoughts? Did you actually hear anything I was thinking?"

"What I had wasn't what you'd call a genuine E.S.P. experience, Andy. No, I didn't hear or read your thoughts. I've thought for a long time now about what it would be like to go to bed with you. I could tell that you were aroused while we were dancing. So I just guessed, and when you blushed after the first 'Gotcha,' I knew what you were thinking. The second one was just to play along and make the joke better. Turned out OK didn't it?"

"You bet it did. I do love you, Rosalie. I asked you if you would marry me earlièr and you haven't answered me yet, why not?"

"I'm just not ready to make a decision like that. I think I'm in love with you, too, Andy, but I don't think I know you well enough yet to get married. Let's talk about it later, not right now, OK?"

She quickly changed the subject. "I've been thinking about what you told me after you woke up there in the Cantina, Andy. I think you need to go to the Sheriff if you have any information about Carmelita being killed."

"No, Rosalie I can't go to the Sheriff or his deputies right now because the voices I heard back in the Cantina belonged to him and Ms. Charles. In that conversation, they pretty much admitted killing Carmelita and now they want to kill me. I can't prove it and no law officer would believe the story. I have to get more proof first.

After I told her of my suspicions and why I thought Ms. Charles and the Sheriff were involved this murder and cover-up, Rosalie became agitated and then very frightened for my safety, and then angry again.

"I know someone who might be able to give you some more proof of their guilt, Andy. Wait a minute till I make a phone call." She crawled naked off the bed, walked to the phone and dialed a number. It was a long time before she started to talk.

"Jose, Rosalie here. I'm fine. Are you busy right now? Good. Look Jose, I have a good friend who needs your help again. Yes, you know him and what we have been talking about. Can you come over here tonight and bring all the stuff you showed me? I think that is what we'll need. OK good. I'll see you in about fifteen minutes. Love You."

Hanging up the phone, she turned to me with a glint in her eyes and laughter in her voice and said, "We can't be naked when he gets here, Andy, just wouldn't look good."

"You're right. Best not be naked but I have to tell you, Rosalie, you are beautiful and all that I expected. But we don't have time to get tangled up again so let's just get dressed."

"He'll be here in about fifteen minutes," Rosalie said as she hurriedly pulled her black silk panties back on. Jose just lives around the corner but he has to go and get his stuff. He never keeps it at his house in case someone breaks in and tries to steal it."

"You know from the pictures he gave you of Pablito, that Jose is an excellent photographer as well as a reporter for the *Bullsnort Press*," she said as she fastened her bra around her breasts. "He takes pictures of the desert which is his specialty. He must have a thousand pictures of all kinds of sunsets, animals, and different scenes out there. He has tried to explain to me what those long lenses do, but photography isn't something I'm interested in. Jose calls them telephoto lenses. You saw the pictures he took on the day Pablito was shot. They had to have been taken from a long distance away. He said that with the long lenses he can take a perfect shot of a bird from almost a mile away. That way he doesn't have to get too close and scare them away. He's good at what he does, too. He also develops his own film and makes all sizes of prints."

FIFTY-FOUR

After we had finished dressing we went to the kitchen where Rosalie made a big pitcher of iced tea, sliced some lemons, and made a bunch of sandwiches out of ham salad with pickles.

I snatched one of the first ones and gulped it down saying, "I have to rebuild my strength for later tonight, and maybe you should too Rosalie," I said, hoping that maybe I'd be staying another night and we'd continue our adventures in bed.

"I'm fine, Andy. You look a little weak in the knees are ya huh?" she said, with that now familiar lilting laugh, mocking me.

"You'll have to admit Rosalie, that we took very good care not to have another 'tits' problem didn't we?" I joked.

She laughed a little giggle and said, as she went to open the door for Jose, "Yes you took care of the tits all right."

Jose came into the living room carrying a brief case.

"Wait a minute," I said, as he took a seat on the couch. "Before we get started, I will call Martin to see if he is free now and can come over here."

I dialed the number at the Tribal Police Station and Martin answered. I told him briefly that we had some pictures he should see without mentioning who had taken them or how we had gotten them. I added that I was at Rosalie's house with the photographer who had taken them. I told Martin that I thought he should come over.

Martin begged off saying that he'd see us later after he and his deputies had completed their investigations of some new leads in the disappearance of Carmelita. Then we could meet to put all the information together and build our case. I relayed what Martin had said to Rosalie and Jose.

I found several of the second set of pictures that Jose had brought very interesting. They would definitely add some very useful evidence to our case against the Sheriff and his lawyer friend. The pictures were the Sheriff and the Lady lawyer in a hotel dining room together on three different dates. The others were of the Sheriff and Carmelita at the same hotel on two different dates.

They would be very damaging to whatever story they conspired up between them to cover themselves. As with the first set, the date was imprinted on the bottom of the pictures I was looking at.

Then, I just about went into shock when I saw a picture of a young woman lying in the sand and another picture of what looked like a dead rattlesnake lying near a horse. There were several other pictures showing the walls of an arroyo. Other pictures showed the same woman lying under an overhang with a water bottle beside her. There were a couple close-up shots that showed a bleeding wound on her face and her eyes were closed.

Rosalie cried out, "My God, that's Carmelita!"

With a grave look on his face Jose said, "Yes, that is Carmelita. These are pictures that I developed today from a roll of film in a camera Pablito has been using. When Pablito regained consciousness, I went to see him at the hospital. He told me where to find the camera he had borrowed from me. It was under the front seat of his truck."

We didn't like having to wait several days for Martin to come to us, but it would be worth the wait because we would also get a chance to see some results of what Martin and his deputies had been doing for Carmelita. Since we really couldn't do anything without some advice from law enforcement, we said our goodbyes and Jose went home with the promise that when Martin came he would again bring the packets of pictures to show him. I thanked him and closed the door.

As I turned again to face Rosalie, I could see her moving down the hallway to the bedroom. There was a trail of clothes that led the way for me to follow. As if I needed a trail to follow. I said to her as I made my way down the hall, "I've got a calculus problem that I want to work on."

"What the hell you talking about, Andy? I'm not interested in Calculus right now." Somehow, I knew she wouldn't understand so I dropped the subject.

FIFTY-FIVE

I was lying on my bed the next day reading the remaining five chapters in the book about the Clan Fathers that I'd neglected since returning from the mesa. The phone jangled and ruined my train of thought.

"Andy, Martin Begay here. I have some good news for you. I contacted the Shaman and he has finished listening to your tapes. After completing his interpretation of your visions and experiences out on the mesa, he has decided to hold the formal naming ceremony for you. Can you come to the reservation and be at my office at six o'clock in the morning on Friday?"

My anxiety level was on the rise again as I said, "Sure Martin, as long as I have your assurances that since you are asking me to arrive there before dawn, I won't be taken out some remote place and left to starve again."

I had to laugh when I recalled the situation. I heard Martin laugh too.

"I promise Andy. I won't take you anywhere other than to a dark, deep hole in the ground. We'll go to the Kiva where the Shaman will announce your Indian name after an appropriate ceremony of honor for you. How does that sound?"

After only the slightest hesitation I replied, "Well, Martin, that's what I went out there for. I can't very well refuse now can I? I'll be there at dawn on Friday. What do I need to bring and should I be dressed in anything special?"

"Just bring yourself and dress as you always do. Nothing special, like a suit, is required. I have also called Mrs. Hernando and invited her. Do you have anybody you want to invite? If you do, that's acceptable."

Since Rosalie and I were back on track again, I thought of her. "I might want to bring Rosalie. Is that OK?"

I wanted to include her since she was now involved deeply in the investigation with me. I also needed her self-assurance to help me get through whatever the Shaman had planned for me. (I did say before that I am a devout coward, didn't I?)

"I don't think that will be any kind of problem, Andy, glad to have her here," he said with understanding. "That's all I have for now, see you on Friday, Andy, and congratulations!"

"Thanks Martin. I certainly could not have survived the Cleansing

Ceremony and everything that happened to me out on the Mesa without you and Mrs. Hernando. I'll be there."

I was a little more than apprehensive about the Naming ceremony. After what had happened to me so far, I wouldn't be surprised to see all twelve Clan Fathers in attendance. I doubted if the Sand God would resurrect himself to be there but that wouldn't have surprised me either.

On the appointed day we were all at the Tribal Police Station on time. I found both Martin and Mrs. Hernando waiting. They said friendly hellos to Rosalie, who had been a bit uneasy about coming with me. I had brought my carved cedar pole because it had played such a significant role in my visions and besides, I felt like I needed it. Sort of like a security blanket. I was a little wary about what was about to happen to me, but I wasn't nearly as scared as I was when I was left alone out on the mesa.

Both Martin and Mrs. Hernando tried to assure me that nothing quite so unnerving would happen and that all would go smoothly with the ceremony. I wasn't quite as assured as they would have me be.

Mrs. Hernando looked proudly at me and asked, "Well, Andy, this is the day you've been looking forward to. How do you feel?"

After taking a deep breath I replied. "I am all right, I guess. I've been waiting for two weeks now for the Shaman to make his decision. I'm nervous because I don't know what's going to happen next. Can you tell me Martin, what's going to happen? You went through this ceremony as a boy."

"Yes I did Andy. I remember my Naming Ceremony vividly. First of all, I need to tell you that the women will not be allowed into the Kiva. That is a sacred place reserved only for men. The women can wait here in one of the houses for us. One of the Shaman's assistants will come and take you to one of his rooms to get you prepared. You must remove your shirt and shoes. They will give you moccasins to wear. You will be blindfolded and led down the ladder into the Kiva."

Martin continued his detailed explanation to make sure I understood exactly what would happen.

"There will be a fire going in the center of the large ceremonial room. All the men of the tribe will have already thrown sweet grass and sage into this fire as their part of the ceremony. It will smell great but the air will be filled with smoke, and it will be hard to breathe at first. All the men from the tribe will be there, including me. Someone will be beating a drum and someone will play Indian music on a flute.

Some of the men around the drum will be chanting songs of honor for you. You will hear it but not see any of it."

I must have had a very puzzled look on my face because Martin immediately said, "You must remain blindfolded during the entire ceremony."

"There are sacred paintings all over the walls and since you are an Anglo, you cannot be permitted to see them until you receive your Indian name. The Shaman will utter some ritual chants as he throws purifying sweet grass and other, great smelling things on you for purification. There will be a pipe lit and passed around for all to smoke.

When you feel it being placed in your hands, take one small drag on it and pass it on. Blow the smoke skyward so it will go out the smoke hole at the top of the Kiva. The Shaman will use some natural colors to paint your name sign on your chest and arms. This sign will be one that came from one or more of your visions. Then the Shaman will tell all present what your new name will be. The blindfold will then be removed."

"The removal of the blindfold symbolizes a teenager's rebirth into the tribe as a man," Martin continued. "For you it will symbolize your acceptance by all the men as a member of the tribe. From this day forward you will not be called Andy by any of the tribe members. They will call you only by your new Indian name." "But that is not all. The last part of this ceremony will be dance called the Naming Dance which will be in Your Honor. All the men of the tribe will participate, including you. You do not have to say anything afterwards unless you want to, but if you do, I will be there to translate for you. Understood?"

"Yes, I understand, Martin. I just want it over with now."

The solemnity of the situation was beginning to sink in and I was in awe. Right at that instant an Indian man outfitted in full ceremonial dress, approached the four of us and motioned for Martin and me to come with him. "It's starting," I thought to myself. "Here we go!"

The events happened exactly as Martin said they would.

I was given new handmade leather moccasins to wear and my cowboy shirt was removed. My chest and arms were washed with something that had a very sweet odor. I was then blindfolded and led, by someone on either side who had taken hold of my arms. I was apparently taken towards the Kiva. When we reached the Kiva my hands were placed on the two poles of the ladder that I assumed went deep into the hole. I stumbled a little then regained my balance and footing on the top rung. I almost fell down the ladder a couple more times, but I made it down the ten log rungs and was relieved when I felt solid ground under my feet again. The smoke inside the Kiva was heavy and thick, but sweet, just as Martin had told me it would be. I choked a few times but my breathing soon adjusted to the heaviness and was all right after that.

The drums, the chanting, and the flute music were soft and very soothing and mystical somehow. The flute music seemed to be just offset tones with no discernible rhythm at first but after listening for a few minutes I could hum along with it. The music was mesmerizing me. I felt someone use what felt like a cloth woven from grass, or something just as rough, to rub something on my chest. I wondered what was happening.

This was probably the cleansing sage brushes. I didn't think the signs were being painted on me just yet. After this I was gently nudged into a sitting position against what must have been the outer wall of the Kiva. I felt the earthen walls shake a little as the drumming became louder. I could feel the radiant heat from the fire.

I could hear the other men as they began dancing around the fire. I recalled the vision I had seen in Mrs. Hernando's shop of the large bonfire and the Indian warriors dancing to the thumping drum beats. The music and the dancing must have gone on for ten minutes or more as I sat there, unable to see anything that was going on.

Suddenly the music, as well as all the other activity and sounds, stopped. The Kiva became deathly quiet. Something was happening but, of course, I couldn't see a thing. Suddenly a gravelly voice started to speak in a language I couldn't understand.

The Shaman was performing the Naming Ceremony, giving me my new Indian name and making me part of the tribe. I heard it but I couldn't understand any of it, let alone, pronounce any of the words. I felt something very sharp and wet, touch my chest and move slowly in some kind of pattern there. I assumed that the name sign was being painted on me now. My chest swelled proudly at that thought. I didn't think I could repeat any of the ritual if my life depended on it.

When I have a chance to, I'll ask Martin to translate what the Shaman is saying for me, I thought to myself.

Just as I finished that thought the blindfold was taken from my eyes. At first I could see nothing but the light that came through the hole in the roof and from the glistening fire. As my eyes adjusted to the darkness, I looked around the Kiva. There must have been forty or fifty men inside with me. I noticed that there were sand paintings on the walls and all sorts of things like feathers, knives, and bows and arrows as decoration. The place was beautiful, to say the least.

As I sat there the Shaman took a flaming ember from the fire and lit the tobacco in the prepared ceremonial pipe. He puffed three times and then passed the pipe to me. I remembered what Martin had said, puffed once, blew the smoke upward and passed it on to the Indian next to me. As I watched the pipe go around the Kiva I noticed that each person touched the ceremonial pipe to their lips but not all smoked from it. I would have to ask Martin about that later. It made its way back to the Shaman who then placed it on a little deer-antler rack in front of him.

As the honored guest I didn't know what to do so I just watched the dancers start up again along with the drum, chanting, and flute music. The Shaman motioned for me to come to his side and I followed him round and round inside the Kiva. I tried to shuffle the way I had seen the Indians do it. I hoped I didn't embarrass myself.

The whole ceremony lasted about an hour and a half by my best estimate. Then the Shaman said a few more words and motioned for all to follow him up the ladder and back outside. Going up was a whole lot easier than coming down without wearing the blindfold.

Mrs. Hernando and Rosalie, and all the women and the children of the tribe who weren't allowed into the Kiva, were waiting for the ceremony to end as the men emerged into daylight. I guessed they were getting hungry for the feast that awaited them. They had arranged the feast in my honor. My stomach growled a little at that thought. The main dish turned out to be primarily mutton stew, but there were fried breads and other goodies which tasted great.

When the feast was finished, Martin motioned that it was time to leave.

I asked if I could say thank you to the Shaman for what he had done.

Martin assured me that he'd translate whatever it was I wanted to say. I told the Shaman that it was an honor for me to be allowed to have this Naming Ceremony and become a part of this tribe. I promised that I would not dishonor the privilege in any way. I asked the Shaman if it were acceptable for me to have the images on my arms and chest made permanent with tattoos. If there were no objections, I would have it done as soon as I got back to Albuquerque.

After Martin had relayed the messages to the Shaman, he turned back to me and said the Shaman had no objections to a tattoo of the sign. On the way back to town I asked Martin what the signs meant and what my new tribal name meant.

I looked at the signs the Shaman had painted on my arms. They looked a lot like the arrows I had made but they were different somehow.

I had no idea what they symbolized. I couldn't see the signs on my chest very well, but Martin said he'd explain later about what they were and what they meant.

When we arrived back at the Tribal Police station, Martin told me that the arrow signs meant shooting at nothing which was a sign for peace and that I was now to be a peacemaker for the tribe. The message from the Sand God was interpreted to mean that I was an arbiter of disagreements and that any tribe member could come to me to ask for my help in settling a dispute with another tribal member. The messages from the Clan Fathers were interpreted as an indicator of my ability to see things that others could not even envision. I would be consulted for advice by the Tribal Police when a particularly complex event needed some outside interpretation.

The animal carvings on the pole meant that I was an animal relative and a lover and keeper of all animals. That didn't mean that I was a healer, but a keeper of relics and tokens, especially important fetishes that brought people luck of some kind. The relics and tokens wouldn't be given to me to actually keep but when a need occurred for something to be done that included animals, I was to be consulted for advice.

The Shaman did not tell Martin what all of the other symbols meant that I had carved on the pole, but the Indian's head was described as a religious fetish that was used during feast days. As a new member of the tribe, I now had a standing invitation to attend all feast days and ceremonies, if I was available. I was to bring the pole to these ceremonies.

I was very proud and deeply grateful that my visions could be used for the benefit of the tribe. I wanted nothing for myself by way of benefit or special treatment. I was happy to be the chosen conduit to help whoever needed it.

The two signs, painted and later tattooed, on my chest I cannot reproduce. Martin told me that under no circumstances should I reveal to anybody, except close friends and relations, what those signs look like. I reassured Martin that I would honor the Shaman's wishes and was glad I had gotten his approval to have a tattoo artist see them so

I could have both them and the arrow signs that had been painted on my arms made permanent.

Martin also told me what my tribal name meant.

My new name is "Wartegil Yawipa". In Lakota Sioux it means Kills and Comes Back. I couldn't figure out what the name had to do with my visions. Maybe that's why I'm not the Shaman. I would have come up with something like Carver of Images, or Sees No Horses, or something like that.

Martin pronounced my new name several times but when I tried to say it I always got my tongue tangled around the pronunciation. It just didn't come out like what he had said. I let it go at that. I was very proud to have it-my new Indian name.

FIFTY-SIX

After an uneventful trip back to town we all went to the Cantina to celebrate. The music was great and we danced and drank all night. Rosalie mentioned something while we were close together that I found intriguing. The town of Bullsnort was the county seat. That bit of information surprised me and I said," I can't believe it."

When I looked it up on the map the dot was so small and I thought it may have even disappeared.

She got very indignant at the slur on the town and pouted up like she was going to cry. I soothed her as best I could by making many apologies and swearing never to belittle the town again. I didn't want to turn off whatever feelings she had for me by not being respectful about the town she so loved.

"Gotcha! Don't you think that all of us here know how small Bullsnort is, without you reminding us of it?" She laughed at my discomfort and apologies.

"You have to stop doing that to me," I said in fake anger.

She came right back with, "Just you wait till tomorrow, you disbeliever."

"What's going to happen tomorrow that's so special?" I asked her.

"Well, Bullsnort is the county seat, and as such, there are judges sent up here from Santa Fe to hold special trials once a month. The public is invited. I really don't think they could keep us away anyway, because all of us go to see what is going on. It can be great fun, or very boring, depending on who is being tried and for what. The trials are held one after the other and last all day but you don't have to stay for all of them if it doesn't suit you. Do you want to go?"

"Sure I do. Wouldn't miss it for the world if that's what you want to do." I was a little overenthusiastic, maybe, but she bought it all and said she'd come get me at the Motel at 8 O'clock the next morning.

I slept well after all the beers, the good food and the rhythmic music of the Cantina's Mariachi band. I tried to say my new name several times but got it so tangled up I just gave myself a headache before falling asleep.

I heard a loud pounding on the door and my name being called. Is it dawn already? I thought as I struggled awake. I looked at the luminous face of my watch and it read 7:30.

Apparently, Rosalie was out there pounding and calling.

I slept in the raw and couldn't very well answer the door in that condition so I hollered, "Just a minute." I slipped on a terrycloth bathrobe and opened the door to bright sunshine.

Someone I assumed to be Rosalie made a very nice looking shadow as she stood there.

"Come on sleepyhead, time's a wasting. Let's get to the courthouse so we can get a good seat right up front," I heard a familiar voice say to me. I guessed that it was Rosalie because I couldn't see a thing but a shadow with the sun in my face.

"OK, give me a minute to get dressed," I said, as I ran my fingers over my eyes. As I turned to go back in I felt her slip in beside me and close the door.

"I'll just wait and watch if you don't mind." I heard her lilting laughter as I dropped the bathrobe, and pulled on my underwear and T-shirt, and finished dressing. I couldn't do much more than agree to her demands. I didn't look directly at her because I didn't want to show her how much I blushed at this situation. I don't normally have women watching me dress.

FIFTY-SEVEN

We arrived at the Bullsnort Courthouse, which was the only red brick building in town. It was behind the Sheriff's office away from the view from the street. That's why I hadn't seen it before. There were a few people already in line ahead of us. The line behind us grew rapidly as we waited for the doors to open. We were indeed lucky and were able to get front row seats. We immediately settled in and waited for whatever mysterious things were going to happen. I had to admit to myself that this certainly was a strange way to spend the day and one that I hadn't considered doing, ever. But then again, I wasn't from a small town where there was virtually no excitement other than what you made yourself. "Whatever floats your boat," I always said.

As we sat there talking we heard a voice speak out over the rumble of the people in the room.

"Hear Yee, Hear Yee, Hear Yee. The Municipal Court for the District of Santa Fe, Honcho Aquia County, is now in session, the Honorable J.D. Weir, presiding. All rise."

When everybody was on their feet the judge entered the courtroom from a rear door. He just kind of swooped into the room with his big black robe billowing behind him and sat down on the high bench. The door he entered from reminded me of those hidden doors that are shown in movies about old English castles. Everything that goes on behind them is very mysterious and spooky.

His Honor Weir took his seat on the bench and the dislocated voice said.

"Now be seated and come to order."

Everybody was looking at the small cluster of people seated at the tables in front of and directly below the judge.

There were three people at each table.

The Defendants and their lawyer sat at one table and the Plaintiffs, and their lawyer at the other. Clearly Rosalie recognized some of the people seated there, but didn't say anything about them.

"Mr. Clarke, are the Plaintiffs ready to proceed?" the judge asked, looking at the table to his right side.

"Yes, we are ready Your Honor," was the reply.

"Mrs. Bonilla, is the Defense ready to proceed?"

"Yes, the Defense is ready, Your Honor."

"Good then, let's proceed. Mr. Clarke, call your first witness."

"I call Mr. Herman Blunt to the stand."

A very athletic man about medium height, medium build, with light brown hair came out of the gallery and approached the witness box. He was obviously in pain and sort of limped his way to the stand. When he got there he moved with obviously great care, not to mention trepidation. I wondered why.

"Do you swear to tell the truth, the whole truth, and nothing but the truth, so help you God?" asked the Bailiff.

"I do," he responded.

"State your full name for the record."

"My name is Herman Blunt."

As Mr. Blunt said his name for the Bailiff, his attorney acted like he was spring loaded, jumping to his feet. He immediately began asking him questions.

"Mr. Blunt, what is your occupation?"

Mr. Blunts' reply surprised me as he said, "I am a professional golfer."

The attorney said to him, "Please state briefly why you have brought this suit here in County Court."

Mr. Blunt started his response.

"I make my living, and a very good one I might add, by playing in tournaments around the country. I see listings for tournaments in the pro golfer's magazines and I sign up for a lot them, as do a lot of my fellow pros. I saw the one that the City of Bullsnort had advertised and thought it would be a good one to sign up for, so I did. The prize money was a great inducement so I paid the $2,000 entry fee and received the brochure from the tournament officials that stated the rules of play."

"The rules were a little strange but, what the heck, it looked to be a fair tournament, or so I thought, so I didn't even consider backing out of it. I know now that I should have."

"What do you mean, now you know that you should have? Please explain that," the attorney led his witness.

"Well, this was no ordinary tournament. There were about forty pros signed up for it and the ones I have had contact with, said later that they will never come back up here to play. I brought suit to get back my entry fee and ask that the City of Bullsnort pay some of my doctor bills associated with this tournament along with some of my other expenses."

"What Doctor bills do you have? Why should the City of Bullsnort be responsible for paying doctor bills for injuries and expenses that you incurred playing in a golf tournament? I don't understand, and please explain what these other expenses are that you incurred and that you feel should be paid by the tournament sponsors."

"Well, as you can see, I am sunburned rather badly. I wasn't told a hat would be needed so I didn't wear one. I had to see the doctor three days running to have several very sharp needle-like spines removed from various places on my body. Rather painful removals, I might add. I still find it hard to sit for long periods of time."

The entire gallery erupted in laughter at his last remark.

"I had no idea how the needle-like spines were associated with the golf course, but apparently the townsfolk understood and they had a good laugh at my expense."

I also noticed that he turned a bright red in his current embarrassment.

The lawyer attempted to clear up the confusion, but just added insult to injury when he asked, "What kind of sharp needle-like things are you talking about, Mr. Blunt?"

"Cactus spines removed from my backside. About twenty of them," was the very low-keyed reply. "That was in addition to having both ankles twisted and sprained as I tried to walk over the rocks and holes."

"What other expenses did you incur that you feel should be paid by the City of Bullsnort?" the attorney continued.

"My very expensive leather golf bag that had my initials on was pretty much destroyed, Mr. Blunt declared. It was a Christmas present from my wife. She'll kill me if she finds out that it is damaged like it is. Also, a really good pair of my spiked golf shoes was destroyed out there. A couple of pairs of expensive pants were also destroyed as I played on this so-called golf course. These damages to personal property are not normally expected when one plays golf, Your Honor!" he said as he looked toward the judge.

"About how much would your total expenses be Mr. Blunt?" the attorney asked.

"I will accept nothing less than four thousand dollars in payment for what I've gone through. I don't imagine that the rest of the pros, who played in this tournament, will accept any less either."

For a minute I thought Mr. Blunt was going to cry right there on the stand.

The judge was busy taking notes and when the witness stopped talking, he asked him to clarify a point in his mind. "You say you have had twenty cactus spines removed from your backside? How did that happen? Weren't you on a golf course?"

"I sure was on what was supposed to be the Bullsnort golf course, Your Honor," said Mr. Blunt after taking a moment to regain his composure. "I got several of those spines when I tripped over a log on the fairway and more of them when I stepped into a hole and flipped onto a cactus. I got some spines in my arms when I tried to retrieve my ball from inside a cactus on the seventh hole. Yes, it was advertised as a golf course, Your Honor, but it is nothing like any golf course I had ever played on before. I will never play on anything like that again, I'll guarantee you that."

"I have no further questions for this witness, Your Honor," the attorney said as he addressed the judge.

"Are the rest of your witnesses all prepared to affirm what this witness has just presented to this court?"

"Well, yes they are basically going to say the same thing, Your Honor," the attorney declared.

"In that case, I don't see any reason why we have to hear the same story thirty nine more times. This witness is excused."

The judge turned to address the Defense. "Mrs.Bonilla, call your first witness if you please."

"Thank you, Your Honor." She responded. "I call Mr. Sevilla to the stand."

Everybody in the court room heard the same litany from the Bailiff that the other witness had gone through. Mrs. Bonilla addressed her witness.

"Mr. Sevilla, will you please state your involvement with this trial and the golf tournament for us?"

"I was the owner of the land that is now the town's golf course," stated Mr. Sevilla. "I helped arrange for the town to purchase the land, helped in the development of the course, and am now the manager of the Bullsnort Golf Course. I did the advertisement for the tournament, and I also managed, for the most part, the entire operation of the First Annual Bullsnort Golf Tournament. We plan to make this an annual event to attract some new businesses to our town," he added.

"Please tell us some of the specifics of the course and the tournament." Ms. Bonilla directed.

"Well, as advertised, the entry fee for all professional golfers who wanted to enter was set at $2,000. The prizes were dependent upon the entries.

One half of the entry fee paid by each player went into the prize money. A $40,000 prize was set for the golfer who came in with the best time and had the fewest strokes under the time limit after completing all eighteen holes. The other half of the prize money, another $40,000, was set for the golfer who returned under the time limit after all eighteen holes with the most usable clubs and the largest number of balls returned. The main stipulation was that the winners complete the course under the time limit. No one golfer could win both prizes. If nobody came in under the time limit, then, as stated clearly in the rules, the prize monies would not be awarded."

"Don't those requirements seem a little strange for a professional golf tournament?" the lawyer inquired.

"No, we don't think they are strange at all, but very reasonable, considering the course, he replied. As I said before, all of the rules are stated clearly in the pamphlet that was sent to each golfer who entered the tournament."

"Please tell the court about the course, if you will," the Defense attorney instructed.

"This course was the town's project," stated Mr. Sevilla. "It took us three years to design and build it. We wanted to build a unique and challenging golf course. The golf course project was actually started by the town of Bullsnort because of a rivalry with our neighboring towns. Katpan, a town just up the road about ten miles, heading North, and Hornbeak, about the same distance heading East have both started projects to bring business and money into their treasuries.

The Katpan officials decided to build a football stadium with lights for night games so all the surrounding high school teams can play there. They got building monies from the school system, the monies from selling the tickets, and all the concession money from the games. Hornbeak, to compete against Katpan, decided to build an Olympic sized swimming pool so that Olympic athletes can come there to practice at the high altitude. You know, like the place in Colorado for skiers to train. The town makes a lot of money from their new pool."

"Well, after they did those things, we had no choice but to build something to increase the money coming into our Bullsnort town coffers. We had a hard time choosing between a tennis complex, definitely smaller than Wimbledon, but adequate, a baseball diamond, a golf course, or a basketball court. We all know how golfing has exploded in popularity so that's why we chose to build a golf course. Bullsnort needed the cash that visitors would spend to attend a really good tournament so, after the course was ready, we advertised all over the United States and got forty pros to sign up. That gave us the $80,000 prize money," Mr. Sevilla stated proudly.

"Why do you think all the pros are trying to get their money back plus expenses?" Mrs. Bonilla asked.

"I think it's because they call themselves professionals but are actually 'molly- coddled' folks who can't play on anything other than the manicured courses you see on T.V. where, when they hit the ball from the tee it bounces and rolls for fifty yards before stopping. That won't happen on our course. I guess they didn't really bother to read the rules that are clearly stated in our pamphlet that was sent to each of them." Mr. Sevilla stated in a matter-of-fact tone.

"Please explain that, Mr. Sevilla."

"Well, you see, as I said before, our course was built to be a challenge," Mr. Sevilla continued. "It is raw desert out there where we built our course. There are gullies, snake holes, rodents of all kinds, birds of all descriptions, an occasional mountain lion and once, even a bear on that piece of land. We couldn't very well plow it all smooth and plant grass. Without adequate rain it would all revert back to desert in no time. We did move some of the larger boulders off the course, though. We lined the fairways with little red flags so none of the pros would get lost out there."

The golfers are well protected, too," Mr. Sevilla added. "We have our caddies ride along with them on ATV's with all the necessary supplies, and each caddie is even armed with a rifle just in case the golfers get into some kind of real trouble they can't get themselves out of. Like once, a golfer was attacked by a large eagle who thought the ball was one of its eggs. The caddie fired off a shot and scared it away. Same thing happened with a mountain lion one time. It came too close and the caddie scared it off with a shot. Nothing more serious than a couple of sprained ankles, busted clubs, and lost balls ever happened before. But, we make it clear in our pamphlet that this is a challenging golf course and the golfers should not expect to stroll down a lush grassy fairway between shots."

"As I said before," Mr. Sevilla continued. "Our brochures make the layout of the course and the rules about finishing within the required time very clear. The course is rugged and sometimes the golfers do get lost even with the flags that mark the course. The brochure we send to each golfer explains the reasons for the time limit, which in fact is four days."

At this point the judge leaned over the edge of the bench and asked the witness to clarify his statement. "Did you just say that the time limit was FOUR DAYS for the tournament?"

"Yes, I did Your Honor. The tournament is limited to four days and nights," Mr. Sevilla stated once again. "The other requirement is that the golfers bring back as many balls as possible and the one returning with the most balls and usable clubs wins the second prize. We give each golfer a box of thirty six balls to begin play. They are allowed to carry only two drivers and three sand wedges in their golf bag. Of course, they can carry an umbrella if they choose to, but nothing else."

"We don't want them loaded down with too much stuff that is unnecessary out there. The caddie has all they need for their survival. The fact that Mr.Blunt damaged a leather golf bag is really immaterial. Each golfer was told, both in the brochure we sent them, and verbally, what they should expect out on the course."

The judge leaned over the railing again like a hovering Devil ready to devour those at his feet, and asked another question. "Why should they be concerned for their survival? I don't understand that."

Mr. Sevilla replied without hesitation,

"The playing time limit is four days and they have to stay out there the whole time. They need food, water, a place to sleep, and a tent. We provide all of this. I've already explained about the wildlife that we cannot possibly control. We also cannot insure that the golfers are in good physical condition, although we do recommend that they have a physical examination before deciding to play in our tournament."

"We designed the course to be a challenge Your Honor. It really is. For example, the seventh, tenth and eighteenth holes are twenty three hundred yards long. The others are just a little shorter but none are less than fifteen hundred yards long. We left the terrain in as much of a natural state as possible. That means gullies, holes, boulders and wildlife. We didn't clear anything away except for the very large boulders. We did move them out of the direct path. We also caution the entrants that some cacti out there are heat sensitive. I believe they are called Jumping Chollas. If a heat source, like a hot and sweaty human golfer, gets within five feet of one of these cacti, the spines just seem to jump at the heat and are very painful to remove because they are like very fine needles."

As he said this, the gallery erupted in loud and continuous laughter.

Mr. Sevilla paused a few moments until the courtroom became quiet again and then continued.

"The reason a prize is awarded for the number of returned balls should be obvious. There are gopher and snake holes, gullies, arroyos, and all kinds of places that a ball can get into that make it very difficult to recover. One cactus out on twelve has about ten balls stuck in it right now. We have to go out there every once in a while with long tongs to get the balls out of it before the damned thing grows around them."

Again the gallery erupted in laughter and I have to admit, I joined right in.

After signaling once more for quiet in the courtroom, the judge reacted again.

"Did I hear you correctly, Sir? You said there are three holes out there that are twenty-three hundred yards long, and the rest are no shorter than fifteen hundred yards long?" He paused a minute as he did the math on a pad. "That makes the long ones each more than a mile and a half long! How long is the entire course?"

"Well, Your Honor," Mr. Sevilla replied with a shrug, "As best we can measure, the whole course is a little over twenty-three miles long. That's why we put a four day max time limit on the tournament. We have had only one person who completed the course under the time limit and he did it in three days and twelve hours. He also returned eighteen balls, two wedges and one driver. That is the standard to beat."

"How are the strokes verified?" the Judge asked.

"Well, the course has no putting greens for obvious reasons, so when a golfer gets within five feet of a "hole," which is a very large tin can painted red and tied to either a bush or a piñon tree, he is allowed to drop the ball into the can. The caddie tallies the strokes for each hole," Mr. Sevilla explained.

"As I mentioned already," Mr. Sevilla continued, "every golfer who enters the Bullsnort tournament must be in good physical condition. If a golfer has problems and can't walk the entire distance, there is one way that he can avoid doing that. He has the option of surrendering two balls to the caddie after teeing off and in return he gets a ride in the ATV to the ball. This is allowed for only one hole and only once for each golfer, on what we humorously call the long and short nine of the eighteen holes. So, he relinquishes four balls for the rides. It's all very fair."

I thought, "No wonder everyone in Bullsnort comes to these trials. This is the best comedy show I have seen in years."

The people in the gallery showed their enjoyment as the courtroom erupted in laughter again.

"The services provided for our golfers are like none provided anywhere else," Mr. Sevilla stated after the court room had quieted once more. "The caddie has all the supplies needed for overnight stays. He puts up the tent and cooks the meals over an open fire. Just like camping without all the mess. We acknowledge that most of the pros today don't know squat about camping in the wild, or even basic survival, so we can't in all good conscious, leave them out there alone. Out of forty who signed up, I would guess that only about five would make it back if we didn't provide the caddy and the ATV services."

"Did you award a prize for this tournament?" Mrs. Bonilla asked.

"Nobody came in under four days. Some had more balls to return than others, some had **fewer** strokes than others, and some even returned clubs undamaged, but in answer to the specifics; no, we did not award either prize. Nobody won either prize because nobody came in under the time limit."

"Do you think the town should be liable for the damages and injuries to the golfers?" continued Mrs. Bonilla.

"Well, Your Honor, no, I do not. We did all we could to insure that they understood what the course was like before teeing off," he answered. "We even offered them a tour of the course before they paid their entry fee, but nobody asked for one. They just assumed, I guess, nothing could be as challenging as our course and it would be an easy win. Well, it separated the pros from the golfers, and it seems to me that the pros lost."

The crowd behind us broke into a raucous laughter and applauded the defense witness for his super defense of the town against the outsiders.

It was now up to the judge to decide the merits of the case and make a decision. The judge finished writing whatever notes he felt necessary and told the waiting public that he needed some time to make his decision. The court was in recess until ten o'clock. The proceedings so far had taken less than an hour. We all rose as he left through the back door to his chambers.

I had been taking notes on the trial hoping that it would possibly make a good short story to submit to Dan and assure him that I wasn't wasting our time up here. I had all the specifics, I'd just have to flesh it out when I had time to think and write. It would make a humorous story, that I might get reprinted in Golf Digest.

I laughed out loud as I re-read my notes.

Nobody in their right mind would sign up for a tournament on a course that is twenty-three miles long. These guys must have been nuts!

Meanwhile, we had about an hour to wait for the decision, so Rosalie and I decided to return to the Cantina for some much needed breakfast. I hoped that the people, sitting behind us, hadn't heard my stomach growling. I also wondered if this golfing trial was the usual type of stuff that went on in the court room up here. If not, what could I expect later in the day with the remaining cases? If they were all as laughable as this one I'd have enough material for several articles and maybe even a few humorous short stories.

FIFTY-EIGHT

Rosalie and I walked and chatted about many things as we walked away from the courthouse. I asked her about the Sheriff and the lady lawyer, the deputies, and specifically about the old man at the Motel.

"He's a strange old bird isn't he?" She said with a nervous laugh. "I've talked to him a lot over the years and I find him very interesting, full of the history of the town, and a fascinating person to talk to. Do you know that he hybridizes roses and sells them to the florists in Santa Fe? He also writes mystery short stories and sells them to magazines. He told me once of story he wrote that basically was true but he had to change some of it so the cops wouldn't come and arrest him. Wow! You ever hear anything like a person committing multiple crimes, especially murder, and then have the guts to write a short story about them? Well, that's exactly what he told me he did. That was several years ago and I was younger then and didn't really believe him. It could all be true though."

I instantly became more alert when she told me about her experiences with the old Sheriff.

"What was the story about?"

"Why do you think he committed murder? And how was he able to get by with it? There might be a police record somewhere of the investigations of those crimes. Since he is free now, obviously, he was never arrested and convicted."

"I was pretty young when he told me about it." Rosalie replied, "But as I recall, he said he was teaching at the Agricultural School at UNM in Albuquerque. That was after he retired from the Sheriff's job here in Bullsnort. He had a couple of female students that he became sexually involved with there. That is unacceptable behavior for University staff and could have gotten him fired if the school officials had ever gotten wind of it. Well, at the same time, he was doing experiments with plants. Carnivorous plants, I think he called them. He told me the Latin names but I didn't pay much attention because I found it incredulous that he would be telling me about all of this. He had the plants locked up in one of his offices and only he had the key to it. Apparently, nobody else in the department had an inkling of what he was doing in there, or what he had done, even though there were some suspicions."

"From what he told me," continued Rosalie, "he didn't remember exactly what year it was, or maybe he just didn't want to get too specific, but three female students, who just happened to be enrolled in his classes, disappeared under very mysterious circumstances. He said that the police knew he had been seen in the Student Union with all three of them at different times, but never with all three at the same time. Being seen in the Student Union with a student might have raised some eyebrows, but most people would probably assume that it indicated some kind of student-professor conference, discussion about a project, or maybe grades. He told me that his behavior apparently didn't raise any red flags at the time, but when these students didn't show up for their classes the next semester the University Officials and their parents became alarmed and an investigation into their disappearance began."

"According to what Rosalie said the old Sheriff had told her, there was a lot of gossip about him seeing all three girls for the entire semester they were in his class. He was questioned about his relationship with these students and as a result, he guessed that the police thought that one, or all three of them, may have made demands on him that he was not willing to meet. Apparently, detectives accused him of having inappropriate relationships with all three girls and when he tried to break off his relationships with them and they said the bad words like blackmail, and loss of job, and paternity suits, and some other rather nasty things that he wasn't ready to listen to. All of this was conjecture of course, because, according to the old Sheriff, the police found no trace of any of them anywhere. There was nothing to link any of them to him, either in his apartment or his office."

"He had bragged to Rosalie that he, very succinctly, showed his off-limits plants to the detectives, along with everything else in his apartment and office. Since the police could find absolutely no evidence of a secret connection between him and any of the girls, he was not arrested or charged."

"He also said that the girls' bodies have never been found, nor have they ever come back home to their families. They are gone and nobody knows where."

"He told me that the police did find some things in his office that they were very interested in, though," Rosalie said. "He laughed when he described their interest in a white paper that he was going to submit to some botanical group explaining his experiments. He told me that one section of the paper was on his roses and the hybridization techniques he had developed but what interested them the most, was the section on carnivorous plants and his experiments with them. I have no idea where you might be able to locate that paper," she said, "but maybe you could find it at the UNM archives. Might make very interesting reading."

She had said that last bit so that I immediately made up my mind to try to locate the white paper. I decided that the library here might just have a copy of it. I would go there after the trial was over.

We had completely lost track of time, as I listened to that weird story, and had to run like rabbits to get back to the courthouse before the decision was given by the judge. We got there just in time to get the last two seats in the very last row.

"All rise. Court is now in session!" We heard the Bailiff exclaim just as we sat down.

In came His Honor Weir, again swooping like Batman, and took his place high on the bench above us all.

"I have reached my decision," Judge Weir began in a very somber sounding voice.

"The facts of this very peculiar case are clear, as is the law that governs my decision."

"Fact one, the rules of the tournament were explained explicitly and legally by the advertisements and the stipulations in the contracts that were signed by those who entered the Bullsnort golf tournament."

"Fact two, the professional golfers who signed the contracts did so willingly without the benefit of counsel and apparently without actually reading the brochure provided to them when they signed up."

"Fact three, the tourney committee had no hidden agendas to meet; everybody who signed up was treated equally and fairly."

"I also conclude," continued the Judge, "that the tournament officials took extensive precautions to insure the safety of the golfers. The town of Bullsnort should not be held responsible for the injuries suffered by the players because they chose to ignore warnings and refused to protect themselves by taking advantage of the services provided to insure their safety."

"The town is not, nor shall it ever be, compelled to award a cash prize when clearly the limits, set by contract, are not met.

Therefore, I find in favor of the defendants against the plaintiffs in this case. We stand adjourned. The next trial will commence at eleven O'clock sharp in this courtroom."

As soon as the Bailiff uttered his command, "All rise!" the wraith-like judge swirled his black robe like a gigantic bat, and quickly disappeared through the hidden door and was gone.

It took the audience about two minutes to fully digest what the judge had said. Then there was a grand and tumultuous roar of approval and applause. The town had won. The professionals had lost. There was to be no award money given.

Then the look on people's faces turned sober as reality began to sink in and thoughts turned to the down side of what that meant. There would never again be a professional golf tournament at the Bullsnort golf course, but what else could be expected. Most thought silently, "Well, what the hell, we won. We can build something else that will be a bigger attraction than the golf course ever could be."

Some even decided to try the course to see if it was really as tough as the pros said it was. Some people would try it but not nearly enough to keep it from reverting totally back to a desert habitat.

After the decision and the contemplation caused a great lethargy among the townsfolk, Rosalie and I retired to the Cantina for a couple of beers and an early lunch. All the time we sat there, she continued relating her impressions about the motel owner. We were sitting close enough so that I would catch a slight scent of her perfume and I could also feel the warmth of her as our thighs touched. I put my hand on her shoulder and pulled her to me and kissed her hoping that she would respond in kind. She did. We felt each other responding and as I started to think about making love to her again, I stopped abruptly and pulled away from her.

"Hey, what's wrong? I was enjoying that and I hoped that you were too," she said with a look of concern on her face like she thought she had done something to turn me off. She sure hadn't turned me off, quite the contrary. I was very ON right then with her. I had thought about making love to her and suddenly remembered the two "Gotchas" and I didn't want to go through that again. I made a lame excuse that I knew she would see through easily.

She proved me right once again. "What were you thinking just now as we were kissing, Andy? I definitely got a very short message then it stopped quickly. I think it had something to do..."

"OK, just stop reading my mind, will you?"

I must have turned a shade of pink because she picked up on it readily.

"Were you thinking about us in bed again, Andy? Did I 'Getcha' again?"

I thought to myself, "If she doesn't stop that I'll never dare be with her again because she can pick up on all my thoughts about her."

She looked at me with a sort of crying frown on her lips and said, "You will most certainly not stop seeing me, Andy, not if I have anything to say about it."

"There!" I thought, "She's done it again." I looked at her and said something super lame. "I'll love you till the middle of next week if you'll stop reading my thoughts. It's becoming a little embarrassing. I can't think anything sexy about you that don't come shining through. Some things are meant to be private, you know."

She just laughed at me in that beautiful prankish way and I sank back into a deep love for her. It must have been love since my knees seemed to turn to mush, I started to sweat, and my hands became clammy to the touch. I definitely didn't turn to clammy over very little, and this was new to me. I quickly steered the conversation back to the old man at the motel, or at least tried to.

"When did you say the disappearance of three girls in Albuquerque happened?" I asked.

Rosalie humored me and said, "He was never arrested or anything for the girls' disappearance. That must have been in the late seventies since it was about ten years or so after that he retired from his job as Sheriff, but before he came back up here and bought that Motel and set up shop."

"Luckily, there hasn't been anybody who disappeared from Bullsnort," she added, other than Carmelita, in all that time, that I can recall. I don't think he could be involved with her disappearance. He's much too old now for her to become involved with. No, there's something else going on here that probably doesn't even involve the old man. We'll just have to look at other possibilities to explain what happened to her."

I didn't tell Rosalie then what the Lawyer had told me about the three missing girls from Santa Fe, nor did I explain my suspicions about who might be responsible for what happened to Carmelita. I needed to do a lot more work before I confided in her. I would also have to get to the old man somehow and get whatever information I could relating to the crime in Albuquerque almost thirty years ago before I could hope to link him to the disappearance of anybody.

The sharp horns of the dilemma poked me again. How could I breach the subject about carnivorous plants to the old Sheriff? I knew absolutely nothing about them. Some research in the library was needed. That's just where I went after I left Rosalie at her door with a puzzled look on her face.

The librarian saw me coming and tried to leave her desk as I approached, but luckily I caught up to her before she got out of sight. For some strange reason she didn't seem too happy to see me. I wondered why. I asked her if the library had a botanical research section that had any materials on carnivorous plants.

The look she gave me would have withered any plant but she reluctantly said, "Yes, we do have a section like that," and led me into the stacks. She pointed at a very small section that I estimated held about forty or fifty books, magazines, and a few pamphlets and walked away leaving me there. I hoped that the old man's white paper would be included in this small collection, if indeed, he had actually told Rosalie the truth about writing it. If it wasn't here, I'd call Dan and have him check at the Central Library of Albuquerque or the archives of white papers at UNM.

The arcane titles in the section the Librarian showed me made absolutely no sense until I saw one entitled, "On Methods of Propagation and Hybridizing the Viktoria von Pruessen, Kron Princessin Rose and Selected Species of Carnivorous Plants" By Jose Fuentes, PhD.

I had hit the jackpot! Amazing! Doctor Jose Fuentes! That's his real name! I took the little pamphlet to a nearby desk, flipped on the light and opened the flyleaf. I should be so lucky, the table of contents listed exactly what I was looking for. Another jackpot was on the back flyleaf. A picture and a short biography of the author. It was the motor court owner, thirty years younger.

He hadn't said anything to me about being a PhD or about working with carnivorous plants. I knew he was extremely proud of his roses, but the first connection with carnivorous plants had come from the Lawyer's story about kids and what they saw when peeking through his fence.

I flipped through the pamphlet until I found the section called "Propagation and Maintenance of Carnivorous Plants." Three carnivorous varieties were listed for consideration: "Utricularia," "Sarraceniaceae D. Californica," and "Dionaea Muscipula". I immediately knew that some very diligent reading, and maybe some additional research might be in order.

I spent the next hour reading and making two copies of the pamphlet at the copying machine. I found one other reference book and diligently went through it getting more and more familiar with these plants. I had hit a gold mine of information. I had good evidence now, but evidence of what? I would have to work on that a little more.

As I made my way back to the Cantina for another cold beer, I thought about what I had learned. Was it significant that the motor court owner had written a paper over thirty years ago on these plants and then moved up here after leaving UNM? I knew then that somehow I had much more to learn before I could either prove or disprove my theory about the motel owner.

FIFTY-NINE

I was sitting in a booth at the Cantina looking at the menu, when I heard my name and "you have a phone call in the office," being announced.

I dropped the menu on the table and looked around wondering, "Who would call me here?" Well, I guessed maybe Martin is trying to find me and is just calling several places where I might be. I had not given this number to Dan. I didn't know if the motor court owner would actually pass along a message if anyone had tried to call me there. Knowing his nature, he probably would have said there was no such person registered and hung up. No, he wouldn't do anything like that. Would he? I thought.

I walked up to the bar and around the side to the office. The clerk handed me the telephone and I held it to my ear as I said,

"Hello, this is Andy Bling, how can I help you?" I didn't have a clue what or who would come from the other end of the line.

I hoped it wasn't an anonymous threat telling me to mind my own business or get the hell out of town by sundown. In the flash of a second I envisioned myself wearing a six-gun in a holster on each hip, walking down the center of the black street facing a roughneck from town, dressed the same way, coming at me with an evil sneer on his face.

There was no reply right away and my imagination started to soar. In my mind I pictured a scene like the old time Tom Mix movies at the Drive in. Or, God forbid, the mean looking characters I'd seen on the posters in the motor court office with "WANTED DEAD OR ALIVE" printed under their very ugly faces. Was I to be in a gunfight just because this turkey coming toward me wanted me to stop looking into things here in the town? In my mind, I looked closely at the face under the brim of the hat and saw that it was the Sheriff coming toward me. OOPS, I'm in big trouble now, I thought, Here I am, in a shootout with the Sheriff. I'm a dead man!

My thoughts were finally brought back to reality by the voice I heard on the other end of the line.

"Hello, Mr. Bling. Sorry to bother you at lunch," the male voice on the phone said. "You don't know me but my name is Pablito Dornock, and I need to talk to you about something very important. I can explain a little over the phone but I would rather speak to you face to face if that's all right with you."

My erratic breathing brought on by my imagined gunfight with the Sheriff began to slow to normal with this request just to talk. I had envisioned a threat that wasn't going to happen.

"Mr. Dornock, I would be happy to meet with you anywhere you say. What do you want to talk to me about? I don't believe we've met since I've been in town." Somehow, though, the name, Pablito sounded familiar. I knew I had heard it before.

"No, we haven't met yet," came the reply. I know who you are by hearing the gossip being spread all over town. You have been dating Rosalie and have been looking into Carmelita's disappearance haven't you?"

OK, I thought, here it is. A jealous boyfriend of Rosalie who is going to kick a vital part of my anatomy all the way out of town if I don't stop seeing her. Or maybe it's something worse. Maybe he's going to threaten me with bodily damage and severe hurt if I don't leave her alone." My imaginings went wild again and I swallowed twice, hard, before answering him. "Yes, Rosalie and I have been dating since I got into town. Do you have a problem with that?"

"No, I surely do not. Rosalie and I have been good friends for many years and what she does, and who she dates, is her business. I know that Rosalie and Carmelita were good friends and I wondered what she had told you about her. I have something that will definitely help you if you are serious about finding out what happened to Carmelita. I haven't been able to get to you because I have been in the hospital from the day she disappeared until two days ago."

The mention of his being in the hospital rang a very loud bell in my memory. I visualized the first newspaper article I'd read the night I arrived in town. Pablito Dornock! Of Course!

That was the name of the young man who was found wounded out on the desert in the bullet riddled truck. He was the subject in all the pictures Jose had taken of the shot to hell truck and the bloody body in it had been Pablito's.

I was definitely more interested in talking to him now that I knew who he was. I wondered how he was connected to whatever had happened to Carmelita.

"Yes, I understand fully now, Mr. Dornock, why you hesitate to talk on the phone about it, and I would like very much to talk to you. Where are you now? Do you want to come to the Cantina or meet me somewhere else?"

"I am at my home right now," Pablito said, "and I am not really able to leave and go anywhere. I am still recuperating from the bullet wounds. Would it be possible for you to come here? I would feel more secure here than any place else in town right now, anyway."

I did not hesitate to tell him, "Yes, Pablito, I can do that if you will just tell me where you live."

He gave me his street address and his phone number and then said, "After we talk I'm sure you'll understand. How long will it take you to get here?"

I was excited about the prospect of finally getting some new information, so I wanted to see him as soon as possible.

"I have to go back to my room to get some things but I should be at your house in no more than twenty minutes. Is that OK with you?"

"Fine with me," he replied, "I'll be waiting for you. Ring the doorbell two long and one short so I'll know it's you. Right now, I don't want to open my door unless I know who is there."

I hurriedly finished the remainder of my lunch, including the cold beer that I had wanted so badly, and made my way, at a trot, to my room. I wanted to get my recorder and some tapes. If Pablito permitted, I wanted to make sure I got his version of the events leading up to the time he was shot, and any other evidence that could be useful, on tape. I didn't want to miss anything by just taking notes.

I had to stop at the gas station and ask directions to the street address he had given me. The attendant on duty knew Pablito and gave me explicit directions on how to get to his house. I was close to the mark of twenty minutes when I arrived.

SIXTY

It was a typical adobe house very much like the rest of the houses in town, on the end of a row of them along the street. It probably had a central courtyard with all the rooms running off of it. Outside was the standard six foot wall of adobe that surrounded the house.

I opened the wrought iron gate and walked up to a door that had been painted brilliant blue. There were windows flanking the door. Each window had a window box with flowers that reached almost to the ground. It smelled like a botanical garden. I was beginning to like all the flowers and colors of this place.

I did as I had been told. I pressed the buzzer two long and one short and waited for someone to open the door. No one did. I wondered if someone was watching from one of the windows and if I were in the crosshairs of a scope mounted on a very powerful hunting rifle that would blow my head apart or puncture my heart easily at this range.

After about a minute's wait I heard someone inside yell. "Come on in! The door's unlocked."

My panic indicators went wild, racing up and down my back, giving me many warnings. Was Pablito being forceably held by someone who wanted me in there so he could kill both of us together to make it look like a murder/robbery? Will I be looking down the barrel of a gun when I open this door? I thought as I looked very carefully at the doorknob on the blue door. Should I do as I was told and open it or just wait till someone from inside opened it? At that point I had no choice but to open the door and take a chance on being taken hostage or shot dead. My nerve endings didn't stop their erratic dancing at all. I didn't very much care for their antics as I stood to one side and cautiously opened the door.

What I saw was a long hallway stretching maybe twenty five feet straight ahead of me. About five or so feet from the front door on both sides of the hallway were double doors. I had no idea which one to enter. I was thinking about knocking on the doors on both sides to see what would happen, when I heard a voice call out again.

"Open the door to your right and come on in please."

I didn't know if the voice belonged to Pablito or not, but I couldn't very well back out now.

I opened the door as instructed, and came face to face with a very round, black, and menacing hole at the end of what appeared to be a

260

large, powerful rifle. As I looked carefully down the barrel I saw a finger on the trigger.

I was always amazed at how far you can see down a rifle barrel when it is pointed at your face. I thought to myself that I've made a serious mistake coming here. I'm a dead man! A very panicky inner voice said. My fright levels were quickly reaching a new high looking at that very large black hole. I had to swallow several times before I could speak.

"Pablito?" I asked cautiously, "I am Andy Bling and you asked me to come here. Would you please put the rifle down? It is making me exceedingly nervous to have to look down that barrel."

I didn't know if I had wet my pants or not in my initial shock at seeing the rifle pointed at my face. If I had, there wasn't anything I could do about it now.

"Sorry about the gun," the person sitting in a wheelchair who must have been Pablito, said apologetically.

"You will understand the need for it after I tell you some of the things that I have been through in the past few weeks. I don't need any more attempts to kill me. They've already had two tries. The next one might just be successful. Please sit down. Can I get you something to drink like a coffee, or a beer, or a soda?"

That sounded like just what I needed to put some moisture back into my very dry throat, so I said yes, "a good hot cup of coffee would certainly help to settle my nerves thank you. I take cream and sugar too."

As Pablito wheeled himself back from the kitchen a few minutes later with two filled cups, I waited for him to start talking.

I explained my need to record what he said to insure that I had everything he told me straight in my mind. I assured him that no one else would listen to the tape without his permission and he told me he had no objection to it.

I very carefully started my tape recorder that I had concealed in my jacket pocket and asked, "What exactly do you mean, Pablito, when you say that you don't need another attempt on your life? Would you please explain that?"

"I will in the course of the rest of the story," he assured me. "I have talked to Mrs. Hernando and she says that you can be trusted with whatever I am going to tell you. I couldn't go to the Sheriff or his deputies because those three men, I do not trust. You'll understand why as I reveal the rest of the story to you."

"I will thank Mrs. Hernando for recommending me to you," I

assured him, "especially if the information you have helps in any way to put the killers behind bars."

I didn't reveal any of the evidence I'd gathered so far; maybe later I would.

"Mrs. Hernando and I have talked many times and she is right. I know how to keep a secret. I will not put you or anybody else in danger just for a story. I don't work that way. I am anxious to hear what you have to say about Carmelita."

I hoped that would make him more open to talking about everything he knew. I sat back, took a drink of coffee and waited for him to begin.

After about a minute of seriously considering what I had just said, Pablito began his story.

"I know exactly what happened to Carmelita the day she disappeared. I was there. Yes, right on the same spot with her. I also know exactly where her body can be found because she is where I put her. I definitely did not have a hand in killing her but I know the people who did it and why. I know all the details of why they wanted her out of the way."

"You know who killed her and why?" I said in a very surprised voice. "I'd like for you to give me as much of the details as you can remember, OK?"

After taking a drink of his coffee, Pablito continued, "Oh I know all the details all right. I have seen them in my nightmares every night since I was shot. Yes, I'll tell you!"

He took another long drink of his coffee and continued. "You don't know much about her or what went on in this town before you got here do you? Probably nobody is going to volunteer much information to a stranger either. If I don't tell you, you'll never find out. Carmelita and I grew up together. We went through grade school and high school together. We dated in high school for about a year. We planned maybe to get married and have a couple of kids after graduation but it didn't work out that way. I went away to college and she went to work for the lawyer."

"I wanted more than this town had to offer me then. College was the only way to get it. She seemed happy just staying here being a clerk. Then the tragic accident that killed her folks happened and that sealed her resolve never to leave here. I couldn't blame her but neither could I talk her out of it. We just sort of fell apart after I left and couldn't get back together after I got back. We met a couple of times and she said we couldn't keep seeing each other because she was seeing someone else now but she didn't tell me who it was."

"Did you find out later who it was?"

I hoped, beyond hope, that Pablito would say it was the Sheriff.

"Yes, I sure did," Pablito said as he nodded. "She told me she had been sent to Santa Fe by Ms. Charles to do some minor company business two or three times. She told me that the person she was seeing came there to be with her. She also told me that she knew Ms. Charles was suspicious of her because she had been seeing the same person."

"Are you telling me that the man she was seeing in Santa Fe was also dating Ms. Charles?" I asked.

"That's it exactly what I'm saying, Andy. She told me this twice after she got back from down there. What's even more interesting is that I also worked part time for Ms. Charles as a courier. I helped get her case files to the court house wherever she had a case come to trial, both here and in Santa Fe."

"You worked for her too?" I asked in amazement. "Did you hear her say anything about the affair her boyfriend was having? Who was her boyfriend anyway??

"You get ahead of the story, Andy. Just hang on a second and it will all become very clear. I was hired by Ms. Charles to do some undercover work for her because she knew me."

"During the times when Carmelita was sent to Santa Fe alone on company business, I was sent there to spy on her and to verify who her boyfriend was. I did this twice. I reported my observations back to Ms. Charles in writing. This included a list of where they went, what they ate and how often they were together.

What Ms. Charles did not know is that I had borrowed a camera from Jose and had taken pictures of Carmelita and her boyfriend dining in a couple of Santa Fe's best restaurants. For some reason, I felt I should not give these to Ms. Charles. I never got them back from Jose, who developed them for me."

"Ms. Charles gave me three hundred dollars a trip and she also paid the entire hotel bill for my stay. She really wanted the goods on her cheating boyfriend. Do you have any idea who it was, Andy?"

"From what I've uncovered so far my best guess would be that it was the Sheriff. Am I anywhere close?" I asked.

"You are right on the head of a very sharp nail" Pablito confirmed. "She was so angry that she threatened to kill them both the first time I reported back to her. The second time she just threatened to kill

Carmelita. I don't know if she confronted the Sheriff with my evidence or not. If she did, the Sheriff has kept a very low profile around me. He never asked me about what I'd done. I just know that Carmelita went to Santa Fe those two times so I don't know if they kept up the affair when they were here in Bullsnort or not. I never talked to Carmelita about it."

"What do you know about her disappearance?" I asked, encouraging him to continue.

"One or two days before Carmelita's disappearance Ms. Charles told me that she knew that the two girls were going riding out into the desert. Don't ask me how she knew it. I don't know for sure how she knew. My guess would be that Carmelita told her that she and Rosalie were going riding and that she'd be back to work late that day. Maybe the owner of the stables called and told her that the girls had reserved horses for that day."

"Ms. Charles told me that she wanted to rent my truck for a couple of days and offered such a good price, I couldn't turn her down. She told me to take my truck out of town about four miles and leave it and she followed me to bring me back to town. I didn't know then why she wanted me to take my truck out there, but I did it because she offered to pay me well. I just figured she must need it for something she wanted to bring back to town."

"Anyway, the day Rosalie and Carmelita were to go riding, Ms. Charles called the stables and reserved a horse. I thought it was for her but it wasn't. It was for me. She then told me to follow the two girls and report back to her on where they went. Then she said something that made me feel very uneasy. So uneasy that I took the camera I borrowed from Jose with me. She said that she wanted me to do whatever I had to do to get Carmelita out of the picture. She didn't come right out and say she wanted me to kill her and dispose of her body, but the look on her face and the tone of her voice that was rancid with hatred for Carmelita sure pushed my thoughts in that direction. I sure was not willing to do anything to help her do something like that. She didn't pay me anything up front for what she wanted me to do. I assumed that she would pay me later when I reported back to her as she had always done."

"I work for her doing odd jobs to help with her court stuff, but I don't kill for her. I wasn't about to commit murder that would put me in jail for the rest of my life or get me strapped into an electric chair. No way in hell was I going to be that stupid. I thought maybe, as an old friend, I could just tell Carmelita that she was putting her life in danger and persuade Carmelita to end her affair with the Sheriff."

"What happened after you followed them out into the desert?" I asked eagerly.

"I was about a mile or so behind them but I had a pair of binoculars so I could follow them closely without them seeing me. I saw Rosalie take her horse down into an arroyo. Carmelita's horse shied away from climbing down the wall for about five minutes. Rosalie was climbing up the far wall when Carmelita finally got her horse moving down the steep path. Rosalie didn't stop or look back for her. She probably assumed that Carmelita was right behind her or would catch up as quickly as she could. She sure didn't act like she knew Carmelita wasn't there behind her."

"I kept watching Rosalie. I didn't see Carmelita come out. When I got to the rim of the arroyo there was no sign of Carmelita. Her horse was up against the far wall standing in the shade near the mutilated body of a rattlesnake. I immediately caught the reins of her horse and followed what looked like its tracks down the arroyo because I was concerned that maybe the horse had reared up throwing her off."

After pausing to sip his coffee, Pablito continued.

"It wouldn't do for her to be stranded horseless in the heat of the day. Then, after walking another hundred yards down the arroyo, I saw her lying in the sand unconscious with what appeared to be blood on the sand around her. After checking to make sure she was alive, I took pictures of her there that included all of the area around where she was lying. The rattler and the blood. She was obviously unable to ride a horse back to town."

"She was alive when you found her? What about the wound on her head, was it life threatening?" I said as I encouraged him to continue.

"Yes, she was very much alive and breathing normally. As for the wound, I don't know, she was unconscious when I found her. I saw a pretty large cut on her face and a big lump on the back of her head. I noticed then that the waters of the latest flood had dug a washout on the arroyo wall that was big enough to lay her down in the shade. I carried her over there and put a bottle of water beside her. I took some more pictures of her there just in case the rescue team needed to see what she looked like so they could bring the right equipment. I knew I had to go get some help, and I took several pictures of the place as I rode away so I could be sure I found the exact spot quickly when I returned with help for her."

"Then I got on my horse, a Pinto, and led the other one, her Appaloosa, out of the arroyo as I tried to decide how I would get her the help she needed. I knew that my truck had been left pretty close to the arroyo. If Ms. Charles hadn't taken it already, I figured that I could use it to get back to town faster than I could go on horseback. I hoped that Carmelita would be OK till I got back with help. I felt very bad about leaving her there alone, but I couldn't do anything to help her. I know that now."

"Did you see anybody else nearby, or in the arroyo when you climbed out to go for help?" I asked.

"I really didn't look around to see, I just wanted to get help for her. As I rode away, it must have been ten or twelve minutes later, I guess, I heard what sounded like a shot. I slowed down a little and then spurred my horse faster to get to my truck. I didn't want some nut taking a shot at me. That's exactly what happened when I got to my truck though. I let both horses go hoping they would find their way back to town and was sitting in my truck trying to get it started, when I was shot in the shoulder. A second shot hit me in the abdomen and I felt the third shot hit my leg. As I fell over onto the seat I put the camera under it and must have passed out after that."

As he said that, I recalled the picture that Jose had shown me of the bloody body of a man lying on a truck seat.

"If you passed out, how do you know who it was that shot you?" I questioned.

Pablito shifted in his wheelchair as if in pain and replied.

"I was sprawled out over the front seat and I came to a little when I thought I heard voices. They're coming to help me, I thought. I came to a little more but I lay very still on the seat. I was very groggy and in a lot of pain. I had covered my stomach wound with both hands to stop the bleeding. As I heard the voices get closer I understood what they were saying and I recognized both voices. I certainly didn't want to take a chance on moving after I heard what they were saying to each other. One voice was a male and the other female."

Pablito said he had heard the woman ask, "do you think this bastard's dead yet? Maybe I should pump a big one into the top of his head just to make sure. He's a damned trouble maker and good riddance."

"I heard the male voice say, No, he is already dead and won't be telling any more lies about me and that bitch back there in the arroyo."

"He told the woman that he had made sure the bitch was dead before he buried her in that ditch where nobody would ever find her. He advised her to just pray for a storm up in the mountains that will wash away all the evidence and told her they had better get out of there. She walked over to the window of my truck and fired a bullet from a huge pistol into my leg, laughing as she said that she just had to get revenge someway."

"I can't tell you how relieved I was to hear them ride away."

"After that their voices faded away and I just lay there hoping that someone had heard the shots, would see my truck out here, and come to find me. Otherwise, I was sure I would bleed to death. I had to face the fact that from what I'd just heard the Sheriff and Ms. Charles say about both of us, that Carmelita was already dead and beyond my help. With that thought in my mind, I passed out again."

Pablito refilled our coffee cups and continued his tale.

"The female voice that wanted to pump a big one into my head belonged to Ms. Robin Charles, the Lawyer, and the male voice that was bragging about the bitch in the gully belonged to the Sheriff, Bill Johnson. As true as I'm sitting here, Andy, I'm telling the truth about this. You can see now why I can't go to the deputies with this story. The Sheriff would just deny it and then make more plans to get rid of me. Can you help me stay alive and at the same time get them arrested for Carmelita's murder?"

"Yes, I can see that you are in a very dangerous situation here. Why didn't the Sheriff try to kill you once you were out of the hospital? Or did he?" I asked.

"Yes, he did try to kill me again. I can show you a couple of shot out windows where he took pot shots at me the day after I was released from the hospital," Pablito assured me.

"I didn't actually see him but with that scoped rifle of his, he could have been hiding hundreds of yards away behind a tree or something and I never would have seen him. Maybe he thinks he killed me, but I know he will make sure and when he finds out I'm still alive, he will try again. I have the bullets that were fired at me, too. I'm sure they are 30-30 slugs that came from his rifle. That's why I sit here with this rifle, ready if he tries again. If I get a chance to shoot back at him I'll take it. I won't miss or give him a second chance either."

"Who found you out there in your truck and brought you to the hospital?" I asked to see if he knew about Jose.

"I don't know who it was but whoever it was saved my life. Do you know who it was, Andy?"

Without waiting for my reply he continued, "I must have been out a long time because when I came to I was in the Emergency Room at the hospital and they were getting ready to take me to the operating room to get the slugs out of me. They said the wound in my stomach was the most dangerous one of the three so they'd take care of my shoulder and leg after the stomach wound was taken care of. I didn't argue with them at that point." I asked one of the nurses if I could have all of the slugs, for a souvenir. They all laughed and said that the slugs were evidence and must be turned over to the Police. I requested that they give them to the State Police and not the Sheriff, and I also asked them to ask the State Police to go and look for Carmelita. Jose came by to see me and I told him to look under the seat of my truck for his camera that still had the film with the pictures I took in it. He assured me that he would develop the pictures for me."

"Later when I was in the recovery room, one of the nurses slipped one of the bullets into my hand. I still have it. I'm not a ballistics expert or anything like that but to me this thing looks a lot like a 30-30 slug. I have a Winchester 30-30 and I have boxes of bullets that look a lot like this one. Of course this one is a little flat but here, look at it and tell me what you think."

He pulled the slug out of a pocket and handed it to me. It was in a little plastic bag.

"I put it in this plastic bag to help preserve any fingerprints that might be on it," he said.

"I know nothing about examining used rifle slugs, Pablito, but I sure know someone who does. Can I have this as evidence? If the person who shot you and Carmelita is arrested, this slug will help convict them."

I just hoped the surgeons had not turned the other two slugs over to the Sheriff.

"Sure you can have it, Andy. Now, what can you do to help keep me safe from the Sheriff and Ms. Charles? I don't doubt for a nanosecond that she will try to "pump a big one" into me if she gets a chance."

I wondered to myself if Mrs. Hernando could help.

"Can I use your phone to make a call?" I asked as I turned toward the phone on the table beside Pablito.

"Sure can, it's there on the table," he replied with a motion of his hand.

I dialed the number of the shop. Mrs. Hernando picked up on the second ring. "Indian Arts shop, Mrs. Hernando here. How may I help you?"

I didn't identify myself but just said, "This is the Koshare and since you are the person who sold me, I have come back to you for some advice and help."

The transformation of my voice into a voice of a Clan Father was amazing. I hoped she would understand. It surely wasn't any kind of code that we had worked out in advance, but I was afraid that Pablito's phone might have been tapped by the Sheriff.

I needn't have worried.

She didn't miss a beat as she replied, "I understand, Koshare, and I am ready to help in any way I can. Where are you now? Do you need anybody else that I might bring with me?"

"I am looking for Mars right now with a friend who was just released from the hospital a couple of days ago and, *yes,* I need whoever you can bring to help."

If the Sheriff was listening, I hoped that what had just been said would sound like so much gibberish to him. I knew that Mrs. Hernando would know what it was she was to do because we had joked about the reservation being as different from Bullsnort as Mars was from the Earth.

"I have to make a couple of calls but I can be in contact with Mars and have the help you need there in about twenty-five minutes," she replied. She apparently had understood what Mars meant and that she should try and get Martin to come here.

I didn't much care that he would have no jurisdiction off the reservation to arrest anybody for the shooting of Pablito, but the more solid facts, as Pablito had just revealed them, proved the murder and his shooting had been done on reservation lands so Martin had legal authority to be involved. Martin could provide ways to get Pablito to safety. He could also call in the State Patrol and the F.B.I. to help. He would need help with the forensics and ballistics and they could provide it. What I wanted at this point was help in saving Pablito's life. He and all concerned now knew that the Sheriff along with the Lawyer would try again to get rid of him.

SIXTY-ONE

After twenty minutes or so had passed I heard the front doorbell ring. "That must be Mrs. Hernando now. I'll let her in," I said as I walked toward the door.

Pablito followed me to the hallway entrance and sat with his gun trained on the door. He was taking no chances.

I quietly asked as I stood to one side of the door, "Who's there?" and heard the quiet voice of Mrs. Hernando answer. I slowly opened the door. She was alone. I motioned for her not to say anything with a finger on my lips at the same time I held out my other hand and motioned for her to stay where she was until I got out of Pablito's line of sight and he recognized her as friendly. He saw who it was immediately and lowered the gun down across his lap. He apologized for having to greet her with a gun and invited her to come in as he turned around and wheeled himself into the front room. She indicated that she understood fully about Pablito taking the precautions necessary for his own protection.

We prepared to talk about what he had to pass on to all of us. Then I asked her where Martin was and she replied that he was on his way over but it would take him awhile to get here.

My relief was instantaneous. I knew I could depend on her and Martin to bring this murder investigation to an end.

I gave her a brief summary of what Pablito had told me. I showed her the tape recorder and said it was all right there. While I had it out of my pocket, I changed the tape just in case the story wasn't finished yet.

Pablito said hello and as he extended his hand to her asked if she'd like a coffee. She said yes and he rolled his chair into the kitchen. While he was gone I explained that he couldn't go to the deputies or the Sheriff, but I felt he would talk to Martin if he ever got here.

When Pablito got back and had given her the coffee, he started to explain his part in what had happened out on the arroyo. Mrs. Hernando was very eager to hear what he had to say. She wasn't disappointed.

"I know now why Ms. Charles had me take my truck out on the desert the day before." Pablito concluded. She wanted make it look like I had planned to murder Carmelita and had tried to make it look like I was trying to cover up my real reason for being out in the desert. It would look like I wanted people to think the only reason I was out there was to shoot holes in my truck for the Bullsnort festival."

"You see, I've been in some of the escapes that we stage every year. We buy these older, run down trucks from junk yards and fix the engines so they will barely run. That's why so many of them smoke like trains. Why bother to put new mufflers on them when the whole truck may collapse in a pile if you hit a bump a little too hard on the way home? Those of us who are selected to participate in the escapes take our trucks out on the desert about a week before the event for target practice with our 22's and pepper them with holes."

"We shoot out both the rear windows and side windows," Pablito explained. "That way we can fire our pistols out of them easily. One or two shots go into the windshield so that they aren't the only thing without a bunch of holes, but we don't try to destroy it. On the day of the escape everybody, hopefully, fires blanks at us as we drive out of town."

"One time there was a guy who was shot, I think on purpose, and had his ear blown off. I personally think that it was an attempt to actually kill him. I have no idea who fired the shot there were so many people firing at us. As far as I know the Sheriff has never said anything one way or the other about solving the shooting. It probably could have been another perfect murder. That was three years ago. Nobody's been hurt in an escape since then. You can also check my truck for larger holes now as proof that a larger rifle was fired into it three times. It's out back now."

"I'm sure Martin will want to examine it." I assured him. "Can you think of anything else about that day out there when you were shot?"

"I didn't see anybody out there but the Lawyer and the Sheriff must have followed me. The lawyer wanted Carmelita dead and told me so three or four times in her anger when I had given her my report from Santa Fe. When I found Carmelita alive and decided to get into my truck to go after help for her, they apparently decided to take us both out, but I am sure they moved Carmelita's body after they killed her so no one would connect my shooting with her. They assumed she would never be found and it would look like someone had just murdered me. They laid a pretty good trap for both of us and I fell right into it for them."

"If they rode horses, they had to get them from the stables," Pablito continued. "If so, then there will be some kind of record unless the stable owner is somehow beholding to either of them. I am sure they think that they will never be arrested. The Sheriff would never find any reason to charge anybody with my murder or with Carmelita's murder. They were counting on rain to wash away the evidence in the flood that always follows in those arroyos. They thought they would both get off scot free. All the more reason I want to see them behind bars for shooting me."

Mrs. Hernando reassured him that if we have anything to do with that, they will both be behind bars for a long time. "We just have to wait for Martin to get here so you can tell him what you've told us," she said.

After we had waited abut thirty minutes for Martin to arrive, he called instead. He explained to Mrs. Hernando that he wouldn't be able just then to come to Pablito's house until tomorrow and that he had some very interesting developments to tell us about. Mrs. Hernando said that she'd call him and arrange a meeting place. Meanwhile, Mrs. Hernando and I agreed that Pablito would stay with me at the motor court and Mrs. Hernando would send a couple of her Indian friends to stake out the room so we both would be safe. We left the house immediately in case someone had been listening on the phone. Pablito slept in the spare bed in my room at the motor court. We did not sleep too well that night even under the protection of the Indians.

SIXTY-TWO

We were all very curious about the new information that Martin had for us. We had already called him twice telling him we had some very important information to share with him, and we were getting anxious. We had nobody in the world to turn to if Martin couldn't, or wouldn't, help us. We definitely knew now who the killers were, had proof, but were helpless and really at the mercy of the Sheriff. I doubted if the deputies would act on this information against the pair of killers. We depended on Martin. I hoped he'd come through for us, and Carmelita.

About nine-thirty the next morning, after spending a sleepless night, luckily, without any shots being fired at us, I received a call from Rosalie. She had already talked with Jose and said she had set up a meeting at her house at noon if I would like to meet with him and anyone else I felt needed to be included. I immediately called Mrs. Hernando and passed the information to her. I asked her to call Martin and ask him to meet us there, instead of at Pablito's house just in case someone had learned of our plans. Pablito said that he'd definitely wanted to be there. We were all there when Martin arrived.

Martin knocked on the door and when Rosalie opened it he was standing there beside a State Patrol Officer. Martin had told us that he had contacted both the State Patrol and the F.B.I. We hadn't the time to ponder the reasons. We had a long story to get from Martin. We also had a long story to tell him, along with the slug from Pablito, pictures of the Lawyer and the Sheriff out on the desert, and best of all, Pablito's eye-witness testimony. We let him tell us what had kept him so busy for two days while we waited anxiously.

Rosalie got everyone a cup of coffee and Martin started telling us about the latest information that he had collected.

He began his story with a grim expression on his face. "I have some bad news that we learned earlier this morning. Carmelita has been found, dead, in one of the arroyos out on the desert about five miles from town."

That immediately got our attention, although it came as no real surprise to us.

"I can't tell you all the facts right now because we are still investigating them," he stated, "but she died of a bullet wound in the head from either a rifle or a high powered handgun at close range.

Her body had been buried in a shallow grave. She was probably killed and buried the same day that she disappeared, which explains why the search parties sent out by the State Patrol did not find her."

"Whoever did it was in a big hurry and didn't do a good enough job of burying her," Martin continued. "Yesterday, three coyotes were seen by a mother and daughter from the reservation, who happened to be in the arroyo gathering firewood and clay for pottery. The coyotes were trying to dig something out of the ground."

"Out of curiosity, the mother and daughter went to investigate and scared the animals away, but they certainly weren't prepared for what they found. It was Carmelita's body. They immediately came to the station on the reservation and reported the discovery. I've still got a team out at the site right now. I called the State Patrol for any forensics help that might be needed."

"As soon as the State Patrolmen arrived in his office, the daughter had led them along with Martin and his own team of deputies, out to the arroyo." The detectives and coroner's office staff were still at the site collecting evidence even as he sat talking to us.

Martin relayed what the mother and daughter had told him and assured us that both of them had signed a statement attesting to it being the truth.

"Their story is that they were gathering firewood and clay for making their pottery from a secret location used by their family for years. They were delighted with finding dried buffalo chips in the arroyo that they could use in the firing of the pottery they made. They are used to give the finished pots a luster that reflects the essence of those great beasts. Assuming that buffalo chips were what the coyotes were digging for, they decided to take advantage and collect the chips for themselves."

"But that is only the end of the story," said Martin. "The mother and daughter said they had seen two girls riding into the arroyo several days earlier and didn't see anything unusual about it. They noticed the girls, but went on with collecting wood and buffalo chips on the flat desert area. People are often seen exploring the desert on horseback so they did not see anything unusual about the girls heading toward the arroyo."

"This particular arroyo is many miles long, about fifty feet deep and about a hundred feet across from wall to wall," Martin said, indicating the relative size with the motions of his hands. "It takes a long time to get in and out of it because of the steep walls and the loose sand. The mother and daughter don't go into it regularly because the walls are so steep it can be very dangerous when there is a storm up in the mountains. The water tends to come rushing down the arroyo sweeping away everything in its path. It's just too dangerous to be down there for a long time."

"The witnesses said that one of the girls had gone down into the arroyo ahead of the other one and they saw her come up on the far side and ride on. The other girl's horse had shied away from the rim and didn't want to climb down. It had taken her about five minutes to get her horse to go into the arroyo. They did not see the second girl come out and ride on after the first girl. The first girl didn't wait either, but rode away. They didn't think too much about it; maybe the other girl had decided to take another way back to town and had come out farther down the arroyo where they couldn't see. They were too far away to hear any talking or noise from them."

"About ten or fifteen minutes after the first girl came out of the arroyo, they went over to the rim to see if they could see the second girl. When they got to the rim they saw a horse standing against the far wall in the shade. The girl was nowhere to be seen. About ten feet from the horse they saw a dead, smashed up rattlesnake the horse had obviously trampled."

"They guessed that the girl had left her horse in the shade while she went off exploring the arroyo as so many Anglos do and when the snake had approached it, the horse reared and the killed the snake. The horse had apparently wandered over to the shady side of the arroyo where it waited for the girl to return. They were concerned that maybe the girl had been hurt or bitten by the snake, so they went down the steep side and tried to investigate," Martin continued.

"They saw no clear footprints that could have belonged to the girl in the loose, windblown sandy bottom," Martin said with a shrug. "They called out asking if anyone needed help and got no reply. They decided that the girl must be off exploring like so many Anglos do or maybe she was meeting someone. Besides if she didn't show up back in town when she was supposed to, they thought that someone would surely be sent out from the town to look for her."

Martin continued his story as we sat with eyes glued to his face.

"The mother and daughter, concerned about getting back to the reservation before dark, decided they should get started toward home. After climbing back up the steep trail, they gathered up the materials they had left on the rim of the arroyo, but before they could start back to the reservation, they saw a rider, who they guessed was experienced because of the way he sat his horse, coming toward the arroyo. He was about two hundred yards away, but they said they did not call out to him because they knew that two women, alone in the desert, had to be very cautious about talking to people they didn't know. They said they assumed, with feelings of relief, that he was searching for the girl and her horse so they backed away and hid behind a large piñon bush so as not to be seen and watched him."

Martin continued to tell us the tale that boosted our confidence in finally getting justice for Carmelita.

"When the rider reached the bottom of the arroyo, he approached the loose horse, grabbed the reins, and started further down into the arroyo, obviously in search of the girl. He had gone about one hundred yards when they saw him dismount and move towards something that was out of their line of sight up against the wall of the arroyo that was below their hiding place. They waited and watched from behind their bush for about fifteen more minutes until they saw him come out of the arroyo. He was riding his horse and held the reigns of the other one as he headed off toward town at a gallop. They assumed he must be going for help in finding the girl."

"They could not give us a description of the man, but they could describe the two horses," said Martin. "The horse the girl had ridden into the arroyo was an Appaloosa and the one he was riding was a Pinto. They are very familiar types of horses; the kinds of horses that we see every day on the reservation," Martin added. "And yes, they are certain concerning the types of horses they saw out on the desert that day."

"The mother said she had looked at her daughter and asked what she thought they should do. Should they go into the arroyo and see what it was he found? The daughter, about sixteen years old, said that she felt that they should go look at the place where the man had stopped and if anything was wrong there, they should go and report it to Sergeant Begay at the reservation Police Station."

"They said they nudged their horses back into the arroyo to roughly the spot where the rider had found the horse. When they got to the place where they had seen him dismount they looked around very carefully but didn't see any sign of the girl. There were hoof prints all over but the man's horse had just been walking around this spot so that was normal. They didn't see anything that would alert them to the girl's location. It was getting very late, so they climbed back up the steep trail and started home, believing that the man had gone to get help in searching for the girl."

Martin asked Rosalie for a refill on his coffee and continued to tell us what the mother and daughter had told him.

"About five minutes after riding away, they said they heard what sounded like a single gunshot. They had looked questioningly at each other and both had said, at the same time, 'that's a rifle shot." They said they started riding faster toward the reservation and about three minutes later they heard three more shots that were very close together and then another shot about two minutes later that sounded just like the first shot they had heard."

"They couldn't see who was doing the shooting but it scared them so they raced their horses all the way back to the reservation stopping only when they got to the Police Station. They reported what they had seen and heard to the Deputy on duty that day."

Martin emphasized, "I was not working that day for some reason but I always check the records for days when I am not at the Station. A Deputy was sent out the next morning to look over the area around the arroyo. According to his report, he found nothing suspicious, and, although he did find the dead snake, there was no evidence a shooter had been there and no sign of the girl. He filed the report and thought no more of it."

Martin shook his head as he said, "There's always somebody out on the desert shooting at something, especially now that it's almost time for the town's Escape Festival and men are out there shooting up their trucks."

As Martin continued his story, I thought, our day in court is approaching, along with justice for Carmelita!

"The mother and daughter went back to the same area again over the next couple of days and said they had pretty much forgotten the incident in the arroyo but, yesterday, when they looked into the arroyo they saw three coyotes digging frantically under an overhang where the rushing waters had dug an undercut."

"As I said before," Martin reminded us, "they told me they thought maybe the coyotes had found some buffalo chips and so they kicked their horses towards them to scare them off."

"They said they came close to where the coyotes had been digging but did not dismount. The coyotes had uncovered something and it was sticking out from under the dirt. It looked very much like a human arm that they assumed must be attached to a dead body. They wanted no part of a dead body so they spurred their horses and rushed back to the reservation Police Station to tell us where this body was."

"This took place yesterday morning about ten thirty," Martin said as he took another long drink from his coffee cup. "They got to my office about a half hour later and managed to overcome their fright enough to tell me what they had found. I immediately sent two deputies to check out their story."

"About twelve twenty the radio on my desk crackled with a message from the deputies, who were in the arroyo. They told me that they found a female body right where the mother and daughter said it would be. There was a bloody wound on the back of the dead woman's head. Maybe from a fall where she could have hit her head on a rock, or something like that, but a bullet wound in her left temple alerted them to her possibly being murdered. There were powder burns around that bullet hole, and her hands were tied behind her back, execution style. She didn't have a chance. This was, without a doubt, a violent act of Murder," Martin said with conviction.

"I told them to stay there and search the entire area until I could get the Coroner to come out and collect evidence before removing the body. I also told them to let me know immediately if they needed help from me."

"I told them to use their camera and take the usual set of pictures of the surroundings and the body, and yes, stay there. I called the State Police and told the deputies that as soon as I finished questioning the mother and daughter, I would come out there with those Officers and bring the rest of the equipment we needed to secure the area."

"After taking care of those details, Martin said, "I called the mother into my office again and asked her specifically how many shots they had heard and to estimate how much time had lapsed between when they rode away from the arroyo until they heard each of them. Our office staff had typed their statements and both the mother and daughter read and signed them after repeating the exact same story they had told me a few minutes before."

"She told me that they were about ten minutes from the arroyo when we heard the first shot. It was not very loud, like a large pistol makes, but maybe like a twenty-two the boys use to kill rabbits and prairie dogs. The first shot was separated from the next three by maybe fifteen minutes. These three shots sounded like they came from a lever action rifle like men use when they want to kill a bear or a deer. She even demonstrated as she described the sequence; shot-pause-shot-pause-shot. She thinks it was definitely not an automatic. A short time later, a fourth shot followed that sounded just like the first one. After the fourth shot, all was quiet."

"When the State Police Officers arrived on the reservation, we went out to the location armed with the information the mother and daughter had given me," Martin said. "We went out to the arroyo, and sure enough, the deputies and the Coroner's staff had uncovered the body of Carmelita. I immediately called the F.B.I., too, since the murder victim was found on reservation property. They will assume responsibility for the investigation and we won't have to rely on the local Law Officers from Bullsnort anymore. We still have officers in the area collecting evidence. I can't tell you any more than that right now."

Martin took a deep breath before asking, "What is it that you have discovered that you feel is so urgent, Andy?"

SIXTY-THREE

We all just sat there in stunned amazement for about ten seconds before I answered him. Martin had just corroborated the story that both Pablito and Jose had told us. I knew I had both of their stories on the tape. We had the slug from Pablito's abdomen that the doctor had given him. It was still sealed in the wrapper with the hospital label on it. I also knew Martin would be amazed that we had both Jose's photos and Pablito's photos to back up what I had on tape. Now it was our turn to surprise Martin with the information we had. I didn't think he would have any inkling of the connection between Carmelita, the Sheriff, and the lawyer. I introduced both Jose and Pablito to Martin.

"Martin, we have some surprising and interesting information for you," I began. "I have been talking with Pablito and Jose here. They have been telling me a very interesting story that sounds very much like the one the mother and daughter told you today. I hope that the evidence we have dug up will insure the conviction of the killers, who, by the way, we have been able to identify. We have very incriminating evidence that will tell you who they are."

Martin had no idea what I was talking about. I had not shared the specific details or confided in him about what my investigation had uncovered so far. He waited expectantly for what I had to tell him and I couldn't keep him waiting on the edge of his chair any longer.

"Pablito can explain the reasons why. He can tell you who killed Carmelita and made two attempts on his life. You will definitely need to talk to him. But first, I have to ask for your help in protecting him. We spent last night barricaded in my hotel room with two of your friends keeping watch for us. Someone attempted to kill him at his house the day he went home from the hospital. His life isn't worth a plug nickel if he stays in town now, especially after he tells his story to you. Can you possibly take him some place on the reservation until the murderers are arrested? Or maybe the Feds can help out and take him into protective custody somewhere away from here?"

"I can't make any promises at this point, Andy, but if his story seems feasible, maybe something can be done. I need to hear what he has to say first."

Pablito was more than cooperative. He explained the facts exactly as he had told them to me earlier. Martin was taking careful notes and asked questions as Pablito described how he had been involved and what had happened to him. I hadn't told Martin about the tapes or the photos yet. They would be the cement that would hold all the clues together.

When Martin had finished interviewing Pablito, I told him about the pictures Pablito and Jose had taken and Jose confirmed that he could verify what was in them. I also told him that I had the tapes of Pablito's story as it was told to me, the 30-30 slug from his abdomen and the five slugs that I dug out of my car seat along with the handful of casings I had found on the ground. I told him we were confident that and the slug from Carmelita's head would be a match for the others we had. Martin wasn't aware of the shooting into my car, so I filled in the details as I knew them.

The case was building very securely against the murderers of Carmelita. Somehow he didn't seem surprised that the evidence pointed to the Sherriff and the lawyer as the murderers.

Martin and the State Patrolman got together and talked for about five minutes. The patrolman then got the phone, dialed a number, and spoke for another five minutes to someone on the other end. When he hung up he turned to Martin and said, "before we can make an arrest or a search anyone's office or property we need some help from the office in Santa Fe. They will be sending some more people up here to help with the investigation. Just so we don't alert the Sheriff that there is a bunch of lawmen in town, they will be in civilian clothes."

"They will be here tonight, hopefully with the arrest and search warrants so we can proceed with the arrests early tomorrow morning." Seeing the hope on our faces, he continued, "I think we have enough information and evidence to convince a judge to issue search warrants and arrest warrants for both the lawyer and the Sheriff before they try to get out of town and go into hiding. What we need to do immediately is get these slugs to the State Police lab in Santa Fe for comparison to see if they might have come from the same gun or guns. Carmelita's body has been taken to the Coroner's lab and he has instructions to remove the bullet and send it to the State Police lab so a comparison can be made. All of that will take time," he said.

After a brief pause to dial his phone, the State Patrolman continued. "I will have a State Police helicopter take me along with the pictures and the tapes to the Prosecutor in Santa Fe immediately so he can approach a judge to get the warrants. Once the warrants are issued, we can hold both the Sheriff and lawyer for questioning while their houses and offices are searched."

After walking away from us and speaking with someone on the

phone for a few minutes, the State Policeman turned back to us and said, "I just called the Prosecutor's office and alerted a judge to get the process started to get the warrants issued. We should have them in a couple of hours."

Martin acknowledged this information and spoke to all of us, "Now, what can we do about finding Pablito here a safe place to live until the trial starts? I'll have to work on that little problem. We have a house on the reservation that we might be able to use, but I have to check to see if it is available. I'll be able to do that by tomorrow."

As the patrolman left to meet his helicopter, Martin spoke to him to make sure he had the photos and tapes as well as the statements from the mother and daughter. We were all greatly relieved when he got into his patrol car and headed to the landing pad at the State Police Station a few miles away.

"The Feds should be here early tomorrow and, hopefully, the judge will have issued the warrants and the State Patrolman will be back with them in a couple of hours," Martin said as he turned back to us. "That OK with everybody?"

Martin looked at each of us to see if we had anything to add. We didn't. All of us had smiles that reflected the hard work of our investigation and the conclusion that had just been verified by both Martin and the State Patrolman. We had the killers dead to rights and they would go to jail for a long time.

We all could tell from their sour expressions that both of the State Policemen didn't like the idea of arresting a law enforcement officer for murder and attempted murder. We would just have to wait for justice that would eventually come. And, right at this minute, we all felt that justice would finally be done for Carmelita. Mrs. Hernando and I said our goodnights to everybody there and left Pablito with Martin.

We drove to the Cantina and had a big dinner, on my expense account. As we ate we talked about the murder and I explained more of what Pablito had told me. I also told her about the other information I had gotten from talking to the lawyer.

Early the next day the entire Law Enforcement Team was ready to go. The required warrants for the Sheriff and the lawyer's arrest, along with warrants authorizing the search of both of their houses and offices had been obtained and were now in the hands of the State Police. I wasn't part of the Team so I lagged behind just close enough to hear and see what went on.

Martin worked with the State Police Commander and the F.B.I.

representative as they divided the Patrolmen and deputies into two groups; one team would arrest Ms. Charles, while the other took the Sheriff into custody. Both Ms. Charles and Sheriff Johnson had been under surveillance since last night so the Teams knew that they were both in their offices and were apparently unaware that Carmelita's body was with the coroner. They were both in custody before the teams began the search of their offices.

Both arrests were made without too much of a problem, although the lady lawyer very loudly told them that they were making a big mistake and she would see that they all lost their jobs. The Sheriff looked almost like he had expected it to happen. The searches were made and proved to be very successful.

A rifle was found hidden under some discarded blankets and other junk in the basement of Ms. Charles' home. The receipts for Pablito's two stays in Santa Fe, in addition to the two cancelled checks for three hundred dollars each, made out to Pablito Dornock were found in her private files in the house.

The receipts for Carmelita's two stays were found in a box of miscellaneous records in Ms. Charles' office. Surprisingly, the Sheriff had also kept his receipts for the two times he had met Carmelita in Santa Fe when he went there on business. They were found in his desk drawer in a folder marked expenses. All the dates matched perfectly and very nicely verified the information we had dug up and had given to Martin.

The rifle was identified as the one missing from the gun rack in the Sheriff's office and it was test fired at the State Police lab along with the Sheriff's personal handgun. When the slugs from the lab test firing were compared to the slugs that were taken from Pablito, Carmelita and my car, there were some exact matches. The rifle slugs matched the three from Pablito and three from my car. The Sheriff's fingerprints were all over the rifle. The one mangled slug from Carmelita's head did not match the test shot from the rifle or the Sheriff's service revolver, but it did appear to match one of the slugs taken from Pablito, and the other two from my car. Apparently the Sheriff had not used his service revolver in the crimes, but had definitely had help from someone, when he shot up my car trying to intimidate me. It didn't take too much for me to figure out just who that someone was after hearing, via my ESP experience, what he and the lawyer said when they were talking in the Cantina.

There had to be another gun somewhere. The big one the lawyer had said she wanted to use to pump one into Pablito's head? It hadn't been found yet. So the team went back and searched Ms. Charles's house and office again. This time they found a .44 magnum Ruger Blackhawk in a well- hidden safe. Only her fingerprints were on the gun.

They test fired it and compared the slug from Carmelita, the so far unmatched slug from Pablito, and the other two slugs from my car, to the test bullets from the Blackhawk. They were all a perfect match.

Ms. Charles had killed Carmelita. Her anger had obviously gotten the best of her. The Sheriff had helped her cover up her crime when he buried the body. Both she and the Sheriff were now in custody and would be questioned further about the shootings in order to round out the motive, timing and all the details yet uncovered.

After these developments, the questioning turned to getting more of the specifics and, if possible, their confession as to exactly what happened that day in the arroyo.

Ms. Charles was the first to be questioned after the irrefutable evidence of the slugs was found.

At first, she continued to be adamant in denying her involvement, insisting that she had no part in either crime and that the Sheriff must have had done them without her knowledge. Then, when she was shown the pictures that Jose had taken of her and the Sheriff riding into the arroyo and standing next to Pablito's truck with her extended arm thrust into the busted out window, she broke down in tears and slumped in her chair.

After seeing the picture of Pablito lying in a puddle of his own blood in the truck, she began to talk about what had happened.

"We had set up Pablito to do the killing for us. I had gotten the information that the girls were going riding at noon from the guy who owns the stables. He owes me several favors and this was one way of paying me back. I rented a horse for Pablito and sent him out to follow them. He was supposed to take her out of the picture however he chose to do it."

"He chickened out and left to get help for her after she fell off her horse," Ms. Charles said with a sneer. "We saw him leading her horse out of the arroyo and assumed he had done his job. We followed him on horseback about a mile behind him, but, when he left the arroyo with no shot being fired, we knew we had to make sure she was dead. It didn't take long to find her and when we saw that he had put her under the rock overhang in the shade with a bottle of water to drink, we knew we had a problem and had to finish the job ourselves. I was the one who tied up her hands. I guess I just couldn't stand to see them together, even there in the arroyo knowing what had happened between them so I didn't wait for him to kill her. I raised my own gun and shot her. Then I told him we had to go and get Pablito, after we had made sure the bitch was dead and buried."

After the lawyer had completed her confession, the Sheriff was called in for interrogation. He was belligerent at best and at first refused to answer any questions without his lawyer. When the Sheriff did start talking he corroborated Ms. Charles's story up to the time she had shot Carmelita and they tried to kill Pablito.

"After she had shot Carmelita, we knew we had to get Pablito because he knew too much about our plan," the Sheriff said quietly. "We rode after him and almost caught up to him but he'd heard the shot and was racing towards his truck. We had to do something before he got the truck started or we would never catch up with him. I dismounted and after I let the horses go, I knelt down, sighted in on him and fired three times through the windshield. I saw him fall over on the front seat and thought he was dead. When we got to the truck he looked dead to me. Ms. Charles wanted to put a shot directly into his head she was so mad at him for not killing the girl, but I said no, let's get back to town now! She settled for pumping a shot into his leg. We came on back to town and Ms. Charles hid her gun in the safe in her office while I hid my rifle in her basement."

"Both of us then went on about our daily business. Hell, we weren't worried until that bastard from Albuquerque showed up. I assured her that we would never be caught because I was in charge of the investigation and could invent clues, and facts as it pleased me. I could direct the entire investigation away from us. I planned to just let it fizzle out with nobody being arrested for lack of sufficient evidence. It would have been the perfect crime if it had rained up in the mountains. Then the floods would have washed away all the incriminating evidence. My deputies weren't involved with the investigation at all," he added, "so I didn't have to worry about them finding anything."

"The plan was that if someone found Pablito in the bullet-riddled truck they'd assume he'd been in a gunfight and someone had finished it out there on the desert. We would be in the clear there, too. What we didn't count on was that someone was watching us and found Pablito. After we left him for dead, they brought him to the emergency room. I couldn't very well try to kill him again in the hospital with my own deputies watching him, so I waited until he was discharged and tried again to kill him at his house. Obviously I missed him." he said with chuckle.

All the while the Sheriff was confessing to his part in the crimes, a court stenographer was busily clicking the keys on the machine and getting it all recorded verbatim. Both confessions were exactly the same in content. Only Ms. Charles's attitude was still vicious whenever Carmelita's name was mentioned. How could anybody have so much hate they could murder Carmelita in cold blood and hate her still after she had been dead all this time? Not only had she been killed but the Coroner confirmed that she was in fact pregnant. This was a double murder. New Mexico is one of only a few states with a law on the books that makes killing a fetus murder.

That made it a double murder in the first degree. Malice was a for-thought in this case. It was obviously well planned.

Both Ms. Charles and the Sheriff were charged with two counts of murder in the first degree in the deaths of Carmelita and her baby, conspiracy to commit murder in their deaths, conspiracy to commit murder in the shooting of Pablito.

Mr. Johnson was also charged with two attempted murder charges with the two attempts to kill Pablito. They were also charged with conspiracy to commit murder for the attack on my car.

They would never see the light of day outside the razor wire confines they would call home for the rest of their lives.

We all could hope that a jury of their peers would give them both the death penalty for their vicious acts but the thought of them spending the rest of their natural lives behind bars was a very comforting thought.

I could not leave town now that I had been instrumental in finding the killers. I would have to be here for the trial. I convinced Dan to let me stay until after the trial. I promised him three more stories; one on the conspiracy angle to include all the evidence and especially the pictures, one on the trial and conviction, and one on how the town readjusted after the murder. He OK'd my prolonged stay in Bullsnort. There were several loose ends I had to wrap up before the trial began.

I had to talk a lot more to Mrs. Hernando about all that had happened. I especially had to go and talk to the old man at the motor court. I now knew his true name to be Jose Fuentes, not Ordonez. I knew he could help allay my fears and doubts about several of the people in the town whose stones I found at the new cemetery.

SIXTY-FOUR

I got up early in the morning, at a time when I knew Jose Fuentes should be at home, and went to the front office at the motor court to see him. I hoped the dogs were chained up out back, or wherever it was he kept them. I stood looking at all the wanted posters again as I waited for him to respond to my yelling his name. He came up behind me silently and scared the hell out of me again when he spoke. I would never get used to him doing that. He must be a wraith to get so close without making a sound. Like he just floated into the room and settled behind the desk.

"What do want now sonny? If you're here to keep asking me questions about things that are done and past then you're wasting my time. I'm not interested."

He looked like he was about to turn and walk back down that long dark hallway and leave me with my bare face hanging out. I couldn't let him get away without asking him some important questions that just had to have some answers to. So, in my haste to keep him there I put my mouth in motion before I got my mind in gear (I seemed to be doing that very often these days.) and blurted out what was a really stupid question.

"Are you a ghost or just what the hell is going on with you? I found a gravestone in the cemetery that had the name of Sheriff Ordonez, and the dates on that stone indicate that when he died he was exactly the age you said that you were the last time we talked. Are you that Orlando Ordonez or are you really Jose Fuentes, PhD?"

There, I had at least stopped him from leaving. I felt like a fool accusing him of being a dead man. Why the hell should he even bother with someone as stupid as I appeared to be? I wouldn't blame him if he just kept on walking and ignored my questions.

I didn't like the ominous look on his face when he turned around to stare at me. It must have been three full terror-ridden minutes that he looked at me. I almost wet my pants again I was so scared that he was going to pull out a six-shooter and kill me for asking a stupid question like that.

The old man just looked at me for a minute and then the biggest grin I had ever seen on a face anywhere was followed by a long loud guffaw and he started to choke on his laughter.

"What the hell did you just ask me Sonny? Am I dead? Did you go completely crazy out there on the mesa? Of course I'm not dead you fool! I'm eighty-nine years old and as healthy as a horse. What made you ask a stupid question like that anyway? Whose gravestone did you find in the cemetery anyway?"

I tried not to look too stupid or to laugh as I stammered and stuttered and tried to think of an intelligent answer for him.

"I found one for Orlando Ordonez, born 1830 and died 1919. The epitaph indicated that he was the Sheriff here, but didn't say exactly when. You said that you were the last of the originals of the town and implied that you were Sheriff here in the eighteen hundreds and lived to tell about it. You told me that you are eighty-nine years old and that is the same age Orlando Ordonez was when he died."

I took a deep breath and shuddered because I knew I would just have to suffer the consequences of my statement now.

Somehow I got the nerve to continue as I said, "Ms. Charles told me a story about when she was a kid that she came over here and you looked like you were dead then, or had just risen from the grave. You scared the bejesus out of all the kids then. You scared them so bad, in fact, that she has never set foot on this side of the street since that Halloween night, almost twenty five years ago. What do you have to say about that?"

I knew what I had just said was all circumstantial and wasn't worth anything as far as proof of anything. I just wanted him to clear it up for me, because I couldn't get it off my mind unless I heard his story in his own words.

The old man shook his head and the grin disappeared from his face as the said, "first of all, Andy, I can assure you that I'm alive and well. I'm not been dead and haven't risen from the grave, ever. I was born in 1891 in South Dakota. My family moved here to New Mexico about 1900. I was taken by the BIA to the local Catholic School a few weeks after we arrived. I told you the whole truth about that story."

"When I come back from that school, I was selected as a Deputy Sheriff of this town. Let's see, that must've been about 1911 or so, when I was about twenty years old. And my name's definitely not Orlando Ordonez. It is Jose Fuentes."

Things began to become a bit clearer to me as he continued.

"I knew Ordonez because he was the Sheriff here when I came back to this town. I wanted to be his Deputy and he agreed to teach me the ropes. We didn't have Police Academies in those days. It was all sort of what you'd call on the job training. If you happened to get shot and killed then the training ended. If you didn't get killed, chances were you'd be the next Sheriff in line after the current one did get killed or retired. Ordonez was lucky, he retired."

"Sheriff Ordonez was the one who told me all about those men you see on those wanted posters there," he said as he pointed to the wall behind me.

"He was the one who went through the shootouts with those outlaws. When he caught them, he hung most of them outside on the porch. As far as me saying that I was the last of the originals of the town, well, I'm the oldest in town and came here the earliest."

"The shootouts I went through weren't with the men on the posters but with the likes of Bonny and Clyde, and all the car driving crooks who thought that a sleepy little town way out here in the mountains would be a good place to hide out from them big city cops, the marshals, the F.B.I., and all the other lawmen who were chasing them. They sure did come here after hitting stores and banks in Santa Fe and Albuquerque, but they didn't stay long," he declared.

A grin appeared on his face and he chuckled as he continued again, "As far as scaring the kids around here at Halloween I guess I did do that because they expected it and enjoyed it. They thought the place was haunted and that I was a ghost. I just lived their fantasy for them. I painted the outside of this place with hog's blood and put on face paint and some old clothes. Made all the right electric connections, too, so that whenever the bell was pushed the creepy sounds would start. I dressed like a corpse as best I could. I was having a great time. Most of the kids came back to check on me after Halloween and found me alive and well. We all got along pretty well. If they chose to believe I was a ghost, then I couldn't stop them, could I? I even was invited to the school to tell them kids some of the history of the town. Too bad the lawyer hasn't been on this side of the street for all these years. She must've really been scared. After I retired from being the Sheriff I got my degree and went to UNM in the Agriculture Department and taught there for a while."

After I finished laughing about his stint as a teacher, he asked me, "Does that answer most of your questions about me?"

"Yes, it does Mr. Fuentes. I'm really sorry for asking you stupid questions. I guess that I owe you an apology for thinking what I did, but I have to admit, since I have been in this town, some weird things have been happening to me so I'm not sure what is real anymore. You are a little scary and not a real friendly person to talk to, let alone be a motor court owner. Do you always try to scare away people who want to stay here like you did to me?"

"When you rang the dinger I was in the back yard working on my roses and was a little aggravated that someone was interrupting me. Course I was dirty so I didn't look so good, but was planting new plants in my beds. One thing you will learn, Andy, is that when you mess around in dirt, some of it sticks to you. You want to see my roses?"

He motioned for me to follow him down the hallway.

I hoped that I wasn't agreeing to a suicide mission with me being another victim of this ghoul. With that thought, I started to walk back into the depths of the hallway. I couldn't just let him dismiss me like that. If I did, then I would never know the truth so I blurted out another question I needed answered. I surreptitiously looked for locked doors that might just hold the carnivorous plants in question, but saw nothing out of the ordinary. Obviously he wouldn't post OFF LIMITS signs all over the place now would he? Or would he?

"Sure I would like to see your roses," I said meekly as I followed him through the office and down the hallway to the source of light streaming through the back door. I looked around and did notice one solid wooden door that was closed and probably locked. I immediately thought. That must be where the hideous plants are hidden. How could I possibly get him to open it?

I slowed in front of the door and he saw me looking at it. "That door leads to my study, Andy. I still do research in there. Sort of a lab, if you don't mind. Do ya want to see what's in there, what I'm working on now?"

I couldn't pass up a chance like that so I said "Yes, I'd like to see some of your work," hoping that some of the plants I'd read about in his paper might just be in there.

He came back to me, pulled a huge key ring out of his pocket, chose the right one, and unlocked the door. Believe it or not, the damned thing creaked on rusty hinges like those old Boris Karloff movies about castles, monsters, and dungeons. It scared the wits out of me just thinking about going in there.

But I did, and was amazed at what I saw. It was a professional looking laboratory with what appeared to be a thousand plants in neat catalogued rows, with each container labeled with a scientific name. Some were just shoots, maybe two or three inches high. Some were larger, up to maybe a foot and a half high. In one of the far corners I saw three plants that had very large circular leaves that were almost at ceiling height. The leaves were very dark green, almost black and had curly hair like tendrils on their edges.

As we walked, Mr. Fuentes started to explain what the signs on each plant meant, what stages of development each plant was in, and what he was doing as far as hybridizing them. I noticed that he steered me away from the large fuzzy looking plants in the corner. While he stopped to examine some of his plants, I tried to make my way over there without him spotting me and got close enough to one of them to read the little card on the pot. It was like the one (maybe the exact plant) that he had written the white paper about. I looked quickly at the other two giant plants and realized that he had all three varieties that he had used for his white paper research right here in his house!

There were some bits of detritus on the surface of the soil in each pot so I very carefully picked up a piece of dried leaf or part of a stem from each plant and carefully put them into the plastic bags I had purposefully put into my pocket. I had an idea festering in the back of my mind about what I would try to do with them. I quickly caught up with the old man and followed him around the room and back to the door we had entered.

The whole excursion had lasted no more than ten minutes or so. I could feel the sweat running into my eyes from the nervousness I felt because of my surreptitious actions. I just wasn't a sneaky kind of guy. It bothered me that I had taken advantage of our almost friendship to get what could be evidence against him, but if it was, then I was justified or so I reasoned. I followed him out and he locked the door behind us. He motioned me to follow him and we walked on down the hallway toward the back door.

What I saw when I emerged from the house was the biggest expanse of flowers that I had seen anywhere. I estimated that his garden was at least an acre in size with every square foot covered in roses. The colors ran the gamut from brilliant red to orange, to blues of unimaginable hues, to pinks and yellows.

As I followed him along the path between the plants, my nose was assailed with the most concentrated fragrance I had ever smelled. It was amazing to have this many flowers growing in the desert. I asked him how he did it.

"See them three things over there?" He pointed a gnarled finger in a direction I had not looked before.

There were three things that looked like storage sheds lying on their sides with the doors opening on top.

I had no idea what they were and asked him about them.

"Those are my three stages of compost. Out here where the soil's mostly sand, nutrients and supplements have to be added to it or nothing but tumble weeds will grow on it. See the numbers on them? The new stuff's in bin number one. The second year stuff's in bin two, and the stuff ready to use is in bin number three," he explained.

We walked toward the bins as he continued his explanation.

"Every day I save all the scraps of food I can and put them in bin number one. I sometimes go to the grocery store and ask them to save the stuff they're going to throw away and I go get it and put it in there. Everything but meat goes in there. I let it set and ferment for a year and then I empty out bin number three, fill it up with new stuff and rotate the numbers on the bins so I can tell which one's the oldest. Does a good job on the roses doesn't it?"

I could see he was immensely proud of his garden and I complimented him on it. I asked him what he did with all the flowers.

"I take them to the florists in Santa Fe. I got about seven shops that I keep well supplied. Make a good living at it too. I plant the new hybridized ones over there in my greenhouse after experimenting in my lab," he said proudly.

"My work has let me develop several new strains and colors that have made a big hit with rose lovers. I'm very happy and satisfied with the way most have come to be so popular."

He was amazing! I thought he was a ghost and now I find that he truly is a rose developer. He told me later, in the course of our trampling all around his garden for the better part of an hour, that he had worked in the Agriculture Department at UNM and had worked for the State Agricultural Department for many years until he was forced to retire eight years ago.

During all the years that he worked, he spent his off-time developing this garden so he'd have it when he retired. No wonder he didn't seem to care if anyone rented rooms at the motor court!

I didn't think it was appropriate for me to question him further about the Penitentes so, after an hour and a half of walking around his rose garden with the accompanying lecture, I told him I had some more things I had to take care of so I had to leave. As I walked out of the office he handed me a big blue rose that he said was one he'd developed. I got the unexpected feeling that he was sorry to see me go. I thanked him and went on my way to the Cave for some lunch.

SIXTY-FIVE

I had some very serious thinking to do about how and who to contact for help in my guesswork plot. I decided that Martin would might believe me and offer to help in any way he could. After all, Jose Fuentes was an Indian, although he didn't live on the reservation.

I called Martin at the reservation the next day and explained about the old mystery in Albuquerque. I told him what I thought had gone on back then. If it was a triple murder, and I had no reason to think it wasn't, then there was no statute of limitations. If the plant samples I had proved what I thought they might, then three more victims would find justice and their murderer would find that the long arm of the law worked in mysterious ways.

Martin begged off doing anything immediately, but after hearing my suspicions about the plants, he agreed to take the samples and request the State Police lab in Santa Fe do an analysis on them. I explained that I thought the samples might reveal some very interesting information if the new DNA analysis techniques were used to analyze them.

"This whole thing is unofficial," I heard him say. "I cannot get involved with a thirty year old crime that didn't even occur on the reservation. But I'll try to help."

I was grateful for any help I could get and replied, "Great, Martin, I'll meet you at the Cave and give you the plastic bags of the stuff. Can you meet me at the Cave for dinner tonight?"

He agreed and said he'd see me about six that evening.

I had nothing to do but wait. At six o'clock that night we met in a booth at the Cave enjoyed a great dinner of fajitas and beer. I gave him three small bags of rapidly disintegrating pieces of plants. He looked them over. They all looked like ordinary dried leaves.

"If what you think is true, Andy, this will be more than enough material to do the tests. I'll let you know as soon as I hear something back from the lab."

I expressed my gratitude for his help and he left me feeling as if a great load had been shifted from my shoulders to Martin and the legal authorities with this transfer. I just wanted justice done. I knew it would take a while to get the results, but I was willing to wait because I had some other important things to tend to. He called me a couple of days later with the news I was waiting for.

"Andy, Martin here, I've got some news for you from the State

Police Crime lab in Santa Fe. They wondered where I had gotten the plant residue and why I wanted it analyzed. I guess they accepted my explanation that I was investigating a cold case because they honored my request and did what I asked them to do. You were right on with your guess. They found traces of human DNA in all three plant samples. Now the State Police are getting samples from the parents of the girls for comparison. I have notified the Homicide Division of the State Police in Albuquerque and they agreed that the case should be reopened if this new evidence proves to be a match for any of the girls."

"Well Martin, that's really good news. If the results are positive, are you going to come to town to question him about the plants and the evidence? I know it is probably out of your jurisdiction because the crime happened in Albuquerque?"

"No. I can't question him, and since there is no Sheriff in Bullsnort just now, the State Police will have to do it. I called and told them about the human DNA in the plant samples and they are getting a search warrant for the flower garden and the lab at the motor court. They will want to talk to both you and Mr. Fuentes, so make yourself available."

I told Martin that I was very relieved and grateful for his help.

He cautioned about getting too enthusiastic just yet.

"Even if the DNA match is positive, it will be hard to connect Fuentes to the crime. The detectives will have to find witnesses who can connect him with the girls at the time of their disappearance. Like people who saw them together. That could be a major problem after all these years. If the three girls disappeared at different times, then making the connection will get a bit harder. It'll take a lot of investigative work to find a roommate, a classmate, or a boyfriend, maybe, who can provide information."

"Remember that the crime happened thirty years ago," he said. "The students who might have known the three girls could be at the four corners of the world, or dead by now. We've had two wars since then, Korea and Vietnam. It's going to be tough. But don't get discouraged, Andy, investigative techniques have improved at a fantastic rate since then and that will give us an advantage."

"I've laid the groundwork, Martin. I just hope, that if Fuentes did the murders and disposed of the bodies in this gruesome a way, that it can be proven so he goes to jail for whatever time he's got left. I wouldn't put it past him to have done this thing. He scares the hell out of me every time I go and talk to him. Let me know what happens, even if it is after I go back home, because I want to track it."

SIXTY-SIX

Meanwhile, we had to go through the ritual of talking to the investigators and lawyers as they prepared to go to trial to convict the Sheriff and the lawyer. The evidence had been compiled and was substantiated, so the defense attorneys for both of them would logically be concentrating on avoiding the death penalty and getting the least jail time possible for their clients. The Assistant District Attorney who had come up from Santa Fe, said that she was going for the maximum penalty for two counts of first degree murder, and would ask for the death penalty for both of these two vicious killers. She said that she was also going to ask for extra time for each of them for the attempted murder of Pablito and felony menacing for shooting up my car.

At that time the death penalty was under review by the New Mexico State Legislature which was revamping the wording to meet the Federal Constitutional requirements. But she vowed that wouldn't stop her in this case.

The whole town was relieved when the juries were selected and sworn in and the trials began. Those of us who were supposed to testify as to the evidence were not allowed to sit in on the proceedings of either trial. So, I didn't have to suffer again through seeing the pictures of Carmelita with the bullet wound in her head, Pablito with the three shots in his body, and all the incriminating evidence that I had the satisfaction of helping to put together.

Within three weeks after the trials started both defendants were found guilty of first degree murder. Two weeks afterward, at the sentencing hearings, the judges announced that both Ms. Robin Charles and Mr. Bill Johnson would spend the rest of their natural life at the New Mexico State Penitentiary without the possibility of parole.

Although I felt that both of them should suffer the same fate as Carmelita, I was gratified that they would at least spend the rest of their lives in a steel city that the state government maintains for people like them.

They would be denied the possibility of ever being released to hurt anyone again. I felt relieved that it had been proven, once more, that the guilty cannot escape the tolling peals of the bell of justice. There is simply no place to hide.

Society will exact the required retribution. Society got its due when they brought Mr. Bill Johnson and Ms. Robin Charles to trial for the murders of Carmelita Martinez and her unborn baby.

As the court police officers snapped the handcuffs on both of them the sound echoed loudly. Dirty cops and dirty lawyers are an athema to the many hard working honest policemen and women everywhere. They didn't hesitate to lead them away to prison. The clanking sound of the cuffs ratcheting tight was a sobering sound. The hands they held would never again threaten or shoot the life out of a helpless victim.

I waited around after the trial, along with most of the citizens of Bullsnort, to watch the Police take them away and I'll never forget the significance of the flashing red and blue patterns that the two Police cars made on the street. I knew as they drove away that my time in Bullsnort would come to an end shortly. I had to get back to Albuquerque. Although I might want to stay and to see what might develop with Rosalie, but after our last conversation, I knew deep inside that it would never work out with us. It saddened me to think of our not being together.

SIXTY-SEVEN

I have said my good-byes and conveyed my thanks, especially to Martin for all he had done for me and for Carmelita. I was proud of my new Indian name even if I couldn't pronounce it correctly.

Although I didn't regret for a second having gone through the Cleansing Ceremony and the Naming Ritual, I assured him I would not ever want to go through it again. He told me that he would always have a place in his heart for Wartegil Yawipa, "he who kills and comes back," and assured me that we would meet again someday.

Mrs. Hernando didn't want to say goodbye and didn't want me to leave but she knew I had to go. I thanked her for all her help as I loaded my special drum into my car. I had already wrapped all my dolls and packed my precious books for the trip home. Both of us had tears in our eyes as we kissed our farewell and embraced. When I drove away from her and Bullsnort a few minutes later, she waved goodbye with one hand and wiped tears from her eyes with the other. I watched her in the rear view mirror waving to me as I went down the street and out of her sphere of influence.

As I drove out of town I looked again at the Conestoga wagon and the giant wagon wheels on the roofs above the colorful buildings. I remembered the Indian Arts Store and especially Mrs. Hernando. She was the one person, of all those I had met there, that I came to know well, love, and respect. Her, I knew, I would miss very much. She had been so tolerant of my asking and my probing about the Penitentes as well as all about the Kachinas, rugs, pottery, and paintings in her shop. I had made up my mind, and told her so, that someday I would once again drive down that black street and stop in her shop. Her reply had made me feel welcome any time in her domain.

As I drove out of sight, I recalled the experiences we had been through together. I remembered the day we had been at Pablito's house to listen to his story and then had gone to dinner at the Cave. While we were talking and I had been drinking a cold beer. I must have been extremely tired because I didn't remember anything that happened until Mrs. Hernando shook me and I awoke. When she had told me what had happened there in the booth and it had been unbelievable.

I had apparently passed out or had fallen into some kind of trance. She had said she wasn't at all worried that I might injure myself, but she had looked after me for the time I was unconscious. I had never told her that this was what had happened when I had received all of the twelve messages from the Clan Fathers. I didn't expect a thirteenth one to come to me so I had not been prepared at all for it. She had been able to do nothing but watch and listen. I apparently had a headache, but must have assumed it was because I was tired.

I remembered her telling me that I kind of slouched down and when she started to leave me to get someone to help, I had asked her not to do anything. She had described her anxiety when I had gotten a pen from my pocket while keeping my eyes closed tightly. She told me that it appeared that I went into some kind of a trance or something. Later, when I awoke, the two of us had read what I had written, not in the notebook, but on the white tablecloth.

> "*Tawamiciya*
> *I am the thirteenth and last Clan Father.*
> *I am named Becomes His Vision.*
> *I am the guardian of transformation and transfiguration.*
> *I am the keeper of emergence of the spirit in physical form.*
> *I will help you to become yourself again.*
> *Do not be afraid.*"

After I had received that message, I awoke, and Mrs. Hernando had explained what happened to me. I had never written a Clan Father message like this one before. I had heard the Clan Fathers speaking to me as they gave me the first twelve messages. Then I had written them in my notebook. I had not heard this one at all, but had been guided by the Clan Father while I wrote it, or did the Clan Father just use me to write it? I'll never know the answer to that question.

I realized with regret as I drove on, that this message was the last one I would ever receive. The problem had been solved and the killers found and brought to trial. The Clan Fathers had come to me with their collective messages that have changed me in ways I could not have imagined. I realized that I had never told Mrs. Hernando that I had received some of them in her shop.

I had been the Clan Fathers' student since my first day in Bullsnort. I must have inadvertently called them up when I hit the drum in Mrs. Hernando's shop the first time. As I continued on my journey home to Albuquerque, I vowed that I will live their messages and never forget them. I had tried as best I could to follow their advice and they had led me to Pablito, Jose, and to William Johnson, former Sheriff, and Ms.

Robin Charles, former lawyer. Now both the former Sheriff and the former lawyer were convicted murders setting behind bars, thanks to the Clan Fathers.

As I drove on, my thoughts shifted to the fly infested old man at the motor court and wondered about him. I had thought I would like very much to write his story but that would mean going back there in the future to be with him. I didn't know if I will ever be up to that. Although he had become a little more friendly and talkative about himself and the town, I had to admit that he still scared me. I realized that I will never be all sure of the story he told me about working for the Sheriff who had arrested or shot the men on the wanted posters. My God, was I actually still thinking that I had been talking to, and living in the Motel apartment, owned by a man who had died so many years ago? I still shivered when I thought of it. Best leave well enough alone for now. Maybe that will be the subject of another book, I decided as I wove in and out of traffic.

I knew I was still interested in the Penitente rituals but doubted that I would ever be able to go back there to observe them. I'd just have to wait and see. I would definitely go back to see Rosalie and Mrs. Hernando, but I'd have to think long and hard about going back to see Orlando Ordonez, Jose Fuentes, or whoever he really was.

Pablito had fully recovered from his three wounds and since the trial had come back to live in Bullsnort. He is no longer confined to the wheelchair but will need the support of a cane for a while. He had even asked my permission to start dating Rosalie if she'd agree. I had no objection because I knew that Rosalie and I could never have a future together.

I had asked Rosalie to marry me, but she had refused, saying that I would want to take her away from the town that she could never leave. Her life was there. I had to agree because I could never live there. There were too many bad memories and thoughts that would never go away, ever.

As I drove, I thought about the future. My self-imposed nightmare was over. I had survived the visions. I had thwarted the Sheriff's attempt on my life. I have an Indian name now, and am proud of it, even if I can't pronounce it. I had helped put the killers behind bars. I had even written three headline stories which had been printed about the town and about the problems there, but not my personal experiences in it.

I will always have the mementoes of my stay Bullsnort. I have five dolls from Mrs. Hernando's shop that are well protected in boxes in the trunk. In addition to the Koshare, the Sand God, and the Owl Man, on my last visit to the store I had discovered another two that I just had to have. Mrs. Hernando had given me a good discount on them. One is called the Snow Eagle. It is unique in that it has pure white fur and looks like an eagle. The head feathers are wood and carved to resemble real feathers and painted white with black highlights.

The most interesting thing about it is that the outer head is removable. Under the Eagle head is the head of a man. This one has black fur hair and a painted face. This Kachina fascinated me when I first saw it because unlike all the other Kachinas there, it had white fur hair that reminded me of the Sand God. Then when Mrs. Hernando revealed the removable head I knew I had to have it, whatever the cost, so it is mine now.

The last one I bought is really a strange looking doll but all the dolls have a place in Indian society and this one is no exception. The hair on this one is long, frizzly and stands out from the head in a thousand different directions. The hair is white. The face is a painted mask of grotesque features. It has a nose shaped like an eagle beak, black eyes, white eyebrows, and a red gash for a mouth. The clothes it has on are not typical Indian style clothes. The leggings are cut off at the knee and are cut into strips that extend almost to the crotch of the doll. It wears moccasins that have the heel in front and the toes pointing toward the rear of the doll.

It was odd, to say the least, until Mrs. Hernando told me what the doll is called and explained what it represents.

"In every society, including the Indians, there are those people who just do not fit somehow. They have a plane of existence all their own. They talk to themselves and, when asked why, they reply something to the effect that the voices in their heads talk to them continuously. This doll is made to signify those people who just cannot live a normal life."

"They are called "Contraries."

"Everything they do, whether walking or talking or eating, is done in reverse of the normal way. For instance if you see a Contrary walking somewhere and happen to ask them where they are going, it invariably will be in the direction from which they have just come. Their speech is slurred and backwards. They pour water all over their bodies to get a drink. Nobody ever tries to get a Contrary to conform to the way everybody else does things. They are just left alone in their own private worlds."

I remember that when I first met Martin and told him about the

Sand God, he mentioned Contraries briefly. When I saw it in Mrs. Hernando's shop, I was amazed that there would be a doll as an example of someone that normal society would consider mentally sick, but there it was. I hadn't seen a person who fit the description of a Contrary anywhere and now that I knew of them I surely wouldn't ask Martin if there were any out on the reservation. I had bought this very interesting doll because the story fascinated me.

In my mind I could see my apartment in Albuquerque as I drove. I have the perfect place, a fireplace mantel that will be a great place for all five Kachinas. I have my cedar pole wrapped very carefully in bubble wrap to protect the carvings and it is lying on the back seat. The large drum is in the trunk. I couldn't think of leaving town without it. I know that every time I hit it, I will remember. The one big problem is, will I want to remember or should I let the memory of what happened there fade or at least become dimmer with the passing of time? It will take years for the mental scars to smooth over. I doubt if they will ever go away entirely.

I had the beautiful male mountain lion stuffed in Santa Fe and I made a gift of it to Mrs. Hernando. She has it in her private office now, high on the wall overlooking the lodge poles and buffalo hides. I gave the bow and the three arrows to Martin in appreciation for all of his help. I knew they will be valued and respected. Little did I know, or envision, how vivid the memories of what had happened to me there would be. I wondered if I could remain sane after having all those experiences.

As I drove slowly down the black street I looked into the rearview mirror one last time before I had to make a curve at the outskirts of town. The town would be gone from my sight at that turn. I slowed down. I hesitated to leave it all behind me. Why? I should have welcomed getting away. But was I actually getting away and from what? I knew it would be with me always from there on out, till when?

SIXTY-EIGHT

Now that I am away from that place, will I go completely and irrevocably insane, while nobody believes the stories I tell, or maybe write?

Or will I hear the sounds and visualize the memories once too often and commit suicide somewhere alone, sinking into a dark deep hole of my own mind where I can't possibly retrace my normal steps. The normal steps that began with a simple phone call that came, oh, what seems so very long ago, when I was a fledging reporter for a newspaper, are clear in my mind. I can't say the same for all that followed.

Will I ever be able to bury the memories of that town and what I experienced there somewhere deep into my psyche?

I know I don't want to go back there, even in my thoughts. But I will because it is an unfinished part of my story and I always finish my stories.

I read in the local paper that a memorial service for Carmelita was held the Sunday after I left with interment following at the cemetery. Regrettably I could not be there to pay my last respects to a woman I never knew but helped vindicate. She has been finally laid to rest. I made a donation to the fund to get a nice headstone for her. I never had the pleasure of knowing her but that was the least I could do. I did have some satisfaction knowing that I had helped find and convict her killers.

I vividly remember making the turn that led out of Bullsnort slowly and all was gone from my view, but not from my memory. Never from my memory!

I had made the drive back to Albuquerque slowly on I-25 instead of the back roads that took me there. Why? I guess I was a little terrified that I might just have to stop in another small village on the way home and get stranded there. I surely never want to have another experience like what happened to me in Bullsnort. I made the outskirts of town at Bernalillo in record time. I was home again but I somehow didn't feel any more secure or safe than I did in Bullsnort.

SIXTY-NINE

But my life is better now, though. What had come to haunt my life those years since I left Bullsnort has not followed me here, to the asylum, where I know I am safe from experiencing them again.

After I returned to the paper I talked a lot with Dan about the happenings up there in the mountains. Nothing specific though. He suggested that I was a changed man and that I should find help of some kind so that I could deal with those memories. He hoped that they would start to fade into the background and that I would come back to work on the Indian Desk soon.

About a month or so after I got home I received a letter from Martin. The letter itself wasn't totally unexpected. What fell out of the envelope as I opened it but before I had a chance to read the letter, utterly flabbergasted me. It was a check made out in my name from the First Bank in Bullsnort, New Mexico, and it was from the City's account. The amount written in at the places required took my breath away and forced me to sit down as I looked at the check more carefully the second time. Yes, I had read it correctly. It was made out to me for the sum total of $10,000.00. Below in the left hand corner was written For Reward. Hopefully, Martin, or whoever had written the letter, would explain the reason for the check. I read the letter.

Dear Andy,

Mrs. Hernando and Rosalie send their love. They asked me to pass it on to you when I told them I was going to write this letter. They are both well and happy. Rosalie and Pablito are planning to get married in a few months. He has fully recovered from his wounds and is going to run for Sheriff of Bullsnort. Mrs. Hernando said to tell you that you have a standing invitation to come back anytime, and that she misses the booming of the drum.

I am writing to let you know the progress of the investigation into the alleged disappearance of the three girls from Santa Fe that Rosalie told you about. I greatly appreciate your help in getting the samples of the plants. I just got the results back from the lab yesterday.

It seems that you were right. The human DNA in the materials you collected did, in fact, match the DNA of the three missing girls. The search warrants for the garden and lab were granted and the State Police found substantial proof that those plants had been hybridized and had been in the care of the motor court owner for many years. The authorities in Santa Fe were able to locate witnesses that could testify that the girls had all been seen in his company on the days they disappeared. Mr. Fuentes will definitely be arrested and brought to trial. Your handiwork was extremely important.

You are probably wondering what the check is for, aren't you? (He had guessed correctly on that question.) The check is for your efforts to find and bring to justice the killers of Carmelita and her unborn baby, as well as the attempted murder of Pablito, not to forget the destruction of your own car.

The town is also appreciative of your efforts in finding the main evidence that links the motor court owner to the murders of the three students. Without your diligence in getting the DNA evidence, Dr. Fuentes would have continued to get off scot free for his killing the three women. Now, at least, he is in custody and will have his day in court.

Jose also got a reward check for $5000.00 for his efforts in taking the photographs that became the corroborating evidence and proof against the former Sheriff and the former lawyer in both the killing of Carmelita and the two attempts to murder Pablito. The town decided to reward both of you using some of the funds taken in from the Bullsnort Golf Tournament entry fees.

I have placed the bow and arrows you made in a glass case in the Tribal Police office so all who want to look at them can. I frequently go into Mrs. Hernando's shop and look at the beautiful mountain lion you gave her.

Well, that's all the important news from here, so, I'll close. You have a standing invitation to come to any tribal ceremony on the reservation. We'll be expecting you.

Martin.

Nobody in Bullsnort knows of my condition because I have not been up to writing, but I did appreciate Martin's letter. Maybe one of these days, when the shaking and the hallucinations slow down, and maybe even stop altogether, I'll either write them all a collective letter, or maybe, if I can get up enough courage, I'll go back to Bullsnort. That is something that will take a lot of courage that I just don't have at this juncture in my wanderings.

Of course, I had to tell Dan about what had happened up there because he wanted me to assume my job as soon as I returned. I didn't have the wherewithal to just be normal so soon. He said he understands and that I have all the time I need to recuperate and get my health back. I have to laugh at that. He understands? I doubt that very much. The second time I talked to him I did gain a better appreciation of his ability to understand some of the things I experienced, though.

"You know, Andy, that I sent you up to Bullsnort for a personal reason, don't you? You do know that it wasn't your true assignment, just to find that girl. Hopefully, the police would have eventually found her."

"No, my true assignment for you was to experience what you did. Have you ever thought about my last name? Or did it never occur to you to equate it to the place on the reservation where the finest grade of turquoise comes from, Morenci? Yes, I am an Indian, with a real Indian name too. I am Sees Many Elk. I am known to Martin Begay, whom I know well, as Miniconjou."

"You see, Tawamiciya, I do know, and understand much of what you have been through. I too have gone through the Cleansing Ceremony and the Naming Rituals. I had visions out there on the mesa too, but nothing nearly as amazing as what happened to you, happened to me. I'm glad you are back. Jose was also meant to watch over you and to help guide you in your search."

I was amazed at what I had gone through and could say nothing more to Dan about my experiences.

Dan had undergone some of the same things I had. He knew what could be in store for me when he sent me to Bullsnort to find the girl. He had arranged for Jose to be there at the paper in case I needed help from him. It was all pre-arranged.

EPILOGUE

Within in a week of my return, I took Dan's advice and found myself a good psychiatrist and have had many sessions about my experiences. Nothing helpful has come out of those sessions because I inherently felt like the psychiatrist thought I was making it all up. The doctor said that I just wasn't receptive to therapy, and I would just have to be patient.

I didn't feel that his sessions with me had resulted in any improvement at all. The nightmares were still just as vivid after two years, and then after four years as they were the day they happened. The psychiatrist finally suggested that I admit myself for long term intensive care at his clinic. He assured me that if I voluntarily admitted myself I could leave at any time.

That's where I am now. I have been here for one year under my doctor's care at his private asylum. I can leave at any time I want. I just don't feel secure enough to do so. I may be here the rest of my life. I relive my Bullsnort experiences every day. I just don't want to re-live them anymore. Sometimes I shiver uncontrollably, while other times I sweat buckets. I know that if I physically experienced it all again, it couldn't be any worse the second time around than the first, but thank you. I'd just as soon never do that. I don't want to bet my life that I would survive it a second time.

I just hope that I have made enough sense out of what happened to me to make the narrative of it interesting enough to have at least one person buy the book you have just finished reading.

The cover photo was taken by Roch Hart who was born in Santa Fe, New Mexico. He is a retired Albuquerque Police Department Detective who has helped solve many homicides. most recently, some on the ranch he manages. Roch is currently a photographer and the ranch he manages has many Ancestral Pueblo Ruins, two ghost towns, and thousands of petroglyphs within its borders.

Printed in the United States
by Baker & Taylor Publisher Services